ADRIFT

DAW BOOKS PROUDLY PRESENTS THE SCIENCE FICTION NOVELS OF W. MICHAEL GEAR:

The Donovan Series

Outpost

Abandoned

Pariah

Unreconciled

The Team Psi Series

The Alpha Enigma

*Implacable Alpha**

The Spider Trilogy

The Warriors of Spider

The Way of Spider

The Web of Spider

The Forbidden Borders Trilogy

Requiem for the Conqueror

Relic of Empire

Countermeasures

★★★

Starstrike

The Artifact

*Coming soon from DAW

ADRIFT

DONOVAN: BOOK FIVE

W. MICHAEL GEAR

DAW BOOKS, INC.
DONALD A. WOLLHEIM, FOUNDER
1745 Broadway, New York, NY 10019
ELIZABETH R. WOLLHEIM
SHEILA E. GILBERT
PUBLISHERS
www.dawbooks.com

TO

BRIAN AND LEXIE YARRINGTON

FOR ALL THE YEARS OF BEER, FOOD, AND FELLOWSHIP.

ACKNOWLEDGMENTS

Special appreciation goes to my old and dear friend, Sheila Gilbert, for standing by me through the insanity of a changing literary world. By the time this is published, we can only hope that political censors are a thing of the past and authors can write from their hearts without fear of reprisal. To better days and a return to freedom of speech. Thanks, Sheila, for helping to weather the storm and for your continued faith in the Donovan books.

As always, my beloved Kathleen—center of my heart and the axis of my universe—has supported, been critical of, and kept the creative blood flowing through the Donovan universe. All that I am is because of her. You wouldn't be reading this if Kathleen hadn't been willing to seize the dream all those years ago when we were eating pizza on our first date. I owe her so much.

The long ocean swells might have been on Earth. Physics are physics after all. The same on Donovan as in the Pacific, Atlantic, or Indian Oceans; though the water here was a deeper blue—a sort of royal turquoise. These waves were running about a meter and a half, occasionally cresting into whitecaps as the foam was wicked off in streamers.

The warm wind, too, could have been on Earth; it carried odors of salt and spray. It blew in from the northeast, gusting against the curved walls of the Maritime Research Unit's Pod. The Pod was essentially a two-story sialon tube set north-south on pilings. With a small landing pad on the roof, a deck that could be raised or lowered to sea level on the northeast, and the Underwater Bay, a submerged submarine hanger and ocean access, the wind-blown tube now functioned as humanity's lonely base for the exploration of Donovan's oceans.

If Scientific Director Michaela Hailwood was any judge of the weathervane atop the station's high mast, it was blowing from about forty degrees and pushing close to ten knots. Overhead, low puffy bits of cloud rode the zephyr. Torn and twisted by turbulence, they seemed to dance against a background of higher cirrus in Donovan's deeper-blue sky.

Born on Apogee Station, Michaela had taken an improbable path to scientific director. Her African and European ancestors had come from industrial and urban stock, not to mention that station-born folk were rarely drawn to such fields as oceanography. She had reached the ripe age of forty-eight, stood right at six feet, and her build remained rail-thin—as did the rest of her team's—after the years of privation during the ten-year-long transit from Solar System aboard *Ashanti*.

Michaela centered her attention on the restless sea. Swells were all about friction: the interface of moving air on water. Donovan's moon massed more than Luna did back in Solar System, so Donovanian tides could be fierce. But here, five hundred kilometers east of the nearest shoreline, and at this latitude, the effect was ameliorated.

More than a million years ago, a meteor strike had forever altered the continental landform. Blasted out the five-hundred-kilometer crater like taking a giant bite out of the coastline. Michaela's research station had been situated on a narrow reef created by the ejecta. It was one of a line of shoals that ran like a string of beads around the Gulf's eastern circumference. A million years of wave action and tides had worn down the land that had once protruded above the ocean's surface.

Donovan was a living world. The triangular sails of what her people had named seaskimmers could be seen in the distance. To date, Michaela and her team were unsure what they were. The closest analogy was that the seaskimmers were a Donovanian equivalent to the terrestrial Portuguese man-of-war, the small bladder-topped siphonophore. But there the comparison stopped. Seaskimmers were nearly thirty meters tall and similar to a lateen-rigged sailboat. Unlike a man-of-war, they had no subsurface tentacles but seemed to use wind power to chase down prey. The sail itself appeared to be a membrane, stiffened by something analogous to cartilage ribs that trailed filaments at the tips. To date, Michaela's team hadn't managed to get a closeup image of the creature's lower and buoyant body, but it was streamlined, reminiscent of a racing hull. From the single blurred visual they'd taken, the creature had three eyes and a triangular mouth. Based on morphology, at least three different species of seaskimmers could be distinguished.

And then, off in the distance, they'd also seen something that looked like a glowing cone with tentacles. The thing floated, apparently dangling its tentacles into the water, though what it might harvest outside of plankton was up for grabs.

Michaela rubbed her arms against the chill coming off the water. The distant seaskimmers flipped in the wind, tacking eastward in unison. Capella's light shimmered in the iridescent colors that rippled over the sails. Brilliant reds, yellows, greens, and blues flowed across the membrane in complex patterns.

"Probably some form of communication," she whispered, taken by the beauty of it. Communication by patterns and colors was one of the givens on Donovan. At least, that was the case on land where people now knew that quetzals and mobbers communicated by color and pattern. There was speculation that the invertebrates and perhaps even the plants did as well.

She heard the hatch cycle behind her and turned as her second-in-command, Lee Shinwua, Shin for short, stepped out into the wind. Still looking half-starved, the man's clothes hung on his broad-shouldered body. The stiff gusts played with his spacer-short black hair, and he squinted his nut-brown eyes into the wind, which accented their Asian cast. He was thirty-six with a PhD from ScrippsCal University. As with her origins in Apogee Station, Shinwua's Uyghur roots wouldn't have predisposed him to a degree in oceanography. Somehow, however, he'd managed to navigate the Corporate system, aced the exams, and landed a coveted appointment to the SCU. That he'd graduated magna cum laude, published prodigiously on deep-water resources, and cultivated the right sponsorship on the Board had wrangled him a place on Michaela's team.

Shin stepped up beside her, squinting into the wind's bite. "Thought you might be here. Got a problem with the main refrigeration unit. Got Tobi Ruto working on it. Looks like it's some sort of fried circuit. We don't have a spare. Tobi's not sure how to fix it."

She glanced at him. "No spare? Again?" Seemed like half the equipment they tried to fix didn't have a spare, or if it did, it was the wrong part. For the first maritime expedition on Donovan, they were off to a rocky start. They had only been in the Pod for a week, unpacking, setting up, testing equipment, and preparing to initiate the first study of Donovan's oceans. They had suffered one malfunction after another.

Shin shrugged. "If we have one, it's not in the listed inventory. I guess from what Tobi tells me, it's a common sort of part that rarely fails, and if it does, you just order one. Dharman called Corporate

Mine. They don't have one. Not sure Port Authority does, either. But they're asking around."

She chuckled dryly, eyes on the endless swells that rolled toward them to vanish beneath the platform and slosh against the Pod's pilings. In Capella's harsh light and crystalline water, she could see the reef three meters beneath the surface. Patterns of vegetation—in a mosaic of green and blue—mottled the water-worn rock. Something big, torpedo-like, jetted from under the pod to vanish from sight. Who knew what it might be?

Michaela told him, "Have Tobi call Sheyela Smith, that electrician in Port Authority. If she doesn't have the part, she'll know how to jury rig something to make the refrigeration work."

"Um, doesn't Sheyela Smith need to be, like, paid? You know, part of this market economy they're so proud of? We have some sort of deal worked out with them?"

"Supervisor Aguila said she'd dicker something until we could figure out a suitable method of compensation." Michaela gave him a shrug. "It's so weird. So different. Haphazard and chaotic. Back home everything was ordered. Even on *Ashanti* we knew where we fit, how it all worked."

Shin stuffed his hands into his back pockets. "Scary, huh? This whole world. I don't get it. After everything we've been through. All the hell we lived on *Ashanti*: knowing the Unreconciled were eating each other down in Deck Three; the starvation; the years of being locked in that little space. We should be prepared for anything. You know that everyone's on the edge of panic, don't you? That it's sinking in that we're here. All alone."

She nodded, staring out at the waves. "It's never been just us, Lee."

"Not on *Ashanti*, that's for sure. We were surrounded by crew. And back on Earth? The whole of Solar System was just a short shuttle's ride away." A pause. "You been sleeping? Well, I mean?"

Did she dare tell him?

Taking a breath, she said, "It's a new environment. Takes getting used to. Different sounds, different smells. Hell, even the beds are different. Brand new . . . never slept in. Everything's clean and fresh. Like this air. It doesn't stink of ship and human. And then there was that briefing Aguila and that Perez woman gave us back at Port Authority. Watch out for this monster, watch for that monster. Be careful of the wildlife. Donovan will try to kill you. Give it a while for our people to adjust."

He grunted, then said, "The kids are having nightmares. Lot of them wish they were back on the ship." A beat. "And it's not just the kids."

"Back on the ship? We prayed for ten years, desperate to get the hell out of *Ashanti*." She didn't dare tell Shin that she, too, dreamed of being locked back in the limited confines of *Ashanti*'s Crew Deck. And she did have nightmares. A recurring theme was of water cascading into her cramped quarters, rising, and there was no way out. Which was absurd; there wasn't that much water aboard *Ashanti*.

"It's this." Michaela waved an arm out at the endless waves marching their way. "The vast immensity of it. Nothing but water. In all directions. Endless water, endless sky, with no roof, no safe walls. And here we are, with just the Pod. Our little universe. Shouldn't be any different than being locked in *Ashanti*, right? Or being out in the middle of the south Indian Ocean back on Earth."

"But it is." Shin's gaze fixed on the swells. Gave the impression that the Pod was moving instead of the water. "Okay, so I know the specs. I know what kind of forces the Pod can endure. The thing's essentially crush-proof, can withstand just about anything the ocean can throw at it. Solid sialon casing and floors." He rapped a knuckle against the white wall behind him. "But it's like this thin shell is the only thing between us and drowning."

"You having nightmares of your own?"

The dull acquiescence in his brown eyes provided all the answer she needed. Played right in concert with her own tortured dreams of sinking into dark water, of holding her breath. Desperate. Then finally gasping, sucking in an endless rush of cold ocean. Even awake and aware, she could still feel the cold filling her lungs, the terror of drowning . . .

Michaela shivered. Shook it off. Appalled that Lee had seen, knew her weakness. All of which triggered her sense of frustration and fury. Damn it, she was the Director of Scientific Research, second-in-command only to Board Supervisor Kalico Aguila. The Board had appointed Michaela to the Directorship because of her iron will, her expertise in the field. To show any—

"It's all right," Shin interrupted her thoughts. "After all that time in *Ashanti*? There're no secrets left. You can be human like the rest of us."

"No secrets left," she whispered in agreement. "Isn't that the truth?"

They'd been packed together on Crew Deck after the Unreconciled had tried to seize the ship: twenty-three people jammed into four small cabins.

They'd had no privacy. Had to live cramped together—ass to armpit as the saying went. Had to endure all the trials humans inflicted upon each other in close proximity. They'd fought, formed alliances that shifted through time, hated each other, loved each other, swapped partners, squabbled and made up, and finally sorted themselves into a sort of extended family. One that tolerated each other despite the histories, jealousies, sexual complications, and remembered slights. Well, all but Dr. Anna Carrasco Gabarron. She was like the despised aunt that everyone stoically endured as a sort of cosmic punishment for his or her sins.

"You kept us sane, you know," Shin told her. "Otherwise, we'd never have made it. You were the one who ordered us out of Deck Three. Sided with Captain Galluzzi before we could make any other choice."

So, did that make her any less timid now that they were dirtside, alone on an empty and hostile planet in the middle of an uncharted and unknown ocean? An ocean that, if they could trust the briefings the Supervisor had given them, was full of creatures that would try to kill them?

A violent gust hit her, fluttering her coveralls, causing her to stagger. She ran a hand over the tight curls of her short black hair. "We'll be fine. All of us, we've trained for this. We're the best Solar System had to offer. Wind, waves, wildlife, we're the experts. If anyone can make a go of it, it's us." A beat. "We just need to get out

there, Shin. Get our hands dirty, start doing research, and everything will fall into place."

Shin studied the waves with shining eyes. "You're right. Once
we start exploring, get the subs and UUVs out, I think the nightmares and fears will fade away. It's just knowing that if anything
goes wrong, there's no Corporation a com call away. No Coast
Guard. No other ships. No search and rescue."

A large swell—one that almost reached the deck—swept beneath
them, crashing on the Pod's duraplast pilings. To Michaela's relief,
she didn't even feel its impact. The Pod was solid. Dreams of drowning in the darkness were just plain silly.

Then, as if spiraling out of the back of her mind, the words of
Wejee Tolland—who'd been on guard at the Mine Gate back in
Port Authority—repeated in her head: *But if an old hand can give you
any advice, Dr. Hailwood, you'll live a lot longer if you'll take for granted
that everything on this planet is trying to kill you.*"

Damn it, they *had* to get out there, start cataloging. Of course, it
would be different than being on Earth, but if they couldn't figure
out Donovan's oceans, no one could. They'd be careful; they'd been
dealing with sharks, rays, eels, sea snakes; and they had the best
technology available.

"What's that look?" Shin asked, fixing on her expression.

"Nothing." She pointed where the colorful seaskimmers were
tacking against the stiffening wind. They'd passed over the horizon
now, their triangular sails fading behind the line of rising and falling
swells. "No matter what Supervisor Aguila tells us, how could
something that beautiful be dangerous?"

"Michaela," Shin chided, "the situation here, it's not like life on
the mainland. We're in the Pod. Not directly exposed to the wildlife.
In the sub—which is a pretty tough piece of equipment—we'll be
perfectly safe. It's made to withstand pressures down to thirty thousand feet. Nothing on this planet could crush it. And most of our
work is going to be with the UUVs." UUV stood for unmanned
underwater vehicle, the AI and remote-controlled drones that would
be doing the majority of the underwater survey and exploration.

As her gaze fixed on the water, a gap in the high cirrus let Capella's light fully illuminate the shallows. It could have been a trick, an illusion created by the pattern of the waves and the undulating vegetation beneath, but something large seemed to flit away with remarkable speed, as if it had suddenly determined she was looking at it.

"Now what's wrong?" Shin asked.

"I keep thinking of something Wejee once told me. He works gate security in Port Authority. He said, 'Nobody has ever died of old age on Donovan.'"

2

Water ran around Corporate Supervisor Kalico Aguila's boots as she sloshed up the inclined adit. They called the sloping tunnel the Number Three. It had been driven into the base of the mountain three hundred meters below Corporate Mine's fenced compound.

Her muscles ached. She still hurt from her frantic escape from the Unreconciled. Now, barely having time to catch her breath, her engineers had asked her to take a look at the Number Three. Damn it, she had too much to do. And Michaela Hailwood kept asking when she'd be out to inspect the Maritime Unit, said she had issues that needed to be dealt with.

Issues? Who the hell on Donovan didn't have issues?

Around Kalico, the rock walls had been intricately shored with timbers that supported zones of shattered rock. In principle, the adit had been a good idea. Drive a tunnel at an inclined angle from the base of the mountain to just below the expanding stope in the Number One mine. In the stope, water had become an increasing problem, one that was rapidly overwhelming the Number One's single-pump capacity. Better to use gravity as a drain than to keep building pumps, pipes, and hoses. Additionally, instead of hauling ore out in the skip, winching it to the surface, and transporting it by tram, her crew could dump ore into a hopper and drop it down a vertical shaft into a waiting ore car. The ore car would unload it into a tipple that would fill a hauler at the adit's mouth, or portal. From there it could be driven to the smelter for processing. And finally, the adit would give her people another egress in the event of a disaster as well as improve ventilation now that they were working deeper and deeper into the mine.

A simple solution to a lot of problems, all of which had proved to be an incredible headache.

She and her engineers had understood that opening a haul road between the adit mouth and the smelter would be a battle. On Donovan, trees moved. And this was deep forest. Kalico and her people had barely won the fight to keep the relentless forest from overrunning her measly seven acres of farmland and its contiguous smelter. Fortunately, she had been able to secure enough terrestrial pine trees from Mundo Base to establish a line. Something about the chemistry in pines repelled Donovanian plant life. Her road would have to be lined with pines, which meant she was harvesting every cone that matured down at Mundo Base. Once sprouted, the seedlings were nurtured with extra care. Armed patrols planted the seedlings where aquajade, chabacho, and ironwood was cut for shoring. Meter by meter, the haul road was being established. Might be another three years before enough pines could be grown to line the entire route.

Next came the problem of the adit. Her engineers, Desch Ituri and Aurobindo Ghosh, had carefully surveyed the slope, determined the angle and distance, and begun driving the Number Three adit. What they hadn't counted on was the zone of shattered rock they hit two hundred meters into the mountain. This was, after all, the edge of a crater. One caused by an asteroid impact powerful enough to penetrate the planet's crust. Shattered rock wasn't a big surprise. And it was remarkably rich in valuable metals, so it was profitable to extract. On the downside, it also crumbled the moment it was undercut. The technical term for the roof collapse was *goafing*. Problem was, once excavated, the tunnel roof just kept goafing its way up through the shattered rock zone. What Ghosh called "void migration." Like hollow rot eating its way up through the mountain's guts, or a bubble of empty space rising through ever-collapsing rock. Leave it go for long enough, and the whole volume above the adit would consist of loose fill that had to be supported.

The solution was that shoring had to be built bit by bit as the adit was drifted into the mountain. They fought a constant battle to keep the adit roof, or head rock, supported.

Structural stability wasn't the only problem with shattered rock. Unlike higher in the Number One and Number Two mines, the shattered rock in the Number Three had the porosity of a sponge. Water trickled out of it by the bucketful. Because of the incline, Ituri had cut a ricket, or gutter, into the floor that now ran a full stream of toxic heavy-metal-rich water. What Ituri called the "watermake" was now just over one hundred and twenty gallons a minute.

For the time being, they let it drain into the forest. Didn't seem to hurt the trees. But eventually Kalico was going to have to do something with it. Figure some way of processing it for the metals. She didn't want it contaminating her farmland, toward which it would eventually drain. Heavy metals in their diet were already a problem that required constant vigilance and chelation therapy.

Kalico nodded to Tappan Mullony where he was fixing a jury-rigged light as she climbed up to the mucking machine with its waiting crew. Ahead of her, she could hear the clattering of the pneumatic hammers as they drove a length of steel rod into the brittle head rock at the top of the working face. The steel would stabilize the roof while fragmented rock was removed and shoring built. Once the shoring was extended, and the potential for cave-in was stopped, the pipe would be withdrawn and carried forward to be driven into the ceiling rock for the next length.

Five foot four in height, and built like a black-haired block of a man, Aurobindo Ghosh stood in the center of the tunnel, lights silhouetting his hazard-suited body. He had his hands propped on his hips, helmeted head cocked as he watched Jin Philon and Bill Masters run the pneumatic hammer. The two men were perched atop a scaffold, each bracing the heavy piece of machinery. Kalico stuffed her fingers in her ears, deafened by the noise. The others all wore hearing muffs with integral com.

"That's it," Ghosh called as the rod was driven even with the last length of chabacho-wood shoring. The sudden silence left Kalico's ears ringing. She lowered her hands, calling, "How's it going?"

Ghosh turned. "Hey, Supervisor. We're making ten feet a day through this rotten stuff. Talovich is out with the sawyers dropping trees along the haul road. We're shaping every timber and fitting it before hauling it in to be placed." He pointed. "Got to shore along the top as we muck out the ore. Sort of like extending a ceiling before building the room. Then we pull back, muck another meter or so, back the machine out, set more timbers, and do the whole thing over."

"Monotonous," Jin called, a smile on his wide lips. He had an arm slung over the top of the large pneumatic jackhammer as if it were his best pal.

"What the hell else you got to do?" Kalico asked ironically. "Go gamble at Port Authority?"

"Naw," Masters called derisively, "Ol' Jin here, all his plunder goes to keeping his man-part vertical while the rest of him is horizontal at Betty Able's."

"Don't be jealous, Billy Boy," Jin chided. "At least I got something that will go vertical. Bet you wish yours did."

Kalico shook her head. "You're both what I'd call hard luck cases."

They laughed at that, jabbing each other in the ribs before muscling the heavy pneumatic hammer off of its platform and easing it down onto the broken rock on the tunnel floor.

Ghosh had an amused look on his face.

"What?" Kalico asked. She stepped aside so Jin and Masters could maneuver the bulky hammer past. It was a makeshift thing that they'd had Tyrel Lawson up in Port Authority cobble together out of parts scavenged from who knew where. Water dripped and spattered on her helmet as she squinted against the bright lights to inspect the mazework of cracks crisscrossing the ceiling.

Ghosh waited until the two miners were out of hearing. "Long way from *Turalon*, aren't we?" A beat. "Listening to you bantering with the guys, I wonder if we're even the same people."

"A long way." Kalico agreed, stepping forward to get a better look at the metallic shine that reflected from the cracked stone: gold, silver, lead, antimony, maybe some copper, and a host of the rare Earth elements like rhodium, beryllium, scandiums and the like. Those took a better eye than hers to identify with the casual glance. "Why do you bring that up?"

Ghosh indicated the departing miners with a jerk of his head. "They'd crawl through hell for you, you know. We all would. Watching you just now, you're a million years away from that woman who came here on *Turalon* figuring she was going to whip the whole planet."

She snorted in a half laugh. "Just because I'll engage in ribald banter with my people?" A pause. "Yeah, I know. Donovan does that. Knocks you down, beats you into the mud, and waits to see if you'll get up or be eaten by a slug."

"No slug's gotten you yet."

Though the mobbers had come close once. The four-winged fliers traveled in colorful hoards; they had come within a couple of seconds of slicing Kalico into ribbons while she stood in the supposed safety of her fenced compound. She fought the urge to reach up and run a finger along the scar that ran the length of her jaw. It was one of many that crisscrossed her skin, this way and that, in a pattern not so different from the cracks in the shattered rock that surrounded her. The miracle was that she was still alive.

"Tell me about this." She pointed at the face where water seeped from the colorful rock to drain down the stone in silver trickles. "We're way behind schedule. By now we were supposed to be driving a manway and chute up into the Number One. The pump up there is running twenty-five hours a day, and the stope is filling. How far do we have to go?"

"Depends, Supervisor." Ghosh stepped forward, plucked an angular yellow rock from the working face. "If this rotten rock keeps going, it might take a whole lot longer. When we drift our way under the Number One, we'll have to crib our way up as we go. We hit stable rock again, it's just a matter of drilling, shooting, and mucking. We'll be making twenty-five feet a shift." He paused meaningfully. "If we hit good rock."

Absently she ran a finger along the scar in her cheek. "Didn't figure it would take this long."

He gave her a knowing squint. "What's your hurry? Got a shipment going out to Solar System that I don't know about? Ituri's making metal down at the smelter, and we're shipping it up to orbit for holding in vacuum. Didn't know we were behind on tonnage. Uh . . . assuming we ever see another ship from Solar System."

She grinned back, amused with herself. "Maybe part of me is still that same woman who stepped off *Turalon*. You're right. *Ashanti* couldn't take everything we had to ship as it was."

Ghosh slipped his glove off, wiped a drip from the end of his nose. "Do the math. *Turalon* spaced for Solar System five years ago. If everything worked, if she inverted symmetry and ran the equations backwards, she would have popped back inside right on cue three years ago. Would have taken her a couple of months to make the transit from Neptune orbit to Transluna. Wouldn't have needed more than a couple of weeks to unload her. Meanwhile, all of Solar System is hearing about the missing ships. They still think seven of the big cargo vessels have vanished. They won't have a clue that *Ashanti* or *Vixen* made it. The stories will be running wild about *Freelander* showing up as a ghost ship. The powers that be will be watching the holographic record of the temple of bones, seeing that spooky hallway with all the weird writing, and Jem Orten and Tyne Sakihara's corpses in the welded-up A.C."

"That ought to send shivers through the Board. Almost wish I could be there to see their faces," Kalico told him. "They'll control a lot of the images. Keep a lid on most of the more gruesome details, like the fact that the crew murdered all the transportees."

"What about the returning contractees?" Ghosh lifted an eyebrow. "Marston and his bunch with all their plunder. That's going to make a splash. And they'll tell the whole story."

"Oh, you innocent babe in the woods," she chided him. "We're talking about The Corporation. What principle was it founded on?"

"Control, distribution, and management for the good of all."

"Key words: control and management." Kalico winced as a large drop of water spattered on her helmet and exploded into silver mist under the harsh lights. "All the returning transportees will be handled with total efficiency, and believe me, the Boardmembers will be on top of any rumors as soon as they get a hint of trouble. By the time the first of the transportees step off *Turalon,* they'll have been completely versed in what to say and what not to say. Not to mention the consequences to themselves and their families if they go telling tales that are not officially sanctioned by the Board. What The Corporation won't be able to squelch is that something's wrong with the way we're inverting symmetry, that seven ships are missing and presumed lost. That *Freelander* suffered some catastrophe, and everyone died. And finally, that the colony has survived, if not prospered. But most of all, they can't stop the knowledge that Donovan is a treasure chest of potential wealth."

Ghosh pulled on his glove. "You think it's enough to make the Board turn *Turalon* around, put another crew on her, and send her back?"

"I don't know." Kalico watched a loose piece of rock break loose from the ceiling and clatter to the floor. It shattered into pieces when it hit. Rotten, indeed. "They'd be running the figures. Seven ships? That's a huge capital loss to write off. *Turalon*'s cargo? Most of it was clay. Remarkable clay, and enough to build two starships to be sure. And then there was the plunder. That, along with the geological reports, will have the Board intrigued. Of course, they'll trickle the gemstones and precious metals into the economy slowly so as not to disturb the markets."

"Oh, yes. Mustn't disturb the markets," Ghosh growled.

"But whether they'll turn *Turalon* around? I really can't say, and I've given it a lot of thought. Depends on the politics and backstabbing. On who has the power on the Board these days and what their agenda is. Who has the most to gain or lose? What's the political situation out among the stations? Social unrest? If so, it's a lot more likely they'll make the most out of *Turalon*'s arrival. Use the wealth as a distraction, disseminate glowing reports, and hope to ship as many radicals off to Donovan as they can manage to cram aboard. So, it's a tossup."

"Until *Ashanti* arrives," Ghosh added.

She gave him a conspiratorial wink. "If *Ashanti* arrives."

He shifted uncomfortably, gaze fixed on the crumbling rock.

"All this speculation about what the Board would do? It's just wishful thinking, Supervisor. For all we know, *Turalon* never made it back. Maybe she's lost somewhere in some other universe. Like *Freelander*, all of her passengers and crew are dead, and all that wealth is floating somewhere in blackness."

Kalico could well imagine. She could see it. The image of *Turalon*'s familiar decks. Dark. Cold. Rimed with ice crystals. Corpses, frozen for eternity, lay sprawled; or if the ship were totally dead, the bodies floated in free fall. And *Turalon*, hurtling through some dimensionless universe where the laws of time and space didn't exist. And she'd do it forever.

"Supervisor?" Ghosh prompted.

"Sorry." She shivered. "Take as long as you want. Do it right. Suddenly schedules aren't quite as important as I thought they were." Except for getting her butt out to the Maritime Unit. She should have been there a week ago, but for being up to her neck in cannibals, treetop terrors, and mayhem.

As she turned to walk away, the overhead rock gave off a loud crack, and another couple of angular pieces fell to clatter on the floor.

3

Kevina Schwantz let the wind blow through her long blond hair as she sent the motor launch skimming across the waves. Having just turned thirty-five, her tall body remained thin, still malnourished after all the long years on *Ashanti*. Too thin to her way of thinking, but she had always been body-conscious. During her undergrad years at University of St. Petersburg, and through her PhD work at Moscow Tech, she'd had to rely on her brains, but being drop-dead gorgeous had never hurt. They'd jokingly called her "the ice-blond goddess of the Arctic." The latter referred to where she'd done most of her dissertation and postdoctoral research.

Flying across the water, Capella's light warm on her face, the wind in her hair, *this* was what she lived for. She'd argued like a woman insane to get this chance, to get out under an open sky. It had been twelve years since she'd been at the controls of a boat. A seeming eternity since she'd been on the water. And this was a whole new world.

"We don't know what you might run into out there," Michaela had told her, expression worried.

"Nothing on this planet is as fast as the motor launch," she'd replied in her most reasonable voice. *"Director, if I encounter anything, I'll peg the throttles and run. It's a simple trip out and back. And the weather's perfect."* She'd shrugged. *"And I've got thousands of hours in motor launches. And that was in the Arctic."*

She shot a look over her shoulder to make sure that her son, eight-year-old Felix, was in his seat. Michaela hadn't thought to ask if she was taking the boy. And if the Director said anything, forgiveness was always easier to attain than permission. Besides Kevina had promised him. Told him for years that she'd take him on his first boat ride. To have left him behind today? It would have broken the little guy's heart.

Felix appeared mesmerized by the water. And well he should, he'd been born on *Ashanti*. Had known nothing but Crew Deck until they'd set foot on the landing field at Port Authority. Since that day, Felix's life had been one magical moment after another. Now he was taking his first boat ride, out in the open, across sparkling water. The look on her son's face was pure rapture, and that filled her heart with a kind of joy she'd rarely known.

Behind them, the Pod, looked like an elongated white egg where it perched on its pilings. Shoal waters swirled beneath and along the length of the reef where it stretched to the south.

Capella's light burned down from a partly cloudy sky, the golden rays reflecting on the low swells with their glassy surfaces. The horizon made a sharp line in the distance. There the sea looked like the finest of lapis lazuli where it met the lighter turquoise of the sky. A trio of aqua-blue-speckled-with-white flying creatures glided along to her right, effortlessly matching her twenty-knot speed. To Kevina's amazement, they had four wings—two per side—with what looked like a third set consisting of two stubs that protruded from the keel-shaped belly. The beasts had three eyes and a triangular mouth consisting of three jaws that narrowed to a spear-shaped snout. The tooth-studded jaws were open as they flew, apparently to act like a funnel. She wondered if—like so many of the land creatures—the gaping mouth functioned as an air intake. And, yes, as the closest swooped past, she could see the vents at the root of the thing's trailing tail.

"Felix! Look!" she called to her son as she raised her recorder to get video.

Felix spun from where he now was hanging over the gunwale. He had been watching the white foam splashing out from the launch's hull. Felix fixed his soft brown eyes on the fliers, his mouth forming an O of amazement. Bracing his arms, rapt, he watched the closest of the fliers soar over their heads, then veer off with a flap of the wings. The other two followed, cutting behind the boat. One dove, snatching something from the wake that twitched and flipped in its needle mouth. With a gulp, the beautiful blue flier swallowed its prey and sailed off after its comrades.

"What was that, Mama?"

"Felix, I don't have a clue. You and me? We're the first human beings to ever lay eyes on one. You want to name it?"

He stepped up beside her, barely kept his balance as the launch planed over a larger set of swells. "I don't know. Polka dots?"

"Polka dots? What kind of name is that?"

"It had those white spots on the blue."

"Okay. That's as good a name as any." She wondered how Soichiro Yoshimura—their marine biologist and evolutionary theorist—would react to naming an entire order of flying creatures as "polka dots."

"Did you see?" Felix asked soberly. "It ate something from the water."

"I did. That's called predation. You've always lived off ration. But way back in human history, we lived off prey. That means that humans hunted and killed and ate other creatures. Back in Solar System, meat is grown in factories, so we don't have to kill things. But, when they first started Port Authority, they brought animals to kill and eat because it was easier than a factory. There were cows, chickens, and pigs."

Felix made a face. "Yuk! That's sick."

"Yeah, well, Donovan made short work of the livestock." She turned her attention to the course, keeping to ninety degrees.

The launch—a thirty-meter V hull—was powered by a five-hundred-horsepower electrical engine, and Kevina pushed the throttle up a notch. The launch leapt ahead, planing across the swells.

Felix grasped onto the grab bar, wide-eyed, as he was thrown back. Then his face burst into a wide grin and he began to whoop with joy. "Faster, Mama. Faster!"

"That's thirty-five knots. That's fast enough for now."

Her attention being fixed as it was on the far horizon, she first caught movement at the edge of her vision. Focusing just ahead of the bow, she saw them. Darting images beneath the surface, like arrows that sped away at perpendicular angles from her course. Not that Kevina was the world's best judge of speed, but if she was doing thirty-five knots, the things zipping away just below the surface had to be twice to three times as fast.

Her PhD had been in oceans system theory with a specialization in the Arctic, so she'd had considerable training in marine biology. On Earth, a sailfish might hit an incredible seventy miles an hour in a short burst of speed but couldn't maintain it. Try as she might, she could think of no terrestrial fish or mollusk that could move as fast and far as these. Nor did this creature leave a gas trail like a hyper-cavitating torpedo would. She couldn't wait to catch one, see for herself what magical traits it possessed.

Just over the horizon, perhaps six kilometers off the port side, Kevina could make out the triangular sails of seaskimmers. She was contemplating their nature when something erupted from the ocean's surface not more than fifty meters to her left.

Kevina started at the proximity, at the intrusion to the perfect morning. Then she gaped. The breaching thing was big. Huge. Water ran in sheets from a midnight-blue head that had to be twenty meters across. She had a momentary glimpse of dark, water-sleek hide, and a midnight-black eye the size of a dinner plate. Some long, thin, and moon-blue creature thrashed in the giant's three-jawed mouth. One of the torpedoes?

As the launch barreled past, Kevina thought to reach for the recorder. By the time she pulled it up and hit the record button, only foam-white turbulence and spray remained where the beast had been. It had vanished as quickly as it had appeared.

"Zambo!" Felix cried. That was kid-speak on *Ashanti* for "Wow!" He was staring back, unease reflected from his posture. "What was that, Mama?"

"I don't have the first idea," she told him, thinking of the way a great white shark came from below to nail a sun-basking seal. But this leviathan had taken a moving target. And it had been huge. A shiver tightened her spine.

What if that monster wanted to take the launch?

She tried to calculate the size of the great three-jawed mouth. Big enough to engulf a thirty-meter boat? Maybe. The torpedo in its jaws had looked to be about ten meters in length.

Suddenly the morning, the sunlight, the smooth rolling water had taken a more ominous turn. Kevina couldn't help herself; she clicked the throttle up a notch to send the launch flying across the swells.

She remembered Michaela Hailwood's warning. *"You're just taking the launch out and back. Drop the sensor buoy and collect your water samples. Don't deviate from those two things, and in particular, don't get too close to anything that might be alive. We'll have time for that after we develop a protocol."*

"Wish Daddy had come." Felix interrupted her thoughts. "He would have liked to have seen that Big Mouth Thing."

Big Mouth Thing. The shorthand would be a BMT. She couldn't think of a better name for it.

"Daddy is putting a submarine together today. He's going to test it this afternoon."

Truth be told, Kevina would have liked to have had Yee come. Ever since they'd hooked up aboard *Ashanti*, they'd hardly ever spent time alone. Well, maybe a few stolen moments in an empty corridor, but nothing significant. And since Felix's birth, there had been nothing that resembled "family" time.

Their relationship had just happened. If she were going to choose a mate, it wouldn't have been Kim Yee. His training had been in sonar, remote sensing, deep-sea resource extraction and drilling. Nothing in his character was particularly outgoing, engaging, or charismatic. Yee was, well. . . . Okay, so he was boring.

But he'd been available and unattached. Outside of phenomenal sex, her affair with Derek Taglioni had been a disaster. She'd just broken up with Yoshimura, and she'd been desperate to prove to herself that she was still desirable, still the ice-blond goddess. Not just a discard. That first time, she'd practically ripped Yee's clothes off and wrestled him to the floor. For a month, she and Yee had carried on what was clearly "convenience copulation." And then *Ashanti* had popped back into regular space.

Out in the black.

Way off course.

The same day Kevina discovered she was pregnant.

The change in Yee had been immediate. He was always there. Good old boring Kim Yee. Say what you might about him, he stepped into the role of father without a second thought. Brought her food during the starving times after the Unreconciled failed to take the ship and were relegated to Deck Three. Placed her welfare and the baby's before his own. And as the years passed, the man doted on Felix.

Kevina had been the volatile one—and more than once when she and Yee were having trouble, she'd taken up with one of the others. Sometimes with Dek, sometimes with one of the other men in Maritime Unit. A lot of mate swapping went on over the years, but she always went back to Yee. Because of Felix. Because Yee loved his son with all of his heart.

She took a deep breath, eyes on the gently rolling swells they now shot across. The planing launch slapped them with rhythmic impacts she could feel through the hull.

What did the relationship mean for her now? For Felix? For Yee?

Since moving into the Pod, they'd been constantly at work. She'd been setting up, testing, and calibrating her sensors, studying maps, plotting wind patterns, and wondering where the currents ran. He'd been endlessly working with Shinwua on his robots and UUVs.

So, if Yee had come, what would it have been like? Left to themselves, alone as a family at last, could she and he have found anything in common outside of their son?

The beeper on the GPS sounded, indicating that she'd reached her position fifty kilometers out. Throttling back, she let the launch slow, the wake lifting the stern and rocking them forward.

"We're here?" Felix asked, looking around at the ocean.

"We're here." She stepped back to the buoy where it rested just forward of the fantail. "Want to help me?"

"Okay."

She bent down to where the sleek metal tube lay in its cradle and flipped on the power pack, GPS, transmitter, and beacon. Pointing to the glowing readouts, she explained, "See the numbers? They tell us that the transmitter is communicating with both the Pod and the locational satellite *Ashanti* placed in orbit. It's keyed to all of our buoys, the seatrucks, and launch. The GPS will allow the buoy to stay on station. If it gets blown, or the current tries to move it, the motors will keep it exactly where we drop it. Meanwhile it will be sending data through the satellite on temperature, current direction, wave height, wind speed, and water chemistry. All that in this one machine."

"Zambo."

"Help me now." She got her arms under the curved length of the buoy and lifted. Felix helped, and together they muscled the fifty-kilo cylinder onto the gunwale and rolled it over the side to splash into the lapis-blue water.

The thing sank, bobbed up, and righted itself, the readouts glowing a bright red on their screens.

Kevina could hear the faint whine of the motors as they stabilized the buoy. She picked up her com. "Michaela? Can you hear me?"

"Roger that. We're getting a clear reading. You're right at 50 kilometers out. We're calibrating now. Should take us about five minutes to fix the position and run the diagnostics."

"That works for me." She glanced around. "I suppose there's worse places to be."

"Like being the main course at a meal hosted by the Unreconciled?"

"Not even close. It's peaceful out here. Water's smooth as silk. Not a hint of wind. Smells like a faint perfume." She forced any thought of the Big Mouth Thing out of her mind. "I'd forgotten the magic of sunlight on water."

Kevina glanced over, smiled at Felix where her son was leaned over the gunwale, watching the buoy as it rose and fell in sync with the launch and the swells. As he did, she heard him humming the melody to *"London Bridge is Falling Down."*

"Roger that," Michaela replied with a laugh. *"Next time, I get to go. I've had enough of control rooms, light panels, and air conditioning."*

"What's this, Mama?"

She stepped over, propped herself on the gunwale, and looked down. On Earth, her first thought would have been a sort of algae. Here, who knew?

"Don't touch it, Felix. No telling what it is."

"It doesn't look scary, Mama."

"We won't know until we study it." She found her sample containers with their five-meter cords. One by one she lowered them over the side as far as they would go. A stiff tug on the cord pulled the mouth shut to seal them at depth. Then she pulled each jar in hand over hand.

She saw another blob of the floating algae, and out of impulse, fetched a container and scooped it up. Then she carefully labelled each sample jar, recording the time, date, and provenience.

On the other side of the launch, Felix was still hanging over the side, staring down at the water. Kevina was about to pull him back, when Michaela's voice over the com said, *"We're reading five by five, as the old saying goes. Water temperature is thirty-two degrees Celsius. Depth at your location is two thousand three hundred meters. Wind is point two knots with an ambient air temperature of twenty-nine degrees. Swells are running point six meters from crest to trough. I'll save the chemistry until you get back, but wow, it's like nothing on Earth, that's for sure."*

"Roger that. I'm headed back."

"Good. Don't linger. Word is that Bill Martin is feeding us lasagna tonight. Like, the real thing. Noodles, tomato sauce, garlic, parsley, spinach, and the fixings. All but cheese."

Kevina smiled. "Wouldn't miss that for the world. See you at the dock."

She turned. "Kiddo, you aren't going to believe what we're having for supper tonight."

He was still on his belly, rubbing his fingers together. He studied them thoughtfully, and then rubbed his hand on the fabric of his overalls.

"Felix? What's the matter?"

"My fingers itch."

He wiggled back from the gunwale and offered his hands. She studied the delicate skin of his fingers, seeing nothing more than a greasy sheen. "That looks pretty good."

Nevertheless, she used the rag to wipe them dry. "There, good as new. But you do me a favor. Don't touch anything. It might be dangerous?"

"How do you know?"

"Well, little man, you don't. And you don't want to find out. I know you were fascinated by that stuff that looked like algae. What if it had started to eat the skin off of your fingers? Hmm? That would really hurt, and all it would leave behind is bloody bones."

"Okay."

"Good, because if it had eaten your fingers, you couldn't have lasagna tonight. You wouldn't be able to hold a fork. Not with just bones left."

"What's lazanna?"

"Lasagna. It's wondrous and tasty like you've never known."

"There's more, Mama."

"More lasagna?"

"Of that sticky stuff," he told her. "It's on the side of the boat."

She glanced over, seeing little greenish-blue blobs sticking to the launch's hull at the water line. More of it floated around them. Curious stuff. She wondered how it managed to survive, then figured from the color that it must have some manner of photosynthesizing. The chemistry required to use sunlight to create proteins and sugars was the same on Donovan as it was on Earth.

"Come on. Let's go eat lasagna." She throttled up, spun the launch around and took her heading back toward the Pod.

Felix stepped up beside her as they headed west, the launch rocketing over the low swells. Felix kept rubbing his fingers on the pantleg of his coveralls. Probably thinking of what it would be like to have acid eating his skin off. Good. It was a lesson well learned.

4

Derek Taglioni lay on bedrock, at the edge of the canyon rim. His head was reeling from the pain. What the hell? How had he come to . . . ? Yes. Mobbers, it had been mobbers. He'd been down, a couple of meters below the rim, working his way along with a geologist's pick hammer, testing samples of ore. Had heard the chittering call of the mobbers, seen the flock coming, a remarkable swirling column of multicolored, churning flying beasts.

Dek had been hurt before. Thought he knew pain. He didn't. Not even close. Fire and agony might have been mutilating his left calf. Tears squeezed past his lids as he clamped them shut. Looking down he should see his lower left leg in shreds of ruined meat and splintered bone. Nothing else could explain this kind of agony.

Dek blinked, remembered throwing himself flat, covering his head. How they'd come, fluttering around him. Wings beating, chittering, squeaking, whistling. The patting and batting of his clothing, the vulnerable back of his neck.

And all the while what felt like acidic fire had started to eat into his left leg. Like burning needles that seared the flesh.

But I didn't dare move. Not with the flying death hovering, trying to decide if he was prey.

And then they'd flown on, a last few pausing to flutter above him, uttering a high-pitched harmonic of curiosity before following the flock on their way toward mayhem.

Only then had he been able to look down, horrified to see the gotcha vine shooting spines into his leg and foot. He barely remembered the fight to free his leg as he slashed and hacked with his long knife. Or the crawl that followed as he whimpered, cried out in agony, and screamed each time he jarred his leg.

Somehow he'd made it to the caprock. Here, to this bit of bare basalt. And consuming pain.

His leg had to be tattered ruins. But when he dared a glance, his leg was whole. Horrendously swollen, skin pulled tight and shiny as if it would pop open, but whole.

Dek leaned his head back and screamed.

Out of instinct, he reached for his knife. Tried to crush the handle in his grip.

The knife. That was the solution.

God! Yes! He could reach down. Cut right at the knee. Sever the whole calf. Slice it clear off. A body couldn't take it.

Fucking gods, get it over with!

"Dek?" Talina's voice cut through the haze.

"I want it off. You do it. Cut it off!"

"Hey! Look at me!"

An iron grip tightened on his wrist. He felt the knife wrenched away as it was peeled out of his trembling hand.

He blinked through the tears, managed to fix on her face where it was lit by the dying light as Capella sank below the canyon wall to the west.

Talina? Here? Yes. It had to be Talina. A whimper broke from his throat as a wave of pain sent him into a spasm.

How did Talina get here?

Through glazed eyes he glanced around. Chabacho trees and aquajade. Sunset. He could barely hear the chime, rising, mocking. He couldn't feel the rock he lay on. Pain. Only the blasting damn pain.

Rock? Basalt? How did he get to the cap rock? He now lay at the edge of the canyon. Could see it drop off into a wilderness of trees no more than a meter from where he lay. Last he recalled he'd been under the canyon rim. Below the capping strata of basalt. On the steep slope. Surrounded by plants. Picking his way along the vein. Found a chunk of quartz that gleamed with nodules of gold. And then. . . . And then . . .

"I climbed," he whispered, remembering. If only his thoughts weren't wheeling and reeling.

Focus. It's Talina.

Talina Perez filled him with awe; the most exotic woman he'd ever known. Quetzal genetics made her that way, TriNA, or trioxy-nucleaic acid. The Donovanian analog to terrestrial DNA. The stuff had turned Talina into a hybrid. One mostly human, but her angular cheekbones, the large dark eyes, and the intensity with which she watched him most assuredly had an alien quality.

"I'm not cutting your leg off."

He fixed on her voice, an anchor in a burning sea of misery. Somehow he got a swallow down his throat. Yes, look at her. Concentrate.

She had the richest black hair. Thick. Pinned behind her neck, it still spilled down her back.

"This is going to hurt," she told him. Capella's sunset light had turned her skin into gold, shot fire along the edges of her black coveralls.

Hurt? Too late for that. He'd have laughed if the mind-killing agony had left him any wits.

He screamed as she lifted him. Tossed him over her shoulder. Screamed some more as Talina pounded down the trail. She dodged the sucking shrub, veered wide around the tooth flower, ducked the blood vines with their crimson tentacles, and hammered her way heedlessly across the writhing roots. With each step, his leg exploded anew. Kept bursting, the meat blasting away from the bone. Nerves splintered into an infinity of fire. Time after time.

The world started spinning, his vision a blur of aquajade, squirming roots, reaching branches of green and turquoise leaves blurring as they whipped sideways.

At a particularly hard jolt, pain stunned him. Couldn't help it. His stomach pumped. Acid bile filled his mouth, clogged the back of his nose. He coughed and coughed, each wracking of his body beyond endurance.

"Stop! In the name of God, just kill me," he heard some dissociated part of him plead. "I can't stand this."

"Hey, Dek," her voice came from somewhere beyond the pain. "You'll make it. It's the gotcha vine. The thorns shoot poison into you. Paralyzes the local critters, just burns like liquid fire in humans.

Let me get you back to camp. I've got something that will make you better."

Each breath broke into a whimper.

Falling.

Falling into pain.

The blur around him darkened, softened. Until . . .

5

A faint sensation of impacts hammered through Dek's sternum. Air was being blown into his lungs, inflating his chest.

Something on his mouth. Movement on his lips. More air.

A taste of overpowering and bitter peppermint.

Dek gasped, jerked.

He blinked his eyes open. Stared into Talina's anxious gaze, her face hovering close over his as her lips left his mouth.

Starved for air, he gasped a lungful, almost gagging at the overwhelming peppermint that filled his mouth, his lungs.

"You back with us?" Talina asked. "That was quite a scare you gave me."

"I . . . ?" He blinked some more; mouth filling with saliva, he swallowed the bitter taste.

"You stopped breathing. Couldn't find any heartbeat. Thought I'd lost you." Talina shone a penlight into Dek's eyes, watching him critically for a few moments, and straightened.

How long had he been gone?

Dek felt like he rose in the gray haze. Floated.

His left leg throbbed. Distant. Dull.

A crackling. He knew that sound.

Yes, fire.

The flicker of it teased the backs of his eyelids, and he blinked. Fixed glassily on the fire. He was back in his camp, and lay supine atop his bedroll. Behind him, his airplane glowed whitely in the firelight. The night sky above was frosted with a million stars; opaque blots of dark matter and alternating swirls of nebulae interspersed with patterns of cloud.

He gasped, glanced down. Talina was bent over his left leg. Her hair pulled back over her shoulder.

He remembered her hair. How soft it was. Her lips on his, blowing life into his empty lungs.

She'd carried him. Tossed him up over her shoulder like a sack of flour. That, too, was the quetzal in her. The woman was as strong as two men.

The slight breeze chilled his bare legs. What had happened to his pants? His boots were missing.

If he could just think.

Why the hell did his left leg ache so? What was Talina doing? Why was she here?

"Tal?" Damn. Why couldn't he find words? His whole fricking body was floating.

Couldn't think.

"You're going to be all right," Talina told him, looking up from his hugely swollen left calf. The thing looked as if it were overinflated, the skin so tight it would burst at any moment.

"Wha . . . ? What?" He blinked, tried to focus. Seemed to drift sideways as the ground went rubbery.

"Relax," she told him. "Don't try to think. You can't. You're doped up past your gills. It's a painkiller. One of Dya Simonov's concoctions made out of blue nasty."

"But I . . . ?"

"I said, don't try to think." She shifted enough to take his hand, the side of her face golden in the firelight. "Just listen." She squeezed his hand as if in emphasis. "You did fine, Dek. You were prospecting. When the mobbers flew over, you played dead. Even though a gotcha vine grabbed hold of your leg. That took some real guts. Don't know how you endured it. Then, when the mobbers flew off, you fought your way free of the gotcha vine. But its spines were embedded in your calf and foot."

He blinked, struggling to remember. Wondered if the kaleidoscopic images cartwheeling through his memory were real. Had to be. Those four-winged creatures, alternately glowing in laser-bright patterns of blue, red, yellow, green, and orange? He'd never seen a live flock of the feared predators. This had to be a memory.

"I threw myself flat on the ground. Remember that. Roots were wiggling under me. But the mobbers were fluttering around, making that odd chitter. Checking the trees, looking under branches, trying to scare up anything that would move. Saw one get a tree clinger. Sliced the poor guy into ribbons as the things flew off with it. Left the bones to fall back to the ground."

"Sounds about right." Talina gave his hand a squeeze again.

"Pain started in my leg," Dek told her. "I couldn't let myself move. Not until those flying bastards had moved on."

"If you had, that tree clinger's bones wouldn't be the only ones out here." Talina gave him a ghostly smile. "The first time I got into gotcha vine, it was just a couple of spines. I thought someone had poured boiling acid into my arm. Second time left scars on my hip and upper thigh. It's your whole lower leg, Dek."

"Did I really try to cut my leg off?"

"I stopped you."

"How'd you get here?"

"Sheer dumb luck. You were down in the canyon. *Vixen* just happened to be overhead when you called out a mayday. They relayed your signal to Two Spot. You were still lucid enough to give your location. Said you were going to try and make it to a basalt outcrop at the top of the canyon. Closest aid would have been Chaco and Madison, but they were on the way to Port Authority and didn't have enough charge to turn back."

She gave him a half-hearted shrug. "Step Allenovich and I argued over which one of us was going to have to fly way out here and save your scrawny ass. After a couple shots of whiskey, finally we drew straws. I got the short one, and Step wouldn't go two out of three."

"The fulfillment of dreams," he whispered.

"How's that?"

"I've fantasized about spending a night alone in the bush with you." Oh, had he ever!

"Okay." She arched a thin eyebrow. "So, like, a lot of men fantasize about spending a night with me. Most know it wouldn't end well. None of them, however, are dumb enough to let a gotcha vine chew on them just to get the chance."

"Then they're fools."

Her oversized dark eyes fixed on his with a curious intensity. "All right, tough guy, now that you've got me here, what are you going to do about it?"

He tried to fix his thoughts on the question, but they just seemed to drift aimlessly until an image of her popped into his head: Under a star-filled sky she lay on her back as he made love to her; her hair was spread on the ground in a midnight wave. Her legs were locked around his hips, her arms crushing him to her. He was staring into her eyes, drinking her soul. Lost in the image, he said, "You are beautiful, you know. Unlike any woman I've ever known. You're so . . . fantastic."

She laughed, flashing white teeth, which brought him back to the night, the camp, and the fact that she was fully clothed beside him. "Raya warned me. Said that you'd be drugged past any good sense, and anything might come out of your mouth."

"I mean it. You are. I'd be honored to take you anywhere in Transluna. Can't think of a single one of the courtesans who would merit more envy than if I walked into the Three Spires with you on my arm."

Talina leaned back on her haunches, releasing his hand. "Now, that's an aspiration I've never striven to attain. Wonder how it's slipped my attention over all these years?"

"You mock me." God, why couldn't he find his wits? The drug? Really? If he could only think.

"Besides," she told him, "I thought you were interested in Kalico. She's the Supervisor. And you had a thing for her back in Transluna, even if you were a spectacularly crass boor about it."

"I understand now."

"Understand what?"

"Why she went to Miko's bed. She's remarkably competent to have played Miko the way she did. Of course, he knew she was using him for her own advancement, just as he was using her to sate his rather perverse sexual appetites. I suspect he'd have had her murdered eventually. If he hadn't, she would have ruined him. Left him trailing in her wake like broken flotsam."

Talina considered him. "Tough world you folks have back in The Corporation. And I thought quetzals played rough."

The breeze cooled his naked legs. "Where are my pants?"

"Folded yonder. I had to be able to pull the gotcha spines out. Can't do that through coveralls. I think I got them all. Just for good measure, I shot you up with an antibiotic along with Dya's anesthetic to keep the pain at bay. Still, if I'd known the stuff would shut off any good sense you might have had, I'd have considered letting you scream."

"You don't like me, do you?"

Again she gave him that intense inspection, the firelight playing on her face. "Yeah, Dek. I like you." She patted him on the thigh before rising. "And that's probably not a healthy situation for either one of us."

"Why not?"

She paused where she'd headed for her aircar, turned, looking back in the firelight. He thought she looked marvelous in the flickering yellow glow. Her raven hair, the slim body in its form-fitting black fabric, the muscular poise and almost feral balance. And those eyes, those marvelous eyes that stared right down to his soul.

He was adrift in his mind now, feeling a euphoria as he asked, "I wonder what it would be like to hold you, love you?"

She retrieved something from the aircar, walked back and knelt beside him. As she slipped the needle under the skin of his arm and injected the fluid she said, "Think it through, Dek. I'm a sort of hybrid freak. And you? You're a Taglioni."

"That doesn't . . ." He was falling into gray clouds, eyes closing . . .

"Good night, sweet prince," he heard her say from some incredible distance.

6

I n a very real way, the children were the heart and soul of the Maritime Unit. Michaela had understood it from the very beginning. That Kevina Schwantz had been pregnant had figured into Michaela's calculus clear back when she'd ordered her people not to participate in the Unreconciled's attempt to seize *Ashanti*. Thinking of her people as family, she'd ordered them off Deck Three the moment the insurrection failed. She had directed them to throw their lot in with Captain Galluzzi and the crew.

Michaela had stifled any protest when Galluzzi locked the rest of the transportees behind the hatch down on Deck Three. In Michaela's mind, if Kevina was pregnant, it meant the ship's birth control was breaking down. Something was wrong with the dietary progesterone supplement. Kevina would only be the first, given the realities of men and women in close confinement.

After Felix came Sheena and Felicity. A year later, Tomaya was born. Almost one baby a year followed, including Breez, now five; Toni, who was three; little Kayle had just had his second birthday; and then a spate of infants. New life born among them in spite of the poor nutrition and the numerous miscarriages. The children had given her people a separate identity, one that the surgically sterilized crew would never mimic. And now, eight years and nine kids later, she could see the fruits of her wisdom. A certain enjoyment came from watching the parents treating their young to lasagna. Of watching the children's faces screw up, or the smacking of their lips.

For her part, Michaela wasn't sure if the lasagna was as good as she remembered. With no dairy, cheese was only a memory. These weren't egg noodles after all. There were no chickens on Donovan to lay eggs, but the rich red tomato sauce was so good she didn't care.

In a very real sense, the children belonged to all of them. A living

legacy to their survival of *Ashanti*'s near-disastrous passage. A coun-
terbalance to the horrors of the Unreconciled, of the starving times,
and an affirmation that they had made it across thirty light years of
space to continue as a species.

The first-level room where they ate was located on the Pod's
north end, and served as mess hall, auditorium, commons, and—
when the tables and benches were folded flush into the floor—as the
gym/playroom. The kitchen where Bill Martin held court opened
off to one side. Through the central doorway was the landing. A
hatch behind the stairs opened out onto the dock where the seatrucks
and launch were stowed and could be lowered to sea level.

The second set of stairs—opposite and through the pressure
hatch—went down the tube and through a second pressure hatch to
the Underwater Bay five meters below sea level. Continuing down
the length of the Pod, beyond the stairways, was gear storage on
either side of the hallway. Past storage, on each side, were the personal quarters. Finally, the hallway ended at an observation blister
with its clear dome looking out over the water.

Opposite the tube access, a set of stairs led up to the second-level
labs, clinic, com center, and offices. From there, yet another set of
stairs opened to the landing pad on the roof.

This was Michaela's kingdom: six thousand three hundred square
meters of living space, labs, equipment, and life-support systems. A
solitary terrestrial outpost in the middle of Donovan's trackless and
unmapped oceans thirty light years from Solar System.

A burst of childish laughter intruded on her thoughts. Sheena, who
was Kel Carruthers's and Vik Lawrence's seven-year-old daughter,
had tomato sauce smeared on her cheeks as she wolfed down a whole
lasagna noodle. The thirty-eight-year-old Lawrence held a PhD in
marine microbiology, taxonomy, and genetics. For a couple of years
after Sheena was born, Vik had taken up with one of the *Ashanti*
crew, but ultimately had come back to Kel, who in the interim had
moved into Kevina's bed. As if by unspoken rule, the children had
remained, more or less, community property; steps had always been
taken to keep the adult drama from their already-fragile lives.

Funny thing how relationships had worked out on *Ashanti*. She'd once explained it to Miguel Galluzzi with one word: complicated.

The miracle was that during the turbulent years—and despite numerous promises to do so—no one had been murdered. Ultimately a live-and-let-live we're-only-human-so-lets-make-the-best-of-it philosophy had developed. Michaela had been uncommonly lucky. By chance she'd been given the right mix of personalities that they'd finally coalesced into a close-knit and pragmatic bunch instead of exploding into violence and retribution.

Well, all except Dr. Anna Carrasco Gabarron. She was second only to Michaela in age. Along with having a smattering of medical training, Gabarron was the marine chemist and aquatic system's specialist. Decidedly single, surly, and bitter, she'd avoided the squabbles, gossip, and tumultuous relationships during the years they'd been crammed into *Ashanti*. The woman was just plain anti-social, but brilliant in her field. Now she sat in the last seat by the door, eating thoughtfully and watching the rest feasting on their lasagna. Hard to tell what lay behind Gabarron's dark-brown gaze. As always, the woman's expression was fixed, slightly disdainful. For tonight she'd pulled her hair back into a severe ponytail that revealed the silver at her temples.

Iso Suzuki stepped out from the kitchen, the large lasagna pan in her hands. "Can you eat more, Michaela?" she asked. "Bill doesn't want leftovers."

"Sure." Michaela offered her plate and Iso served up another of the kitchen-sized spoonfuls before marching on to dish more onto Shinwua's plate. Of course Shin would have seconds. Anything to support Martin. Captain Galluzzi had married the two of them a couple of years back.

Nor would there be leftovers. After *Ashanti* no one took food for granted. They were all still thin, weak, lacking in stamina from the endless malnutrition and barely sufficient ration. And then there was taste. Like this marvelous lasagna. Rich with tomatoes, spinach, and spices.

Michaela launched into her second helping. After the endless monotony of ration, this was pure bliss—though she and the rest were still struggling to come to terms with Port Authority's preoccupation with hot peppers and garlic. So, what the hell if it burned the skin off her tongue? Taste was everything!

"You'll adjust," Raya Turnienko—the MD at Port Authority—had informed them. "And the garlic is necessary as a chelation agent for the constant exposure to heavy metals. Believe me, you'll stay healthier for it."

Michaela had to admit, the profusion of garlic in the lasagna wasn't nearly as overpowering as some of the dishes Bill Martin had been serving up. Since he'd finally been turned loose in a real kitchen, the man was a marvel. Maybe Shinwua was the smartest of them all when he married the man.

The lasagna was also a celebration. Today they'd actually started their research in earnest. Schwantz had taken the first of the buoys out. Jaim Elvridge had piloted the submarine for its rather limited shakedown dive while Casey Stoner had manned the recorders and cameras to take the photos of the fantastic creatures that called the reef home. To see the stunning array of life forms was overwhelming. They had no frame of reference for the creatures and plants. No terms to describe the colors, the incomprehensible shapes. Casey had been speechless—a wonder given that she'd specialized in kelp-forest ecology and trophic systems theory.

And then there was video of the polka dots, and Kevina's report about the torpedoes and Big Mouth Thing—whatever kind of creature that might have been. Kevina hadn't been quick enough to get video of the deepwater leviathan.

"Wish she had," Michaela muttered under her breath. Anything as big as Kevina described it—not to mention as fast as she claimed it to be—would be well worth further investigation.

"Have to think about how we record these missions. We need some sort of three-sixty video record." She made a mental note to discuss it with Shinwua.

Baby steps to be sure, but the first for their exploration of Donovan's oceanography.

She was reveling in the feeling of euphoria when Bryan Atumbo wiped his mouth, pushed his plate back, and rose from his seat. The man walked over asking, "Got a minute, Director?"

"Hey, I've got all night, Bryan. But I'm going back to watch that holovid that Casey took of the reef. That purple thing with a thousand eyes just can't be for real."

He pulled out the chair next to her, sat, and laced his fingers together. "I did the after-action check on the motor launch. Pulled it out of the water and onto the dock according to protocol. I asked Kevina if she noticed anything weird about the boat while she was out dropping that buoy. Any funny noises. Felt anything through the hull. Asked if she'd hit anything floating. Or maybe a reef. She said no, but there's gouges. You know, like someone has taken a chisel and scraped it down the hull a couple of times on either side of the keel."

"There aren't any shoals out there. Nothing she could have hit unless it was floating debris."

Atumbo shrugged. "I'm just telling you that those gouges weren't there when I lowered the launch into the water this morning. It's my job to notice these things. The launch has a duraplast hull, so it's not like sialon, but that's still pretty tough stuff. Whatever peeled those slices had to be really sharp and really hard."

"Okay, I'll go over the charts again. They were generated a couple of decades ago, not to mention from space. Maybe they missed a shallow, something volcanic that bubbled up from the ocean floor after the impact. Anything else, Bryan?"

"Just some slimy stuff that was on the hull. Sort of like the tar we see stuck to hulls in the Gulf of Mexico or maybe the Persian Gulf. You know, where there's oil seeping out. But it's slimy and greenish blue. Didn't feel like tar. It washed off with a power spray."

"Bryan, make note of the gouges, put it in the service records."

"Already done, Supervisor."

Michaela glanced down the table where Kevina was in conversation with Lara Sanz. Beside her, Kim Yee had little Felix on his lap, holding the boy with one hand, using a slice of bread to sop up the last of the tomato sauce on his plate with the other.

Felix was telling Sheena something. Showing the little girl the tips of his fingers, letting her touch them. When she did, the little boy let out a giggle, and loud enough for Michaela to hear, cried, "That tickles!"

Gouges in the hull? Surely if Kevina had hit something, she'd have put it in her report.

7

The official name of the tavern was The Bloody Drink. Everyone on Donovan called it Inga's for the owner proprietor, Inga Lock. Inga was a big-boned woman, blond, and buxom. Her personality matched her body; it came on strong. Across the alley, behind the tavern, Inga brewed, distilled, and fermented the finest beer, spirits, and wines on the planet. All of which she dispensed with a smile. At least she did as long as her patrons had coin to cover their food and beverages. What made Inga's unique was that it was Donovan's one and only tavern.

Sure, you could get a drink at The Jewel casino, or Betty Abel's brothel, but they didn't have the amiable sit-down atmosphere where you could bring the family, let alone order a meal cooked to order. Not to mention that both of the aforementioned establishments catered to a rather unsavory clientele. On Donovan—when it came to the social center of the planet—Inga's was *urbs et orbis:* City and world.

Kalico Aguila perched on her usual bar stool. She had flown in with the weekly rotation of workers from Corporate Mine, having worked out a deal with the triumvirate years back. Her people needed the skills, manufacturing, and amenities of Port Authority, such as they were. Port Authority needed the production of her smelter, access to *Freelander's* free-fall manufacturing, and the additional income from Corporate Mine. One couldn't survive without the other.

In the beginning, when Aguila had arrived on Donovan, she'd almost destroyed Port Authority's independent-minded leadership. Had actually arrested Talina Perez, Shig Mosadek, and Yvette Dushane. Was going to convict them of treason and shoot them down in the street as a lesson meant to put the rest of the local hardheads in their place. The memory brought a smile to Kalico's lips. She lifted her glass of whiskey in a salute to her scarred image where it reflected from the back bar. "To lessons well learned," she toasted herself.

The scars were proof of that. She'd been a ravishing beauty before the mobbers sliced her into ribbons. They would have killed her but for a handy sialon crate. She had barely managed to dive into it. Even as they continued slashing her open and chewing on her flesh, she'd had to stomp, strangle, and crush the hideous beasts she'd trapped inside the box with her. Not all of her people had been as lucky.

Behind her, Inga's was half-filled with patrons who sat at the long chabacho-wood tables. Outside, night was falling. For the most part, the families had retreated to their domes and houses, but the boisterous element was here. Sheyela Smith sat with Tyrell Lawson and Toby Montoya, mugs of beer in hand as they hovered over a tablet. Some sort of skull session to cobble together a jury-rigged kind of machine for Lee Halston's sawmill.

As Kalico pondered that, Shig Mosadek climbed onto the bar stool beside hers. She gave the Indian a sidelong appraisal, taking in his brown face, mushroom-mashed nose, as well as the wild and unkempt hair that was graying at his temples. The comparative religions scholar barely stood five foot three. One of the triumvirate, he was the last person one would expect to be in a leadership position in hard-knuckled and rough-and-tumble Port Authority.

"How's life?" Kalico asked.

"Very good. I sold two squash to finally pay what I owed Rude Marsdome for these new boots." He pointed to the knee-high quetzal-hide footwear that shot rainbow patterns of light up and down their length. "The old ones were getting a little worn."

"Understatement of the year, Shig. Your old ones looked like hell. How long you had them?"

"Let's see. Ten? No, must have been twelve years at least. Wait. It was before the arrival of the *Tableau*. That was what? Fifteen years ago?"

"No wonder they looked like you'd stolen them off a corpse. But then, you've never really been a slave to sartorial perfection." She took in his use-polished quetzal-hide cloak, the embroidered claw-shrub-fiber shirt and scuffed-and-stained chamois-leather pants.

He ignored the barb. Said, "You had an amused look on your face. Am I to interpret that to mean that things at Corporate Mine are running with unusual efficiency?"

She laughed, studied the light reflected in her glass of whiskey. "Hardly. The Number Three has us at wits end. It's a nightmare of shoring, mucking, and driving rod. My people are half-spooked to work it, and I don't blame them. But it's paying, and if we can drive that bore under the Number One, it will make everyone's life so much easier." A pause. "And richer."

Kalico lifted a finger when Inga glanced her way. The burly blond woman was pouring beer from a tap in one of her kegs. Kalico pointed to Shig. Inga jerked a short nod and went back to her pour.

"Actually," Kalico told him, "I was thinking back to the time that I had you, Yvette, and Talina arrested for treason. I was sitting right there." She pointed to the backside of the middle of the bar. "Holding court. Ready to sentence the three of you to death."

Shig smiled wistfully. "We did teeter on the edge of disaster, didn't we?"

"Talina stopped it. It would have ended in a bloodbath. Only the marines would have made it, and not all of them, I suppose."

Shig smiled at Inga as she brought him his customary half glass of wine. Kalico had rarely seen the man even drink that much, and never had he had a second glass. He treated the drink more like a toy, something to amuse himself with.

Shig tossed out an SDR coin that Inga snapped up. She dropped it in a pocket, took a couple of swipes with the bar rag she had slung across her shoulder, and asked, "Anything else? Supervisor, you all right?"

At Kalico's thumbs-up, the woman hurried back down the bar— an irresistible object in motion.

Shig lifted his wine, studied the light through the red liquid. "That was not just Talina, you know. She gave you an out, one that you were smart enough to take. A more obtuse personality might have failed to recognize and seize such a solution. Such a person might have made it a point of honor, no matter what the cost."

Kalico sipped her whiskey, let it run over her tongue. Alcohol wasn't allowed at Corporate Mine. Her rule. One she chafed over but wouldn't change. It made her visits to PA more enjoyable. "You once said that if I could put my cultural baggage aside, I would be capable of great things. Seems that I also remember you saying that lunacy was catching."

Through a placid smile, Shig told her: "That woman who arrived on *Turalon* knew nothing but the rage and anger of tamas. You now have a leavening of sattva gained through suffering, responsibility, and self-examination."

"I don't want to hear all that Buddhist crap."

"Hindu. You're as bad as Talina."

"Speaking of which, where is she? I would have expected her to be here given the hour and all." Kalico indicated the empty barstool next to hers. The one everyone in Port Authority reserved for the nominal head of security and local legend.

"She's out in the bush. Apparently Dek Taglioni got himself in some sort of trouble. Tal took her aircar and headed out that way a little after noon."

"What kind of trouble?" Kalico felt every nerve stand on end. Mention of Taglioni did that. She still wasn't sure what to make of the guy. Back in Solar System, he'd been a foul-mouthed bit of walking human flotsam. Make that *ultra-privileged* walking human flotsam. A scion of the politically powerful Taglioni family, he'd been first cousin to Miko Taglioni, the Boardmember to whom Kalico Aguila had bound herself. Her encounters with Derek had been anything but pleasant.

Shig was watching her closely. "He called in on the radio, said he'd had a bit of a scare. That a pack of mobbers had flown over. Story is that he'd dived to the ground. Covered his head. Problem was that his left leg was within range of a gotcha vine. By the time the mobbers had passed over and he could take his knife to the gotcha vine, it had eaten through his boot and into his calf. Apparently the plant was pretty adamant about not letting him go. It kept grabbing hold of him as he cut his leg free."

"Shit." Kalico slapped the bar. "I'd better get to the shuttle, get out there. Cancel the trip to the Maritime Unit tomorrow, and—"

"It's dark. The gate to the landing field is locked, and you'll never get past the guard." Shig indicated the dome overhead, Capella's light having vanished from the sky. "And Talina's out there. She's had dealings with gotcha vine before. She'll have him loaded up first thing in the morning. He'll be in the hospital and under Raya's care by midday."

Kalico rubbed her brow. It figured that Dek had finally gotten himself into a mess. One of her worst nightmares was that she'd be the one who would have to tell Miko how his cousin died, that she hadn't been able to keep the prick alive.

Prick?

Well, that was the question, wasn't it?

Images flickered through her memory. Dark forest. Fear and thirst. Dek Taglioni handing her an energy bar when she was on her last legs. His infectious smile, the dimple in his chin. How his green-ringed yellow eyes—genetically designed for effect—twinkled when he shared a joke with her.

"That's a tortured expression," Shig noted.

"Trying to figure out what to do with Dek. Wondering who he is. What he is."

"I heard that you didn't think much of him back in Solar System." Shig fingered the stem of his wineglass. "Dek doesn't think much of who he was, either."

She took another small sip of whiskey to keep her tongue fresh. "Shig, do leopards change their spots? Do the evil ever truly become good? Can a onetime monster become a saint? He stays with you when he's in town. What do you think?"

"Dek is a man in search of himself. What he endured in *Ashanti* should have broken him. Instead, he held on, grasping onto something he never knew he had."

Shig lifted his wine to his lips, but Kalico wasn't sure he actually drank any.

"And now?"

"Supervisor, he is no longer the man he was back in Solar System. Nor is he the man who scrubbed toilets and worked hydroponics aboard *Ashanti*. As to why he is risking his life out in the bush? I think it is to prove something to himself . . . and perhaps partially as an act of the penance he insists he doesn't believe in."

"I don't know what to do with him."

Shig dryly added, "In more ways than one, I think."

"What's that supposed to mean?"

"He is your only social equal on the planet. You enjoy his company. You share a common origin and can speak honestly about a way of life that only a select few can aspire to. But each time you find yourself drawn to him, the reminder of who he was back in Transluna rises to haunt that most-analytical-and-cautious brain of yours. That same world that you share, the one that brings you commonality, haunts you both."

"You think I have a crush on him?"

"*Crush* is an unseemly and unsuitable word. I do think you are attracted to him for all the above-mentioned reasons. And as the Corporate Supervisor, you remain separate—apart from your people despite the camaraderie you have managed to cultivate. Just because you rely on your strength of will, your determination and faith in yourself, doesn't mean you don't wish that you had someone to share the burden."

She laughed at that. "I share my burden with you, Yvette, and Talina. Which makes the irony that once upon a time I was going to shoot you even richer."

Nevertheless, it bothered her. Irritated her that Shig could see her confusion so clearly. Damn it, she did enjoy her time with Dek. They did have a lot in common to talk about. And she did, on occasion, have those fantasies about what it would be like to have a man again. One trained in the arts of sex, who spoke her language, and understood her history and needs. A man she could be *intimate* with on all levels.

She'd also spent way too much time worrying that the fool was going to come to grief out in the bush, and now she learned that

Dek was hurt? Badly? While she was sitting here in the safety of Inga's, he was in excruciating pain.

"We're sure that Talina made it out to Dek's?" she asked.

"She called in. Had a conversation with Raya about Dek's leg. My understanding is that Dek died on her, and Tal brought him back. Last I heard, Tal had him stabilized. By now she's got him in, under cover, and will be battening down for the night."

"Died?"

"Like I said, Tal got to him in time. He's stabilized. Could have been worse, mobbers and all."

Kalico fought the urge to finger the line of scar on her cheek. "At least he had enough sense to play dead for the mobbers." A man had to be tough to hold still and not even quiver while a gotcha vine was eating into his leg. That was the thing about Dek. He listened. Learned.

Her fingers tapped on the side of her glass. Part of her really wanted to stay in PA, to be there tomorrow when Tal brought Dek in. You know, just to be sure that he was all right. He was, after all, a Taglioni. Her loyalty lay with the Taglionis. Miko was her patron. He'd ensured that she got the assignment to *Turalon*. Dek was her responsibility.

Fleeting fantasies of her meeting him at the hospital, overseeing Raya's care. Ensuring that Dek got the best of everything. That she could ease his recovery, care for his . . .

What the hell am I doing?

Kalico shook her head to rid herself of the sappy images of her playing nurse.

Shig watched her with amusement, his wide lips pinching off a smile.

"I'm going to the Maritime Unit tomorrow," she declared. "Michaela Hailwood has been after me since she got the Pod placed. Would have been out there a week ago, but for the mess down in the Number Three."

When she glared at Shig, he avoided her eyes, lifted his wine to his lips in an effort to hide the smile.

Yes, that's what she'd do. Dek had gotten himself into this mess, he'd just have to live with it.

Nevertheless, it rankled that Talina would get to play hero. And Dek had always had a thing for Talina.

Kalico could just wait long enough in the morning to ensure that Dek was made comfortable in the hospital. Get Raya's take on the wounds and . . .

"I *said,*" she told herself, "that I'm going out the Maritime Unit in the morning."

"Yes, you did." Shig gave her that infuriatingly beneficent smile.

8

Throwing another chunk of broken aquajade onto the fire, Talina waited for the flames to catch and rise. Not that she needed the light. She could see just fine in the infrared and ultraviolet ranges. Another benefit—and curse—of her quetzal TriNA. The way the molecules had remodeled her ocular physiology gave her that alien look that spooked even her closest friends.

Rolling the syringe between her fingers, she studied it in the firelight. Should have put him to sleep in the beginning, but she'd had no clue how unsettling his utterances would be. Talina had always taken for granted that Kalico had the inside track when it came to Dek. Kalico was his kind of people. Came from Dek's world. And they'd been spending a lot of time together when Dek was in PA.

Talina replaced the syringe in its case, returning it to her aircar. As she did, she took in the camp. Dek—no doubt with Chaco Briggs's help—had picked a sound location. Surrounded by low chabacho, aquajade, and dwarf stonewood trees, the camp sat on eroded basalt bedrock, free of roots. But, taking nothing for granted, Dek had parked his airplane on a tarp to keep any questing roots from wrapping around the landing gear. Smart trick, that.

This was deep bush, maybe forty kilometers northwest of the Briggs homestead and mine. The canyon where Dek had staked his claim—and above which she had found his pain-wracked body—was a good two hundred meters to the west. Port Authority lay just over three hundred klicks to the east. About a four-hour flight by aircar in good weather. Hardly an hour in Dek's airplane.

By rights, Derek Taglioni should have died.

In Donovanian terms, the guy was "soft meat." A newcomer who'd spent but a few months dirtside. Nevertheless, he'd listened, learned. Immediately recognized the mobbers for what they were:

flying death. That he'd dived to the ground and froze was smart. That he'd been on rocky colluvium, without a thick root mat had been chance good fortune. That he'd stuck it out as the mobbers flocked over him and the gotcha vine began chewing on his leg took extraordinary resolve. That he'd fought off the carnivorous vine with his knife was sheer pluck. As to *Vixen* having been overhead to receive his signal? Again, just dumb luck. And, finally, he'd been ballsy and courageous enough to climb out of the canyon and onto bedrock where she could spot him from the air. In brain-numbing pain, he'd kept his wits. Been smart. Smart had kept him alive.

On Donovan, anything else was a death sentence.

Talina crossed her arms, stepped over, and stared down at the comatose man. Derek Taglioni had sandy-tan hair, a perfect patrician face, and a dimple in his chin. The pinking scar on his cheek—left by shrapnel from an exploding drone—gave him a dashing and exotic look. With his yellow-green eyes, the guy was drop-dead handsome, muscular, and graceful. Everything that an elite program of monitored breeding and advanced genetics could bestow on a pampered and entitled Corporate male.

She could see the healing wound on his arm where he and Flute had exchanged blood. The guy had willingly infected himself with TriNA. Here she was, wishing she could be rid of the shit, and he was letting a quetzal pump it into him.

She should have hated him for who he was. But the guy charmed her, not to mention that Dek was willing to take on Donovan's challenges with the full knowledge that the planet would try to kill him at every turn. That the odds were, it *would* kill him. Today—but for the thinnest sliver of luck—it almost had.

"He wants to mate with you." Demon whispered from his lair down behind her stomach.

"Go suck on a toilet, you piece of shit," she told it.

It only felt like the quetzal lurked beneath her liver. Demon—and its antithesis, Rocket—existed inside her as TriNA molecules. The stuff communicated with other TriNA through recombination, transferRNAs, microRNAs, and proteins. Raya Turnienko and her team were still struggling to understand the intricacies, but the notion that intelligent molecules could live within a human being was sobering.

For Talina, it wasn't academic. She was full of the stuff. Some of it—from what they called Whitey's lineage—wanted her dead. That was the Demon identity who lived in her gut. The TriNA Rocket had infected her with actually had a soft spot for humans. The Rork quetzal lineage was mostly just curious, and she had her own infection of Flute's Briggs lineage.

Factions among intelligent molecules? Who would have thought?

Using transferRNA, the various "identities" of TriNA had learned to communicate with the language centers of her brain, talked to her, and often times interacted with her limbic system. In the years since her first infection, she had developed defenses that allowed her to maintain her sanity and personality while she waited for Raya—or someone—to figure out a way to scrub her blood and body of the alien genetic material.

"And you want to fall in love with me?" she asked the somnolent Dek. "Typical male. All you see is the packaging. Not what a fucked-up mess I am on the inside."

Talina chuckled at herself. Told Dek, "While you may not have a clue about who I am, you're an open book, and I can read you page by page."

Especially with her augmented sense of smell. She couldn't have missed the sexual musk that poured out of him when he told her she was fantastic. Not that a sexually excited man without pants was a tough call in the first place.

Looking back at the history of the species, maybe it was adaptive for humans to have methylated most of their genes for olfaction. People gave off too many pheromones. It would have led to murders in closely packed cities. She could always smell when a man or woman was interested in or had had sex. Some were worse than others. She had seriously considered nose plugs when she was working with Step Allenovich; the guy was in a constant state of rut.

Raya had warned her when she gave Talina the drug. *"This stuff numbs the inhibition centers of the brain. Don't be offended by anything he says."*

But the last thing Tal had expected to come out of his mouth was a protestation of love.

"Hard to think I'm more desirable than a courtesan." She was cosmopolitan enough to realize that in Transluna's rarified corridors of power, the courtesans were a special caste. Each belonged to a specific guild, was highly educated, trained in the arts of music, poetry, sex, history, geography, culture, and etiquette. Training began in childhood, and but a handful of the men and women managed to qualify for the registry by the time they reached their late teens. Of them, only a few would survive the cutthroat world of Board politics to make it to the top of their profession. The kind who would appeal to a Taglioni like Dek.

Talina took a deep breath, tossed a triangular chabacho limb onto the fire, and seriously contemplated the sleeping man. The night chime was rising and falling, the stars partially obscured as the clouds drifted in from the east. Out in the forest, something screamed. On Donovan, the hunters never slept. She could hear the soft rustle of the leaves as they shifted out in the deeper forest. There the trees wrestled with each other, repositioning their roots. Far off, she thought she heard a distant crash, the kind made when a group of the forest giants toppled one of their foes.

"And you chose this world?" she asked Dek. "Knowing it's going to kill you?"

She reached down, ran her fingers through his hair, felt the tingle inside her.

"*Yes!*" Demon hissed down in her gut. But the thing had always been intrigued by human sex.

Reproduction was a lot less complicated among quetzals; three of them shared TriNA through an interchange of saliva. The TriNA was sucked into the reproductive tract where it recombined with strands from each of the donors. The new TriNA was incorporated into a prokaryotic germ cell that began dividing, developing, and a couple of months later a juvenile quetzal was popped out the reproductive orifice atop the tail. The whole process held no emotion, no agonizing choice of mate, none of the drama characteristic of human sexual relations.

At times, Tal envied the beasts.

Talina could feel Rocket's presence shift on her shoulder. Like Demon, Rocket was no more real than a feeling. Was it something in the human psyche that insisted on giving her infection a physical presence, a manufactured identity? But then, Shig would say that all identity was *maya,* a form of trickery or illusion.

"And what do you think?" she asked Rocket.

"You are tired of being alone."

"I'm never alone. Half the time I'm sharing your dreams. Same with that piece of shit in my gut."

"You know what I mean."

That was the thing about having an intelligence inside her. Dek's pheromones might give away his sexual interest, but the damn quetzals knew her innermost thoughts.

"Yes!" Demon insisted.

Before being infected by quetzals, she could tell herself any damn thing she wanted. Pretend she believed it. Having intelligent molecules that knew better running around in her blood really sucked toilet water.

Yes, admit it already. She *was* lonely. The quetzal molecules in her blood, the physical changes in her body, her almost superhuman strength, reflexes, and senses, made her suspect. And there had been some pretty rocky incidents while Whitey's molecules were trying to manipulate her body into becoming a weapon. Like the time she thought she was shooting Sian Hmong. Thank god it was only a hallucination. But she'd still blasted a damn hole in a shipping container.

She *missed* human companionship. Ached for the old camaraderie. Wished that she could walk down the steps in Inga's, slap people on the back, be invited to their tables to lift a cold glass of beer. She'd fought for them. Been one of them.

"Now you are outcast!" Demon chortled.

"Oh, go fuck yourself."

"Poor . . . sad . . . pathetic."

"Eat vomit and die, you piece of shit."

Demon chittered in quetzal laughter where he slipped around down behind her gallbladder.

She could sense Rocket giving her that three-eyed look of com-miseration. He often did these days. And the look was new. Almost human. Another piece of her personal weirdity, she imagined that she really did see Rocket on her shoulder, could feel his weight. But only when she was looking for him.

"How screwed up is that?" she asked Dek, thankful the drug had knocked him out.

She laughed, answered herself. "As screwed up as having an inti-mate conversation with a man who's so out of it, he isn't hearing a word I'm saying."

If there was ever a symbolic moment of how alone Talina felt, this was it.

Well, there was Kylee. As far that went. She and Kylee shared quet-zal molecules, even shared memories—some of them damned un-comfortable for Talina's part. But Kylee was just coming on fourteen. She was more quetzal than even Talina, and her youth at Mundo Base had been limited to immediate family. While Rocket's death might have torn her in two, Kylee had never buried a husband or a lover, never shared that ultimate intimacy that came of an adult relationship. She'd never been one of a team, a valued member of a community.

For all the things they had in common, Talina and Kylee had even more differences that left them in separate hells.

Just thinking about it, she remembered the morning sunlight on Cap's face as it poured through the window. He was lying in her bed, still lost in dreams. With that came the memory of how they'd made small talk after sex, his reassuring hand on her breast. For those few days she'd had a partner, a man she could treat as an equal and a soul mate.

She didn't dare allow herself to recall her days with Mitch. That had been young, heady love. The stuff of fairy tales and head-over-heels passion. Talina had lost herself in Mitch, her heart had beat within his, her soul had wound around his until the two were one. And his death had almost killed her.

The firelight played in yellow and shadows as it toyed with Dek Taglioni's features. What was it about him? Some innate quality that

Talina hadn't been able to finger. Not even that first night when she and Stepan Allenovich had half carried the blind and stumbling Dek back to her dome.

That had been Kalico's work. The wily Supervisor purposely got the guy so intoxicated he couldn't see straight. She'd figured it was the best way to ferret out Dek's furtive goals, given that Board politics might have sent their dirty tendrils some thirty light-years across space. Turned out that Dek was just running away from home. No power play.

"He's a Taglioni. Can't let anything happen to him," Kalico had said. *"Can you keep an eye on him?"*

Which meant Talina had taken him home. Put the guy in her bed and prayed he wouldn't puke on her sheets.

The next morning she'd found the hungover wreck soaking in her shower. Having not had a man in her house since Cap, something had felt complete in her as she fed him breakfast, watched him devouring her tamales. Sure, he'd been soft meat, but something about the guy had been game. For days afterward, she'd caught his scent in the bedding, on the kitchen stool where he'd sat.

"Oh, Talina," she told herself. "Even if he isn't interested in Kalico, he's still a Taglioni."

9

The way Felix Schwantz saw it, the Pod was a miracle. He'd been born on Crew Deck in *Ashanti*. All he'd ever known was the crowded warren of rooms he had grown up in. He missed the old Maritime Unit ship's quarters where people slept in beds that were built—one on top of another—into hollows in the walls. He and his mom and Yee had lived in a lower bunk, just up from the floor. All the families with kids had low bunks. It was that way so none of the little babies could accidentally fall and hurt themselves or be killed and have to go to hydroponics.

On *Ashanti*, Yee had taken Felix down to see what hydroponics was. He knew it was bad, that it was on Deck Four, which was beneath Deck Three where the cannibals lived. Cannibals ate people. Killed them, cut them into pieces, and cooked them. So, being even further down, those yuck-suck green tanks of goo were pretty horrifying.

A lot of babies had been born dead and had been dropped into the hydroponics chute. Some were called miscarriages and were really small and bloody. Others were what they called "closer to term," and some, because of the mother's health were something called "aborted." When any of those things happened, it had been a sad time, with a lot of crying and people hugging each other. The old saying, "The child is in hydroponics now, it will be part of us all soon" was said over and over afterward.

The Pod had a hydroponics, too. But this one was different. It was just behind the kitchen where Bill Masters made the best food Felix had ever eaten.

Felix had been to the Pod's hydroponics several times, and to his complete mystification, it was just a line of tanks full of green and stinky water. Nothing horrible or scary about it at all. Not like the tanks aboard *Ashanti* that seemed to reek menace.

He was just leaving hydroponics, stepping out into the bright and big hallway that ran through level one. The lights here amazed him. As did being outside. Outside light—coming from the sun they called Capella—hurt his eyes. And he'd got something called a "sunburn" on his skin from the boat ride he'd taken with Mother.

In the hall, walking aimlessly, was Sheena. She was his best friend. Probably because she was seven, and every year for almost a month they were the same age before he got older. Sheena had red-gold hair that hung down her back. Her parents had let her grow it when most everyone on *Ashanti* had to either shave their heads or keep their hair short. And even though he was older, she was taller than he was by about five centimeters. He knew because he and Sheena had measured it on the living quarters bulkhead in *Ashanti*.

"What are you doing?" she called. "You can't be in hydroponics. They might throw you in."

He gave her a grin, thumped his chest. "Naw. I had to take a mug of tea in to give to Tobi Ruto. Bill Martin asked me to. Tobi can't get away because of some stirring thing he has to do in the tanks. Something with algae. You do know what algae is."

Sheena screwed up her nose, which she always did when Felix annoyed her. "I do so. Mom talks about it a lot."

Sheena's mom was Vik Lawrence. She did stuff with tiny living things that could only be seen under a microscope. Felix knew what a microscope was now. He'd seen the big white one in Vik's lab. It made little things big enough to see.

"Algae only lives in hydroponics," Sheena said with absolute assurance. "That's why Mom was down in *Ashanti*'s hydroponics so much. She was always trying to keep it alive."

"Yeah, well, it's in the oceans here, too."

"Is not."

"Is. I've seen it." He lifted his fingers. "I wasn't s'pposed to, but I caught some out in the ocean. It was in the water. It makes your fingers tickle for a long time."

Sheena's blue eyes were giving him that suspicious look. She did that a lot given the tricks he played on her when he could. "No, it doesn't."

"If we could see the water, I could point it out."

"Bet you can't."

"I could. If they didn't have the hatch locked we could go out on the seatruck dock and see some. It's probably just floating like it was out where we left the buoy."

She gave him that familiar I-don't-believe-you stare. Said, "You're lying, and I can prove it."

"How?"

"'Cause I can show you, liar." She turned. "I know how to get down to the Underwater Bay. Kel showed me."

Kel was her father. He was the pod engineer. Knew how it all worked and made sure that everything, like the air conditioning, the pumps, and stuff ran. For some reason, she never called him Dad. He was always Kel, and he seemed to like it that way. Some people whispered that Kel wasn't really her father, that it had been Dek. But who cared who anyone's father really was? They were all Maritime Unit. That was what mattered.

Sheena started off in an exaggerated walk, her steps almost stomping. Felix followed, watching the dress she wore jerk back and forth, and hearing Sheena's homemade shoes clap on the deck.

At the companionway stairs, she stopped before the pressure hatch that led down to the Underwater Bay. With sure fingers, she punched in a 7-6-7-8 code. The hatch clicked, and Sheena reached up to wrestle the dogging latch open.

"We're not supposed to go down there," Felix told her. "Not without a grownup."

Sheena turned on him, jabbing a finger at his nose, which she always did to make him mad. "Told you there's no algae anywhere but the hydroponics tanks. You don't want to go 'cause there's no algae!"

"Would you know algae if you saw it?"

"Sure! It's green and slimy."

"Well, the algae here is kind of green-blue. I know 'cause Mom told me what it was when I caught it."

"Then prove it!" Sheena jammed her fists against her hips the way her mother did when she was making a point.

"But we're not supposed to go down there!"

"If you don't go, it means you're wrong. And you're a liar."

Felix made a face, his heart starting to pound. He stepped over, stared down the tunnel that slanted into the depths. It was called the tube. Feeling like he was going to die, he stepped onto the first step and started down. The adults were all in the cafeteria, doing some kind of planning meeting with maps and stuff. If he and Sheena went fast . . .

Committed, he hurried down the steps. Steps were still new. Until they'd shipped out of *Ashanti,* he'd never been allowed on them. Now they were a fun challenge to leap down one at a time.

And the tube was marvelous, a white tunnel that went down into the water. Curving, oval-shaped transparent windows in the sialon allowed him to see the underside of the Pod, and as he went lower, the water lapping around the tube. Then, underwater, he could see the reef, with all the living creatures and plants beneath the silverish patterns of the waves. Sunlight filtered through the water, shooting magical rays of light that glowed on the colorful creatures swimming around out there.

"Zambo!" he cried, staring up in awe.

"Wait 'till you see the bottom," Sheena pushed past him. "C'mon."

She led the way, hopping down, step by step, to the pressure hatch at the bottom. Again, she entered a code. 5-3-3-5 this time. It took both of them to pull the latching dog around, and the heavy door let them into the pressure lock.

"Got to close the hatch behind us," Sheena told him in her authoritative tone. "It's going to hurt your ears as the lock pressurizes. See, the air pressure keeps the water out of the Underwater Bay."

"I know that," he retorted. "Like the escape module hatch on *Ashanti.*"

"That's in space where air rushes out into vacuum. But this is underwater, otherwise the ocean would flood the Underwater Bay."

With the first door closed, Sheena stood on tiptoes to press the big red glowing button.

A whooshing sound filled the air lock, and Felix made a face as his eardrums compressed. And then the button turned green. Sheena threw her weight against the dogging latch and managed to pull it to the open position.

Felix followed her out into a large room; his nose filled with the odor of salt and water. The walls were white, covered with equipment, lockers, monitors, benches with tools, diving suits, and helmets. The big yellow submarines rested on rolling cradles in the middle of the floor, their transparent round noses pointed at the water. In the glare of overhead lights, the curved sides gleamed with their bulbous tanks and pipes and frame-mounted lights. In front of the submarines was what looked like a square pool of water that opened to the sea. A line of UUVs rested on racks all the way to the far wall. Both the submarines and UUVs could be rolled forward on tracks and lowered into the water. Felix walked past the submarine's clear nose and looked down through the still water, seeing the reef bottom below sloping away into a darker and translucent blue.

"Zambo!"

"They picked this place because the reef drops off. Like this." Sheena had a serious look on her face as she held her hand vertically and made a slashing motion downward. "It goes way, way down really fast."

Felix could believe it. He saw something long and thin flash through the depths. Thought it looked kind of like a big, pointed tube. And then it was gone.

"Okay, liar. Where's the algae?"

Felix turned his attention to the glasslike surface. "Different water here."

"Liar, liar!"

He wanted to hit her. Didn't dare. Last time he'd got mad and socked her, she'd beat him up. Lara Sanz had come at his screams and howls, had saved him. And all it got him in the end was a day of ridicule and a terrible lecture from his mother about hitting anyone.

"Wait," he pleaded, walking slowly along as he peered into the water. "I tell you, this isn't the right kind of water. You need waves. And to be out in the launch."

"Liar, liar!"

He made a face, getting ever more desperate as he searched his way along the edge of the pool. It had to be here. It just had to!

He could feel his fingers tingling, as if in memory of being in the launch. He rubbed his thumb and fingers together, feeling that oily texture, as if it were the day he and Mother set out the buoy. Absently he tried to scrub his fingers on his coveralls. He just couldn't wipe off the oily stuff.

"We're leaving!" Sheena called. "You had your chance. You were wrong. I was right!" She pirouetted around in the way she did to celebrate a victory. As she did, she sang,

> "London Bridge is falling down, falling down.
> "Namby Pamby.
> "Felix lies and he's going down, going down.
> "My fair lady."

"It's the wrong water!" he protested. "Just let me look a little . . . Wait! I see it!"

He broke into a run past the noses of the UUVs to the far edge of the pool. Dropped to his knees and pointed. "There, see!"

Sheena had stopped her twirling, half stumbled from making herself dizzy, and charged over, her shoes slapping in the quiet room. She knelt down beside him, peering. "Where?"

"Right there!" Felix pointed to the small green-blue splotch that clung to the wall right at waterline.

Sheena squinted. "That's not algae!"

"Keep me from falling in," Felix told her. "Grab my waist. I'll get you some."

As she did, and he leaned out over the water, he caught movement down below, as if something big had just disappeared from sight. Felix hoped it wasn't one of those Big Mouth Things like what had eaten the torpedo. He wasn't nearly as big as a torpedo, so he'd never have a chance.

Reaching out, he hung, suddenly terrified that Sheena'd let go.

Let him fall headfirst into the water where he'd drown. And no one was there to save him. He'd sink. And some monster would eat his body.

"Liar, liar," Sheena chimed behind him.

But she kept her grip as he strained out, clawed his fingers through the slimy green-blue stuff, and cried, "Pull me back!"

She did, and they both dropped onto their butts. Felix lifted his fingers, showing her. "Algae. Feel it."

Even as she pinched some off of his fingers, he could feel the weird tingle. But this time it ran through his fingers, down his hand, and partway up his arm.

"You feel that?" he asked. "Like little prickles in your fingers?"

She was rubbing the slimy stuff between her thumb and first two fingers. "It tickles. You sure this stuff is algae?"

"It's the same thing I caught out in the ocean. Mother called it algae. So . . . you calling her a liar?" Felix gave Sheena that look that said she'd better not or else.

"No." Sheena gave him a look of utter defeat. "Okay. We better go. We've been here too long as it is."

"Look." Felix pointed. "There's little bits of algae all along the pool edge. See where it's sticking at the water line?" It looked like splotches here and there.

"We're leaving now!" Sheena told him in a huff as she got to her feet and scampered off for the latch. "If you don't keep up, I'm leaving you behind!"

Felix, shaking his arm to stop the tingle, leaped up and ran full tilt to catch her.

10

Kalico enjoyed the view as her A-7 shuttled circled the Maritime Unit's Pod. In her imagination the research base looked like an elongated white bubble that floated above the crystalline shoal waters. From this altitude, the reef could be seen extending to the north and south as far as the horizons. The shallows marked the eastern boundaries of the Gulf—the body of water created by the great Donovanian crater. From this altitude the crater's edge appeared as submerged, elongated ridges. Over millennia the rim had been scrubbed away by wave action and tides to leave shoal waters. Occasional white lines of breakers were visible in the distance where more-resistant rock shallowed. Seen through the transparent water, the underlying geology made a patchwork of light and dark where strata had been thrust up. In the distance, where lava once had welled and cooled, vulcanism created a chain of islands that stretched away to the north before curving back toward the mainland.

Looking down, Kalico could see the seabed drop away to either side of the reef; the colors changed from the mottled browns, greens, and tans to darker shades and then faded into the gemlike royal blue of deep water.

In the pilot's seat, Ensign Juri Makarov banked the shuttle wide, descending to approach the Pod from downwind. From her portside seat next to the window, it seemed to Kalico that the ocean rose up to meet them.

From this angle, the Pod appeared like a gleaming white cocoon left by some unmentionably huge insect. Only as the shuttle closed the distance did the windows, antennae, decks, and struts become visible. The Pod seemed to hover over the pale shallows on stilt-like legs. From this angle the damn thing looked like a big bug, and the observation bubble on the end might have been a single eye. As the shuttle rose slightly, Kalico caught a glimpse of the landing pad—a flat square on the north end of the Pod's cylindrical length. Compared to the width of the big A-7, the pad was ridiculously tiny. No wonder Makarov had balked at flying her out here.

"Supervisor?" Makarov called. "You sure you still want to do this?"

Seeing the tiny target, she really didn't. But damn it, they were here. The Maritime Unit was expecting her. And she should have been here weeks ago. To fly off now . . .

She bit her lip, leaned forward in her seat. "Yeah, you call it a 'feather dusting.' The landing platform can't support the A-7's weight. So, instead of setting down, you'll lower the aft ramp. Hover so the ramp's barely above the landing platform. I scurry off, try to keep from being blown off my feet, and duck into the access door. At my all clear, you lift off and book it for home."

"It's the 'blown off your feet' part that worries me." Makarov followed it up by craning his neck to give her a warning glance from over his seat back. "You understand, you'll be between the full-thrust downdrafts from the jets. I call this foolish, dangerous, and likely to end up with you either hurt and floating in the water. Or maybe dead if you get blown off and tumble down the side."

She extended far enough to give his shoulder a slap. "Juri, even if you weren't the best pilot in The Corporation, the A-7's automatics can hover within a millimeter's variance. I'll be fine."

He shot her another worried look.

"What?" she countered. "All I have to do is duck, run straight to the access hatch, and slip inside."

"You take too many chances. You get killed out here, and I'm the one they're going to blame."

She gave him a saucy grin. "What's living without a little risk to life and limb?"

"Yeah, anything happens to you, it's my life and limbs."

"That was the point I was making. Just set me down. This visit is way overdue."

"Hey, as I remember, on your last adventure, you were out in the forest, chased by cannibals, being hunted by monsters. That didn't work out so well, either. Lost good people. Don't want to lose you."

She bit off any reply. Let the silence hang, and finally ordered, "Get me over that platform."

Hell, it hurt too damn much when she thought about Dya Simonov and Mark Talbot. It had been her decision to fly out to Tyson Station without armored marines. And they'd walked right into the Unreconciled's trap.

You have to trust your instincts, she told herself. *Get to second-guessing every decision, and you'll be paralyzed.*

She watched as Makarov eased them around, approaching along the Pod's long axis so the thrusters blasted down on either side of the tube-shaped structure. Below them, water churned out in circular waves as the downdraft intensified.

"I'm headed aft," she told Makarov. "I'll be off as fast as I can."

"Please don't do this."

"See you in a day or two."

"Roger that."

She grabbed her bag and passed through the hatch into the cargo bay. In the rear, she took a position at the head of the ramp. Felt the faintest of shudders as the A-7 slowed, stopped, and hovered. The ramp whined, the back of it dropping down. As it fell, a sliver of daylight widened around the edges and the deafening roar made her wince. Kalico started down the ramp, felt the blast tugging at her pantlegs. She descended into a thunderous gale, bent low, and staggered into the vortex. The step down from the ramp wasn't more than ten centimeters, and she was on the Pod's landing pad.

A blast of hot air sent her staggering, almost blown off her feet. She caught her footing an instant before being blasted sideways off the pad to tumble down the Pod's curved side. If the fall didn't kill her, hitting the water from three stories would. Another gust blew her a couple of feet to the left. Crouched as she was, only dropping and bracing herself with her hand saved her from being tossed off her feet. Panic froze her. Another buffet left her weaving, even bent double as she was. At any instant, the combination of blasting air was going to blow her, tumbling, over the edge.

God, fucking damn! This is a mistake.

Through squinted eyes, she made out the roof hatch, grabbed at her blast-savaged hair, and struggled forward at a low crouch. It was like trying to run while big old Step Allenovich was punching her with roundhouse blows from each side. All of her concentration went into keeping her feet while the oscillating blasts of hot air beat her back and forth. Then came a blow from the rear, sent her tumbling.

Somehow, she kept hold of her bag, scrambled on hands and knees.

All right, Kalico. Not your brightest choice ever.

But she made it. Grabbed the hatch, swung it open. Leaped inside . . . and it took all of her strength and weight to shove the thing closed. Heart hammering, breath coming in gasps, she let the adrenaline drain from her quivering muscles. She'd be damned if she'd ever do that again.

In the relative silence, she accessed her com, saying, "Juri? I'm in. See you in a couple of days."

"Roger that, Supervisor. We're headed for the barn."

The roar of the thrusters changed; the Pod trembled under the blast, vibrating and rattling. Then it lessened, softened, and began to fade as the shuttle cleared the structure and lifted.

"Shit on a shoe," she whispered to herself. Fought to pull the tangle of her hair into some kind of order. Gave it up for a lost cause.

Once upon a time, she'd have rather died than made a disheveled entrance. Since her landing at the Port Authority shuttle field that first time, those pretensions had slowly given way to the realization that a hand on her holstered pistol, the scars on her face and hands, and her steely laser-blue glare carried a lot more authority than any sartorial perfection.

Michaela Hailwood was waiting at the bottom of the steps with Lee Shinwua and Kel Carruthers in tow. Hailwood had an amazed look on her face. "We were watching on the monitors. We thought you were going to be blown away at any second. Can't believe you just did that."

"Yeah, hell of a way to arrive," Kalico told them, fingers still combing out her hair. "That's the last time *ever* that anyone is going to try that trick."

"It was a bit interesting in here, too, ma'am." Hailwood told her. "Perhaps we can find a less exciting means of transport back and forth to the mainland. But in the meantime, welcome to Maritime Research. We're delighted and honored to have you, Supervisor."

"It's our distinct pleasure having you aboard," Shinwua added. "Can we get you anything after your flight?"

"Let me take your bag," Kel said.

The way they were looking at her, she must have made quite the sight with her wind-blasted hair, quetzal-hide cape and boots, and, under her suit jacket, the claw-shrub-fiber shirt that Yvette Dushane had embroidered with colorful tooth flowers and crest images. Her scars always grabbed their attention. And then there was her utility belt with the aforementioned pistol, large knife, survival pouch, and various tools.

Kalico indicated the hallway that led to the women's locker room. "Give me five. Then I'll meet you in the cafeteria. A cup of hot mint tea will be fine." God, she wanted a whiskey.

Kalico found the facilities to be immaculate, still so new the duraplast walls gleamed. Stepping inside, she dropped her bag on the floor, stumbled over, and braced her arms on the sink. Her heart was still racing, pulse pounding in her ears.

"Damn it, woman," she told her tousled image in the mirror. "You came within a millimeter of getting yourself killed out there."

Once she got her racing blood and adrenaline under control, she took stock. That last mad scramble had taken its toll. One elbow and the left knee were torn out of her natty black suit. Her *last* formal dress. Not to mention that her hair looked like something out of a horror holovid.

"You'd think I never learn," she muttered to herself.

Well, hell, after an arrival like this, nothing the Maritime Unit could throw at her would come as a challenge.

11

Shinwua, standing in the Pod hall, gave Michaela a measuring sidelong glance. "Did we really see what we just saw? I mean the Board Supervisor just jumped out of a hovering shuttle. The woman was knocked off her feet. She crawled, made it to the landing pad access by fricking luck." He shook his head in disbelief. "*That's* the Board Supervisor? I expected . . ."

"What?" Michaela asked when he couldn't finish.

"More decorum." Shin stared thoughtfully at the women's locker room door. "Listen, I've only met her a couple of times. So, like, she didn't strike me as the kind who'd let herself be blown off her feet and walk in the door looking like she'd been dropped out of a rock tumbler. You know her, spent time with her in Port Authority. Is she mentally deficient to pull a stunt like that, or what?"

Michaela glanced down the level one hall and back toward the cafeteria where everyone was waiting. Like Shin, they would have been watching on com. Seen the Supervisor's most undignified arrival. If there was anything that would lead her people to question Kalico Aguila's leadership, that hellacious first impression might be it. She'd looked more like a demented buffoon than a self-possessed and dignified Corporate Board Supervisor.

Michaela considered her words. "The woman I spent time with in Port Authority struck me as a no-bullshit, tough-as-nails, jack-me-around-and-I'll-kill-you hard-ass."

"That's not what I saw scrambling for the hatch." Shin crossed his arms, expression skeptical. "And the scars, they creep-freaked me the first time I ever saw them. Makes her look like some kind of monster, all crisscrossing her face and hands. I mean, the woman's a Board Supervisor, for God's sake. Why doesn't she have them fixed? Or does she keep them just for effect? You know, to scare people. Maybe because she needs all the help she can get?"

A pause. Then he added, "Like that big pistol on her hip? Come on! What's she need that gun for? Here? On the Pod? We're a bunch of scientists for God's sake. What's she expect? To get jumped by monsters in the cafeteria? Who's she trying to scare, anyway? And what's it say about her that she thinks she has to?"

Michaela pursed her lips. Let the thought run around in her head. Granted, she'd only spent a half day with the Supervisor, mostly in a debriefing about the situation on *Ashanti,* discussion about the Unreconciled, and planning for the Maritime Unit's disposition and placement. The meeting had been focused on who, what, and how. Michaela had done most of the talking; Supervisor Aguila had listened, offering only occasional questions, asking for clarification. Pretty much a nuts-and-bolts meeting. Hardly a social situation, and the scars and pistol had been a distraction the entire time. Shin had a point there.

She said, "I don't know what to think. Never met a Board Supervisor before I met Aguila. She comes across as a tough woman, has from that first communication from *Ashanti*'s AC. But you're right. Watching her being blown around the landing pad didn't inspire confidence. Her reputation is as a really tough and hard-bitten leader. As to the pistol? I heard that she's shot people who didn't measure up to her standards. That said, her crew at Corporate Mine worships her. The people in Port Authority respect the hell out of her."

"Maybe they've been left out here for so long they've forgotten what it means to be a Board Supervisor? When she came through that access just now, she looked like something tossed out the back door of a Hong Kong bar."

Michaela bit off a reply before she could agree. Made herself say, "Don't rush to judgement, Shin. It's a whole new world and a new set of rules. My advice, and what I want you to share with the others? Let's keep an open mind until we have a better feel for the woman."

Shin, cocked an eyebrow, his longtime way of saying, "All right, but I'll wait to be convinced."

She grinned, slapped him on the shoulder, and said, "Go get Bill

Martin to make the Supervisor a cup of tea. I'm going to go in and make sure she's got everything she needs. All she has is that one bag."

"Got it. While I'm at it, everyone's in the cafeteria so I'll get a feel for the general mood. See if the great Supervisor Aguila with all of her tales of monsters under the bed has them trembling in awe."

"Shin? Whatever else she is, or thinks she is, the woman is still a Corporate Board Supervisor. Make sure the rest of the team greets her accordingly." She watched him go. Wondered what she'd do without him and turned for the locker room door. Pushing it open, she stepped inside and stopped short, gaping. Kalico Aguila had just pulled off her black suit and was fingering the hole in the knee.

It wasn't the sight of the woman, half naked, but the scars. Kalico Aguila had the kind of body only the elite could buy: lithe, muscular, and perfectly formed. Call her statuesque. She would have been a beauty in anyone's book—but for the horror of the scars running across her stomach, hips, along the outsides of her thighs, on her back and arms. To Michaela's dismay, the ones on the woman's hands and face were hardly worth mention compared to those disfiguring the rest of her body.

Michaela gasped. Horrified. Her stomach went queasy, and she instinctively placed a hand to her throat.

Aguila glanced up, blue gaze startled, only to be followed by a knowing smile. "Sorry. Had to change into something without holes. Pisses me off, really." She wiggled a finger through the hole in the knee of her suit. "My last good 'official' dress outfit. Maybe I can have Pietre Strazinsky figure out a becoming way of patching this. That, or it's a whole new claw-shrub-fiber outfit. Some of the weave they're making now is coming pretty close to a quality fabric."

"Those were mobbers?" Michaela couldn't take her gaze from the tracery of scars. "I just didn't . . . I mean, I never . . ."

"Saw the like?" Aguila's smile thinned, her laser-blue gaze cooling. "Donovan plays, for keeps, Director. So take a good look and don't forget. Your next question is, 'You're a Board Supervisor, why don't you undergo the cosmetic surgery to repair them?' The answer is: 'If I were back in Solar System, I would. But here, on Donovan, that kind of cosmetic surgery is outside of Raya Turnienko's expertise. Her specialty is keeping you alive, and she's pretty good at it.'"

"So you live with them?" Michaela wondered, her skin crawling at the disfigurement.

Aguila reached for her bag, removed a set of utilitarian coveralls, and pulled them on; her scarred hands zipped the fasteners closed. Then she attacked the rat's nest her hair had been blown into. As she did, she said, "Director, even after the orientation we gave you in Port Authority, and despite everything I've tried to tell you about Donovan, I have a pretty good idea where you're coming from. What your expectations are for the Maritime Unit and how you expect life to line out for you and your people. Now that you've finally made it here, you think it's all going to be nice and cozy science filled with wonders. Oh, you'll get plenty of wonders, not all of them pleasant."

Michaela couldn't get the scars out of her memory. Now, here was her Board Supervisor, dressed in utilitarian coveralls, pulling the knots out of her long black hair like she was a schoolgirl after gym class. Who the hell was Kalico Aguila, anyway?

"We were expecting . . ." What? Michaela remained at a loss for words. Everything about the Supervisor's arrival had her off balance.

"Forget your expectations." Aguila tossed her glossy black hair over her shoulder, dropped her brush into the bag, and snapped it closed over the black suit. "I've tried to beat this into you from the beginning: All you need to know about your expectations is that they are wrong."

"But, we've read all the—"

"Forget it all," Kalico slung her pistol belt around her hips, picked up her bag. "Everything you think you know from the reports is in error. You're about to run headlong into Donovan."

Michaela kept herself from bristling. "I have the best team The Corporation could assemble, with some of the finest minds and young scholars in Solar System. After what I and my people have been through, I think we're even better prepared to tackle our mission as a cohesive and flexible unit. All that time in *Ashanti* knit us together in a way I've never seen before. I can't think of a more adaptive and self-reliant team than what we have here."

Aguila's slight smile bent the scar along the line of her jaw. "Director, if all it took was a bunch of scars to have you creep-freaked, what are you going to do when you face a real disaster?"

"Oh, I wouldn't say that I was—"

"Come on," Aguila headed for the door. "After that spectacle of an arrival, it's time to go see if the damage to my image is as easy to repair as the holes in my good black suit."

As Michaela followed, she wondered: *So, is Kalico Aguila the monster her scars suggest, or just simply mad?*

12

With her hair in order and most of the damage repaired, Kalico sauntered her way down the hallway. Director Hailwood followed a half step behind. The woman remained unsettled. The fact that she'd been so affected by the sight of the scars set Kalico's nerves on end. Hailwood had been repulsed. Almost to the point of being ill. If a mazework of healed scars was enough to make Michaela Hailwood want to spew her breakfast, how would she handle a real emergency?

Time to find out just what the Maritime Unit is made of.

Again, Kalico cursed herself for the spectacle of her arrival. Not only had she scared the sucking snot out of herself, but who knew what that humiliating scramble across the landing pad had cost her in credibility. Not to mention putting holes in her good black suit, painful abrasions on her knee and elbow, and the loss of dignity.

She'd faced worse. Like the time Shig, Yvette, and Talina had humiliated her during their trial. In comparison to that calamity, this was a piece of fluff. She strode into the cafeteria as if she owned the place. Which, in a sense, was indeed the case.

As she did, someone announced, "Board Supervisor Kalico Aguila."

The men, women, and children rose respectfully to their feet; many stood with lowered eyes and their hands held before them. All were silent, unmoving. The solemnity was only marred by one of the infants who made a "whaaaaa" sound.

The gesture of respect took Kalico by surprise. It amused her that she'd been on Donovan for so long that a display of Corporate protocol seemed alien. Made her uneasy.

But then, the Maritime Unit had only been in Port Authority for a few days before flying out to the Pod. Hardly enough time for the corrosive libertarian ethic of the place to dissolve their lifelong training. In addition, while they'd been in PA, they'd been boarded in the Corporate Mine barracks; their exposure to the rowdy locals had been limited and supervised.

"Thank you," Kalico strode across to the head table where Hailwood and Shinwua stood to either side. "Please, be seated."

As they lowered themselves into chairs, the parents shushed the children, tried to explain that they couldn't talk, Kalico took her place. Standing behind the table—Hailwood and Shinwua seated themselves at either side—she said, "I apologize for taking so long to make the journey out here. Events on the mainland precluded any opportunity to get away."

"We've heard," Hailwood said soberly. "At least what we could garner through chatter on the radio. It is especially welcoming that you survived the Unreconciled. Had they all perished, none of us would have shed a tear. Nice to have you back in one piece from the forest and the man-eaters. Your safety was paramount in our thoughts."

Good, the woman had recovered her poise.

"That's Donovan for you," she said wryly. "But I do thank you for your kind wishes."

Kalico gestured to indicate the surrounding room. "You have done wonders here. I sincerely appreciate the hard work and dedication. The Pod is a remarkable piece of equipment, and it's a delight to walk down a hallway again where all the lights work. After my last years at Corporate Mine, and your long confinement aboard *Ashanti,* we can all rejoice in the words 'clean' and 'functional' coming together in the same sentence."

She got laughter out of that. Could read their skepticism.

"Seriously, it's nice to step back into the twenty-second century. Take good care of this place. It may be all that you've got for a long time to come."

She let that hang, then said in a more sober tone. "You all went through orientation when you landed dirtside at PA. You know that The Corporation has lost six of the big cargo ships. *Freelander*'s crew and transportees met with disaster when they were in whatever universe they passed through. Your own ten-year passage on *Ashanti* was proof of the dangers involved in inverting symmetry and popping outside the universe. I'm serious when I tell you that you may be on your own for years without seeing another ship. The Pod is now your lifeboat, your haven, and your long-term hope for the future."

Kalico stepped out around the table to better face the people. Could see that they were waiting to be convinced of her leadership. "There are only a thousand humans, give or take, on Donovan. Here is a list of our assets: We have Port Authority, Corporate Mine, some outlying research bases, and now we have the Maritime Unit. Everything on Donovan revolves around Port Authority. It's the center of our social life, manufacturing and trade, food production, medical care, and our spaceport. For its part, Corporate Mine, with its smelter, is the heart of extraction and raw materials. In orbit, we have *Freelander* for limited free-fall manufacturing, but you've heard the stories. They're true. *Freelander* is a spooky place to spend any time.

"The survey ship *Vixen* is compromised by a navigational error in its programming. Though the crew experienced an instantaneous transition to the Capella system on the outside, when they reversed the asymmetry and popped back in, fifty years had passed. So, though it remains our absolute last link to Solar System, any return trip may, and I stress *may*, be instantaneous to us, but *Vixen* will probably arrive off Neptune's orbit fifty years in our future."

Yeah, they were getting it. Uneasy looks were being passed back and forth, knowing lifts of the eyebrows, the faint shrugs. A lot of the communication was subtle—the sort that developed among people who knew each other intimately. Well, all but the sour senior woman in the back who had remained standing with her arms crossed. That, Kalico remembered, was Anna Gabarron.

Kalico raised her hands. "So there you have it. It's not the Garden of Eden promised by The Corporation. It's only a thousand people spread across a world that will kill us in an instant. Welcome to Donovan."

She paused as she looked them, one by one, in the eyes, then said, "Now, given the grim reality of this planet, you might wonder why

Ashanti wasn't packed with people desperate to get back to Solar System. Why anyone, given a choice, would stay. We're here, I'm here because, for all of its dangers and privations, Donovan is a fabulous opportunity for all of us. I came with the intention of using Donovan as a stepping-stone to catapult myself onto the Board. Maybe I still will one of these days."

She gave them a grin, knowing how it stretched her scars. "So, can you picture that? Boardmember Kalico Aguila, striding into the Board, scars on my face, quetzal-hide cape over my shoulders, and one hand on my pistol."

She struck a pose, adding, "Bet those white-assed candy-dicked bastards wouldn't sleep for a week."

That got her uneasy laughs. And, as she'd hoped, it broke the tension. "Some people stay on Donovan to become rich. Some stay because Donovan has seduced them with its challenges and beauty. Others, like you, are here for the science. You all want to be the first to discover and catalog new species, be the first to understand an entirely new ecosystem. Write that pivotal paper. Make full professor. Or just fulfill your contract so you can go back to Solar System on a full-ride retirement. Whatever. That's your business."

She had their full attention. Even the children. Well, all but the infants, one of whom kept making "goooo goooo" sounds.

"We told you all of this at orientation, but I'm telling you again. Here's the way it lines out: This planet was named for the first man to set foot on it. You saw his grave when you disembarked on the shuttle field. What was left of him was buried under that stone cairn up on the rise. Within two hours, good old Donovan was eaten by a quetzal. He wasn't the last. And there's no telling what's in the oceans."

Kalico watched them shift nervously.

"Barring a miracle, which rarely happens here, some of you are going to die. Maybe a lot of you. This place plays for keeps, and we don't have a clue about the rules out here on the water. Be smart. Think. Take no chances. Do *not* assume that anything here follows the same rules of behavior as creatures or plants do on Earth. Never consider anything that looks like it's harmless, to be harmless. Treat *everything* like it will kill you, and you have a chance."

The air conditioning kicked on, the soft hum of fans almost loud in the still cafeteria.

Kalico gave them a grim smile. "Sorry to deliver that without any sweetener, let alone to keep harping on it, but that's just the way Donovan is. You can see my scars." She pointed to the ones on her face. "The first time the mobbers came, it was just dumb luck that I was standing next to a crate. When I jumped inside, I locked five of the little bastards in with me. Had to kill them with my bare hands. Three of my people weren't that lucky. And that was inside the Corporate Mine fence, inside the compound. And from a known danger."

Michaela Hailwood cleared her throat, breaking Kalico's stride to say, "Director, don't think we take your warning cavalierly, but remember that you're addressing some of the most talented researchers in oceanography. We've worked with just about every dangerous species in Earth's oceans. That includes great white sharks, orcas, sea snakes, and just about every poisonous species on the planet. You won't catch us making any mistakes." As if to make her point, Hailwood told her: "We know what we're doing. We have all been trained in safety protocols. We'll be damned careful."

"See that you are," Kalico insisted, aware that the men and women in the audience were smiling in that superior, almost bored, "yes I know my business" manner of specialists being lectured by an amateur.

God, I hope they're right. But how many ways could she beat a dead horse?

She clapped her hands together to break the spell. "Now that I've reiterated my point, and you've been locked inside the Pod while you brought its systems and equipment online, I'm betting you're wondering if this is all there is. Whether, like the Crew Deck on *Ashanti*, you're locked into this one small universe."

Sudden interest lit in their eyes. Looks of anticipation shot back and forth.

"Well, you're not. You will be rotated out of the Pod to Port Authority at whatever interval you decide on. At Corporate Mine, my people work a ten-four. Ten days at the mine, four in PA. Our crews are staggered, so the mine runs constantly. Work it out with Scientific Director Hailwood. While you are in Port Authority, you must remember it is *not* Corporate. You are a guest in an independent and autonomous community. Now, for the few days you were there after disembarking *Ashanti*, you got a taste of the place. At the time, all the locals were going out of their way to keep you safe and out of trouble. You had a basic introduction to money. And yes, you have to pay for everything in PA."

She could see the question reflected in their faces. "You wonder where you'll get the PA SDRs? You will earn them."

"How?" she heard the man in the front row ask under his breath as he gave the woman next to him a bewildered look.

"You're Corporate," she told them. "I'm the Supervisor. When you landed, despite the fact half of you were out of contract, you all renewed. You now work for me. I know, it's not what you're used to. Back in Solar System, you did as you were told, when you were told, and The Corporation selected and assigned your living quarters, provided food, clothing, entertainment, medical care, and transportation. In PA, you can stay at the Corporate Mine barracks and eat in the cafeteria on a voucher paid by Corporate Mine. Anything else, for example a shirt like the one I'm wearing, quetzal-hide boots, a drink or meal at Inga's, you will have to pay for. It's simple math, people. And most of the folks in PA will help you figure it out if you ask them. They've been in your shoes, they understand your confusion, and with the possible exception of the casino they won't cheat you." She paused. "Questions?"

"What about that casino? The one we weren't allowed to go to last time. Is that still off limits?" Shinwua asked.

Kalico glanced at Hailwood. The Director had made that decision last time around after she received complaints by some of the women. Hailwood said, "Your decision, Supervisor."

Kalico studied the people, considered. "I've had a checkered relationship with The Jewel and its owner over the years, but we've reached a mutual tolerance. The place has just had a change of management, though given the stories, I'm not sure that it's for the better. I will have a word with the woman in charge, but I warn you: not all of the predators on Donovan are native. You enter that place at your own risk."

"What's a casino?" a little brown-haired boy sitting next to tall blond asked.

Kalico gave him a grin. "What's your name?"

"Felix." He watched her with sensitive brown eyes.

"Well, Felix, a casino is where people go and guess if they can make more than they lose. But it's all designed so they lose more than they make."

"Who'd go there?" the boy wondered.

"My point exactly."

13

"Now that Dan's gone, I don't suppose I could ever offer you enough to leave all this?" Desch Ituri asked. He lay on his back in Allison Chomko's bed, right arm up to prop his head on the pillow. His short body was half out of the tangle of sheets and pressed against the wall of her room in The Jewel.

Allison Chomko allowed herself a husky laugh as she ran her long fingernails in patterns across the man's naked chest, then used the thumb and forefinger nails to lightly pinch Ituri's dark nipple. The man gasped, stiffened, and slowly relaxed as she stroked her fingernails down, around his navel and into the damp mat of his pubic hair. As her fingernails continued to trace their way into the man's ultimate erogenous zone it brought a low moan from his lips.

She met his longing gaze with her own steely blue stare. "What do you think would be enough? A berth down at Corporate Mine? The chance to be your kept woman as I reveled in the splendor of the mine's cafeteria? Perhaps took evening strolls along the scenic chain-link fence on the mine perimeter? Or were you thinking of just buying me for all time? Maybe with a couple of gemstones? Rubies are always good, especially if you can find more of the pigeon-blood reds the size of a hen's egg." She frowned. "But wait. Don't I already have a safe full of those? What, I wonder, could you buy me with?"

Ituri made a pained face that drew his dark eyebrows together. "It always comes down to SDRs doesn't it?"

"That, and power, Desch. Though, in a sense, they are two faces of the same thing. Wealth gives power, and power attracts wealth. It's an equation that's as old as humanity. No one, not even The Corporation for all of its vaunted claims of providing social justice, blind equality, and systemic brotherhood for all has ever risen above the sordid reality of wealth and power."

"I know."

She could see him struggling for the right words. Cut him off before he could make a fool of himself. "You don't want to say anything dumb. I appreciate the honesty, and I certainly value your company. Otherwise, I wouldn't take you to my bed for any price. But sex for money is as far as it goes. Don't delude yourself with sloppy romantic shit, or images of love and a caring relationship where you sweep me off my feet. You'll only humiliate yourself."

He nodded, a faint quiver of a smile teasing the corner of his mouth. "That just makes you more attractive, you know? There's never any misunderstanding, no wheedling or play acting. You just tell it like it is. The other women. Dalia and Angelina. They overact, especially when they're bored and just doing a job."

"Maybe I'd better have a talk with them."

"Ali, don't. It's part of the game. Most of the guys coming here are looking for just what they're giving. Right down to the faked orgasms."

She sat up, swung her legs over the side of her bed, and stood. Stepping to the golden sink, she used a cloth and washed before taking her dress from its hook and stepping into it. Pulling it up, she fastened it tight around her body. The material was a fine-silver thread, the fabric reflective so that it accented every curve of her toned body.

Ituri watched her with that now-familiar longing. Good. She had him right where she wanted him.

"Sure you gotta go?" he asked.

"The Jewel doesn't run itself. For a lot of the patrons, they're still feeling their way. Wondering how it's going to work with Dan gone. Vik, Shin, and Kalen have pretty well figured out that nothing's changed. They're good with it. Some of the clientele, however, are still coming to grips with the fact that sweet Ali isn't a pushover."

"So I hear."

She checked herself in the mirror one last time. "Ah, so what exactly do you hear? What's the word down at Corporate Mine? Out on the street?"

"That you're one tough bitch, just as bloody as Dan Wirth, and every bit as heartless." He gave her a thoughtful squint. "I know you. You're smart, Ali. And you're anything but heartless. I know that you've done some things. Been tough on some who've tried to take advantage. And you've had Kalen Tompzen beat a couple of Wild Ones. Is that how you really want it?"

She turned, cocked her head. "No other way I can have it. Not and get where I want to go."

"And just where is that?"

"The very top, Desch." She lifted a hand to fix her hair. "And, no, I'm not talking about toppling Kalico from her gilded Corporate throne. I don't want her empire, so you can relax. Believe me, Donovan is big enough for the both of us."

She could see the slight flicker of relief behind Ituri's eyes. The man was as dedicated to Kalico Aguila as the rest of the Supervisor's acolytes. Which was another reason to avoid any kind of confrontation.

Left in the wreckage of Dan's passage, Allison Chomko would either survive by her cold wits, or she'd lose it all. When Dan found her, she'd been wounded, grieving, and vulnerable. He'd seduced her, drugged her, used her, and finally prostituted her. When she'd sobered up, came to, and realized what he'd done—what she'd allowed him to do—either she could finish the destruction he'd started, or take matters into her own hands no matter the cost. She'd chosen the later.

"Desch, I don't have any illusions. Dan beat them out of me."

He sighed, gave a gesture of surrender with his hands, and climbed out of her bed. "You know that part of your allure is being forever out of reach. Forbidden fruit. Beyond the possession of any man."

"Really?" She arched a pale brow. "When it comes to reach, seems you just had your hands all over me. And given what you did with your mouth, the fruit was pretty well tasted. As to possession, we were in delightful harmony that last time."

"A fleeting moment. Tomorrow I'm back to the mine, and you are only a dream."

She watched him as he reached for his pants. "Maybe dreams are all we really have, Desch. Seems like every time I think I've got hold of the dream, on Donovan it turns to shit. My parents, my husband, my daughter, and then Dan. I don't dream anymore. I just set hard and fast goals, and then I do anything I can to make them happen."

He was pulling on his shirt. "I'd say it's working. Look what you have. After Kalico, you're the wealthiest woman on Donovan. You brought down Tam Benteen. People, even the triumvirate, listen when you speak. You've become a powerful woman. Even Kalico says so."

Allison stifled a smile. "She does? Wouldn't have thought she cared."

Desch gave an offhanded shrug meant to minimize any import. "She probably doesn't. Just a passing mention. People talk, you know. Doesn't mean anything."

Allison turned, placed a finger under Desch's chin and lifted it so she could stare into his eyes. "Sorry, lover. You're working too hard here. She knows you are one of the few I bed. She gave you the third degree, didn't she?"

"I don't know about any degree—"

"That means she interrogated you. And, worshipping her like you do, you told her everything. Gave it to her straight up like you're about to give it to me. What did you tell her?"

She enjoyed the growing panic in Desch's eyes. His hard swallow shifted her finger where she kept it firmly under his chin. She let her stare burn into his, allowed the predatory smile she'd developed to curl her lips.

At his continued hesitance, she said, "Oh, come, Desch. Were those wistful words about taking me away from all this only syco-phantic boy-talk to soak off the girl you'd just fucked from stem to stern, or was it horseshit to convince yourself that I was more than an ordinary and convenient whore?"

Desch looked miserable, reached up and removed her finger. De-feated, he dropped to the bed. "No. I wasn't feeding you a line. It's the rules, Ali. What I promised the Supervisor in order to come here. Nothing, not a word of Corporate Mine will cross my lips. That's what I promised."

"So, you and 'the Supervisor'"—she'd noted the change from him calling her Kalico—"can talk about me. But you and I can't talk about her? Clap-trapping hell, what is it about that bargain that just doesn't seem fair, balanced, or equitable?"

"She can order me to never see you again," Desch almost pleaded.

Allison dropped to the bed, took his hand, let her gaze bore into his. "Desch, I can walk over to the door, give a whistle, and have Kalen Tompzen manhandle you right out the back and into the alley. All I have to say is 'Desch never sets foot in this place again,' and you won't."

"Ah, shit." He made a face.

"Fact is, I'll miss you. I like you. I enjoy the intimacy, the small talk, and the sex. Especially the sex. You're a good lover, considerate and talented. But mostly, I'll miss you for being you. The fact that when we're together, we just relax and enjoy spending time."

"Sounds like pretty good reasons not to have me thrown out, wouldn't you say?"

She snorted through her nose. "Not when I think that you're only here, only in my bed, because you're Kalico Aguila's spy. And, truth be told, after Dan compromised Kalen Tompzen, I wouldn't put it past Aguila to retaliate in kind." She let her eyes frost. "God, Desch. Is that what this is all about? Why you came back? So that Kalico could get—"

"No!"

"That really makes me a fool, doesn't it?" she adopted a whisper, letting her eyes go absent.

"Shit on a shoe, how'd this go so bad?" Desch wondered, dropping his face into his hands. Through his fingers, he added, "She knows I have a thing for you. I asked her. Pleaded with her, that I could come back. Made the promise that I'd never divulge anything to you that Dan could use against her. You know how they were? His threat to poison her, her retaliatory threat to blow up The Jewel. Made with *my* backpack!"

She let her voice warm the slightest bit. "I know. I know."

A beat.

"But Dan's gone."

She pulled his hands away, tugging on them. "Here. Look at me. That's it. Now, pay attention. I have no plans to do anything detrimental to Kalico. Nothing. Like you, I respect the hell out of her. Further, I want, I *need* Corporate Mine to prosper."

She could see the confusion in his eyes as he asked, "Why are you telling me this?"

She bit her lip, let him see her thinking it over. Said, "She won't believe me. Like you just mentioned, there's history between her and The Jewel. But I'm not Dan. I mean it when I say if something might compromise Kalico, you tell me. I'll do what I can to help."

"Why?"

"Think it through, Desch. Answer your own question. My only way out of this life that 'you'd take me away from', is by making a fortune and getting back to Solar System to spend it. To do that, and do it right, I need a powerful sponsor, understand? Like a Board Supervisor who will send a glowing recommendation and letter of support. Kalico's imprimatur, if you will."

He was chewing that over, nodding slightly. "Yeah, makes sense."

She gave him a warm wink. "Never know, old friend. We might go back on the same ship. A fresh start for both of us. Might be the opportunity that we really could spend some time together. Like . . . real time. Not just business. You've lived there. You could show me around."

"Yeah, I could see that."

She gave him a quick kiss on the cheek. "Me, too." A pause. "I shouldn't have snapped at you. It just pissed me off. She can ask you, I can't ask back. Not your fault."

"It's okay, Ali. I told her the truth. That you were better for PA than Dan. That you were smarter, and that our people would get a straight deal at The Jewel under your management. That's still true isn't it?"

"God, yes. Dan was a psychopath. He really didn't give a damn who got skinned or hurt, so long as it didn't affect business. Don't tell Kalico straight out, but I'll be keeping an extra eye out for her people. Last thing I want is to get crosswise. Any of them start to get in over their heads, I'll have my people ensure that they don't."

"Figured it that way," Desch said in relief.

"And Desch, remember, I need . . . No, we need Corporate Mine to run smoothly. Anything happens down there, and I mean *anything*, you tell me. I'll do everything in my power to help Kalico Aguila keep that train on the rails."

He was giving her that worshipful stare again, a glow of excitement behind his thoughtful brown eyes. "Deal."

She slapped him on the shoulder, kissed his cheek again, and stood. "Now, I've got to go check on the floor. Make sure that Vik's not overpouring from the whiskey bottle again. You'd think the man had no understanding of profit margins."

She was at the door as he was pulling on his boots.

"Ali?"

She turned.

"Thanks," Desch called. "And bless you for a saint."

"See you next four-day, Desch. Maybe we'll take an extra hour."

She was smiling as she walked out onto the casino floor.

14

Capella's light burned morning-gold as it bathed the bottoms of the clouds, tinged them with a blazing red and yellow, the edges rimed with an incandescent white. The chime rose, the first of the daytime invertebrates harmonizing with those of the night. A musical changing of the guard, even if it reminded Dek of no symphony he'd ever heard.

He lay on his bedroll, a thin emergency blanket thrown over him. The pain that had awakened him was back with a vengeance. The way it felt, he still expected to see shattered fragments of charred and splintered bone, ruined shreds of meat, tendrils of ligament, and tatters of hanging skin. He just couldn't get used to the fact that his lower leg was only swollen to twice its normal size.

A fire spat and hissed beside him; the last of the aquajade had burned down to a heap of ash. Aquajade made a lot of ash, and usually the coals would last a day to a day and a half. Chabacho burned more thoroughly. Didn't leave as much to clean up.

He had his wits back again—though if Talina had offered, he'd have taken another hit of Dya's blue-nasty-based pain killer. Life as a Taglioni back in Transluna had given him a thorough introduction to mind-altering chemicals. And being a Taglioni, he'd been able to afford the best. Dya's stuff had promise; it had kept him from suicide, dulled the worst of the agony. Let him cope.

That Dya Simonov had died just south of here, out in the deep forest, was heartbreaking. A tragedy for Donovan. He'd met the woman a couple of times in Port Authority. Never really gotten to know her. That she was Kylee's mother made her even more of a legend in his eyes. His memory of her would be of an attractive blonde, competent in her movements, and with a ready smile. Though she'd been polite when she'd introduced herself, some preoccupation had given her a distant look, and immediately afterward, she'd shuttled off for the labs to test some hypothesis.

And she died for nothing.

A fact that really angered him. The woman had gone out to Tyson Station to explain to the Unreconciled that their prophets were being killed by a prion. And she'd ended up dead. Talk about divine injustice.

"Someday the wheel will turn," Dek whispered to himself. "The Unreconciled will get theirs."

Or maybe they already had. Batuhan, who led the perverse cult, had paid. The handful of cannibals who were left were pretty much exiled and on their own. Not a good place to be on Donovan.

Unless you were someone like Kylee Simonov, who could survive in the bush.

He smiled at the thought of Kylee. She might only be closing on fourteen, but he had come to dote on her. On her best friend, Kip Briggs, too, though he was a different kind of a fish. Quiet, ever watchful, and where Kylee was eternally wary of strangers, Kip avoided them like they were plague.

"You have a smile on your lips." Talina's voice surprised him.

Dek twisted, seeing where she lay off to his right, her back to a chabacho log. The brown blanket she had pulled up to her chin matched the log. Made her blend into the background. He could see the long outline of her military-grade rifle where it lay covered on her lap.

"Thinking of Kylee and Kip." He shifted, gasped at the spike of pain that sent fire up his leg. "Shit on a shoe, I'm getting really tired of this."

Talina stood, unwrapped the blanket from around her. "It's light enough we can go. I changed out the power pack last night, so my aircar has a full charge. How about I get you back to hospital and let Raya get a good look at that leg?"

"What about my airplane? It will be faster."

"You think I'm going to let you fly? You can't even stand up."

"How do you know? I haven't tried. I can—"

"I only had a few gotcha spines in my arm, and I was almost out of my head. Another time I had 'em stuck deep in my hip and thigh. Hurt so bad I dug the spines out with my knife. Still got the scars to prove it. You remember what they did to Muldare? That was just a brush, barely penetrated her skin. We pulled them immediately. Yours, my friend, were driven deep. Maybe a hundred spines, all leaking poison into your muscles and blood." She gestured for him to proceed. "But go ahead, macho. Get up and walk over to your airplane. Don't let me stop you."

Dek growled, threw the blanket off, and felt pain-sweat pop from his skin. Just that small shift had him biting off a whimper.

I can do this. It's just pain. Pain can be endured. It's only nerves. Shut it off. One, two, three . . .

He sat up, swallowed a scream, and actually got halfway to his feet before the blast of agony flattened him. On the ground, he lay gasping and sucking for breath. Tears leaked from his eyes. It hurt so much the world spun. His gut convulsed, and he threw up. Or tried to. All he got was concentrated bile that burned in the back of his throat.

"Shoot me," he whispered.

In the pain-haze that washed over him, he felt something pushed into his mouth.

Heard, "Swallow that."

He didn't comply through any kind of coherence, just gulped against the pain. Was vaguely aware of a bitter taste mixing with the bile. Thought the combination was really shitty.

"Be about five minutes," Talina's voice cut through the heterodyne in his ears. "Then I'll get you bundled aboard. That latest dose of painkiller should hold you for the four-hour flight to PA."

Dek whimpered, wiped at the tears streaking down his face.

God fucking damn, if only he could just die.

He clamped his eyes. Tried to concentrate on breathing. *Just in and out. Yes, inhale. Don't think of how much it hurts. Exhale. Inhale. Exhale.* He made himself fall into the mantra.

And slowly the brain-numbing agony faded.

"Feeling better?" Talina asked, her voice close.

Dek blinked. "Yeah." Swallowed. "More of Dya's blue nasty?"

"Seems to really work. You ready?"

"Either cut my leg off or kill me."

"Naw. Either way, Kalico would never forgive me. Since she's one of the only real friends I've got, I can't afford to piss her off. Guess you'll just have to suffer."

"You're a hard woman."

"Hey, you were in love with me last night. How quickly things change."

"Still in love with you. It's my leg that I hate."

He felt her arms going around him. Instead of a lover's embrace, she lifted. Drugs or not, the pain left him dry-heaving as she carried him across the clearing, lifted him over the railing of her aircar, and laid him on the seat.

As the agony eased, he managed to suck air, trying to keep himself from screaming.

He must have drifted off, didn't know how long he was out. Coming to, he had an image of leaping onto a fast break, his jaws snapping shut on the back of the creature's neck. And . . .

What? Leaping on a fast break? What crazy part of his brain had *that* come from?

Dek heard the rushing of air. He blinked. Lifted himself on his elbows to stare over the aircar's railing at the deep forest passing below. He figured that they were about a hundred and fifty meters above the treetops, and they were making about seventy knots.

Overhead the morning sky was filled with Donovan's deeper greenish blue, dotted with puffy white clouds. Capella looked to be about an hour above the eastern horizon. Good, he hadn't been out for long.

Talina stood at the wheel, her attention on keeping the aircar's course. Dek took a moment to enjoy the view. If only he could. . .

The thought flew away like thistle down on the wind. Had to be the drug. Made him really stupid. He remembered Talina's lips on his, the way she'd been breathing life into him. Wished he'd been conscious, could have participated.

Damn, Dek. You've been celibate for far too long.

His last relationship had been with Michaela Hailwood. A couple of years back. On *Ashanti* before she'd turned her attentions to First Officer Turner. Ed and she were really more suited to each other, and in the end, even that hadn't worked for Michaela. Maritime Unit had been that way. In the few instances when he'd been in a short relationship with one of the women, Kevina, Vik, Casey, or Michaela, they always went back to the "family."

Dek reached up to rub his eyes. Wondered at the ache deep behind them. When he blinked, a rainbow-like shimmering made a haze at the edges of his vision. He tried to focus on the colors, how they seemed to pulse, only to have his vision splinter as if a thousand stars were falling around him and his body had become weightless. Had to be the drug messing with his senses.

He gritted his teeth, raised himself up to a sitting position on the aircar's bench so that he could see past the white duraplast sides. Ahead the Wind Mountains blocked the horizon, their tall summits jagged against the sky. The highest peaks were spinning threads of cloud that trailed out with the wind. White patches of snow dotted the slopes up above the four-thousand-meter mark, and contrasted with the mixed grays, blacks, and reds of the up-thrust metamorphic and igneous rock.

Talina was headed straight for Best Pass, the lowest and most direct route to Port Authority.

Her lips on his? Wish it had been a lover's kiss. She'd given him mouth-to-mouth. Hammered his heart back into beating, had breathed life into his lungs. Too bad he'd been dead at the time. As exotic and alluring as she was, he'd have loved to participate, savor her lips working on his, run his tongue . . . A sudden flood of saliva filled his mouth with a taste that he associated with astringent peppermint. What the hell was in Dya's drug that it would screw with his sense of taste so?

"Oh, Dek, get real," he whispered to himself.

But for Talina, at this very moment, his dead body would be swarming with invertebrates as they ate their way through his skin, devoured his muscles and organs. And nothing, no appeal to the heavens that he was a Taglioni, would have saved him. But Talina had come. Not because of his family, but because of him. Who he was as a man.

"That's a considerable achievement," he told himself.

"*Yesss,*" a voice hissed.

What the hell? He blinked, shook his head, trying to clear the sudden ringing in his ears. He caught fragments, as if disjointed voices were trying to form in his hearing.

"God," he muttered, "I might be glad for the pain-dulling effects of this stuff, but the side effects are sure crazy."

Talina turned, looked back. "You're awake. How you feeling?"

"Weird. The backs of my eyes hurt. It's screwing with my vision. Like rainbow shimmers. Uh, as if I was looking through an oil sheen on water. Lots of colors that break into stars. And I'm hearing things. Leg's a hell of a lot better, though. Hurts about half as bad as it did yesterday, which I'm taking for a major win."

Talina flipped on the autopilot, stepped back to crouch beside him. She pointed to the barely healed wound on his arm. "How long since you and Flute exchanged blood? A couple of weeks?"

"Yeah. About."

"And why the hell did you do that?"

"To understand."

"Understand what, Dek? We have no clap-trapping clue what TriNA's long-term effects are on the human body. For all you know, you'll end up a freak like Kylee and me."

"And there's that professor on *Vixen.*"

"Weisbacher. Last time I talked with anyone on *Vixen,* he was a mumbling, half-psychotic wreck. He hallucinates that TriNA is eating his brain. Never leaves his cabin. I think if Torgussen had his way, he'd ship the moron dirtside and be well rid of the albatross. But let's get back to you. What the clap-trapping hell do you hope to get out of quetzal TriNA?"

He tried to think, wished to hell his brain was clear. That the blue nasty wasn't messing with his mental clarity. "You, Kylee, Kip, maybe Chaco and Madison, you're the future of humanity on

Donovan. I don't know if we're going to win here, even whether or not we'll survive. But meeting the planet halfway is the best hope."

A hardness lay behind her dark and alien eyes. "It comes at a price, Dek. Kylee, Kip, and me? We're no longer wholly human. You exchanging blood with Flute? I'd say you'd better hope it doesn't take. If it does, you're never going back to Solar System to enjoy all those perks of being a high mucky muck."

"Thought you knew I wasn't going back." He gave her a wry wink, gestured toward the forest passing below. "My future's here. Like Kalico, I'm betting everything on it."

"Hope it doesn't destroy you," she told him as she rose and headed back to the wheel. Over her shoulder, she added, "More than once it's come within a hair's width of killing me."

"But you made it." He blinked against the growing ache behind his eyes. What was that about? Migraine coming on? On top of the pain-sucking leg? What kind of justice was that?

"Yeah," Talina called over her shoulder. "First time you experience that peppermint taste, you'll know you're fucked."

"How's that?"

"Because it means the changes have started, and there's no going back."

15

The way the seatruck skimmed just above the cresting waves filled Kalico with a sense of magic. She had never seen water this color: true lapis lazuli. That blue so remarkable and enchanting. In order to get a better look, Kalico stood mere inches from the transparency that curved around the vehicle's entire front. For the moment, she reveled in the illusion that she was flying over the water. Only if she looked down to see the deck beneath her feet, or sidelong where Shinwua stood at the controls, did the illusion shatter.

Behind her, Soichiro Yoshimura was seated in the cabin's first row of benches, his head bent to his pad as he scrolled through one of the reports penned by Lee Cheng, the biochemist and miracle maker who worked in Port Authority's hospital. Until their arrival at Donovan, most of the information the Maritime Unit had access to was dated, literally decades old. Since their arrival, Hailwood's team had been in a mad scramble to review anything that Dya Simonov, Cheng, Turnienko, Allenovich, or Iji Hiro had written about biological pathways, organisms, and especially the miracle of TriNA.

Granted, the research documented land-based species, but the theory was that life on Donovan—as it had on Earth—developed originally in the seas. That ontogeny still recapitulated phylogeny, or that if you know how life worked on land, you'd have a foundation for your study of maritime organisms.

Kalico had spent the previous night in briefings with Michaela Hailwood's people, refining her understanding of their goals and research designs. From her own experience she was able to help them narrow their focus. Even to the point of discarding entire Corporate mandates for research.

"Don't bother with that gender study," she'd told Michaela. "Life on Donovan doesn't work the way any of the initial reports hypothesized. See Raya Turnienko's research on TriNA. As far as we've observed, all reproduction on Donovan takes three donors, and there are no sexes. No dimorphism. Nothing close to an analog of a male or female. All three donors exchange TriNA. In the reproductive tracts, the molecules split into separate deoxyribonucleic strands that recombine with strands from each of the other two parental TriNA molecules. Each of the parents gestate one or more young after the exchange."

She had added, "Don't expect reef ecology to have any Terrestrial equivalent. Given that the plants on land move, any mapping of aquatic vegetation will probably be a snapshot. And while we're not positive about this, you're going to be a lot better off if you begin your study assuming that the plants are intelligent. Hell, for all we know, everything is."

"You're joking," Casey Stoner had cried.

Kalico had given the woman a thin-lidded appraisal. "What part of TriNA didn't you get? It's a three-strand molecule that processes data at three-to-the-third power. Cheng has isolated some of the microRNAs that TriNA uses to communicate, and he's building a list of proteins the molecules produce and may use for shorthand. Not to mention that the molecules separate into strands of deoxyribonucleic acid that recombine with strands from other TriNA. They copy, compare, or whatever, then separate again and go back to their original molecule. Sort of like they've gone visiting to share notes. I tell you, it's an intelligence at the molecular level that we're just beginning to work out."

Just as they were all shuffling off to bed, Michaela had buttonholed Kalico, a sober look in her eyes. "I want to thank you. You've probably saved us months, maybe a year or more of false starts. I know my people may have come off as obstinate, but for some of them, especially in the biological sciences, they've just had their entire paradigms upended."

"Welcome to Donovan," Kalico had replied laconically. "That happens here. A lot."

Hailwood had steepled her fingers, hesitated, then said, "Don't take this wrong. It's a pleasant surprise to realize our Board Supervisor isn't just some administrator who could care less as long as the boxes are checked off. Your understanding of the planet's fundamental biology is impressive. Don't think we don't appreciate it." Hailwood had smiled. "After tonight, I think my team and I are more energized than ever to meet and exceed your expectations."

"Director, this is Donovan. Nothing here works the way you expect."

The woman had nodded. "Isn't that the truth?"

To Kalico's surprise, she'd slept well in the single-occupancy berth they'd given her. Awakened refreshed and been pleasantly surprised when the biological experts had quizzed her hard all through breakfast. Obviously, they'd spent most of the night mulling over what she'd told them. But knowing intellectually was different than having the reflexes.

Of course, when The Corporation had chosen them, it had picked from the brightest cadre of up-and-coming young scientists available. All of them had been in their twenties, people with drive and ambition who wouldn't mind dedicating a minimum of fourteen years of their lives to the two-year transit time, the requisite ten-year contract on Donovan, and another two-year transit back to Solar System. That they'd all re-upped spoke well for the prescience used by the selection committee back on Transluna.

Given Kalico's choice of the day's duties and assignments, she'd chosen to accompany the inaugural run out to one of the small islands fifty kilometers to the north. Shinwua had assured Hailwood that the seatruck was finally ready for a shakedown trip. The second unit would be kept in reserve on the Pod's dock in case anything went wrong.

To Kalico's way of thinking, that kind of forethought upped the Maritime Unit's chances of success fourfold.

As the seatruck skimmed along a mere two meters above the wavetops, Kalico savored the sight of endless water. She'd missed having a vista that wasn't through chain-link. And in the bush, vegetation created a constant visual barrier.

"What are those?" She pointed to the triangular shapes that had appeared on the horizon to the northeast.

"We call them seaskimmers," Shinwua told her. "We haven't

managed a close look at one yet. Best we can tell, they're like a living sailboat."

As the seatruck closed the distance, the triangular sails shifted colors, patterns of orange, yellow, and dark blue scrolling across the sails. The seaskimmers reversed course in unison, tacking off to the east and away from the seatruck's path.

Kalico said, "You saw that patterning? The different colors? That's communication. Just like quetzals use on land. When you get the chance to watch these seaskimmers for long enough, you'll be able to read what they're saying, at least on an elementary level."

Shinwua said, "I'll take your word for it."

Kalico asked, "Want to bet a couple rhodium bars?"

"What's a rhodium bar?"

"Call it the most valuable metal on Donovan. A two-kilo bar would buy you the premium penthouse at Three Spires and let you live in whatever fashion you wished for the rest of your life. Oh, and your kid's lives. A couple of bars? Well, I guess they wouldn't buy you a seat on the Board, and maybe they wouldn't buy you a Board-member, but you could sure rent one for rest of his or her life."

"And you're betting two of these bars?" Yoshimura rose from his seat and came to stand just behind Kalico's shoulder as he stared at the fleeing seaskimmers. The creatures were now flashing patterns of red, pink, blue, and violet as they caught all the wind they could to escape from the seatruck's path.

"You my taker?" she asked.

Yoshimura raised his binoculars, studying the patterns on the sails as the seatruck passed to the seaskimmers' right. "Not me. Like you said last night. This is not Earth."

"So, if there's all this intelligence," Shinwua asked, "what does it do?"

"What do you mean, do?"

"Okay, granted, I'm a programmer and engineer. Humans are the only major intelligence on Earth, right? I mean, yeah, dolphins, ravens, and apes are pretty smart, and they make some stuff. Simple stuff. If even the molecules are smart here, what have they done with it?"

"I'm not following you," Kalico replied.

"Hey, I don't see buildings, spaceships, electronics, roads, farms, mines, or anything that I'd consider a sign of intelligence. So, if even the TriNA learns, what does it learn? Or does it just hang around thinking planet-shaking great thoughts? Some kind of solipsistic navel gazing dedicated to asking the eternal question of why? So the planet has figured out the purpose of existence, what good is it if you don't do something with it?"

"Good question," Kalico answered. "We've been asking ourselves the same thing over the last few years. We know the most about the quetzals. Used to think they were the apex predators. Now we're dealing with mobbers, and finally, something big, furtive, and deadly that lurks in the treetops out west. Something smart enough to know it was going to be bombed from the air."

"Wait," Yoshimura said. "It *knew* it was going to be bombed? You'd tried to bomb it before?"

Kalico shook her head. "First time. Somehow the treetop terror figured out that we were baiting it from below while Dek circled above in an airplane. It was able to analyze our actions tactically, identify the airplane as a threat, and make the decision to tear off a tentacle in order to escape our trap. That, gentlemen, is a sobering cognitive ability."

"And the quetzals? They do this too?" Shinwua asked.

"Not like that treetop terror. Here's what we know: The quetzal lineage around Port Authority considers itself at war with humanity. We call this the Whitey lineage after the current leader. For the last thirty years, his lineage has been studying humanity, trying to figure out how to exterminate us. It has taken them that long to figure out how to coordinate a massed attack on PA. But quetzals pass information down through transfers of TriNA. Some learning may even be generational, although individuals are highly adaptive. One of the reasons it may have taken them this long is that we've killed a lot of quetzals. We were taking them out of the brain pool before they could share knowledge."

"That doesn't argue for intelligence," Yoshimura noted.

"Rifles, drones, remote sensing, and explosives haven't been in their cultural history until recently," Kalico countered. "It took Rocket--a quetzal from another lineage who bonded with a little girl--for us to begin to understand quetzal intelligence. And through a couple of infected humans, we're learning that quetzal lineages, like groups of people, have different agendas."

"Go back to this infection," Yoshimura said. "I've heard rumors, but nothing concrete. That somehow quetzal molecules are changing people. Like that Perez woman. That her infection was what made her so . . . what do I say? Alien?"

Kalico nodded. "Good word. Tal's a test case, a battleground for competing lineages of quetzal TriNA. Fortunately, she's a tough lady. Was able to come to terms with her unique circumstance. When we get to Kylee, the little girl? Well, she's not so little now, and her history is tragic. Her quetzal, Rocket, was murdered, which turns out to have been a crippling blow in more ways than one. As a result, Kylee is wild, doesn't trust humans. She's bonded with another quetzal, named Flute. But she'll never be a 'normal' human being."

"So," Shinwua asked, "What do the quetzals want?"

"We don't know. And, to be frank, I'm not sure they do either. It's like we're all feeling our way forward in this."

"And what lessons do we take away from this?" Yoshimura asked.

Kalico could see the white breakers ahead, and even as she watched, a thin strip of cream-colored sand could be made out against the horizon.

"Here's your takeaway, Dr. Yoshimura: Whatever you find in the ocean, don't think—even for an instant—that it's simple. What we know about intelligence on Donovan is little more than a feeble candle flame in a universe of blackness. But it's enough to scare the clap-trapping bejeezus out me."

"The what?" Shinwua asked.

"Sorry. Old term." But still just as true.

16

"**H**ow do you get this stuff off?" Sheena asked.

Felix looked up from the pad where he'd been reading. According to the cafeteria clock, the time was 11:05. He, Breez, Felicity, Tomaya, and Sheena were in what the adults called "school." Or sometimes, just "class." This had started for him and the two girls back on *Ashanti*.

There it had been in one of the dormitory rooms where the three of them had been made to sit at the low central table and study on their pads with half the adults crowded around. Given that there was nothing else to do, it had been a community process, to which Tomaya and then Breez had been added when each turned four. Along with the adults, Felix, Felicity, and Sheena had been expected to help Tomaya and Breez learn letters, numbers, adding and subtracting, and then reading. Seemed like Breez had taken to it a lot faster at her age than either Felix, Felicity, Sheena, or Tomaya had.

During the transition down from *Ashanti,* "school" had been a constant. What was different on the Pod was that no adults were lounging around adding bits of wisdom to the lesson. Sometimes, in the past, he and the girls had learned more from the conversations the adults got into about history and science and stories then they did from the pads.

"I said, how do you get this stuff off?" Sheena repeated, giving Felix a hard glare. She lifted her fingers, rubbed them together. "It's like oil. But I can rub it, wash it with soap, scrub, and it's just there. And it itches."

"Told you." Felix shot a glance at Felicity who looked puzzled. "You weren't there."

"What is it?" Breez asked.

"Algae," Felix told her to cut Sheena off. "From the water."

"Like, from hydroponics?"

"No, the real water," he told her with all the arrogance he could muster. "Sheena and me, we caught some."

"How?" Felicity demanded.

"With our fingers," Sheena finally chimed in. "Now it won't come off. Feels like oil."

"Let me feel." Breez reached out a hand, grabbed Sheena's fingers, and rubbed them. "Like grease, huh? You know, like Tobi puts on moving parts."

Breez would know that since her mother, Jaim Elvridge, was an engineer.

"I want to feel, too," Tomaya got out of her chair and walked over to examine Felix's fingers. As she rubbed them, his palms began to sweat; the prickling tingle ran from his hand up his arm to the shoulder. "Hey, easy. That feels funny."

"Why's your palm all wet?" Tomaya wanted to know, making a face as she studied her hand and then rubbed it, as if trying to get his sweat off. "It's kind of slimy. Sort of like spit." She flounced over and dropped with an overemphasized huff into her chair. Still, she kept rubbing her fingers together. "Doesn't feel . . . what did you say? Tingly."

"It will," Sheena warned.

"Did your Mom try and wash it off?" Felicity asked.

"It's fine," Sheena told her.

But Tomaya caught the look that passed between Felix and Sheena. She said, "Oh, you did something you shouldn't have?"

"Must have been bad," Felicity said.

"How do you know?" Breez asked, bending back to her pad as she started rubbing her fingers on her jumper.

"'Cause they did," Tomaya said craftily.

"Okay, smarty," Felix challenged. "What did we do? Huh?"

"I don't know," Tomaya admitted, "but it was something."

"Bet they went where they weren't supposed to," Felicity told them with self-assurance. "Got into stuff the grownups told them not to."

"Did not," Felix cried impulsively.

Sheena had scrunched her lips into a pout the way she did when she didn't want any more questions. Felix knew she was pretending to read from her pad, but all the while she kept rubbing her fingers on the fabric of her smock.

Felicity grabbed at his hand, clamped on tight, and looked at his fingers. "They look shiny. Like they got plastic all over them. Your Mom seen that?"

"No. She's been busy. It'll go away. Like the time I got ink on my fingers and had to wear it off."

Felicity was rubbing her index finger on Felix's thumb and forefinger. "Feels slippery, all right. Is that why you kept dropping your cup this morning?"

"I don't know." He jerked his hand away. "Let go! It's not your business anyway."

Felicity sat back, a frown lining her forehead as she rubbed her fingers together.

17

A s the seatruck approached the island's white sand, Yoshimura said, "Slow us down, Shin. Let's take our time closing on the beach. Maybe follow a course parallel to the littoral? Say one hundred meters out? Give me a chance to get the UUVs in the water and get a look at what's under the waves?"

"You got it, Yosh."

Kalico had to brace herself on the transparency as the seatruck settled into the water, rocking as it rode the rise and fall of the swells. Shinwua steered them parallel to the beach and lowered the two drones into the water.

The depth here averaged around seven meters, visibility excellent in the crystalline water. Not more than thirty centimeters under the surface, a collection of what they called "jellyfish" were expanding and contracting as they moved slowly forward. Like the terrestrial versions, some were nearly transparent, others came in all sizes and colors. Unlike the earthly versions, these scattered as the drones approached. Created a sort of tunnel along the drone's path. As they did, all were changing color, turning to a remarkably uniform orange-red.

Shin immediately sent the second drone deep, dropping it down through the clear water to hover a meter above the bottom. As it descended, colorful, tube-shaped creatures shot this way and that, apparently propelled by jets of water blasted out through vents at their rear.

"Three-sided," Kalico said in instant revelation. "It's a pattern we see on land. Trilateral symmetry. And the basic Donovanian physiology, it comes from the tube shape being used as a means of propulsion. Like quetzals who suck in air and vent it out the back. But here, it's water."

"And perhaps for oxygen exchange," Yoshimura said. "They must have some equivalent of gills inside."

"That's where quetzals, chamois, fastbreak, mobbers, and the rest have their lungs," Kalico agreed. "Look at the way—"

"Um, guys?" Shin called, pointing to the monitor displaying the first drone's transmission.

Kalico shifted her gaze, tried to figure out what she was seeing. The tunnel the jellyfish had made around the UUV was contracting, becoming more of an envelope that shrank down, closing in around the UUV until the camera was blotted out.

"What just happened?" Shin asked as he worked the joystick that controlled the drone. "I've got nothing here. Drone's responding despite a deteriorating signal, but it's lost maneuverability. Like something's grabbed hold of it."

"The jellyfish," Kalico said thoughtfully. "They've swarmed the drone. My guess, Donovan being Donovan, they're trying to eat it."

"What?" Yoshimura asked.

"Bems, skewers, lots of Donovanian creatures use camouflage, then grab or spear their prey before engulfing it." To Shin she said, "Do you have any way of defending your drone?"

"I can run an electrical discharge through the hull. It's meant to discourage barnacles and such from attachment."

"You might want to try it. Otherwise, unless the jellyfish get bored, they may never turn loose of your drone."

"Got it." Shin tapped the screen, displayed a menu, and touched an icon. Red letters read "DISCHARGE" and on-screen, the drone's camera cleared. The jellyfish were backing away, what had been a deep crimson color shifting to yellow. Here and there, dots of black, indigo, and laser-green flashed, only to be repeated by the closest jellyfish and passed along. As quickly the orange-red color began to appear again, spreading through the cluster.

"Get it back now," Yoshimura said. "Before they can grab it again."

And, sure enough, the jellyfish had retreated out to reform the tunnel around the UUV.

"Full reverse," Shin muttered. And the drone went flying back-

wards as the jellyfish turned crimson and began undulating to close
the trap.

"I'll be damned," Yoshimura whispered. "Did you see how well
organized they were? I can't wait to watch the replay. Study it in
detail. That's organized behavior, and the colors, that looks like
they were communicating, orchestrating the hunt."

"Got grapples on the UUV," Shin cried triumphantly. "It's back
in its bay."

"How we going to get that one back?" Yoshimura indicated the
deep drone. Awaiting commands, it hovered at its same location.
Below, the bottom was carpeted by what Kalico took to be greenish-
blue plants. Though some defied description, being composites of
tentacles, branches, bladders, and stems, others hearkened to ana-
logs from land. Like the one that looked like a bright-green lollipop
stand.

"Steer clear of that one." Kalico pointed. "If it's in any way related to the giant trees that live out by Tyson Station, it's a predator.
And, given that the plants move, and if the jellyfish are any guide,
if any of them grab hold of the UUV, it's not going to let go."

"Good point." Yoshimura used a control to swivel the camera
upwards. "Looks like the jellyfish are all staying a couple of meters up."

"Maybe they're restricted to just below the surface?" Shinwua
wondered.

"See these really tall plants?" Kalico pointed to where long turquoise strands rose to a couple of meters below the surface. "The
jellyfish seem to stay above their reach."

Meanwhile, the colorful tubes were darting this way and that
among the plants. One appeared within a few centimeters of the
camera, and Yoshimura refocused to get a better look.

"Definitely trilateral symmetry," Yoshimura said reverently. "Each
of the three sides is exactly the same. One eye on each. What a perfect
adaptation to an aquatic environment. Complete three-hundred-
and-sixty-degree vision."

"Dya would have loved this," Kalico said softly. "I'm not even close to an expert, but I think Iji is going to see one land-based analog after another in the aquatic plants we're observing here."

"If they're really plants." Yoshimura pointed. "See that petal-shaped thing? Looks like a plant, but it's moving, and I'd swear those are eyes. See? Right in the middle of each of the three leaves."

Even as they watched, the three big spatulate leaves shifted, aligned, as if targeting, and faster than Kalico could see, a slim tendril shot out from what she'd thought was the stem. It speared a tube that had its attention fixed on the drone. As the hunter reeled the tube back, the nearest plants shifted, roots spurting sand; the plants extended feelers, leaves, and tentacles as they tried to snatch the prize. The spatulate-leafed creature artfully dodged and tucked its captured tube close, the broad leaves folding down around the prey like a tight wrapping.

"What's that?" Shinwua asked. He hit reverse, then play, skilled fingers enlarging the image on the monitor. "Here, see. Where the sand is kicked up by the roots. Those things. What are they?"

"Look like invertebrates," Kalico said. "But nothing like the ones on land. It's just the colorful shells. These are, well . . ."

Some of the things looked more like impossible crosses between a beetle, a trilobite, and a crayfish. Others might have been three-sided hard-shelled cuttlefish kinds of things. Others defied category, being colorful composites of shells, flickering cilia, and fan-like wings. She couldn't tell the scale, but the biggest of the creatures might have been a couple of centimeters long. And as quickly, they were hidden back in the shadows of the larger plants.

"A wealth," Yoshimura said through a reverent breath. "Even if all we had was this one record, we're going to be engrossed for years. I've got a—"

"Woah!" Shinwua called, his eyes on another of his monitors. "Sonar has something big headed our way from offshore."

"The jellyfish have vanished," Kalico noted. She tapped the replay, watching in fascination as the jellyfish lost all their myriad colors, turning completely transparent. Like they had just faded away and disappeared.

"See if the drone can get a look," Yoshimura told Shinwua.

Shinwua's skilled hands turned the drone, pointed it at the endless aqua of deepwater, and started it forward.

Kalico happened to be gazing at the sonar, seeing an elongated shape coming in from the side. And then it shot forward.

Switching her gaze to the drone's camera, she caught a glimpse of something like three very broad swords, equally spaced at one-hundred-and-twenty-degree angles and attached to a cylindrical central body where triangular jaws . . .

This thing is huge!

The swords flashed down and in, meeting just out of the camera's field of view. The image jerked, went black.

"What the hell?" Shinwua cried. He was jockeying with his joystick.

Kalico stared at the sonar, seeing the elongated shape, maybe thirty meters of it, flash through where the meter-long UUV had been.

She ran to the starboard window, pushed it open, and stared down.

Through the crystal water, she could see it. Patterns of color ran down the tapering body; what looked like lines of stubby wings, but were probably fins, ran the dorsal length of the body, but remained indistinct through the surface distortion.

The plants in the immediate vicinity had faded, as if they'd lost their color. The water's surface around the seatruck was roiling; tubes actually jetted out of the water, sailing for several meters before splashing back, only to jet again. So did several other, larger creatures, including one with four wings that sailed for quite some distance.

Down below the monster turned, and with a flip and twist, it shot back toward the depths and vanished.

"I've got nothing," Shinwua said from the control panel. "The drone's dead. What the hell could do that?"

On the other side of the seatruck, Yoshimura had opened the door. Leaning out, he extended one of his cameras so that the lens was underwater. "Shin, I've got bad news for you. I've got a piece of your drone here. Looks like it was sheered in two. I mean, whatever that thing was, it cut through the plastic hull like it was cheese. Sliced the wires, everything."

"It happened so fast," Shinwua muttered in wonder. "I tell you, nothing on earth can do that."

"What makes you think you're still on Earth?" Kalico called, closing her window. "Dr. Yoshimura, I think the UUVs are going to take some rethinking before we send them out again."

He nodded, pulled in his camera, and closed the door. "Take us ashore, Shin. At least we can get a look at the beach. If we don't come back with sand samples for Lara, she'll just have to make another trip and do it herself. Not to mention that we'll have to put up with the look."

"What look?" Talina asked.

Yoshimura gave her a knowing grin. "It's her 'you're-a-real-piece-of-work' look. The one she gives you when she thinks a five-year-old could have done a better job."

"You don't want her giving you that look," Shinwua agreed. "It's really humbling."

Kalico muttered, "Well, I guess I'd better not get myself in a position where I'm compared to a five-year-old. I get humbled enough as it is."

"That *thing* is just hovering out there, like it's watching us." Yoshimura stared pensively at the sonar screen. "Maybe it's afraid of Lara, too."

Shin chuckled and sank teeth into his lower lip. The man turned the wheel and ran them through the surf, the seatruck's balloon tires extending from their wells in the hull as the vehicle lumbered up on the sand. He brought it to a stop three meters up from the wave line and at the foot of low cream-colored dunes. Bits of scrubby vegetation—something that looked like white-spotted succulents—grew in lace-like patterns across the dune face.

"Wait," Kalico called as Yoshimura opened the door. "Take a good hard look before you step out. Give it a couple of minutes so we can see if anything comes to investigate. Shin, keep an eye on the sky. No telling what those polka dots are that you've seen. Or who knows what else might be flying around."

"It's just a couple of samples," Yoshimura told her.

"Yeah," Kalico agreed. "The good news is that there's no root mat. It's wide open. We can see for a kilometer in every direction. The only place anything big can camouflage itself is back in the dunes, not on this flat sand. And listen, if something pops up, freeze until I can shoot it. Hopefully, like with mobbers, if whatever it is doesn't recognize you as prey, it might ignore you."

"You got it." Yoshimura told her. "Thank God you came along, Supervisor. I mean, we've listened, tried to learn. But having you here, it really brings this place home."

She opened the roof hatch and climbed up until she had a good view in all directions. Fifty meters to the south along the flat strip of sand, she could see some kind of life-forms—maybe the size of footballs—that charged in and out of the surf. In the distance to the north, a collection of flying hunters were diving into the breakers, but they were a good half a kilometer away.

Wind whipped her hair around as she studied the dunes, seeing no movement, no tracks. Nothing made a mound, no shape that wasn't entirely natural.

As she glanced back at the surf, the seatruck's tracks where it had rolled out of the water were being scrubbed away. Out beyond the breakers, something stuck up. Dark, gleaming, like a tennis-ball-sized eye on a stalk. She had no clue what it might be. Then it slipped back into the water, leaving only the long breaker to crest and waste itself on a retreating wave.

"Supervisor?" Yoshimura called up. "You see anything?"

She gave one last look at the sky, checked the flying things up north; they seemed to be going the other way.

"No." She dropped down through the roof hatch. "But I don't like it. Can you just throw these sample jars out, maybe tied to a string or something?"

"Lara's going to want them filled according to protocol. That means opening the jar, using the scoop to take a core, filling, and resealing the jar. She'll want one from the closest dune, one from the tidal sand, and one from where the waves are washing." Yoshimura paused. "Got to take a risk, Supervisor. If we don't, we'll never be able to do our jobs, and damn it, we've spent twelve years getting here already."

"We'll split up," Shin said. "Yosh, you take the dune. Supervisor, you get the tidal zone, and I'll get the wet one. Won't take us but three minutes. Then we can hotfoot back inside, drive around the dunes in safety, or float offshore taking soundings with the underwater sensing gear. Maybe deploy one of the cameras for underwater photography."

"Works for me," Yosh said. "Supervisor?"

Kalico took a deep breath. "We go fast. But I take the dune sample. It's farthest from the seatruck. I'm faster, and I'm armed. Dr. Yoshimura, you take the tidal zone. Shinwua, you're in the wave-washed zone. Each of you: get out, get that sample, and get back. If anything's gone to sucking snot, Yosh drives to the rescue. Got it?"

"Sure thing."

Yoshimura broke out the sample jars. Clear glass with a stainless-steel top, each held a half liter. Attached to the side was the disposable plastic scoop. It looked simple: Drive the scoop into the sand and twist it to take a core. Lift the scoop free and insert it into the jar. Press the tab on the handle, and it would release the sample as the scoop was withdrawn. Then screw the cap tight and record the provenience on the label.

"Any questions, Supervisor?" Yosh asked.

"Nope. Let's do this, people. Just stay frosty and don't linger." Kalico checked her pistol, opened the door, and leaped out onto the packed sand.

She didn't run headlong, but she sure didn't tarry either. Hurrying, she kept one hand on her pistol, the other holding the sample jar.

The first thing that hit her was the smell: musky, damp, almost like a pungency. The odor wasn't unpleasant, but heavy with salt and wet sand, possessed of a tang that might have been from the plants. At each step, invertebrates broke from where they'd been hidden beneath the surface, skittering a meter or more away from her booted foot to burrow without a trace into the creamy sand. They did so with remarkable speed.

The salt-scented sea breeze batted at Kalico's hair, ruffled her coveralls, and patted her cheeks. Capella's light warmed her, the primary's rays reflecting whitely off the beach. She felt inexplicably free. Surrounded by beauty.

Something in Kalico's memory smacked of Yucatan, or maybe South Padre in the Gulf of Mexico. The kind of place that begged for a beach chair, a cooler, and a day of relaxation and decompression.

Yeah, right, she chided herself.

She trotted up onto the first of the dunes, pistol half drawn as she scanned the wind-sculpted rise. Checked behind the slip face. Nothing. And she made sure to stay well clear of the closest of the succulent plants, not trusting their innocent shape, let alone the reach of their roots, however hidden they might be.

She shot a glance back. Yoshimura was filling his sample jar. On the other side of the seatruck, Shinwua was down on one knee, coring his sample. Just a flash of something out beyond the breakers caught her attention. Movement. She thought she glimpsed the eye-topped stalk again, but it could have been a leaping tube or some other sea creature.

Kalico dropped to a knee, unscrewed the lid, and used the scoop to fill the jar. Vacuum simple. Now Lara wouldn't give her that notorious scowl.

Kalico stood as she screwed the lid tight, took one last look around.

It wouldn't be a bad place to come back to. Maybe. After the surveys had been done and the dangers accounted for. It had been a long time since she'd had a place as remote, beautiful, and beckoning call to her.

She turned, started back to the seatruck. Yoshimura was just climbing into the cabin.

Shinwua, however, was standing in the wash of the waves, back to her as he stared out at the surf. His sample jar hung from one hand as he craned his neck, as if searching the breakers for something.

"Come on," Kalico whispered, breaking into a dogtrot. "Whatever it is, we'll look for it with the cameras."

She had almost reached the seatruck, had just taken a breath to call to Shinwua when the creature shot out of the water. Fast. A blurred image of something slashing shoreward through the curl of a breaker. The curving long blades glistened a steely blue in Capella's hard light. As if exploding from the surf, the creature flew up the beach with uncanny speed.

Kalico broke into a run, took in the body behind the three extended blades: cylindrical, as big around as an oil drum and dazzling with shimmering rainbow colors. Stalk-fixed eyes, two of which were raised high and fixed on Shinwua, gleamed like polished midnight. The third was tucked tightly below the gaping mouth. The front of the thing—on which each of the broad blades hinged—enlarged, opening wide to display three tooth-studded jaws and a black gullet.

"Shin! Run!" she cried.

But the man stood riveted, as if in a trance.

The monster sped onto the shore, sand and water flying in spurts as it dug into the beach with parallel lines of paddle-like flippers. It came on like a greyhound, sleek and agile for all of its length.

The creature was gorgeous; laser-bright reds, gold, deep black, viridian greens, and pulsing blues dazzled on its hide, luminous in Capella's light. Kalico had an image of sun-red shading into bright splotches of yellow and remarkable violet patterns that shifted and pulsed on its water-sleek sides.

Shinwua's spell broke, and the man wheeled around. Maybe, if he'd been fit instead of half-starved after all the years in *Ashanti*, he might have made it. He was reaching for the door when the slashing scimitars flashed closed. The lower ones swept in from either side. Caught Shinwua in the hips. The third cut cleanly down the side of his head, peeling the man's scalp and ear off his skull and sheering through the collar bone. As it did the lower two pinched together, slicing up, stopping just under the ribs.

The sample jar dropped from Shinwua's nerveless fingers to thump and roll on the sand.

Kalico glimpsed the man's horrified face, watched blood well and spurt on bared skull where his scalp and ear were sliced away. The skin from his head was hanging limply, mindful of a soggy red rag that flopped on his shoulder.

"No!" Kalico bellowed, sliding to a stop. She clawed her pistol from its holster as the shimmering beast lifted Shinwua and spun. Clutched in the deadly blades, Shinwua's body was flung around and flopped like a limp doll's. The predator was maybe thirty meters in length with a long, tubular body that narrowed into a pencil-thin tail. Water streaked out of vents just behind the line of flipper feet. As the beast turned, the flippers cupped the sand like scoops. One of the stalk-topped eyes was staring at Kalico, keeping track of her as the thing headed for the sea.

Kalico dropped to a knee, sighted. She shot to center of mass. Saw no effect, shot again, and again, and again as the terrible beast raced for the surf.

She continued to fire as the creature charged into the waves with its grisly prize.

When her pistol clicked on empty, all that remained were the endless breakers, curling, crashing, and rushing up to erase the monster's tracks as if it had never been.

18

The dreams had been weird. Images of the bush, slipping through dappled shadows beneath aquajade, creeping over tangles of roots, and hunting. Odors and tastes he knew but had no words for. Flashes of strange but curiously familiar quetzals. Like Dek recognized these beasts he'd never laid eyes on. He kept seeing landscapes, forest images, vistas where he'd never been, but that reeked of the familiar. In some, he was hunting, camouflaged in wait as chamois or crest approached unaware.

In another, even more fantastic, he was seated at a table in a simple earthly kitchen, reassembling an ancient broken bowl. A colorful thing with wavering and shape-shifting images on the side. He witnessed slim fingers carefully fitting pieces together, gluing them, and setting them to cure in a big sand-filled bowl. And in the background, he could smell tamales.

What the hell had that been about?

Dek shook his head. Had to be side effects from Dya's drug. Or maybe hallucinations caused by the gotcha vine poison.

Opening his eyes, he lay on his back—nothing overhead except the hospital-room ceiling. The duraplast was featureless and even more uninteresting because only one of the two light panels still worked. The second one had been removed sometime in the past, leaving only the gaping square hole in the ceiling with the wire capped off. As if they'd been ready to put in a replacement but thought better of it at the last instant.

The rest of the room had been painted in what Dek decided to call puke-beige. That was the thing about hospitals. Whoever picked the colors for the walls must have chosen the least popular, most universally repellant, and absolutely sterile colors they could find. True, maybe charcoal black or bruised dark purple, or perhaps a morose maroon-brown combination might have been worse. Dek decided he'd best not mention the fact to the administrators, because sure as fart-sucking hell, if he ever landed back here, the walls would be painted with it.

Not only that, the place was noisy. Seemed to be humming. Like bad electrical wiring. The equipment out on the shuttle field sounded unusually loud. The loaders might have been right outside his window.

That and the whispers. He kept hearing bits of words, often disjointed and nonsensical. Sometimes they were clearly in his head. At other times, the partial voice was right there, next to his ear. He'd turn, looking for the speaker, only to realize the sound had been nondirectional. Real and imagined at the same time. Like an itch that couldn't be scratched, he just knew that someone was trying to talk to him.

"*Learning.*" The word popped into his thoughts as if it were an answer to an unasked question.

He squirmed around, delighted that moving didn't send him into paroxysms of pain. The bed they'd placed him in, to his dismay, was also a relic. Something that The Corporation must have bought for cheap because no one else wanted it. So they'd shipped it off to Donovan where, even if anyone bitched, it would be thirty light years beyond the hearing of whichever bureaucrat had made the purchase. That, or—knowing how these things worked—it had been a political deal. Someone had paid off someone else to take the Torquemada-inspired thing. He was starting to wonder what he'd offer a procurement officer just to have the contraption hauled away and dropped in a black hole.

"It's early stages," Talina said from somewhere out in the hallway. "Aching behind his eyes. Rainbow vision. On the way in, he mentioned voices, blamed them on side effects from Dya's anesthetic."

"Cheng just ran the blood sample," Raya Turnienko said in return. "His TriNA predominantly has Flute's signature, but he's got others, too, including Rocket's, Rork's, and, unfortunately, Whitey's haplotypes. Any idea on how that might have happened?"

"No, I. . . . Aw, shit on a shoe."

"What is it, Talina?"

"The guy was dying, Raya. No heartbeat. Had stopped breathing. Probably from shock. I mean, you saw his leg. No human I know should have been able to climb out of that canyon, but he did. Probably took everything he had. Add dehydration to the poison . . . I tell you, the guy was clinically dead. I gave him CPR."

"Tasted peppermint?" Raya asked.

"Yeah, but I didn't think anything of it at the time. I was a hell of a lot more concerned with getting his heart started again."

Dek bellowed. "I'm eternally grateful that you did, but would you mind stepping in here, so I can be part of the conversation?"

To his surprise, he heard them approach from down the hall. How far away had they been? Down by Raya's office?

Raya entered, thundered, "How's the leg?"

"Hey, easy. I can hear fine, all right?"

Raya shot Talina a knowing glance.

Talina, in almost a whisper, told him, "You'll learn to balance it. It's the cells that are growing in your inner ear. What your brain hasn't figured out yet, is how to modulate the signal it's getting from all of those new nerve cells. It's a bootstrapping process, takes a couple of days."

"Can we cut to the chase, here?" Dek asked. "I'm turning into a quetzal, that's what you're telling me?"

"You been hunting chamois in your dreams?" Talina asked, coming to sit on the side of his bed. "Maybe had images of the bush? Places you've never been? Visions of crazy things that you know aren't real, but feel so absolutely familiar you just know it can't be made up?"

"Given you know what's going on in my head, I take it I'm not the first."

"You were the one who shared blood with Flute. I told you it came with consequences."

Dek chuckled wearily to himself as Raya used a thermometer to take his temperature. Asked, "How's the leg?"

"Hugely better," he told her. "What's the prognosis?"

"On the leg, or the quetzal TriNA that's working its way through your body?"

"Leg first."

"Okay, Dek. You're not going to lose it. Part of that is probably the quetzal genetic material doing its thing. It changes the organelles in your muscle cells so that they process lactic acid more efficiently and contract with greater volume. There might also be some gene that recognizes gotcha poison and processes an enzyme that oxidizes or denatures it. I've taken samples. If life ever slows down enough, I'll even get around to studying them sometime in the next two or three decades."

Talina was giving him an eerie stare, as if she was looking right inside him. Seeing . . . what?

"How soon am I out of here?" Dek asked. "The idea of leaving that airplane out at the claim is eating a hole in my gut."

Talina cocked an eyebrow. "Not that I'm particularly looking out for your welfare, but that's too important a piece of equipment to leave at Donovan's mercy. Step and Bateman took an aircar out to your claim this morning. Bateman is rated. He can fly it back." A baiting pause. "Don't know what they're going to ask in return for the favor, but you being a Taglioni, you can bet, it will be big."

"Yeah, probably will." Dek answered her mocking smile with his own. Step wouldn't be the problem. Step liked to play poker, and Dek was really good at poker. Bateman, however, didn't have any vices that Dek could really use against him. That might take more thought.

"Meanwhile," Raya told him, "you're to stay off that leg. At least for a week. You got a place to lay low? If not"—she gestured around—"welcome to home sweet home."

Dek took in the drab walls, gave the missing light panel in the ceiling a scathing glance. No pus-sucking way. He said, "Shig's got that study out in his garden. I've stayed there before. Even Shig's futon might be an improvement over this torture rack of a bed."

"Figuring you'll have Shig bringing your meals? Let him fetch and carry for you day in and day out? Allow yourself to become a burden?" Talina made a tsking sound with her lips. "Raya and I know you better than that. You'll be up and hobbling around after a day, figuring that you don't want to put him out. And, after all, you're a tough Taglioni."

"Could do some serious long-term damage to the nerve cells," Raya told him. "I mean it when I say you have to stay off that leg. And quetzal TriNA is jacking around with your brain. It's already started filling you with hallucinations, weird thoughts. Playing with your free will. Last time I had to deal with that, we ended up with a gunshot-blasted shipping container, and I got ignominiously strapped to that very same bed that you're now lying in."

Talina's lips crinkled in a guilt-ridden wince. "Sorry about that."

"Your day will come, Tal," Raya told her darkly. Then the good doctor fixed on him again. "Seriously, Dek. When Talina went through it, but for luck, she'd have hurt someone. Thought she had."

"Madison and Chaco still in town?" he asked, thinking he might catch a ride out to their homestead.

"Left this morning." Talina told him. She slapped hands to her thighs, looked up at Raya. "I'll take him. Put him up at my place. Makes the most sense. Even got my old set of crutches, so he can hobble to the bathroom. Besides, I've been through this. If Dek starts hallucinating out of control, I can take him down. Restrain him until we can get him sedated."

"Whoa!" Dek cried. "Listen, I'll be fine. Come on, Tal. You don't want to be playing nursemaid. And what if someone else gets into trouble out in the bush? Or there's a riot or something? What are you going to do if you have to run down some criminal? Break up a fight or hunt a quetzal? You have responsibilities."

Talina's alien-dark eyes seemed to bore clear through him. "I may not have done you any favors out there, Dek. After that CPR, when you came to, was your mouth filled with a taste of peppermint?"

"I, uh . . . yeah."

"Know what that was?"

Dek made a face. "Yeah, tasted that once when Flute jumped into the airtruck and stuck his tongue in my mouth. Like really bitter and really concentrated peppermint extract. But there wasn't any quetzal this time. Just you, bent over me."

"Giving you mouth-to-mouth. That taste? That was you reacting to a load of Demon's genetic material as well as the combined TriNA from the Mundo and Rork lineages. Sorry, Bucko me boy, but there's no telling which one is going to come out on top. You just damned well better hope it's not Demon's, because as you're no doubt going to find out, it will do everything in its power to destroy you and as many people around you as it can."

"*Yesss,*" the voice hissed so loudly Dek started.

"Struck a chord?" Raya asked knowingly.

"Didn't you hear that?"

Talina leaned close, her stare even more eerie. "What did it say?"

"Yes. As if agreeing with you about Demon's line."

"Sort of a hissing 'yesss'?" Talina asked.

"You did hear it!" Dek cried in relief.

Talina's expression didn't change. "Welcome to my nightmare. That's Demon. How he talks inside me, and it seems that he's the first to figure out how to interface with the language centers in your brain. But then, he's had the most practice with that."

"Well," Dek said, sinking back against the pillow, "I guess that just sucks toilet water. What happens next?"

"He's going to work on taking over your vision centers, screw around with your hearing and sense of smell, and when you least expect it, he's going to try and kill you."

"Kill me how?"

"Best bet? He'll use your limbic system against you. Paralyze you with fear at the wrong moment. Like when you're being charged by an angry quetzal. Overload you with a consuming anger that makes you do something stupid. Maybe bend you double with crippling pain when you can least afford it. And I mean pain. Sort of like you just experienced with your leg but centered in your gut."

"He can do that?"

Talina gave him a faint shrug of the shoulders. "Hey, Dek. You've got a totally pissed-off quetzal loose in your blood and brain. Your little adventure on Donovan just took a really nasty turn for the worse."

"How bad could it get?" he wondered.

"Bad enough that you might end up wishing I'd let you die out there in the bush."

19

Back on the beach, when Yoshimura had stepped out of the seatruck's door, he'd turned on the cameras. He wasn't thinking of Donovanian wildlife as much as to maintain a record of their field methodology as they took samples. That would have been critical back on Earth. All research was meticulously recorded for peer review.

Kalico was thankful for that as she looked out at the stunned and devastated expressions in the Pod cafeteria. Bill Martin, having been married to Shinwua, had somehow managed to sleepwalk his way through the kitchen during preparation of the evening meal. The food he produced might have been cooked, but it was singularly tasteless, as if he'd forgotten any kind of seasoning. Now that people had finished eating, Martin stood, braced against the kitchen doorway, eyes fixed on eternity. His face might have been an emotionless mask.

When Michaela Hailwood noticed the direction of Kalico's stare, she said, "Bill and Shin had been together for years. Had Galluzzi marry them." She reached up, rubbed her dark brows. "This is a blow. I mean, we've known the risks, heard the warnings, but this isn't fair. Shin was just taking a sand sample. He wasn't doing anything that should have gotten him killed."

"Welcome to Donovan," Kalico told her. She pointed at the UUV, where it rested on a cradle next to the cafeteria wall. After they made it back to the Pod without further incident, it had been Yoshimura who stepped down and noticed the UUV in its grapples. He'd walked over, stared at the plastic casing in disbelief.

So they'd wheeled it up here where everyone could examine it, see the etchings in the plastic where the "jellyfish" had chewed away at it.

"Didn't expect that, either, did you?" Kalico asked gently. "Or to have the first UUV sheered into pieces. Granted, the exterior casing is plain old plastic, not sialon or steel, but it's still pretty tough stuff. If Shinwua hadn't been able to electrify the hull, we wouldn't have brought that second UUV back either. And the jellyfish were closing for another attack even as we evacuated the drone."

Michaela rubbed her hands together nervously. "Shin was such a part of us. I just feel stunned. Like this is all suddenly going sideways."

"It's Donovan, Director. You step back, you think, and adapt to the new reality. While stupidity is an immediate death sentence, losing hope or surrendering to despair pushes the inevitable back a couple of days. You end up just as dead. So, you with me when it comes to harsher measures? Or do we close this place down and evacuate everyone to Corporate Mine?"

"Corporate Mine? To do what?"

"I've got an unstable drift that's way behind schedule. I can put your people on third shift. They're smart enough to run mucking machines. Drills, packing shot holes, and shooting magtex will take a bit longer to learn. And there's always ore sorting or logging details. Reactor maintenance. Cleaning the barracks. Upkeep on the haulers and equipment. No shortage of work, even in the garden. Some of your people could farm."

Michaela took a deep breath. "With respect, Board Supervisor, we'll consider that a last resort. So, what's next in your book?"

"Dealing with reality." Kalico stood from her chair, braced her arms on the table, and stared out at the room. It went immediately quiet. Not that there had been a lot of chatter to start with, just whispered conversation, mostly about Shinwua, and things they remembered or had shared with him. Mixed in among the looks of disbelief and loss were the periodic tears.

"All right, people," she called. "We had a tough day. You've got more of them coming. So let's take a look at what we've got." She triggered her old Corporate implant, thankful it interfaced with the Pod's system.

On the wall, the camera footage taken from the seatruck displayed as the lights dimmed. A couple of the infants cried out, only to be hushed by their parents.

"I'm not going to run all of the footage. You'll be spending enough time going over it as it is. Rather, I'm fast forwarding to the jellyfish attack on the UUV."

Kalico stopped the image as the tunnel formed around the UUV, the jellyfish all turning red.

"What you see here is communication through color and patterning. I'll leave it to you to work out how they do it, but here's what I want you to see and understand. First, the UUV is an entirely new phenomenon in their environment. Maybe it resembles some prey species of theirs, maybe it doesn't. What's important is that they've never seen a drone. What they do, however, is form a trap, capture it, and try to kill it."

Kalico let the vid run as the jellyfish wrapped themselves around the UUV. On the recorder, it registered Shinwua's discharge and the attackers backing off, the flashes of colors and dots as they reacted.

Kalico froze the image. "Okay, they got shocked. Backed away. See the spots? My call is that they're discussing what to do. Communication, people. Dr. Yoshimura? You want to add anything?"

Yoshimura stood, looked around at the people sitting at the tables. The man took a moment to pull his trembling expression together. As if he finally got his brain re-geared from Shinwua's death and into the more comfortable paradigm of a scientist, he said, "This is a highly ordered, disciplined, and cooperative hunting behavior. It's being orchestrated among what we would consider an unsophisticated phylum of invertebrate organisms. The more I watch this, the more unsettled I become. If we misjudged and underestimated something that looks simple, like a jellyfish, what else are we going to mistake?"

Kalico said, "I'll leave that to you all to figure out. Meanwhile, let's get a look at the predator that got Dr. Shinwua. We didn't get a complete image of it to begin with, but I think it's the same creature that sonar picked up while we were still off the beach, the thing that sheered the second UUV into pieces. All I could see down through the water was a long and very colorful shape. We recorded this"—she displayed the UUV's final video of the three slashing blades and tooth-filled mouth—"and then the drone was destroyed."

The room was so quiet Kalico thought she should be hearing their hearts beating.

She stepped out around the table. "When we were ashore, I saw an eye sticking out of the surf. Watching us. I think the creature—Dr. Yoshimura and I are calling it a scimitar—destroyed the UUV, withdrew, and monitored us as we went ashore. My call is that it waited, watched, and studied us."

Yoshimura swallowed hard as the video showed the three-bladed predator launch itself out of a curling breaker. "Nothing hunts like this. Except maybe the crocodile, and it doesn't race inland this far, let alone this fast."

Kalico froze the frame just shy of the scimitar-like blades slicing together around Shinwua. "Nothing, Dr. Yoshimura? This thing does. People, we have to rethink predation. It's not in our mental framework to be hunted from the water. And this sure as hell is not a crocodile. More to the point, it figured out that the UUV wasn't edible, backed off, and watched us. This is a guess on my part, but I'm willing to bet that it knew the seatruck wasn't alive. Curious, it waited until we got out. Having never seen a human, it still recognized us as prey. It bided its time until Dr. Shinwua was far enough from safety to make it's charge."

Thinking of the kids, she skipped the actual attack, stopped the recording where the beast was sideways, Shinwua's body mostly hidden from view. "Here's what the creature looks like. A riot of color, which is pretty normal for Donovan. Trilateral symmetry. What you would call the dorsal fins are flattened on the top of the body, and the two rows of ventral fins—if that term still applies—are perfectly adapted for terrestrial locomotion."

"And notice the musculature at the mandibles." Yoshimura forced dispassion into his voice, walking over to point at the scimitar's head. "These bulges lateral from the mandibular articulation pivot to provide the kind of biomechanical advantage that could cut through the UUVs plastic."

He glanced at Kalico. "Supervisor, is there any land-based form analogous to this?"

"Not that we've seen so far. But Donovan is a big world. We've barely scratched the surface when it comes to biology. There are whole continents where we've barely set foot. Entire ecosystems that are unexplored. When it comes to the seas, we only knew about the jellyfish because one of the survey ships way back in the beginning scooped one up in a water sample. Even then, as today shows, we've completely misinterpreted how the organism lived based on a terrestrial bias."

"What if there are more of these things?" Michaela asked, pointing at the scimitar. "Maybe even bigger ones?"

Kalico hitched her butt up onto the table. "Count on it, Director. The notion that we encountered the craftiest, largest, and only one of these things swimming around in the sea is statistically inconsistent with reality."

"But you shot it," Lara Sanz's voice was almost a protest. "Why didn't it die?"

Kalico shrugged. "Maybe I didn't hit it in the right place. Maybe I mortally wounded it. Maybe it's so damn tough it soaked up the explosive rounds and is healing as we speak. These are handgun rounds that we're talking about. Not a rifle. That's a change we're going to have to make. Research trips are going to have to be armed, and with a lot more than a pistol."

"That's not . . ." Michaela shook her head. "I mean, we're scientists. The subs, the seatrucks are supposed to protect us."

Kevina Schwantz glanced sidelong at her son, Felix. "I told you at the time that I didn't hit any reef. Maybe one of these scimitars cut the grooves in the bottom of the motor launch."

Jaim Elvridge—who was hands-on when it came to the watercraft—said, "From the angle of those scratches, that scimitar could only have raked the bottom with two of those . . . what are they called? Mandibles? There are seven streaks gouged out of the hull. And the gouges are too close together. I think it had to be something else."

"That's creep-freaked," Lara Sanz muttered.

"We'll just have to stay inside our vehicles," Casey Stoner told them as she ruffled Tomaya's hair with one hand; the woman cradled her two-month-old daughter, Saleen, in the crook of her other arm. "It will be all right. We can work that way. Use the remotes for anything dangerous."

"Assuming the rest of the UUVs don't end up like the ones on the seatruck did." Elvridge sounded half panicked. "Come on, people. That thing sheered a plastic, aluminum, and wire Aquaceptor III into pieces." She pointed. "The second one has chunks missing out of the casing. But more than that, after all we've been through, Shin's dead. Gone, guys. He was . . . I mean . . ." She sniffed. "We loved him."

Kalico watched Jaim Elvridge grab Breez into her arms, sobbing into the child's hair as the little girl tightened her grip. Elvridge's wife, Varina Tam, left her chair to wrap them both into an encompassing embrace.

What the? Ah, yes. Kalico remembered that Shinwua was Breez's father. Where he stood in the door, Bill Martin was now in tears, too, his sad eyes fixed on Jaim, Varina, and the child.

"It's . . . complicated." Michaela noted Kalico's confusion. "Jaim and Varina wanted a child. They chose Shin to be the father. Hey, it's only sex."

People were standing, walking over to comfort Bill Martin or Jaim and her daughter.

Kalico understood: This was somehow a pivotal moment. She was seeing the settling of that hellish realization that, after all they'd been through, they weren't invincible after all. Sort of like the image of a hive coming together.

What bothered Kalico was that instead of rallying her people, Michaela Hailwood seemed totally at a loss, her eyes fixed on the blue-yellow-and-red monster on the screen. In the picture, Kalico could see that stalk-topped eye. It stared back at her, black, shining, and filled with menace.

20

Talina stood in the doorway of her residential dome and looked out as Fred Han Chow descended her steps to the street. He carefully placed the litter back onto the cart and strapped it down. Fred and Tal had used it to transport Dek from the hospital to her place. Figured it lent a bit more dignity to the occasion than carrying him over her shoulder like a dead chamois.

Just a normal Port Authority afternoon in the neighborhood. Up the street, C'ian Gatlin's body looked half engulfed where it stuck out from the engine compartment of a backhoe he was working on. Some of the kids were racing down to the main avenue. Capella's afternoon sun slanted, sending rounded shadows onto the rutted gravel. Clothes had been hung to dry behind Iji's dome across the street. The botanist was currently in the southern hemisphere with Leah Shimodi, getting a first look at some of the vegetation while the geologist recorded potentially remarkable outcrops.

Why did I bring Dek here?

What was it about her and Derek Taglioni?

"Want him," Demon hissed from behind her liver.

Yeah, well, just because the quetzal in her gut was a piece of shit didn't mean he wasn't right some of the time.

From the very beginning Talina had felt an unsettling attraction. Was it real, or some fancy Taglioni trick? Perhaps a genetically engineered pheromone like the storied Transluna courtesans were supposed to have? Some chemical that triggered sexual interest in a woman's limbic system? She wouldn't put such a thing past a Taglioni. Especially since Dek had those dazzling genetically engineered yellow eyes that bordered on green in certain light. And who knew how many other little tweaks had been made to his body?

She watched as Fred Han Chow wheeled the cart off down the street. She didn't figure that good old Dek needed to know the thing was mostly used for hauling corpses up to the cemetery. Or maybe he already knew and just hadn't said anything as he was loaded on and then off.

Closing the door, she checked her racked rifles, unbuckled her duty belt with its pistol, knife, and survival gear, and hung it from the chair in her small living room. Dek's rifle, pistol, and camping gear were stacked in the corner where the breakfast bar jutted out from the dome wall.

Walking into her bedroom, she stopped to lean against the doorframe and cross her arms. "You need anything?"

Dek lay with his left leg out atop the sheets. A bandage covered his foot, ankle, and calf. The man's back was braced on her pillows, arms behind his head. When it came to clothing, he was wearing a claw-shrub-fiber undershirt and shorts. His sandy-blond hair, though mussed, still had a wave to it. She could see a slight pinch tighten that patrician face of his, accenting the scar on his cheek and the dimple in his chin. His designer-yellow eyes were fixed on hers with an almost eerie intensity. Something about him seemed to be daring, hinted at the question: *Here we are, what are we going to do with each other now?*

Yeah, Tal. Good question.

She thought Rocket chittered amusement where he perched on her shoulder.

A faint flicker played at Dek's expressive lips, and in answer to her question regarding his needs, said, "Bowl of Inga's chili with lots of fresh poblano pepper, a tall glass of amber ale, and Madison's wheat bread to wash it down. But"—he raised a hand to forestall her response—"I'd settle for a plate of your breakfast tamales with that remarkable red sauce you make. And don't stint on your homemade achiote."

"Sorry, Bucko. I've been too busy pulling soft meat out of the bush to spend time in the kitchen. If you're thinking I'm cooking, cleaning, and bottle-washing on demand, you're in for a surprise."

He waved it away. "That would be boorish, even for me." A twinkle lit his eyes. "What's the point of having a Taglioni in your bed if you can't squeeze a little juice out of him? When you—"

"Uh, what kind of 'juice' where you referring to? If you're thinking that you and I are going to be sharing bodily fluids, you're—"

"Whoa!" He threw his hands up, laughing. "Back, woman, back! Juice? That's Corporate slang. It's an old term that was recycling itself when I left Transluna. I think it dates back to oranges or some such thing. You know, getting best part of something without having to peel it."

She gave him her best deadly and humorless grin. "Go on."

"As I was going to say, when you hear that Bateman has landed my airplane, there's a sack of plunder under the toolbox in the aft left storage compartment. Mostly high-grade ore. Quartz thick with gold. Pieces of palladium. And I think some of the grayish-silver stuff is ruthenium."

"Just what do you expect in return for all this wealth?"

He gave her a conspiratorial wink. "I could probably buy a whole lot of carnal and licentious joy with it, which is what you are no doubt expecting from a Taglioni, but I've got a better idea."

"Which is?"

"I want you to take that sack over to Inga's, upend it on the bar so that it spills all over, and tell Inga I want it all credited to your account. Tell her that I figure it will cover home delivery of whatever you and I order for at least a week." Dek grinned. "We'll let someone else do the cooking and errand running. That's the 'juice' I was referring to."

"Why do I think you're a scoundrel?"

"Because I am a Taglioni. It's self-explanatory." He stopped, and she saw something flicker behind his eyes. "Well, I was."

"And that bad old Derek Taglioni slowly faded away to nothingness during those years aboard *Ashanti*?"

"Oh, he's still in here. Along with . . ." He squinted as if something distracted him. "Along with whatever the hell is getting in the way of my thinking straight. Now it's whispering something about . . . Shit. I can't quite get it."

His eyes went vacant. "Seeing Kylee now. She's a kid. Young. Golden hair. In the forest. Familiar forest. Seeing her with . . . what the? Like looking through three eyes. The feeling inside. Excited."

"That's Rocket," she told him walking over to settle on the side of the bed. "You'll be getting images of his from when they were both little."

"Got another. Like it just blurred out of the old one. Seeing a boy. Kylee's hiding. The boy is terrified, calling for her. He's on the point of panic."

"I've got that one, too. Kylee told me she was punishing her big brother Damien when he was supposed to keep her safe." She clenched a fist. "Tell me you don't have any memories with me in them."

He hesitated a moment, let his eyes drift to one side. "Riding the death cart over here, watching you walk ahead of us on the avenue. Just a flash. You. Standing in a grave, struggling to lower Mitch's body into it. And it shifted. You were in another grave, lowering another body. Young woman you really loved. Trish. You weren't talking, but I could hear your thoughts. How sorry you were that you'd grown apart. The pain and grief. Regret that you'd lied about her mother's rape and murder. I could feel your—"

"Enough," Talina snapped. "I *hate* this shit!"

"You think it's easy on my end? I've got things inside my head. Things that are not me. Half the time I think I'm going psychotic. Something's *reading* my thoughts. Hey, I've done some pretty shitty things. Stuff that I'd like to forget. And this *thing* keeps digging it up."

"Demon's looking for a handle, a lever it can use to manipulate you. And if it finds it, turns you into a weapon . . ." Talina let it hang, but fixed her eyes on his so that he knew she was dead serious.

"What's with the bowl?" he asked. "It didn't click with me until I asked about your homemade tamales just now. I could smell them in the vision, too. That's from your head, isn't it?"

Talina closed her eyes, reached up and massaged the back of her neck. "You got that, too, huh? How much of it? Don't fuck with me. Tell me the truth."

"There's a kitchen. On Earth, I think. Old-style stove and boiling pots of something. I see fingers, like your fingers, putting a bowl of some kind together. It's been broken. And you're fitting piece by piece back together."

"You see the quetzals?"

He made a face, head slightly cocked, as though in hard thought. "No, I . . . wait. Like maybe an image, a sort of cartoon on the side of the bowl. You're afraid, making some choice. Like your life is in danger. And there's fear. But it's not yours. It's . . . sort of . . . quetzal fear? No, more like frustration. Is that right?"

"Demon," she told him. "Rocket and I worked out a kind of compromise. Rocket's TriNA didn't like what Whitey's TriNA combined with Demon's was trying to use me for. Listen, it's complicated. Quetzal lineages don't like each other. Rocket and the Rork quetzals showed me a way to keep my sanity, block out quetzal thought when I need to. Demon's still in here." She tapped her stomach. "Sort of like a delayed-action fuse. Biding his time. The piece of shit still talks to me. After all, he was the first to figure out how to interact with the speech centers in my brain. But, for the most part, he's currently neutralized."

"Currently?" Dek asked. "You said he had the upper hand in my head."

"What's he been telling you?"

Dek's gaze faltered, shifted, and he willfully said, "Shut the fuck up!"

Talina fought a sour grin. *Good work, Dek. You're learning.*

"Okay, so he's talking to you. Tell me, what is he saying? There're no secrets between us for the moment. I need to know what he's doing to you."

"Keeps telling me to have sex with you." Dek winced. "And he's doing it with words I stopped using long ago."

"Figures. He was always amazed by copulation."

"Why?"

She took a deep breath. "Demon thinks it's a weapon. Something to use against me. He's good that way. Picks right up on grief, rage, any feeling of injustice. I think he uses them as a pathway to the limbic system. Maybe it's how quetzals think of the world . . . that emotion can always be used as a tool or lever."

"So, how do you live with it?"

"Me? After I hallucinated the Sian Hmong shooting incident, I was strapped into that bed you just got out of. I sort of switched places with Raya—"

"Who obviously hasn't forgiven you."

"Yeah, well, we've brokered a sort of truce. Anyway, I escaped to Mundo Base, figured Kylee could help. She did. At least her molecules kept me sane enough to get the two of us out to Rork Springs . . . where I took on another load of quetzal TriNA that sort of flooded Demon's influence."

She took his hand, saying, "Pay attention here. I found a way to come to terms. Used that bowl as mental metaphor, a way to piece my brain and consciousness back together. Most days I'm in charge, but not in my dreams. That's when Demon is loose to terrify me, to haunt me with all the horrible things I've done. And he dearly loves to torture, to make me squirm with self-loathing."

Dek lowered his eyes. "He's starting to have the same fun with me. Trying to figure out how to access those memories."

"Dek, understand that what I call 'Demon' is a community of related TriNA molecules that communicate with each other through molecular and recombinant means. It's an incorporeal intelligence, one that utilizes memory and transferRNA to access and operate the cells in my body. Those RNAs are the same on Donovan as they are on Earth. Organic chemistry is organic chemistry no matter what planet you are on. Eventually, Demon's going to dig out those memories. It's going to find all the weaknesses and vulnerabilities"

"Then maybe I'd save myself some agony if I just put a bullet in my brain?"

"Maybe." She hesitated. Did she tell him the truth? "I won't lie to you. You could end up a psychotic wreck. Maybe some zombie-like mindless weapon. On the positive side, you couldn't have crawled out of that canyon with a leg full of gotcha vine spines if you didn't have one hell of a lot of guts and courage hidden away in there. The kind that might see you through this fight."

"And what if I don't?"

She locked gazes with him. "We're being honest, right? So, here's how it lays out: I like you. Maybe, if things work out, and we both come out the other end, I might even come to love you. But I know what's inside you, growing, learning. So, you have to understand: If Demon wins, and I see you lose yourself, if you become a threat to Port Authority or anyone here, to Kylee or the Briggses, I'll shoot you in the back of the head."

"You mean that, don't you?"

"Sure, I'll have some hard days afterward, struggle with my regrets and a little guilt. Given some of the things I've done, I'll find a way to cope. All I have to do, though, is look into the eyes of the people I've saved, and tell myself, 'They're alive because of me.' When I stand over your grave, I'll tell you, 'Hey, sorry it worked out this way, but I did you a favor. You're better off dead than made into a monster.'"

21

The wind ruffled Michaela Hailwood's short hair, caressed her cheeks and eyelashes as she stood, eyes closed, and inhaled the ocean scent. So different from Earth, yet familiar, she tried to assess what the pungency reminded her of. Could only think of damp clothes freshly removed from a washing machine. But that wasn't quite right either. Maybe if you'd added cloves to the detergent? Or perhaps a hint of fresh-squeezed lime?

The first time she'd smelled the Donovanian sea, it had been with anticipation and excitement. This time, it was with a clear understanding that everything they'd endured to get here might have been a price too high to pay. Shin was dead. The effect was like having the strong pillar that supported her broken, smashed, and fallen.

Shin. His reassuring smile shone back from her memory. His calm reassurance always propping her up when her resolution began to waver. *"Easy, Michaela. We'll make it through this."*

"No, old friend, we won't," she told him.

I feel so alone.

She opened her eyes to stare out at the turquoise waters, the endless swells as they marched toward the Pod. Just at the horizon, something big thrashed, sending a spray of white water high into the air. Even across the distance, Michaela could see some of the torpedoes shooting out like missiles to arch through the air and arrow back into the waves. Whatever was hunting them was big to spray that much water. Really big.

Her stomach tightened, and she placed a hand to her gut, wishing she could just close her eyes and will this terrible place away. She could order the Pod shut down. Evacuate to the mainland, retreat to Corporate Mine. Farming, cleaning, hauling rock out of a hole in the ground, it couldn't be that bad. Especially compared to what had happened to Shin.

Michaela had forced herself to watch the recording, to see her cherished friend so brutally maimed and hauled off to the water. This didn't happen to people. Not in the twenty-second century. Not to a kind and compassionate man like Shin who had dedicated himself to science.

She heard the hatch cycle behind her, shot a glance over her shoulder. Did her best to hide her disquiet. "Yes, Board Supervisor? Can I help you?"

Kalico Aguila stepped up beside her, thumbs in her belt as she fixed her attention on the water. As the woman's shining black hair caught the breeze, it reflected shimmers of blue in Capella's light. Kalico's laser gaze fixed on the far horizon, her pinched expression pulling the scars on her face tight.

Bracing her feet, Aguila finally answered, "I don't know. Can you help me?"

"I beg your pardon. I mean . . . help you with what?"

"For the moment, my biggest concern is this research station. You saw them at breakfast this morning. Your people are demoralized. Panicked. On the verge of falling apart. They keep looking to you for leadership, and all you can do is wallow in your own grief and despair."

"If it had been anyone but Shin—"

"That's quetzal shit if I ever heard it," Aguila snapped. "Yeah, you're one big happy family. I get that. You all lived together as some tight-knit commune for eight years, and you're all closer than brothers and sisters. So you're devastated because Shin was killed and eaten by a monster. Shin, of all people. The mean old Supervisor will never understand. Outsider that she is. All those warnings we gave you at orientation weren't hot air and wasted breath. Fact: People die on Donovan."

"I know." Michaela fought sudden tears. "We were warned. It's not the same as seeing it. Knowing who that kind and caring—"

"Stop it! If you're looking for justice, fairness, or some scorecard whereby the universe only takes the unworthy, and the good guys always come out on top, I've got news for you. You're on Donovan. Not to mention in the wrong fucking universe."

Michaela swallowed against the sob that tried to start in her breast, bit her lips. Refused to meet the Supervisor's hard gaze. "We'll survive. It's just the shock of it. It'll take time for us to find our equilibrium."

"And how long is that going to take?"

"I don't know. This is the first time one of us has died. That it had to be Shin—"

"We're back to the fucking scorecard. Get over it. You've put everything on hold. Everyone's got the day off while you all 'reevaluate,' whatever the hell that means. I meant it last night when I said I'd shut this place down."

Michaela turned, feeling like her chest would explode. "Don't you get it? I don't know! I've never had to deal with this. People on my team don't die. Not like Shin did."

"Welcome to Donovan."

"I get really tired of hearing that."

"Then you'd damn well better start understanding what it means. Life isn't cheap on Donovan, but it's damned uncertain. If you can't wake up to that, I'm evacuating this station and redirecting its assets to the mainland. We'll cannibalize the subs, the UUVs, and other equipment for whatever we can salvage. Hell, given the water-make in the Number One, I can use the diving gear."

"God, you're cold."

"Yes, I am."

"How do you do it? Just lose all of your humanity? Become like a machine, some Corporate statistical algorithm figuring probabilities of success, predicting which human being is going to die next?"

Aguila's jaw muscles twitched, the chill in her blue gaze almost glacial as she fixed on Michaela. "When I set foot on Donovan, I wasn't afraid of anything. I was coming here to kick ass, restore Corporate control, arrest and execute mutineers and pirates, and cut The Corporation's losses. I was one tough avenging angel come from on high. Lasted me all of a week before this place slapped me right across my arrogant mug and left me terrified down to my bones."

Aguila thrust a scarred finger into Michaela's face. "I've been where you are now. That's why you get this one chance, woman. Because I was so terrified, I opted for what I thought was the easy way out. But I still didn't get it. Took me a full year of Donovan and its people beating the bullshit out of me before I started to come to grips. Enemies became friends, friends turned out to be enemies, but I learned."

Michaela tried not to wince under that eerie blue stare.

Aguila stepped closer, voice dropping as she said, "I understand that you just had your first real dose of Donovan. I understand that you are all scared. Well, sweetheart, it's going to get a lot scarier. On top of 'Welcome to Donovan' we have another saying. It goes like this: People come to Donovan to leave, to find themselves, or to die. Your last chance to leave was when *Ashanti* inverted symmetry on her way back to Solar System. So, let me see . . . Yes, that leaves you with two choices."

Michaela's mouth had gone dry. She turned away, walked to the railing, and stared down into the water. "What do you mean by finding myself?"

"Finding out who you really are. What you have inside now that you're face-to-face with Donovan. Maybe you're the Scientific Director of Maritime Unit's research station. Maybe you're a drill operator in the Number Two mine. Could be that you end up running Corporate Farm. Or you might find yourself scrubbing the cafeteria floor after each shift."

"I see." She tried to keep the misery out of her voice as something long and thin shot across the top of the reef and vanished into the depths.

"The one constant in all of those scenarios," Aguila's relentless voice continued, "is that you will be afraid. This is Donovan after all. Those of us who find ourselves, we live with it. Actually come to value having the shit scared out of us every now then, because it reminds us to be smart, to think, and it keeps us alive."

"So you still get scared?"

Aguila's laughter reeked of bitter irony. "Oh, yeah. After watching that scimitar take Shinwua, I would have rather been anywhere but on that seatruck flying back to the Pod. No telling what might reach out of the water to grab us next." A beat. "But that's Donovan for you."

"You could order us back to the mainland." A sudden flicker of hope tingled in her breast.

"I could. But I won't." A beat. "Not yet." Aguila's hard blue gaze, unforgiving, bored into her. "That's your decision, Scientific Director. I'll back you up, whichever way you choose."

Michaela closed her eyes, wishing she could be anyplace but here. Wishing that something would reach out of the water as it had with Shin. It would be quick. The crushing of her body as huge jaws sheared through her skin, muscle, and bones. And then it would be over.

There would be no more pain. No more fear of the unknown terrors lurking on this terrible planet.

And she'd never have to face the Supervisor's cold and measuring blue eyes again.

22

Better off dead than made into a monster. Talina's words kept repeating in Dek's head. Nor was it likely that he was going to forget that look in her eyes as she'd said them. She'd been serious as a brain hemorrhage.

He sucked his lips in, staring up at the curving ceiling in Tal's bedroom. His first night on Donovan had been spent here. In this bed. Alone. Since then, he'd fantasized about being back here. With her. In this room.

Only, in his dreams he wasn't a convalescent with a swollen-and-aching leg who was infected with hostile TriNA, and she wasn't thinking of him as potential threat to himself, her people, or friends. Oh, no. In the fantasy she was gazing at him with a very different look in her large dark eyes.

"Not to mention that in the fantasy we are doing very different things in this bed," he told himself. Then he slapped the mattress with the flat of his hand in emphasis.

Was that why he had asked Flute to exchange blood with him that day out at the Briggs homestead? Had it been some prompting way down deep in his psyche? Maybe after being with her in the forest outside of Tyson Station? Something about Talina Perez had always ensorcelled him; he figured that she was the first woman he'd ever met who was beyond his reach. Something he'd never even considered with Kalico Aguila—who had rightly loathed and despised him.

From the beginning, when it came to Talina, he'd had the feeling that he'd never measure up, be worthy of her respect, let alone consideration. And—for a Taglioni—the entire notion was not only totally foreign, but entirely unthinkable.

"Fool!" The word seemed to pop into Dek's head from nowhere, and with it came the distinct hint of derision.

"Demon," he whispered. "Not playing this game. Rocket's in

there, too. And so is Flute and his lineage. My call, piece of shit? You better look to your rear, because they're on my . . ."

He couldn't finish as his vision filled with a splendor of color, flashes of laser-bright reds and greens. The room slipped sideways, spinning in fragments that kept resetting, leaving Dek to gulp as his stomach flipped with increasing vertigo.

God, he hated nausea. In the end, he closed his eyes, shifted, and lowered his right foot to the floor.

"Asshole," he gritted through clenched teeth. "You do this to Talina, too?"

"Stronger."

The beast was referring to Talina and not him.

"What's up?" Talina's voice came from the doorway.

"Demon. The fucker just tripped my sense of equilibrium, made the room spin so bad I want to throw up."

"He talk to you?"

"Yeah, said you were stronger. The toilet-sucking little creep likes making me feel inferior."

Dek blinked hard, rubbed his eyes, delighted when he opened them to find that Tal was staring down, her alien-dark gaze fixed on his.

She asked, "Why is he using me against you? In case Demon hasn't noticed, I'm on your side."

Dek bit his lip, let his eyes slide to the side while he tried to find the right words, but suddenly he was a quetzal, surrounded by aqua-jade and scrub chabacho. He was in midair, leaping across a brushy meadow . . . and onto the back of an old and scarred quetzal. Dek's jaws clamped shut, crushing the top of the old quetzal's neck. He could feel the bones cracking and snapping under the rows of his serrated teeth. The two of them crashed to the ground, Dek's weight pinning the older animal. The elder's mouth gaped; the contraction of the lungs could be felt sucking at the constricted windpipes.

"Hey!" Talina's sharp voice cracked through the image. "Where are you?"

The vision shattered as Talina, hands gripping his shoulders, shook him back to. . . .

Yes, her bedroom. He struggled to clear his sight. Brought her face into focus, just inches from his. His heart was pounding, his mouth—no longer tasting quetzal—felt curiously dry.

He took a deep breath, the smell of her flooding through his senses. He held it, savored, and his body began to respond. Her eyes, so close to his, grew larger, filling his vision. The blood pounding through his veins sent a shiver through his muscles. A flood of bitter peppermint saliva burst onto his tongue.

Talina shook him, hard again. "Hey, back down! That's not real. Demon's playing with you. Using your attraction—"

Those lips, so close. He grabbed her by the back of the head, pressing her lips to his. Caught the shock as her eyes widened. His tongue was against her closed teeth, the flood of peppermint overpowering. And then she responded, was kissing him back, her tongue sliding along his. Her body began to melt into his, the hammering pulse . . .

She tore away, the power of it rocking him back in the bed.

"Piece of shit!" she cried, bolting to her feet to stomp around the confines of her room. "You do that to me again"—she knotted a fist, impotently pounding the air—"I'll scrub you out of my body with a wire brush!"

Dek struggled to catch his breath, to slow his triphammer heart. "Sorry," he said through a gasp. Glanced down, horrified, and clawed at the sheet to cover his arousal. Not that the thin sheet really disguised anything.

Talina barely paid it any attention, whipping around to point a hard finger. "He's not using me like that!"

"Victory!" the voice inside Dek's head crooned.

"Some victory, asshole," Dek muttered, the overpowering peppermint clogging his nose and throat.

"What did he say?" Talina asked. "Victory? Is that what you heard?"

"Yeah."

Talina paused, as if listening, and finally said, "We're at the beginning of the fight. It's the last thing he'd expect." She dropped to the side of the bed, her gaze intense. "Two can play at that game. You with me?"

"Huh?" He tried to sort out the confusion in his muddled head.

She leaned forward, hand behind his head, and kissed him. Her lips conformed softly to his, her tongue teasing. Dek worked into her kiss, the flood of peppermint back, seeming to saturate his tongue, expanding into his nose, sinuses, into his very brain. It became the universe.

Identity faded into a pulsing desire. His heart, blood, bones, and nerves charged as he clasped her to him. And through it all, she kept her mouth on his, as if to devour his essence, and merge them into a high-pitched unity.

Just as he could bear no more, as his body verged on an explosion, she violently broke free. Threw herself off the bed and charged to the door. She whirled. He had that image—captured as she met his eyes—of her heated face, the fire in her eyes, her desperate panting for breath.

"If you get out of that bed . . . try to follow me," she said between gasps, "I will break both of your legs and feed you to a slug!"

And she was gone, pausing only long enough to grab her utility belt off the chair out front. Then the door slammed with a finality.

. . . Leaving him to battle for breath, slow his heart, and try and find some semblance of peace.

"What just happened here?" he demanded of the empty room.

A disembodied voice beside his ear clearly said, *"Transformation . . . if you are strong enough."*

23

The children were in the observation dome—a circular room just past the last of the personal quarters on the first level. Separated from the hallway by a weather door, the observation room consisted of a transparent blister that stuck out from the Pod's rounded end. Varina Tam had led them all here, given Felix his orders in the sternest of tones: "You are in charge, Felix. Make sure that everyone stays here and doesn't leave this room until someone comes for you."

She had given him a wink and closed the weather door behind her as she'd left.

The job was important. Felix was fully aware of the terrible responsibility that was his. Because he was eight, and oldest, he was in charge while the grownups had some important meeting in the cafeteria. The little kids and babies, including two-year-old Kayle, and the infants Saleen and Vetch—just months old—got to go to the meeting with their mothers.

That left Felix in charge of Sheena, Felicity, Breez, Tomaya, and little Toni, who was three. Toni was the potential problem. The little boy—barely toilet trained—liked to get into things. Not that the observation dome offered much to get into. It was, after all, a big transparent bubble with padded benches around the circumference so people could sit and look out at the sea.

Fortunately, Sheena—and to a lesser extent Tomaya—helped with the little brat. Felicity always insisted that she wanted nothing to do with the irritating tile crawler. The problem was that Toni was Yosh's son. Yosh, after Shin, was one of the important people. When he spoke, others listened, and the Director herself often deferred to him. Yosh's wife, Mikoru Yamasaki, took care of the personal quarters. She did the laundry, cleaning, and managed all the housekeeping things the scientists were supposed to be too busy to do. She also had plenty of time to ensure that Toni received constant attention, that his every demand was met.

Mother said Toni was spoiled.

"Can't wait until we get him in school," Sheena had confided. "Wait till he has to learn alphabet and Mama can't come say it for him."

That wouldn't be for another year.

"Bad meeting," Breez noted as she climbed up on the cushions and swung her legs. "Mom said it was a Rubicon. What's that?"

"Rubbercon?" Tomaya asked, her disapproving gaze on Toni as he giggled happily, jumped up and down, and pounded one of the cushion tops with a knotted fist.

Felix pulled out his pad, spelling, "R, U, B, I. . . . You think it's a K or a C?"

"Try C," Sheena told him. "More words are spelled with C."

"C." Felix frowned. "A or O?"

"Try O," Felicity came over to stare at Felix's pad. "I like O better. It's easier to draw."

"O, N." Felix frowned as the information filled his pad. "Rubicon. It's river in Italy. Says Ca . . . e . . . sar. . . . How do you pronounce that?" His pad dutifully said, *"Caesar, Julius. Pretender seeking to become the first emperor of Rome, murdered 44 B.C.E.. Crossed the Rubicon in defiance of the Roman Senate."*

"Zambo." Sheena muttered. "Never heard of it. Michaela called a meeting about this? Why?"

"Don't know," Felicity told her. "But Mom was really worried. Said it might take all afternoon."

"No telling." Felix agreed, watching the pictures of Rome, Caesar, and people in armor and dresses flash across his screen. He muted the sound so he didn't have to listen to a lecture about all the stuff the pad would tell him about Rome. What wasn't even a country anymore, but a city. He had trouble with the notion of cities, didn't seem possible after *Ashanti* and now the Pod.

"All afternoon?" Tomaya cried. "What are we supposed to do? Sit here? There's not even a holovid. We just supposed to look at the stupid waves?"

Sheena, who'd been acting canny the entire time, took the center of the room, shooting a wary eye at Toni, who had dropped to his butt and was trying to pull the cushion off the bench. His fingers kept slipping off the fabric as he cried, "No! No! No!" over and over.

"Sometimes he acts like he's still two," Tomaya muttered in disgust.

"Just think. He's going to grow up someday and one of us is going to have to marry him." Felicity had a stricken look on her face.

"Uuck!" Breez cried and made a "get-away-from-me" gesture with her hands in Toni's direction. The little boy reacted with a goofy smile that let drool run down the side of his chin.

Felicity, her disapproving eyes on Toni, sang,

> *"London bridge is broken down, broken down, broken down.*
> *"Gonna toss Toni down, toss him down, toss him down.*
> *"Gonna watch little Toni drown, Toni drown.*
> *"My fair lady!"*

In response, Toni just gave them his "idiot" look.

Sheena announced. "I know what we're going to do. We're going to start a science club. But it's just for us. Nobody who's not five can be in it." She looked scathingly at Toni.

"What are we going to do in science club?" Felix asked, launching himself onto the cushions so that he could press against the transparent curve of the bubble and look down at the waves passing below. From here, he could see the patterns of plants and stuff shift on the rocky bottom as the swells rolled over.

"We're going to do science, Felix. Just like the grownups. Mom's a microbiologist. She studies life-forms that you can only see through a microscope. You know, itty bitty." She made a scrunching with her thumb and forefinger to show just how small she meant.

"Okay," Felicity said with a shrug. "What do we do?"

"Well, first"—Sheena crossed her arms defiantly—"I'm the Director."

"Why you?" Felix demanded, turning back from the transparency.

"Because it's my club, space gunk." Space gunk. That was what they'd heard one of the crewmen on *Ashanti* call one of the not-so-smart cargo techs.

"And," Sheena declared, "I brought the first specimen for us to study."

"You did?" Breez seemed absolutely dazzled by the concept. But, being only five—as Felix's mom said—she bought into anything.

"I did." With a flourish, Sheena produced a small 10cc sample jar from her overall pocket.

Felix crawled across the cushion, looking closely at it through the jar's transparent sides. Even with Sheena's fingers blocking most of the contents, he knew what it was. "That's algae."

"Like what's on our fingers?" Felicity asked. "You know, that stuff never comes off. My fingers are still slippery from when I rubbed yours. I barely touched you. And I washed and washed." She lifted her hand. "And worse. It's spreading across my palm and it itches."

"That's what science club is all about," Sheena said with certainty. "We're going to find out what this stuff is and why it doesn't wash off."

"And why it tingles on our fingers." Breez held her hand up, played like she was trying to pull her slippery fingers clear off.

"Where did you get that?" Felix asked, dropping to his feet to stand next to Sheena. The little jar fascinated him.

"Michaela canceled everybody's work, remember? Everybody was up in the cafeteria talking about Shin getting killed. So I went down to the Underwater Bay and got some. There's more of it now. Spots of it growing along the dock. I didn't even need to reach. I just scooped it up and put it in the jar."

"So, what are we going to do with it?" Tomaya was crowding close beside Felicity to stare at the jar. Breez started jumping, trying to get high enough to see past the older kids.

"First, as scientists, we have to look at it." Sheena opened the lid and let each of them peer down at the bluish-green contents.

"Looks like algae. I'd know. I found it first." Felix swelled his chest to emphasize his importance.

"Does it have a smell?" Sheena asked. "We should record this. A scientist keeps lots of records."

"All I've got is my pad," Felix protested. "It doesn't record."

"Well, we'll do that when we get to the lab," Sheena told them.

"We can't go up to the lab level," Felicity reminded. "That's on the second floor. We'll get in trouble."

Sheena airily replied, "That's why we have a science club. I bet I can get Mom to take us up to the lab. If we're a science club, we're not just kids. Then we can all look at the algae under the microscope. See what it really looks like."

Breez reached out, stuck her finger in the jar before Sheena could stop her. Pulling it back, she looked at the glistening blue-green coating. Rubbed it vigorously between her fingers. "I mean, yuk. You feel how slippery it is? That's nasty." She began scrubbing her fingers on her coveralls.

"Let me try!" Tomaya insisted. "If you don't, I'll tell where you got it."

Sheena, looking incensed, let Tomaya dip some out.

"Ooo. It feels like fresh snot." Tomaya danced around, shaking her gooey fingers. "Snot. Snot. Snot."

Toni, having failed to pull a cushion off the bench, was now watching them from his sprawled seat on the floor. "What?" he asked, eyes on the jar.

"You can't see it." Sheena turned away. "You're not in the club."

"What?" Toni demanded louder.

Felix had seen this before. The little rat was going to scream any second now. "Oh, let him see it. He won't know what it is anyway. Then he'll go back to drooling on the deck plates."

Sheena leaned down, extending the jar. "See! Nothing there, you little creep. Just blue goo. I like that. Blue goo. Blue goo. Blue goo. We all got blue goo."

Sheena should have known better. She'd been babysitting Toni on the odd occasion over the years.

The movement was so fast, Felix almost missed it. Toni whipped his right arm in an overhand arc. The movement a blur, he almost slapped the jar completely out of Sheena's hand. As it was, the contents splashed all over. Most of it landing on Toni.

Sheena cried out in horror, jerking the jar back.

Toni grinned in triumph, the loud "Gaaaaaa" of his laughter like thorn in Felix's hearing.

"Little creep beast!" Sheena cried, shifting the jar to her left hand as she tried to shake the slimy goo off her right. Not much was slung from her blue-green-coated fingers. Instead, she rubbed her hand hard on her overalls, spreading the stuff.

Toni, seeing the consternation, burst into tears, crying in a loud "Waaaayaaaa."

"What a baby." Felicity grimaced as she wiped at the spots of algae that had splashed onto her face. She touched her tongue to where a glob had landed on her lips, cried, "Uuuck!" And scrubbed at her face with her already-smeared hands.

Felix grabbed the jar from Sheena, ordering, "You got him crying. You gotta make him stop."

Sheena rolled her eyes, bent down, and lifted Toni from the floor, struggling to perch him on the cushions. "Hey, there! It's okay. Here, let's play spaceship and dock." She made a fist, swinging it around in circles over Toni's head as she made shushing spaceship sounds with her mouth.

Toni fixed on her, his eyes clearing as he looked up. Grinning he followed her fist in the ever-lowering circles over his head. "Spaaa-ziiip!" he cried.

"And it's going to land!" Sheena whipped it down, play-grinding it into his tummy. Then she tickled him until he was laughing and squirming.

"Blessed ions," Tomaya said with overemphasized relief. "I thought he was going to cry all afternoon."

"We've got to clean this up," Felix said, looking at the splotches of algae on the floor.

They all bent down, trying to wipe up the slippery stuff with their hands, which only spread it wider.

"Use your sleeve," Breez suggested.

That seemed to work a little better, but not much.

"What about Toni?" Tomaya asked, sitting up. "It's all over his jumper and hands."

"It's all over all of us," Felicity snapped as she kept wiping at her face.

"Not anymore," Felix told her.

Toni, eyes fixed on the waves he could see through the transparency, was sucking absently on his algae-covered fingers. Most of the blue-green slime was gone.

That just left the spots on his jumper, and Felix wasn't too worried about that. Little kids got stuff on them all the time. Yosh and Mikoru would hardly know the difference.

24

"I want to kill something!" Talina managed to growl through gritted teeth as she perched on her barstool in Inga's. She knotted her fists, struggled to still the rampaging hormones, quiet the anger and frustration that raged inside her.

When the fuck had she felt this chaotic inside? Demon vibrated with laughter down in her belly.

The tavern thundered with sound. The nightly crowd—along with the latest rotation from Corporate Mine—had packed into the subterranean dome. Talina sat reversed on her stool, her elbows on the bar behind her so she could look out into the big room. She'd often sat thus in order to keep a watchful eye on her people. After the stormy departure from Dek Taglioni's burning embrace . . . well, okay, her burning embrace, too, it felt reassuring, something comfortable and normal.

Hofer's voice, from down the bar, set her off like the squeal of rusty hinges. An image formed of her walking down, pulling her pistol, and clubbing the loudmouth to death.

"Yes! Kill!" Demon hissed as her stomach tightened.

"He's using you," Rocket replied in warning. *"We did the smartest thing we could with Dek."*

"We just condemned the guy," she growled. "We filled his mouth with a hot load of TriNA."

"Our TriNA," Rocket's reasonable voice insisted from her shoulder.

Talina shot a slitted sidelong look at her shoulder, half expecting to see the spectral quetzal perched there. He wasn't of course. No more than Demon was a physical entity down behind her stomach.

"You're a clap-trapping hallucination. It's just how my brain deals with it," she reminded herself.

Clenching her teeth, she fought the sudden urge to scream in expression of her frustration, conflicting emotions, and overall pissed-offishness at things in general. Never, in all of her life, had she felt this sexually frustrated. She'd barely torn herself away from the guy. Ached to race back, rip his clothes off, and screw him to within an inch of his life. Just because Demon kept tinkering with her limbic system, making her pulsing lust worse, didn't lessen the fact that she was naturally attracted to the man.

"I just won't be your plaything, you piece of shit."

"You will . . . in time."

"Go suck piss out of a boot."

Demon chittered another staccato of quetzal laughter.

Not to mention that she was disgusted with herself. She'd just played God with Derek Taglioni's future by giving him that hot kiss. The bizarre irony was that she'd essentially impregnated the poor guy. Shot him full of genetic material as surely as if she'd ejaculated. And unlike human copulation, she didn't need him to be ovulating for it to take. All that TriNA she had secreted through her salivary glands was circulating through his mouth, passing through the mesoderm in his cheeks and lips, and the permeable tissue beneath his tongue, integrating with his cells and bloodstream.

God damn her! As bad as what she'd done out at his claim, this was worse. She'd given him no choice. Just fucked him over. In human sex, a pregnancy could be terminated. This couldn't. The deed was done. Dek was back at her house, lying in her bed, as that flood of genetic material was coursing through his body. No stopping it now.

I am a shit-sucking monster.

Again, she wanted to scream in frustration. Would have but for the fact that the whole bar would stop, gone suddenly quiet, as every eye in the place turned her way. Hell, as much as people feared her these days, it would probably empty the whole fricking tavern.

Inga came striding down behind the bar, a towel over her shoulder. "Tal, you need another?"

"Damn straight."

Inga paused long enough to grab up Talina's empty mug, take a swipe at the dented chabacho wood with her towel, and retreat back to the line of taps.

Down the line, Hofer was bellowing laughter at some joke Tyrell Lawson told him.

Tal was wondering if—given Hofer's early verbosity—she was going to have to clock him one before the night was through.

"Yes, please," Demon hissed.

She was fighting the urge to walk down and strangle the guy when she noticed Shig Mosadek descending the stairs. Tonight, Shig wore a quetzal-hide cape over his shoulders. A tunic-like claw-shrub-fiber shirt that Yvette Dushane had embroidered with squash flowers and patterns was belted at the waist. Loose trousers, tucked into brand-new quetzal-hide boots, completed the ensemble.

Shig called amiable greetings out to various patrons as he passed, stopped to share some words with Toby Montoya, and grinned as he spotted Talina.

Making his way over, he climbed onto the stool beside hers, gave her a pleasant smile, and motioned with his fingers to Inga, giving the big woman an "I'll take one" gesture.

"Red or my new white?" Inga's bellow even drowned the latest of Hofer's garrulous guffaws.

"Red," Shig tried to shout back, as if it would be heard over the din.

Inga—used to reading lips—nodded and turned back to where she was filling Tal's mug with rich black stout.

Shig's amiable gaze fixed on Talina, paused. "From your expression, I would say you were upset. Anything I need to know before you murder someone?"

"Just enraged with myself, Shig. Dek's at my place while his leg heals. I think I just ruined the rest of his life. What really sucks toilet water is that I did it out of fear. That, and Demon pushed me into it."

"How?"

"Okay, so the guy stopped breathing out at his claim. I gave him CPR, right? Now, he had already traded blood with Flute. So he was infected to start with. But Flute's TriNA, we suspect, is benign. No telling how it affects humans yet. When I resuscitated the guy, he got a load of my TriNA."

"And that's a problem because . . . ?" Shig lifted a thick eyebrow.

"According to Dek, Demon was starting to manifest, which makes sense because his TriNA has an in-depth knowledge of human physiology. Now, that's not to say that Flute's TriNA wouldn't have squelched Demon's in the end, given that there's more of it floating around in Dek's body after the transfusion, but I sort of didn't want to take the chance."

Inga lumbered down the bar, the burly woman thumping Talina's mug of stout down, and then carefully placing Shig's half-glass of red wine before him. "Whose tab?"

"Mine," Talina told her. "Shig's a cheap date. Odds are he's not going to finish that glass as it is."

"Got it." Inga turned. "You're still up three siddars, Tal."

Talina watched the woman charge down the bar to where Hofer was bellowing, "Whiskey, by God, for me and my friends!"

"I really ought to walk down there and tell that prick either to put a stopper in it, or I'll toss his ass out in the street."

Shig glanced down to where Hofer was slapping Montoya on the back. "I've seen him worse. Or are you just looking for an excuse to feed your *tamas?*"

"Oh, I've got plenty of rage." She gave him a weary smile. "I just wish I could beat myself up. I never even gave Dek a chance. Should have told him, 'Why, Dek, if you're worried about Demon taking over your mind and body, I can fill you full of 'friendly' TriNA. Stuff that works for me. You know, really jack you up so that you'll never have a ghost's chance in hell of fitting in with real human beings again. Make you as much of a freak as I am.'"

"Talina, you always take more on yourself than—"

"But, fuck no, Shig. As a screw-you to Demon, I bent down and pumped as much Rocket and Rork TriNA as I could into the guy's mouth. Never gave him a chance. So, what does that make me? A rapist? Same result. Just used saliva instead of semen."

"Talina, you—"

"I'm guilty, Shig. Just like Tambuco. Remember him? You put a bullet in his head for raping Angie Feister. Want my pistol? Might as well shoot me right here in front of everyone. Set the precedent for tongue rape."

She felt the self-loathing build.

Demon hissed, *"Yesss. Reap your reward, killer."*

If it hadn't been Demon, she might have agreed with the thing.

"It was the only logical thing to do," Rocket insisted from her shoulder.

Talina closed her eyes, leaned forward, rubbed her face. "I really hate quetzals."

Shig lifted his wine, touched it to his lips. Set the glass back on the bar, looking just as full. "Talina, if you would listen to me instead of wallowing in self-pity and *dukkha*, we are all feeling our way here. So is Dek. Unlike the day when you were infected in that canyon out in the Blood Mountains, Dek chose his Tao knowing full well where it would lead. That he made the choice he did was partly based on Kylee and his fascination with Donovan, but it was partly based on you. He admired the way you and Kylee kept him, Kalico, and Muldare alive out in the bush. He worships you, you know. Me, I think the man would do anything to earn your respect."

"Oh, shit, Shig. He's got it. For soft meat, crawling out of that canyon—"

"I did not express myself well. He wants you to respect him as man worthy of a woman such as yourself." A beat. "And perhaps there is a part of yourself that would give him that chance, even if it meant risking his life in the process."

"Excuse me?"

Shig's knowing gaze met hers. "I understand your fears, Talina. You live increasingly alone, ever more separated from the rest of us."

"Men don't last long in my life." She gestured around the room. "Besides, see these people? I've dedicated my life to keeping them alive. In the doing of it, I've committed acts that I'll never atone for. I told the guy—and I meant it—that before I'd let Demon turn him into a monster, I'd put a bullet in his head. I know what kind of shit he's facing. But for a sliver of luck, I came pretty close to disaster myself, if you'll recall."

A weary smile bent Shig's lips. "Then take him out in the bush while he comes to terms. Rork Springs worked for you. Two Falls Gap is another option, as is Wide Ridge Research Station up north."

"Aren't you forgetting something? Kalico sets store by the guy. For all the distaste she had for him when he arrived, after that stint in the forest, they definitely have a rapprochement. You think I'm alone? So's Kalico. And Dek's her kind of people. He's a Taglioni who can talk to her about all those fancy places, about people she knew back in Solar System. He comes from her world."

"You are correct. Kalico values Dek's company, as he values hers. What you do not yet understand is that the future of their relationship is now set. They will be friends and colleagues and nothing more because Dek has embraced his *bohdichittai*. But, though in many ways he has become a Siddhartha, you remain his arhat. He made that commitment when he shared blood with Flute. Once a Tao is set, there is no other path that one can walk."

"I swear to God, Shig, there are times your Hindu crap makes me want to hit myself in the head with a hammer."

"What I just told you was Buddhist crap." He considered her thoughtfully. "Talina. I never forget that you have a young soul, but so does Dek. He is unaware that he came here to sell water by the river. Like you, he is a *tamas*-filled young warrior seeking to leave the karma of his old self behind and discover his true dharma. To do so, he has already surrendered himself to Donovan. And you."

"Yeah, yeah, I know. What you just said was Hindu." She gave him a sly smile. "Sorry to steal your thunder. You get an unhealthy charge out of correcting me. Given your enjoyment of such childish pleasures, maybe your soul isn't such an old and holy arhat after all." A pause. "But it doesn't change the fact that I had no right to shoot all that TriNA into Dek. Should have been his choice. Especially after it was my doing that infected him with Demon in the first place. I just made the problem worse."

This time Shig sipped his wine when he lifted it to his lips. Took a moment to work it over his tongue. After savoring it, he finally swallowed. "Not Inga's best," he declared. "I'd heard she had a new petit sirah. I should have asked for her old cask of cabernet if she has any left."

"Shig, seriously, what do I do about Dek?"

"There is nothing in the universe which does not either float or sink that remains the same over the course of its existence. You are changing, Talina. Perhaps you should allow Dek to help you over the rougher challenges of your own Tao."

She slapped the bar with the flat of her hand. "I came in here wanting to kill something. Don't drive me to it."

"Would you seriously feel better if you walked down the bar and shot Hofer? I've seen you glance his way every time he mouths off. Come tomorrow, after the *tamas* has dulled, will you awaken refreshed that you maimed or killed him?"

"Well . . . you never know. It is Hofer, after all. If he wasn't such a damn fine builder, maybe no one would miss him."

"There is that. Now, how about we finish our drinks over amiable conversation. After which, you will go home and ensure that Derek Taglioni hasn't come to grief in your absence. I give you permission to find out what Dek means to you, especially since I know what you already mean to him."

"He didn't share blood with Flute just to make me love him."

"No. There is Donovan, and Kylee, and the Briggses, all of whom figure into his calculus, but ultimately, he knew it was the only way that you would ever take him seriously." Shig raised a hand. "Wait, I know where that's going to take you. And it will be a mistaken assumption. The Dek Taglioni I know fully understood that there was no implied obligation on your part. He still would have gone through with the infection and suffered the consequences because he wants to be part of this place."

"You always did have a soft spot for him."

Shig lifted his wine, smiled, and took a swallow. "Fortunately, that soft spot is something I don't have to trip over like some obstacle in the path the way you seem to."

25

For a woman who had come across as broken and dispirited, Michaela Hailwood must have reached down inside herself and found some hidden reserve. Probably that core personality that had managed to get her appointed to the Donovan mission in the first place.

From a chair off to the side, Kalico sat like a spectator as Hailwood stood before the rest of her team. They sat at their accustomed spots in the cafeteria, apparently ready to hear anything but what Michaela was telling them.

"This is it, people," Hailwood's voice was steady now, resolution in her eyes. "So, we've had our first casualty. Someone we all loved, cherished, and relied on. And now we've had the time to mourn, to assess, and wonder what comes next.

"I'm the Director, appointed by the Board, and I have the support of Board Supervisor Aguila. My decision is that we go back to work with the realization that we are going to have to make some adjustments to our methodology. But we *are* going back to work, nonetheless."

Kalico monitored the stirring in the audience, the hooded and shared glances, the shifting and uneasy postures.

Hailwood continued, not missing a beat. "We have to be smart, people. We have to find another way to do our jobs because that's the only option open to us. Since we set foot dirtside, we've run smack into a new set of rules, a different way of living. Some of you may have heard this phrase when we were in Port Authority: 'People come to Donovan to leave, to find themselves, or to die.'"

The shifting intensified, the expressions reflecting frustration, confusion, or dismay, as people looked back and forth.

"Me, I'm not here to die, so I guess that puts me in the position of finding out who I am. Just to remind myself—and you—I'm the

Science Director of the Maritime Unit. That means I'm here to study Donovan's oceans. As are you."

"Deadly oceans, you mean," Bryan Atumbo called.

Kalico remembered that he was a UUV Tech Level I with a pilot rating for the subs, seatrucks, and UUVs.

Hailwood clasped her hands before her. "Deadly oceans. Correct. I would have thought that after what happened to Shin, that fact would be so apparent no one would have to be reminded. Perhaps I'm wrong."

"We know," Yoshimura called in a low but firm voice. "Go on, Michaela."

Hailwood studied her people for a moment, making eye contact one by one. "Like the Supervisor said, on Donovan you have to face reality. Some of us are going to die. Doesn't matter if it's here at the Pod, or on the mainland at Corporate Mine. And if you are thinking of Port Authority, I would remind you that the day after we shipped out to the Pod, they had a quetzal raid where some of the beasts got inside the wire. Killed a couple of people."

Casey Stoner called out, "This is not making us feel better, Michaela. I've got two kids here." To emphasize her point, she lifted the blanket with two-month-old Saleen. "One way, I don't want my kids growing up without a mom. Another, I don't want to end up crying over their dead bodies or knowing that some *thing* killed and ate them. I thought we were past that when we got away from the Unreconciled."

"Here, here," Jaim Elvridge muttered.

Hailwood gave the woman a sagacious nod. "Fair enough. If you don't want to do the work that you signed up for, that's a contractual matter." She turned. "Supervisor, are you willing to entertain any of my people who want to renegotiate their contracts?"

"According to Corporate contract law, they have that right," Kalico agreed. "As the appointed Board Supervisor, I am vested with authority to reassign anyone under contract to a different occupation on an as-needed basis. Should any of your people wish to pursue that option, it will come as welcome news to a lot of my crew at Corporate Mine. I have people looking to advance from their current positions as kitchen help, sweeping floors, cleaning the bathrooms, working the fields, and some of the other chores. By stepping into those positions, your people will free mine for promotion."

Tobi Ruto asked, "What about if we want to break contract? I heard about people at Port Authority who'd done that."

"You remember the penalty clause?" Kalico asked. "You will be required to repay the entire cost of your transportation to Donovan as well as reimburse The Corporation for any training that you might have received at Corporate expense. The upside is that there's wealth aplenty out in the bush. The downside is that soft meat rarely makes it more than a couple of hours before a quetzal, bem, slug, or thorncactus gets them. And remember, assuming you know how to survive alone out in the bush, Port Authority is a market economy. Your food, lodging, clothing, weapons, and drink have to be paid for in Port Authority SDRs. The last time you were there, Corporate Mine covered your costs. This time, you'll be on your own."

Kalico paused for effect, then added, "Oh, and if you are breaking contract, you will have to negotiate your own transportation from the Pod to the mainland. Neither the Director, nor I will be obligated to get you there."

Michaela spread her arms. "People, I keep coming back to the fact that we're here. That's just the way it is. Yes, it's dangerous. Yes, we're going to lose more of us over the coming months. But the best chance we have is with each other. We're family. Bonded by all those years of privation on *Ashanti*. This is what we've trained for. Not sweeping out barracks or being eaten in the bush while we look for gold."

Michaela let them chew on that for a moment before stating, "As your Director, here's what we're going to do: Tonight we're going to occupy ourselves by rethinking survey protocol and methodology. Determine how can we do our jobs with the least amount of risk."

Kevina Schwantz asked, "What about the BMT? That huge thing that I saw eat a torpedo. What do we do about creatures like that out in open water? It was plenty big enough to have destroyed the launch if it had had the chance and motive. Looking back, I think Felix and I were lucky to get back alive."

Hailwood clapped her hands together for emphasis, side stepped, and replied, "Jaim, you're a design engineer. Any ideas? Maybe a harpoon? Depth charge?"

"We have plenty of explosives at Corporate Mine," Kalico offered. "Jaim, you might have Dik Dharman hook you up with Ghosh and Stryski at the mine. If you want, you can work with them and Tyrell Lawson at PA. If you need Lawson to fabricate some kind of device, we'll work out any compensation through Corporate Mine's account."

Yoshimura raised his hands. "Wait a minute. We're here less than a month, and we're already talking about exterminating creatures? Essentially going to war with the planet? Doesn't this sound a lot like what we did to Earth? How we ended up precipitating one of the largest mass extinctions in the planet's history?"

Michaela glanced at Kalico. "Supervisor? Do you have any thoughts regarding this?"

Kalico stood. "Conservationists and evolutionists fought this battle back on Earth. I really don't care about the philosophical aspects. Our problem is this: If we're going to learn anything about Donovan, we have to be alive to do it. Most of you heard about Dortmund Weisbacher's brief sojourn dirtside. His conclusion was that the damage was already done. That humans had unleashed a maelstrom of ecological disaster. In the end, it turned out that Donovan is more than capable of holding its own. For the time being, if we have to kill BMTs, scimitars, or any other predators to keep ourselves alive, we'll do it. The number of predators Maritime Unit's presence will kill for our own preservation isn't going to trigger any extinctions. Instead, the research you people do will lead to a long-term understanding of the ecosystem that will eventually allow humans and Donovanian predators to coexist. But that's up to you and how well you do your jobs."

"So," Lara Sanz asked, "this is it?" She gestured at the room. "The length and breadth of our existence? Just this Pod? I mean, it's barely been a month, but I'm asking myself if I can stand being stuck inside here for another week, let alone years. The feeling of freedom I felt after getting the hell out of *Ashanti* has already vanished. What about those promised rotations to Port Authority? When is that going to happen?"

Michaela pitched it to Kalico with a questioning look.

Kalico pitched if back, saying, "Director, that's your call. You work out the schedule. Our only problem is transportation back and forth. The A-7 can't land on the Pod, and the seatrucks are limited in range. My thought is to create a waystation on the mainland beach. That's a five-hundred-kilometer hop across the Gulf in the seatruck. We can send an airtruck from PA for the second leg of the journey. If we put a recharging station at the way point, the seatruck can recharge for the trip back. Meanwhile, while you're in PA, you can stay at the Corporate barracks. I'll provide you with an allowance of SDRs so you can cover any other costs."

Hailwood looked out at her people. "We'll begin rotations at the end of the week. Meanwhile, that's it. We're going to work so that we can do what we came here to do. If that doesn't suit you, see the Supervisor for reassignment to Corporate Mine." A pause. "Now, let's get at it, people. I want suggestions for revised research methodologies by 17:00 hours."

Kalico watched the men and women getting to their feet, heard them ask each other: "What are you going to do?" "You happy with this?" "What if it goes wrong?" and "This is not what I signed up for." "When did Michaela get so hard?"

A few stopped to ask Michaela questions and then filed out, leaving her alone with Kalico.

"What do you think?" the Director asked.

"I think they'll stick," Kalico told her. "Your job is to give them a direction and keep them focused. Once they sink their teeth into solving the problem, half of your troubles will vanish. Rotations to PA will help. Rubbing elbows with Donovanians tends to scuff off any romantic illusions about the bush."

"I sure hope you're wrong about losing more of my people."

"Wish I was, too."

26

H er name was Sharascina, one of the most coveted and desired talents in the Hetaira guild of courtesans on Transluna. Some said she was the most beautiful woman who had ever lived. To have Sharascina perched on one's arm for the evening brought a man instant notice—made as much a statement about his position, wealth, and power as any clothing, accoutrements, or number of personal retainers.

Sharascina usually restricted her companionship to Boardmembers like Pierre Terblanch, Vioil Radcek, or Xian Chan. That she arrived at the Tiboronne on Derek Taglioni's arm made an even more powerful statement. As Dek stepped from the limousine and Sharascina unfolded from the vehicle like some elegant flower, every eye was centered on the two of them.

Walking through the great platinum double doors and into the restaurant's elegance, they were the definition of a spectacle. Dek could hear the stilling in the room, the hush of conversation, and the cessation of clinking silverware on fine china. And as quickly, the pause faded, people whispering, "Of course, he *is* a Taglioni" and, "Perhaps his star is rising?" But more importantly each and every one of them were asking themselves if they should rethink who and what Derek Taglioni was.

For the evening, Sharascina wore a semi-translucent gown of laser-fiber and microneon that shifted in glowing shades of sunset red, gold, vermillion, and cadmium yellow; the colors flowed with each step of her overly long legs. The exquisite angles of her face reflected the stunning hues projected by the dress's high and flaring collar, while the wealth of her golden, silvered, and glacial-blue hair shimmered with its own radiance.

God alone knew, she was costing him enough. But then, what

good was a family fortune if not to squander it in the name of personal advancement?

Besides, trolling Sharascina through the Tiboronne to one of the exclusive elevated tables in the upper level was about as flagrant a statement of wealth and prestige as a human could make.

Dek studiously avoided the covetous and disbelieving eyes, fixed all of his attention on Sharascina. He laughed, reveled, and enjoyed her famous wit, the intelligent sparkle in her designer-violet eyes with their vertical pupils. Pretending that the crowded room didn't exist was the true art of the game, after all. And, of course, Sharascina played it with perfect pitch. That's what the best courtesans did. They made their companions look good. And Sharascina was the best of the best.

"Truly, Dek," she told him in that marvelous contralto of hers, "if Contrachedo's Concerto in D Minor were ever to be played by a master, it was by Gutiea. His understanding of the violin's role in the second movement might have been as if the very fingers of God were on the bow. You have never heard such a pathos wrung from the strings. Or, perhaps you have, come to think of it. You had Gutiea play Bach at your ascension, as I recall. That night is still talked about. Word was that Fantu was never the same after you bested him in aeropolo during the games that followed the concert."

"Actually, he wasn't all that good. Implants. Father made sure his were jammed. Poor beast, he had to play without them."

Her melodic laughter carried just the right volume to communicate true amusement, the sparkle in her eye conspiratorial. "Amplified heterodyne with multipod microdirectional tracking?"

He almost hesitated, which would have let her catch him off guard, which in turn would have been humiliating. "Ah, used it yourself, have you?"

She gave his arm a conspiratorial squeeze. "You think my life is all about implants and training? Sometimes you just have to admire an elegant solution to what seems an impossible problem." The intimate look was for him alone. "I cheat."

The way she said it stoked his laughter, genuine and unforced. God, she was good.

They were at the foot of the escalator—the velvet ribbon winding up toward the higher levels—when, to Dek's dismay, Dan Wirth came strolling down from above, that boyish grin bending his lips.

"Fucking nice piece of ass you got there, Dek. I tell you, she's one hell of a fuck. Thought my head was going to explode. Considered putting her on the floor at The Jewel. You know, sort of a replacement for Allison now that she's gotten all high and mighty."

Beside him, Sharascina's violet eyes had widened, the slitted black pupils going round in astonishment.

"Friend of yours?" she asked with venom in her voice.

"Get the hell out of the way, Dan." Dek unslung the rifle from his shoulder. Never even gave a thought to where it had come from. *Never leave your rifle out of hand while you're in the bush.* He brought it around.

"Compensating for a limp dick, there, Dekkie boy?" Dan asked, removing a toothpick from his lips. "No wonder Ali couldn't get you into her bed. Hell, even Talina ran. Figured as hot and heavy as that kiss was, she should have melted right around any normal man's prick. Then, just as you get hard as stone, she runs right out of the house."

"You're over the line, Dan."

Wirth gestured to Sharascina, giving her a ribald wink. "Maybe you and me, we'll slip back into Ali's room. 'Bout time you had the kind of fucking a man who doesn't give a rat's ass could give you. Bet you're tired of having to fake it for the powdered-and-fopped pretty boys."

Sharascina's eyes had sharpened, her lips parted, her breathing now deep as a flush crept up her cheeks. She started as Dan grabbed her hand, pulled her close.

"Let her go, Dan."

The whole of the Tiboronne had gone still. People gaped, stunned, forks stopped in midair, glasses frozen in their hands.

"Let. Her. Go." Dek repeated, aware of the scintillating colors in Sharascina's dress as they shimmered like a dancing rainbow, turning a brilliant crimson red, patterns of black shifting and flowing over the conforming fabric in a communication of threat and violence. His lips parted, a long sibilant hiss sounding deep inside.

The surge of instant rage burned through Dek's core, turned maddening as Wirth gave him that infuriating grin. Quick as a snake, the psychopath reached up, grabbed hold of the front of Sharascina's dress and ripped downward.

At the tearing of the fabric, Dek shoved the rifle's muzzle into Wirth's belly . . .

Only to have the ornate Holland & Holland ripped away. Dek staggered, fought for balance as the world spun. Tiboronne's lights flashed in a blur, torn away into darkness and night that dropped around him like a blanket.

Sharascina—glowing in a thousand laser-bright colors—stared down at him through three eyes, her collar flared in crimson and black, mouth opening into a triangular . . .

"*Dek! Damn it!*"

The slap blasted light and pain through his head. He hit the ground hard, the impact slamming up through his spine, bursting more lights through his skull.

He blinked, Tiboronne, with its crystal chandeliers, gleaming floors and transparent walls, the music, and finely dressed diners, was gone.

No Sharascina.

No raging quetzal.

No Dan Wirth.

Only the dark stretch of Port Authority's main avenue.

Dek's rage withered away into confused nothingness. As it did, his butt began to hurt; so did the gravel eating into his hands. Up the street, a couple of streetlights shed lonely cones of white onto The Jewel and Sheyela Smith's electronic shop. Despite the darkness—which should have been absolute given the cloud cover—he could plainly see the new school. The front door was no more than a meter in front of him.

"What the fuck were you doing?" Talina snapped as she bent down to stare into his eyes. His Holland & Holland was held low, crosswise before her. "You were talking to Dan Wirth? And you said, let her go? Let go of whom?"

"Sharascina," he whispered. "She turned into a quetzal at the last instant."

He wiped at his eyes, aware of rainbows at the edges. Shouldn't be seeing rainbows in the darkness.

"Don't listen," a reptilian voice hissed in his ears. *"She ran from your bed."*

"Oh, go eat shit."

"What did Demon just tell you?"

"That you ran from my bed. Why am I here? What happened to me?"

Quetzal laughter seemed to explode in Dek's brain, making him wince. His stomach tensed. Revulsion—a disgusting feeling of self-loathing—rose from his core. Made him bend sideways, the nausea so thick in his belly, he ached to dry heave.

"Dek," Talina was bent down to peer into his eyes. "Stay with me now. Pay attention. Demon is playing with your head. He's using transfer and memory RNA to tap your cerebellum. Pulling up things from your past. He's trying to control you, to make you do his bidding."

"How did I get to the school? I was . . . I was . . ." He rubbed his face. "Wait. Your bedroom. I was in your bedroom."

"I got home. You were gone."

"I don't remember . . ." She was right. He *had* been at her place. Remembered going to sleep despite the prickle of healing in his leg.

"So," Talina mused, straightening, "who is Sharascina? What was Dan Wirth doing with her?"

"She's . . . perfect. Famous. The most sought-after courtesan in the Hetaira guild. We were at Tiboronne." He shook his head. "Dan Wirth came down the escalator, was going to rip her dress off. And then I had my rifle . . ."

"And you were going to blow a hole through Dan Wirth's brand-new school." She thoughtfully fingered his Holland & Holland and dialed down the charge. "Had it set to maximum. Not only would the charge have blown a hole clear through the building, the recoil would have broken both of your arms. And, I don't want to put this any too mildly, but from the direction the bullet would have taken, it would have shot clear through to the dormitory in the back. Be just my luck that you'd have hit a kid."

Quetzal voices echoed hollowly in his head as he dropped it into his hands. Flashes of Transluna . . . people he knew . . . Miko laughing at him . . . anger . . . disgust . . . "I want this shit to end."

"Won't happen, Bucko." She turned, looking down the dark street toward the south. "Shig's right."

"Isn't he always?"

Talina slung his rifle, reached down, and pulled Dek to his feet. His leg hurt, and he winced as it took his weight.

"Yeah, sorry about that," Talina told him. "But then, guess it didn't bother you to walk from my place to here."

"Where are we going?"

"Back to my dome. Then, tomorrow, after I put a pack together, we're headed out to Two Falls Gap."

"What's there?"

"A place where you can't take anyone with you on your way to hell."

"Hell?"

"You don't know it yet, but it's the only way back to sanity. Just hope your version of it isn't as terrifying as mine."

"How do you know?"

"Because I've been there, and hell sucks."

27

Jaim Elvridge was in her late thirties, had ash-blond hair and gray eyes. The woman topped out at five foot nine, with the thin frame so common to the recovering survivors of *Ashanti*'s long journey. Kalico sat to the side and studied the woman as she leaned over the schematics displayed on the light panel. On the screen were the technical readouts for the two submarines. Jaim, Kel Carruthers, and Michaela Hailwood were poring over the diagrams in search of a way to add to their security.

The HVAC system booted up, circulating cool air through the work bay. This was a water-level storage and repair area adjacent to the seatruck dock where both water and aircraft could be serviced and stored. One of the bright-yellow Seascape Model 15 submarines had been transitioned from the Underwater Bay, winched up on tracks, and now gleamed under the shop's bright lights.

To Kalico's eyes, the thing looked like an oversized propane tank covered with ungainly blisters. Four large fins on the thing's rear ended in gimbled-and-caged propellers that gave the machine maneuverability. They were supplemented by jets positioned laterally and forward that allowed fine adjustments to the craft's position. Ballast tanks were positioned radially around the hull, and lights, com pod, and cameras added to the thing's alien look. So did the two retractable arms with their finger-like extensions that allowed the operator to manipulate various tools, including scoops, cutters, shovels, and saws. These were for the collection of geological and biological samples. The only thing that marred the alien look was the transparent nose made of vacuum-baked clear ceramic. Through it, Kalico could see the piggyback operator's and observer's chairs with their manual and pedal controls, the heads-up display, and rows of monitors and computers on the solid walls behind the transparency. The hatch was located on the top.

The topic was how to protect the Seascape from something as potentially dangerous as Kevina's BMT. If the creature truly had a twenty-meter-wide mouth, it could potentially swallow the fifteen-meter-long submarine in one gulp.

"It can't chew the sub." Jaim tapped a finger on the schematic. "The hull can take five hundred atmospheres. Nothing organic has the musculature or mechanical advantage to compromise that."

"No," Michaela agreed. She in turn tapped on the blisters and light pods. "But something big could sure mangle the external hardware. Maybe even bend up the fins and thrusters. No telling what kind of stresses jaws and teeth that size might impart."

Kel considered, said, "All right, so the BMT bites the sub. Tries to chew it up and spits it out. If the sub's thrusters are compromised, if you lose mobility, you can still blow ballast and surface."

"What about the ballast tanks?" Kalico asked. "What happens if they get punctured?"

"Nothing biological is going to compromise those sialon pressure tanks. It would take a high-velocity bullet to get through that shell. No, the tanks are safe. If anything, they add to hull integrity."

"And crush depth on the Seascape 15 is five hundred atmospheres," Jaim told her. "That's five thousand meters. Nothing around the Pod is that deep."

"Can we weld a cage around the sub?" Michaela asked. "Like a big box larger than the BMT's bite?"

"How much does it weigh?" Jaim asked, turning gray eyes on the Director. "We have to be able to generate equivalent buoyancy for every kilogram you add."

"How big does the box have to be? Using tubing, we can do the math. Figure the tube diameter versus displacement and come up with neutral buoyancy."

"Twenty meters by twenty meters?" Michaela suggested.

"That's doable," Kel told her with a nod. "Assuming we can come up with the tubes." He turned. "Supervisor? Do you have anything like that at Corporate Mine?"

"Won't fit in the Underwater Bay surrounded by a contraption like that," Jaim noted. "Maybe if it was collapsible?"

Kalico stood, walked over to the sub where it rested on its cradle. The thing shone in the lights all new and pristine, the bright yellow paint splotched here and there with little smears of what looked like algae. She could see attachment points that might be used to bolt on the kind of frame Kel was talking about.

"I think we can fabricate something. The easiest would be steel. Hardest would be carbon fiber or ceramic." She turned. "But you're assuming a twenty-by-twenty-meter box will be sufficient."

Jaim turned. "Why wouldn't it?"

"What's to say that your BMT is the biggest bad actor out there? We've got a fifty-meter predator living in the trees out beyond Tyson Station. Not that we've ever had a good look at it, but if something that big lives in the treetops, what's to keep something even bigger from living in the oceans where its mass is supported by the water?"

In a half growl, Jaim said, "This just gets better and better. What the hell kind of world is this, anyway?" She pointed at the sub. "That's not food. It's a big chunk of sialon, steel, and glass."

"And sitting in the cafeteria is an Aquaceptor III that was almost destroyed by jellyfish." Michaela rubbed her tired eyes. "And its mate is lying in pieces on the bottom."

"So, what do we do?" Kel asked. "We're working with Earth's best technology. And suddenly we're worried about creatures eating it? Seriously?"

"Seriously," Kalico told him woodenly.

Jaim had her eyes slitted. "The scimitar backed off after it sheared the UUV into pieces. The sub's a lot tougher piece of equipment. Maybe we need to . . . No. That takes us right back to getting the thrusters bent up and equipment broken."

"Equipment that is almost impossible to fix," Kel reminded. "We don't have spare camera mounts or robot arms. Break it, and it's gone for good."

"Lower the submersibles from the surface? They're on a cable, and we could pull them back if something tried to swallow them. Maybe troll them from the Supervisor's A-7? That would certainly handle the weight." Kel had a skeptical arch to his red eyebrow.

"Shit on a shoe, no!" Michaela shot an apologetic look Kalico's way. "That's a scheduling nightmare, as if we could just up and commandeer a shuttle. Not to mention that the A-7 can't land on the Pod. People, we have to solve our own problems here."

"Explosives," Kalico said. "On some kind of delivery system. Maybe a torpedo. A kind of remote control mine. Something you could shoot at a predator if it got too close. A depth charge? You might not even have to hurt the beast. Just scare it. Discourage it."

Kel gave her an incredulous look. "I can't believe were talking about this. Back in Solar System, they'd think we'd lost our minds. We're talking about possibly blowing up an animal that Kevina says she saw, that we don't even have a photo of. A creature that we're assuming is going to eat our submarine. Key word: *assuming*. It might be as inoffensive as a blue whale."

"It's Donovan." Kalico emphasized the words in a way that should have explained everything.

Michaela threw her hands up. "I know. It's just that nothing in our briefings, our training, or our experience has prepared us to think in these terms. It's like the old sea stories of mermaids, krakens, Davey Jones's Locker, and sea monsters are suddenly true. What's next? The Flying Dutchman?"

"Could be," Kel told her. "Got a better explanation for the seaskimmers?"

Michaela laughed. "All right, your point. But seriously, are explosive charges the best we can do?"

Kalico walked along the submarine, inspecting the gleaming yellow hull, the fancy lights, the robot arms with their stainless-steel fingers and flip-out tools. The thing looked glossy and imposing.

"Maybe not," she told them. "But for the moment, I think it's the best option. We have the explosives, can make the delivery technology to either kill or dissuade any creature that might want to attack the sub. My people and Lawson will work with you on that. If we can keep the big stuff away until we figure out if it's hostile, or how to discourage it from getting close, can I assume you can keep the little stuff like jellyfish away?"

"Hey, Supervisor," Jaim told her, "I can use the arms to wave them off. Slice a couple of them up with the knives or saws, discharge a load of bubbles their way, you name it."

"Director?" Kalico asked, turning to get the woman's take.

"Let's go with a weapon instead of a cage," Michaela agreed, stepping over to stare at the sub. "Once we get the countermeasures built, we start slow, follow transects, stay close to the Pod as we map the reef and the drop off. Nothing big until we have an understanding of the risks and what works."

Kel was fingering his chin again. "I really don't like the idea of setting off explosives underwater close to the sub. Water doesn't compress. We're going to have to do the math. Tailor these charges for a specific distance. The bigger the blast, the farther it has to be from the sub. As it is, there's no telling what that kind of detonation is going to do to the hydrophones and some of the sensors. We're going to have to engineer a couple of levels of fail-safe. If one of those things goes off while it's strapped to the hull . . . ?" He winced.

Kalico told him, "I'll have my explosives people work with you. We're to the point that we're tailoring charges for shot holes in the Number Three. Maybe, if we're lucky, all it will take is a small bang and whatever might look nasty will swim away."

"And if it doesn't?" Jaim asked, walking over with a cloth to scrub at the smears of algae on the sub's side. The stuff didn't seem to rub off.

"You get to be an old-time sub commander," Kel told Jaim with a smile. "Just like back in the twenty-first century. You'll have to figure targeting solutions, and we'll give you torpedoes. I'll find some paint and letter it really nicely." He pointed to the rounded protrusion of the hatch on top. "*Das U Boot!*"

"Yeah?" Jaim jammed the rag into her pocket and stuck her thumbs in the belt at her waist. "I like that."

28

Two Falls Gap. The place was even more beautiful than Talina remembered. She circled her battered aircar above the isolated dome and admired the location where it nestled on the south side of the low forested gap between two blocks of uplifted gabbro. A couple of kilometers to the west, beyond the ascending ranks of broken foothills, the high Wind Mountains shot up like an impenetrable wall. Atop the near-vertical slopes, ragged peaks towered a thousand meters above the basin and seemed to be combing clouds out of thin air.

The sheer mountain wall was composed of upthrust formations of granite, gneiss, and schist lined with veins of quartz and crisscrossed by transected dikes. The strata made patterns of gray, pink, black, and white in contrast with the rumpled basalt and gabbro foothills below. Since the escarpment provided such an orographic barrier to the moisture-thick winds blowing in off the Gulf, rainfall was a near constant in the heights.

That precipitation cascaded down the steep slopes in a remarkable series of waterfalls that ultimately fed a trellis-pattern of rivers where gabbro and overlaying basalt foothills had welled up from the broken crust in the wake of the asteroid's impact.

Talina set her course toward the low gap. There, tumbling over uplifted blocks of broken crust, two rivers—one draining down from the north, the other up from the south—sluiced through low spots on either side of the gap. Separated by a resistant block of basalt, each river fell thirty meters to their confluence in a deep pool. The Two Falls River then followed a tortured course through a narrow and deeply cut gorge that twisted and turned its way down to the clay-rich coastal plain with its thick forests. There it slowed, meandering through the lowlands in sinuous loops and finally emptied into the Gulf one hundred and eight kilometers to the east.

Situated just up from the falls, on the rocky bank of the southern fork, Two Falls Gap Research Station had been constructed on an outcrop of gabbro where erosion and weathering had exposed bare stone. Surrounding it, the shallow, volcanically derived soils allowed a fertile garden filled with terrestrial plants to flourish. The dome, placed as it was on bedrock, was twenty-five years old now. The original white had grayed as a result of fungus and weathering, battered by the afternoon showers as warm air from the lowlands compressed against the sheer uplift.

That same rain, collected in cisterns, provided heavy-metal-free drinking water for the small research station.

The single solar collector atop its mast appeared to be aligned with Capella as the primary tracked across the sky. Talina had to hope the batteries still held a charge and that the electrical system remained functional. At least the power had worked the last time she was out here, which was what? Five years? Maybe six? Had it been that long?

"So, that's home?" Dek asked, eyes squinted against the pain in his remodeling retinas as he sat hunched on the worn passenger seat beside her. "It's so beautiful, it's stunning. This has to be one of the prettiest places in the universe."

With the vertical mountain wall topped by high clouds and tumbling white waterfalls as a backdrop for the thickly forested Donovanian foothills, it looked like a vision of Shangri-La. Some of the most stunning scenery she'd ever laid eyes on.

"That's it. At least for the next couple of weeks. Maybe a month. No one but you, me, and the quetzals rampaging through our bodies. As long as you don't shoot the solar collector or blow a hole in the dome that lets in sidewinders and slugs, we're in good shape. You are welcome shoot the hell out of the forest, and no one will care except the trees."

"How's the charge?" He nodded toward the gauge in the dash.

"Thirty-eight percent. That's why I've got a spare power pack. The only pisser will be if the main battery at the station is flat. If that's the case, we're headed south to find a way through the Winds, and then west to Rork Springs. Not my favorite place given what happened to Trish out there, but at least we know the quetzals are friendly and the station still functions."

"I really apologize for causing you all this grief. Wish I could think. I mean, this really sucks toilet water. Every time I try and hold onto a thought, some part of my past starts happening again. Like I'm right there back in Transluna or stuck in some dark crawlway on *Ashanti*. Hard to keep it all straight."

"Yeah, I know. I ended up in my mother's kitchen back in Chiapas. Turned out it was Xibalba."

"Where?"

"I told you. That's the Mayan version of hell. It's in the underworld and ruled by the Lords of Death . . . who turned themselves into quetzals. Psychotic hallucinations can be so creative. Think of the Lords of Death as a delightfully colorful and ethnically charged alternative to the more traditional pitchfork-wielding red devils with spike-tipped tails, horns growing out of their heads, and cloven feet standing in a super-hot fire."

She shot him a sidelong glance. "So, what's your version of hell?"

"Transluna," he whispered, eyes gone hollow. "I didn't know it at the time, but I had a really shitty life. I mean, you'd think if I was going to conjure a version of hell, it would be on *Ashanti*. Maybe the old nightmare of the Unreconciled sneaking up from Deck Three to cut me apart alive."

Talina made one last pass. The dome, the outbuildings, the overgrown confusion of crops in the garden patch, all seemed to be in order. An old generator, a couple of shipping containers, and the elevated cistern appeared normal. She couldn't see any threats, no heat signatures that would indicate a quetzal or bem.

"Let's see what we've got. Keep an eye peeled, and holler if you see anything that looks suspicious."

Dek laughed bitterly. "As if I'd know."

"Your quetzal sense will warn you. Trust it."

Talina settled them over what had been the landing pad—a flat of dark stone marked by patches of soil. She took a moment to scan all the way around, her IR and UV adding to her assurance that no danger lurked in the shadows. But for a column of buzzing invertebrates that swarmed in the air just behind the solar collector mast, she saw nothing between her and the forest.

Talina eased the car to the ground and let the fans spin down. Only then did she pull her rifle from the rack, flick the safety off, and swing her feet over the side.

The chime filled the air, higher in tone, more melodic and lilting than that around Port Authority. She sniffed for any hint of vinegar that might indicate a BEM or spike, but the air smelled of saffron and cloves. From the other side of the cliff just downriver, the twin waterfalls made a constant low roar. Streamers of mist rose from the canyon depths. Capella's light danced through them like fingers of living rainbow.

Talina checked the ground, assuring herself that the patches of soil weren't deep enough to hide a slug, and better yet, the plants that had taken root there were all terrestrial species of cilantro, parsley, and some low flower that might have been a clover.

Dek winced as he leaned forward in the seat and pulled his ornate Holland & Holland rifle from the rack. He seemed to be having issues, his movements awkward, gaze unfocused.

"Dek? Can you stay in the car? Let me check it out?"

"Yeah, right." His eyes fixed on infinity, his fingers playing along the rifle's wood.

For a second she paused, wondering if she should take the weapon away from him. No. Not on Donovan. Any risk that he might hurt himself or the aircar was balanced by the knowledge that at any moment, some marauding quetzal might charge out of the forest, or who knew what other threat might appear?

Talina muttered under her breath, asking Rocket, "What do you sense, old buddy?"

"Strangers. Not recent."

Down in her belly, Demon hissed in agreement.

"Okay, so quetzals have been here, but not for some time." She scanned the sky, fully aware that this was mobber country. All that she saw was a distant band of scarlet fliers, and here and there one of the really large invertebrates hovered over the treetops.

Talina started forward. She placed each booted step with care, her rifle at the ready. The chime rose and fell, seemed to mock her with its slightly atonal symphony.

She approached the dome warily. The door was closed and latched as it should have been. No one left a door open on Donovan. Well, all but that bem's ass, Weisbacher. That was another reason Talina should have shot him.

She turned the latch, heard the locking bolt retract, and swung the door open. The scent of mold and mildew caused her nose to crinkle. Stepping inside, she swept the room with the muzzle of her rifle, seeing a couple of workbenches along the dome's curve, a couch, table, a large desk shoved against the back wall, shelving, and cabinets on the right. The left side of the room sported a table and chairs, kitchen on the back wall, a cooler that was still humming—which was good—and floor-to-ceiling cabinets. Old throw rugs covered the duraplast floor.

Nothing had changed since the last time she was here.

Talina took her time searching the room, encouraged by the lack of invertebrates. If the little creatures hadn't managed to get in, chances were that bigger ones, like slugs and sidewinders, hadn't either.

Entering the central hallway, she opened the bathroom door to find a two-stall shower, twin toilets, a urinal, two sinks, and mold-speckled mirrors. The once-white walls were splotched with patterns of green mold. The room had a peculiar odor that she had no hesitation about locking away again behind the closed door. Across from the bathroom, the usual storage room had cleaning supplies, garden tools, some sample bags, empty buckets, a utility tool chest, and tarps.

Finally, she opened the door to the sleeping quarters. This consisted of the back third of the dome. All the closets on the partition wall gaped empty. Five beds were aligned in a radial pattern, their heads against the dome's curving exterior wall. A small nightstand stood by each.

The beds were just that. Mattresses on frames. No blankets or pillows.

"Maybe we should travel on to Rork Springs," she told herself. "This place is pretty pathetic."

Closing all the doors behind her, she walked back out to the aircar where Dek was muttering to himself, gaze dissociated. "You don't want to make me do that, Tabo. That's demeaning, and I won't stoop to it. Don't need to be a man who . . ." The words melted into an incomprehensible mumbling. Dek's hands clenched and unclenched on his rifle's stock.

Talina looked around, studied the clouds that formed against the implacable mountain wall in a solid bank of cumulus. Their gleaming white surfaces contrasted to the gray-cotton depths inside. Where they billowed against the rugged and vertical slopes, steamers of rain skirted the bottoms.

Did she really want to fly out to Rork Springs? It meant jogging far to the south—almost to Corporate Mine—before she could find a pass low enough for her aircar to cross the Winds. Then it would be another couple of hours flying back to the north-northwest.

Where she'd be forced to relive Trish's meaningless death every time she stepped out the front door. See her dying friend each time she laid eyes on that couch in the main room.

Thunder boomed, carrying down from the heights to echo in the lowlands.

Screw it, by the time they got south, they'd be flying through thunderstorms.

"Come on, Dek," she told him. "Give me your hand."

Dek's eyes remained unfocused, his mutterings so much senseless babble.

Talina reached down, grabbed him by the shoulder, and shook. "Dek! Hey, wake up!"

He blinked. Look confused, and then managed to focus. "Talina? We're . . . I mean, are we at Chaco's place? But it looks . . . not right. Nothing . . . right . . ."

"Two Falls Gap. Come on. Help me here."

Talina slung her rifle, half-manhandled him out of the aircar, and took his weight on the left side as they hobbled into the dome.

Inside, she lowered Dek onto the couch, wishing she'd taken time to wipe it down with a wet cloth first, but too late for that.

"Don't move," she told him, retreating back to the aircar, putting up the top, and grabbing the pack she'd made up back in PA. From the under-seat storage, she pulled out survival blankets and gear. Toting her outfit back inside, she dropped it on the table with a clatter, asking, "How you doing?"

"Kylee's playing with Rocket," he told her with a smile. "Hide and seek, but Rocket cheats."

"He was really something, the little twerp." She could sense Rocket's pleasure where he perched on her shoulder. Imagined him taking a bow, his collar flaring in happy colors of white patterned with pink and orange.

Stepping over to the sink, Talina checked the water. Was delighted to see it run when she opened the faucet. She allowed the brown scaly stuff to cycle through until it was clear, and then ran a sample through the test kit from the survival gear.

"Looks like we're good to go with the water," she told Dek. "A little scale from the pipes, and the occasional algae signature, but otherwise it's drinkable."

" . . . bite my fart . . . gas-sucking son of a bitch . . ." Dek looked delirious again. "Clean your own damn toilet, scum suckers . . ."

His fists were knotting manically, his legs moving, twitching slightly, his feet jerking.

"Learning muscle control," Rocket told her from her shoulder.

"Demon? Or you and the Rorkies?"

"Can't tell without exchanging TriNA."

"Yeah, well, let's hope it's you. If Demon takes him over, I'll be damned if I'll let him live that way."

In her gut, Demon chortled.

Of course he did. The piece of shit knew how much it would hurt her if she had to kill Dek.

29

The coast consisted of a line of exposed dark-brown dunes, partially vegetated, that ran down to the flat expanse of tidal zone. On the beach, breakers rolled in curling lines of white that streamed off to the north. Beyond the surf, the immensity of the Gulf stretched away to the horizon. Past that, pillars of white cumulus formed against the too-blue sky.

Back from the dunes and behind a belt of vegetation, Kalico had ordered a small knoll to be flattened, the trees blown away with a series of strategically placed barrels of magtex. Then she'd flown in a bulldozer from the clay mine at Port Authority and had the cat skinner, old Artie Manfroid—with all of his years of experience—blade the knoll top all the way down to its crumbly bedrock.

Kalico ended up with a three-acre pad of exposed basalt interbedded with a highly friable quartzite-like sandstone. The stuff didn't offer much in the way of a foundation, cracked and shattered as it was. But the pad sat in the geologically turbulent interior of the crater. By blading down to virgin stone, it gave roots nothing to cling to; the trees couldn't encroach. Some of the smaller plants would probably try to creep their way across the clearing, but the big stuff would be stopped cold at the margins of the site where topsoil was piled.

Or so Kalico hoped as she stepped down from the seatruck and stared at her newly created way station. This would be the beginning, and, who knew, it might even grow into a settlement someday. For now, all the exposed bedrock gave them was a somewhat-safe spot to set up a solar charger, a clear field of view against predators, and a place for passengers to change vehicles for their flights back and forth from the Pod to Port Authority.

As she stared out at the trees, she wished she had either Iji or Cheng present. The vegetation here was unlike anything she knew farther inland. Some of the bluer trees might have been a species of aquajade, but nothing looked like any of the varieties of chabacho with which she was familiar. What she saw just past the splintered wreckage left by the explosives and Manfroid's bulldozing were large trees, but instead of towering giants, these grew short and wide. Many—if her suspicion was correct—had multiple thick and low trunks. Sort of like the banyan trees of old Earth but taken to an extreme. Not the sort of thing that could be uprooted en masse by the neighboring trees.

Here—assuming Kalico could read the interlacing of branches and the periodically exposed roots correctly—the forest war appeared to be one of outflanking, engulfing, and lifting an outlying trunk from its purchase. Once loose from the soil, the upended trunk was flipped upside down, roots and all, on top of an older interior section. As the defeated tree scrambled to reorient under the weight of its overturned parts, the victor secured its position by sending its roots deep with the expectation of growing a new trunk.

Michaela Hailwood stepped down from the seatruck; Lara Sanz dropped to the ground behind her. Both women took position next to Kalico as they sniffed the salt-laden breeze and surveyed the bladed expanse. Really, it wasn't much to see, just broken black, brown, and yellowish bedrock marred by the bulldozer's steel-cleated tracks and blade polish where the machine had cut through stone.

Sanz, being a geologist, immediately knelt, picking up a fragment of the broken sandstone.

The breeze coming in off the Gulf flipped the women's hair and ruffled their coveralls. From the height of the knoll, they had a good view of the beach, the dunes, and the narrow strip of forest that remained between the rise and the shore.

Kalico took a moment to once again sweep the sky, as always, searching for mobbers. Instead, all she saw was a distant flock of the four-winged fliers that she'd seen out on the reef the day Shinwua had died. And, like then, these seemed to be moving farther north and away.

"Don't get more than a couple of steps from the seatruck," Kalico ordered. "It's only a hundred meters between us and the end of the clearing. A quetzal can clock out at one hundred and sixty kph, which means it can have you almost before you see it coming."

"Think a quetzal would still be around?" Michaela asked. "I mean, this was blasted. And then the bulldozer pushed it all over yonder in a big pile. That's a lot of disturbance. I'd think the wildlife would have been scared away."

"Or attracted to see what all the commotion was," Kalico countered. "And look where Manfroid piled all the broken timber and dirt. Perfect place for a camouflaged predator to hide. Trust me. Stay close to the seatruck. If I holler, you leap back inside and lock the doors."

"And where will you be?" Lara asked.

"I'll be inside before you are." Kalico gave her a lazy smile. "There are old jokes back on Earth. Something about, if you and I are out for a walk in the forest, I don't have to be able to outrun a bear. If we're suddenly face to face with one, I only have to be able to outrun you."

"Is this one of those 'welcome to Donovan' things?" Michaela asked.

"Very much so." Kalico stared anxiously off to the west, seeing nothing but a riot of low treetops, and here and there in the distance, a forlorn root ball shoved up in the air.

Lara had pulled out a hand lens from her belt pouch and was studying the rock she'd picked up. "Wow. I'd love to get this under the scope. Bet I'd see shocked quartz. And there's some really unique mineralization." She stared around at the exposed stone, all mixed as it was with basalt and some kind of rock Kalico had never seen before.

Lara pointed. "That stuff? See how vitreous it is? Any takers that we're seeing some of the asteroid? I'm going to get a sample of that." The woman started forward.

"Not yet. Stay close. Wait until we're better armed." Kalico accessed her com. "Step? You there?"

"*Roger that, Corporate. We're about five minutes out and closing on your signal.*"

"See you soon."

Michaela was squinting in Capella's hot light, fingers shoved into her back pockets, wind playing with her short hair. "So, how does this work? You're paying these people to make this pad, to put up a solar charger, and buying guns. That's a lot of SDRs. I get it that Port Authority is not part of The Corporation, but you're the Board-appointed Supervisor."

"The short version of a long story is that it was to my advantage to sign Port Authority over to the people who lived there. They'd been on their own for too long and were not going back under Corporate control. I took my people, who'd arrived on *Turalon*, and we went south to the outcrop where Corporate Mine was established. And yes, we had some trouble back in the beginning. Had to work out who was going to stay, who was going to go. But in the process, my people started to get rich. Really rich. And eventually—whenever that might be—they're going to ship back to Solar System as incredibly wealthy individuals. Had seventeen who took a chance on *Ashanti*. If they arrive alive, believe me, they're going to make one hell of a splash."

Kalico cocked a provocative eyebrow, adding, "It would amuse the hell out of me to watch the Boardmembers trying to figure out what to do with these people showing up out of the blue with bullion and jewels worth a couple billion in SDRs. Just serving out contract on Donovan entitles a person to a pretty nice package when it comes to housing, food, and travel. The Board's not going to have the first clue about what to do with a hard-rock miner showing up with all that plunder."

"Will they just seize it? Declare it Corporate property?"

"On first glance, you'd think they might. But thinking a little deeper, it will cause them an unholy amount of trouble if they do. What's to motivate anyone to go off world if The Corporation will just confiscate your earnings? And my people are going back with their plunder listed as 'earnings.'" Kalico chuckled. "No doubt about it, it will cause a firestorm, especially with the value of the cargo." A pause. "Assuming they make it back at all."

"And all this wealth pays for the pad, charger, and guns?"

Kalico stepped out to get a better look around, let her gaze trace the edge of the pad. "Michaela, when you parse it down to the absolute fundamentals, essentially we're all relying on each other. It's a sort of bootstrap economy. We're extracting wealth, true, but we're also manufacturing it. Here's your bit of economic reality for the day: Every sustainable economy, ever, has functioned based on the principle of the creation of wealth. The true economic powers on Donovan don't reside at Corporate Mine. They're farmers like Terry Mishka and Reuben Miranda, the fabricators like Mac Hanson at the foundry and Rude Marsdome, the bootmaker." She pointed to her quetzal-hide boots.

"Hard to think of a bootmaker being more important than you."

"Oh yeah?" Kalico asked. "Answer me this: What has greater value on Donovan? A metric ton of rhodium or a good pair of boots?"

Michaela gave her a wooden stare. "You're kidding, right?"

Kalico squinted at the dot that appeared over the trees. Headed their direction. Had to be Stepan Allenovich. "Kidding? Not at all. You tell me, what can you do on Donovan with a metric ton of rhodium? But you walk over past the edge of the pad, and what's the most vulnerable part of your body?"

"My feet?" Michaela glanced down at her Corporate-issue plastic-flex shoes.

Kalico told her, "Not sure a slug can chew through the soles, even thin as they are. But your ankles are bare. Step in the mud past the tops of your shoes, and you're gone. Not to mention scrambling across the roots. It's way too easy for the roots to pull those nice comfortable slip-ons right off your feet."

"This place is insane," Lara commented as she studied her rock.

"Now you know how I felt when I first set foot here." Kalico stepped out, waving as Step's aircar approached. "Not to mention that the man coming to meet us? Stepan Allenovich? Once, in my early days, he was dead set on killing me. And now? Here we are, old, if not the best of friends."

"Double insane," Michaela agreed with Lara.

Kalico propped one hand on her pistol as Step slowed, hovered, and settled to the ground. The fans blew out bits of sand and angular gravel before the airtruck spooled down.

Step threw the cab door open, glanced warily around, then gave Kalico a smile as he climbed down. "How's life on the ocean, Supervisor?"

"As the saying goes, 'clap-trappin' and nerve-wrackin'.' What's new at PA?"

"Inga's latest batch of rye whiskey came out like acid. She dumped the whole barrel and took her last good one out of storage. Sczui saw quetzal tracks at the edge of the bush. Got a drone up but couldn't find it. Rand Kope brought in a ruby that's the size of a goose egg. Lost it to Allison at The Jewel in what had to be the poker game of the century. I didn't know Allison had any gift when it came to poker, but I guess Dan must have taught her something."

"Oh, he taught her plenty," Kalico muttered. "She cheats."

Step made a face. "How?"

"Kalen was somewhere behind Kope? Maybe watching?"

"Yeah, you know, leans up against the wall so he can keep an eye on the place while Allison's busy at . . ." Step's visage darkened. "You telling me that's how Dan always did it?"

"Along with sleight of hand. And the guy has implants. Allison wouldn't have, couldn't have. But come on, Step. You're not that fricking innocent or naive."

He grunted, scratched the stubble on jaw. "Hey, you know me, Supervisor. But how did you know?"

"Would I be worth spit as a Supervisor if I didn't know when I was up against a rigged system?"

"Naw, guess not." Step walked around, threw open the big cargo door in the back. "Got most of the stuff you asked for. The solar charger is the best I could scrounge up on such short notice. But, hey, it's old. Maybe forty percent efficiency. I'll have Sheyela Smith cobble together something better and more permanent."

"Let us give you a hand with that."

Together, Kalico, Michaela, and Step slid the heavy unit out of the airtruck, rolled it across the irregular and broken surface, and raised the solar panel on its mounts. The needles immediately showed the available charge. Opening the battery case, Kalico found a homemade lead-acid battery in a hand-blown glass case.

"Looks like some of Tori Ashan's early work," Kalico noted.

"Who's Tori Ashan?" Michaela asked.

"Glassblower. Makes our windows and glasses and things," Step told her, giving the woman a sidelong appraisal.

"One of those important people I was telling you about," Kalico added, slapping a hand on the cover as she closed it. "Looks like the water level's good. I'll have Anna Gabarron make us a couple of gallons of distilled water and detail someone to keep it serviced each time we come through."

"Where did you learn so much about old batteries?" Michaela wondered.

"By keeping my mouth shut and listening when I'm in the presence of people who are smarter than I am." Kalico followed Step back to the airtruck, helped him unload the rifles. These came in a blanket-wrapped bundle of four secured on the ends with straps.

"There you go," Step told her. "Everything Frank Freund had in the shop. That's three bolt guns and a single shot. Now, the fifty-caliber bolt gun only has five cartridges, and it was kind of experimental. You have to mix and match with the other ammunition for the other guns, but don't get too wild when you start shooting. Not counting the big fifty, there's only a total of forty-six cartridges."

"Forty-six? That's all?" Kalico asked as Step pulled out the ammo box. "Can Freund make more?"

"Yeah, well, that's where it gets sketchy. Frank figured you were going to ask exactly that, so he was telling me as we were loading the stuff. Gunpowder is nitrocellulose. We can make nitric acid. The problem is cellulose. Most of that is made from either cotton or wood pulp back in Solar System. We've got cellulose in our terrestrial plant stems, but not like you'd need to easily make gunpowder. The best source we've got might be from wheat, oat, and rye straw. But Frank's not sure. I could turn Cheng on it, but he's already overwhelmed."

"What does that mean?" Michaela asked hesitantly.

"It means you'd better not start any long, drawn-out gunfights," Step told her. "And do most of your shooting with the bolt guns."

"These guns shoot bolts?" Lara asked, straightening from where she was picking at some of the cracked basalt. "We've got plenty of bolts. I saw a bin full of them in the equipment storage."

Step's expression went quizzical, and then descended to disbelief.

"What do you expect? She's a geologist," Kalico said by way of explanation. "Not that I'd have known the difference back in the early days myself." To Lara, Kalico said, "Bolt gun refers to the way the rifle loads ammunition. To shoot it you have to cycle a bolt to load and unload the chamber. A single shot only holds one cartridge at a time. It's slower to operate."

Lara gave her a blank look.

"Trust me. You'll learn."

Step gave Kalico a squinty and skeptical look. "So, Supervisor, you're out in the ocean, already had one person eaten, and you're going to trust yourselves with rifles for protection? Not even considering that bullets don't go through water, your people are Corporate scientists. No offense, but in an emergency, they're more likely to blow their foot off than some menacing sea beastie."

Kalico stepped back for the box of spices she'd ordered, lifted them out. "Step, it's all we've got until Kel, Ghosh, and Lawson come up with some way of protecting the subs and seatrucks. That, or I could hire Talina to come out and teach my people about shooting . . . if only I had enough bullets so that they could practice."

"Yeah, well, that's another thing."

"What is?"

"Tal's off in the forest with that Taglioni character. Seems he got himself in a mess out in the bush."

"With the gotcha vine, right?"

"Right."

Kalico set the box down, an unfamiliar quickening in her pulse. "You mean they never made it back to town from Dek's claim?"

"Oh, yeah. But before she did, word is that Dek started to give up the ghost, crapped out completely, and Tal gave him CPR. Now, I just heard the story from Raya, but she says that Dek got a whole rafter of quetzal TriNA in the process. Made him more than a little cucking frazy. Back in PA, Tal ran him down just before he blew a hole in the new school. She figured to save the rest of us from having to shoot his chapped ass after he did something dumb, so she flew him out to Two Falls Gap in case the quetzals took him over."

Kalico's heart skipped. "Why the hell didn't you tell me this before?"

Step arched a scarred eyebrow. "Didn't know it was a matter of Corporate concern given sea monsters and all." His gaze narrowed. "Besides, Tal's the best person he could be with . . . unless you've got other concerns."

Do I? Kalico asked herself.

Michaela was carrying the last of the boxes of vegetables to the seatruck, giving her an evaluative look. But then the woman had had an affair or two with Dek back on *Ashanti*.

Kalico kept her voice casual. "So, Step, what if, as you say, the quetzals take him over? What's Talina's plan?"

"Said she'd shoot him in the back of the head rather than let the quetzals kill him."

"She wouldn't." But, damn it, this was Talina. If she said she would, she meant it.

"'Scuse me," Step muttered knowingly. "Never seen a seatruck before. Think I'll take me a look." The man nodded, ambling off in the seatruck's direction.

Kalico chewed her lip, seated herself on the back step of the airtruck's cargo bay. Dek wasn't just soft meat. He was a Taglioni. And if anything happened to him, there would be pus-bloody hell to pay.

And what will I do? Images of Dek's smile, his roguish dimple and designer eyes, played through her memory. *What does Derek Taglioni mean to me?*

She was trying to sort through her complicated relationship with the man, their rather rocky history, and who he had become when Michaela asked, "Where's Lara?"

Kalico leapt to her feet, started forward, staring around. The pad was empty.

"Where did you see her last?" Kalico asked.

Michaela pointed. "Right over there. Where that lighter streak of stone is."

Shit. Not more than twenty meters from the tumbled rock and splintered trees at the edge of the pad.

"Step!" she bellowed. "Rifle hot, safety off. Lara's missing!"

The man whirled from where he'd been inspecting the seatruck. For a big man—muscular as he was—he proved remarkably fast on his feet. He didn't bother with his rifle in the airtruck but tore one of the bolt guns from the wrap of blankets.

Armed and ready, Kalico led the way to where Lara had been. The only trace was a smear of blood, and from the angles where drops of it hit and spattered, it was easy to see that something had grabbed her and left at a run. Whatever it had been, it had made a leap to the nearest fallen log and vanished into the forest on the other side.

30

The thing about being second-oldest bothered Sheena. People thought she had to be responsible. The same with Felix because he was oldest of all. But he wasn't locked away in the observation room with the little kids. She was. Because she was second oldest. Felix was doing something with his mother in the workshop where her father, Kel, Kevina, and Casey were building a torpedo that would blow up sea monsters. The whole notion of a torpedo was pretty zambo, and that Felix got to see it, even help make it, while she was stuck here with all the little kids made her mad.

Unfair. Unfair!

Sheena made a face; the rounded transparency of the observation dome barely reflected her image against a background of endless moving ocean. Her expression was indistinct, mostly just a silhouette. When she stuck her tongue out, she could hardly see it.

Why did Felix get to make a torpedo? Just because he was a boy? Or because his mother was Kevina, and Mom said that Kevina got away with murder. When Sheena had asked what *murder* meant, Mom had said it wasn't like what the Unreconciled did, but just a way of talking. That Kevina, because she was beautiful, got her way more often.

"*But you're even more beautiful,*" Mother had said, sharing that special wink. "*Now, go take care of the little kids. It won't be long. Just for a couple of hours until Casey, Iso, and Mikoru can finish their work.*"

So Sheena had ended up here, staring out at the endless waves, all looking like liquid silver in Capella's light. And Mom's words didn't make any sense. If Kevina got away with murder because she was beautiful, and Sheena was even more beautiful than Kevina, why was she here, stuck with little kids instead of making a torpedo?

The words of the song echoed in her head,

> *"London Bridge is broken down, broken down.*
> *"Off to prison you must go, my fair lady."*

"Unfair! Unfair!" she declared in absolute rhyming indignity and even stamped her foot. Careful to keep from waking the babies. She might be mad, but that didn't make her stupid.

For the moment, Toni played with a hollow aluminum tube, sitting on his butt on the floor. He held one end to his mouth, making *hooo hooo* sounds that echoed down the tube. Then he'd break into giggles. Next to him, Kayle sat in his diapers, drool running out of his mouth. Kayle was teething, and went wide-eyed each time Toni sounded his horn-tube. It was stupid, but what did little boys know?

The babies, Vetch and Saleen, were miraculously asleep in their blankets on the cushions. Their faces were slack, the little arms raised, tiny fists half clenched. The good news was that they'd both nodded off after Sheena had fed them from the formula bottles. The bad news was that sometime soon they'd crap themselves awake. When they did, Sheena would have to change them both.

Space scuz. That's what it was. She was wiping up baby shit, and Felix was building a torpedo. Unfair. Unfair!

She would have shouted it out, but it would have awakened the babies. If the babies awakened, they'd crap. Sheena couldn't even shout her frustration. And that just made it worse.

With no other recourse, she knotted her fists and jumped up and down, letting her feet pound the floor. Jump. Jump. Jump.

Toni watched, fascinated enough to stop blowing on his tube horn. Kayle swiveled his not-so-steady head around to look, and his brown eyes narrowed, unsure of what this meant.

That was when the door opened, and Felicity came in. She was wearing her yellow dress, the one made of some kind of packing Iso had found while they were setting up the Pod. Sheena had wanted a dress like Felicity's the first time she saw it. The colors were, like, really, really bright. Yellow made Felicity's black hair, eyebrows, and dark eyes look super good.

"Not your color, dear," Mom had said. *"You need a teal or turquoise with your red hair and blue eyes."*

Didn't make sense. Yellow made Felicity pretty, but it wouldn't make Sheena pretty? What kind of thinking was that? She thought it was just as dumb as making her watch babies while Felix built a torpedo.

"'Bout time you got here," Sheena greeted, propping her fists on her hips and frowning.

"Mom made me wash." Felicity seemed half asleep. Like her eyes didn't focus. She held up her hands. "Said I got into oil. Said I was in Bill Martin's cooking supplies. I told her it wasn't me. She made me stay in our room while she went and checked with Bill. When she came back, she said I didn't do it. She made me wash my hands. Over and over."

Sheena stepped close, took Felicity's hand and inspected it. Weird, it was shiny, felt oily. Like hers did ever since Felix had let her feel the algae. Even as she held Felicity's hand, Sheena's palms beginning to sweat and tingle. The more she rubbed her hands on Felicity's, the better the tingle seemed to get. Like that was the right thing to do. It just felt that way. Rubbing the slick between her hands and Felicity's.

"That's enough," Felicity told her, her eyes still staring off at nothing. Then she pulled free of Sheena's grip and turned to Saleen, reaching down.

"Don't wake them! You do, and you'll clean their diapers."

"They won't wake," Felicity whispered, still not seeing anything. Carefully, she took Saleen's tiny little hand and began to knead it between her fingers. When the baby girl's eyes flickered open, Felicity stuck her wet-shiny fingers into the little girl's mouth. Immediately, Saleen began to suckle.

Do it! The impulse formed in Sheena's head, not even like a thought, and she reached down, taking Vetch's little hand in her own. She closed her eyes, feeling the damp slickness, like runny oil as she began to knead the baby boy's hand. When his eyes blinked, and his mouth opened to cry, she thrust her fingers past his lips, feeling his budding teeth, his tongue working on the pads of her fingers. A thrill ran through her, and she closed her eyes as the infant sucked. She could feel his saliva, mixing with the slick moisture clinging to her fingers, beading on her palms. Sighing at the pleasure of it, time seemed to stop, waver, and slip sideways.

When she finally opened her eyes, the feeling was like she'd been away somewhere. Feeling weird, she jerked her hand back, blinked down at Vetch. He was staring up at her, his black eyes like marbles in his three-month-old round face.

On the floor, Toni had Kayle's left hand in his, holding it like they were best friends. Toni's right hand was in Kayle's mouth, and he was sucking it with the same enthusiasm as if Toni's hand was thick with sweet.

Felicity's gaze had come back to focus. She blinked. "Why are we here?"

"Because Felix got to help make the torpedo."

But somehow, Sheena wasn't sure that was the right answer. Even as she thought it, she heard Saleen's squall. The little girl kicked, the sound of her filling her diapers unmistakable.

31

The doors had been flung wide in Dek's memory. The Transluna of his youth filled his head with images, replayed scenes from his past, the sights and sounds. And he relived his days dirtside on Earth. The family had an estate—a re-wilded place called The Tetons in west-central North America. It occupied a long valley bordered on the west by the Teton Mountains, on the east by the Gros Ventres Range, and included everything in the Snake River Valley between. And then there was St Lucia, the family's private island in the Caribbean, with its mansion and grounds situated on the highlands between the two Pitons.

Both strongholds were Taglioni fortresses, empires within whose boundaries the family elders lived as a law unto themselves. There, along with their residences in New York, Hong Kong, and Transluna, they managed their share of the various extractive and manufacturing enterprises that fed The Corporation's ravenous maw.

Granted, the Taglionis only controlled a portion of the economic engine that was The Corporation—the other families managed the rest—but it was enough to ensure their influence. Keeping it? That was the battle.

"Dek?" Talina's voice intruded.

Pulling himself from images of Taglioni Tower in Transluna, he blinked.

For a moment, Dek couldn't figure out where he was. Nothing made sense as the crystalline halls of Taglioni Tower faded into . . . what the hell? A sort of drab room appeared out of a rainbow haze of colors that dipped down into the infrared. His eyeballs ached as if they were about to explode.

He tried to sit up, discovered he was in one of those emergency bedrolls made of heat-reflective material that inflated into some semblance of comfort. The thing crackled stiffly as he moved.

"I was just . . . Where am I?" His voice sounded hoarse; flickers of sunlit Donovanian forest flashed through his mind only to fade back to this horrible and dimly lit room. From the curving ceiling, it was a dome of some sort. Faint gray light—filtered through scummy-looking windows—illuminated a series of beds, including the one he lay on. He could see closets and night tables.

Real? Or imaginary? How did he tell anymore?

"You don't," the voice hissed inside.

Talina Perez was standing over him, arms crossed, looking down with a serious expression on her exotic face. "It's morning, sunshine. You hungry?"

A flash . . . and he was crouched over a chamois. His clawed forelegs were locked in the beast's sides as he twisted his head, pulled, and severed meat and bone with the serrated teeth in his powerful jaws. Savory, rich blood and hot flesh filled his mouth.

Saliva, ripe with the taste of peppermint flooded around his tongue.

And as quickly, the image disintegrated . . . and he was back in the dim bedroom, looking up at Talina. His stomach twisted and gurgled.

"Food?" he asked, still tasting peppermint and raw chamois despite the fact that any memory of eating the creature had to be illusion.

"Baked squash. I stuffed it with poblanos, apples, and purple sweet potatoes, put it in the oven last night, and miracle of miracles, it's ready to eat this morning."

"Beats the hell out of raw chamois," he whispered to himself, throwing back the inflated blanket and swinging his legs out. The swelling in his left was down to the point that the wrapping Raya Turnienko had put on it hung loose. And the tingling pain was gone.

Standing, it felt normal. Taking a step, it was as if he'd never been injured.

"You all right to attend yourself in the toilet?" Talina asked.

"Yeah, I . . ." He fought his way through the haze that packed his skull like thick fog. "Two Falls Gap, right? I don't remember anything after the couch in the front room. It was starting to rain. And now you tell me it's morning?"

"The very same. Figures you don't remember me getting you to bed. If I didn't know what was going on in your brain, I'd have called you psychotic."

"What was going on in my brain?"

Her level stare almost unnerved him. "Um, not that I've got a good psychiatric term for it, but I'd call it image chaos. If we'd had a scan of your neural function, I'm betting it would have shown every part of your brain was active. One minute you'd be crying, the next enraged, then paralyzed with terror, back to crying, then aggressive as hell, just to get maudlin, scream for a bit, and back to crying, and all the while talking about your father, Miko, some relative named Fango, and a whole bunch of people I never heard of. Like, who was Kalay? You kept telling her you were sorry."

Kalay. He shook his head, pulling on his shirt from where it lay on the nightstand and walking for the doorway. He didn't have to tell Talina about Kalay. She was too many years gone, though he could picture her face so clearly. That gorgeous olive-toned skin, her almond eyes, the perfection of her cheeks and high forehead.

He closed the bathroom door behind him to symbolically shut Talina out. At the first of the sinks, he stopped, braced himself stiff-armed, and stared at his image in the mold-spotted mirror. What was it with his eyes, the hollow look to his face, as if the cheeks were thinning? Was that really him?

"See what you are," the quetzal voice inside told him, and his image seemed to glow orange around the edges. Shifting. Flickers of green began to form along each side of his nose. Pale blue was darkening across his forehead. As he watched, the colors brightened, and his face morphed, flattening. The mirror began to warp; the image split into three, which gave him a third eye in the middle of his forehead.

For a fleeting instant, a finger of fear reminded him of Batuhan, which faded into a quetzal's visage. Not Flute, the shape was wrong. And the mouth didn't have Flute's familiar angle. Not Rocket's, either.

"Demon?"

"Your true self. Not even quetzals are so heartless."

"No. I suppose they aren't."

He clamped his eyes shut, arms trembling as he steadied himself on the grimy sink. Swallowing through a sudden knot in his throat, he made himself remember what he looked like. The designer-yellow eyes that shaded into green, his straight and perfect nose, the dimple in his chin. That pink and shiny scar disfiguring his cheekbone. Sandy hair, with a wave on top of his head.

"You're my handsome young hero." Kalay's words took the place of Demon's, her lilting Greek accent filling the vowels with life.

"There are no heroes, my love. They died in another age."

When he forced his eyes open, stared into the mirror, it was to see himself restored in the glass, the image somewhat blurred by the film and specs of mold.

In the stand beneath the sink, he found a rag. Used it to scrub off the mirror, though it still left streaks. His face—but for his eyes and the zygomas of his cheeks—looked the same. Right down to the triangular scar. What was it about his eyes? As if the pupils were expanding. And something . . . wait, it was as if his cheeks were wider. Or was that just the cheap and streaked mirror?

He used the toilet, then washed. Tucking in his shirt, he stepped out into the hall and padded to the main room. Talina stood over the counter, was using a fork to pull apart a large squash. A puff of steam erupted from the split skin, and he could see the thick orange interior, packed as it was with poblano, apple, sweet potato, and garlic.

"Let's eat," Talina told him, dishing it out onto plates. "Don't have my red sauce, but hey, we'll live. Might be able to shoot a crest or a roo later. Add a little meat to the mix."

He sat, trying to center his thoughts . . . only to have Kalay's image fill his vision. Her voice whispered softly; the way her smile parted those full lips exposed perfect white teeth. Her laughter had always been magical.

And with the image came the pain, loss, and sense of self-loathing. And he was there, as he had been that day when he first knew he loved her with all his heart.

Kalay sat across from him, a sparkle in her animated sienna-brown eyes. The wind teased the young woman's long dark hair, curling it over a tanned shoulder to spill down over her left breast. Behind her, he could see the Caribbean where sunlight glittered on the deep aqua tones as patterns of waves faded to the far horizon. He knew that vista. They were on the veranda at the St. Lucia mansion.

"Kalay, want some of this?" he asked, raising his fork with its prize of smoked crab. She leaned forward, snatched the white meat with a quick bite. Chewed. And uttered a moan of pleasure as she savored. He watched her firm throat work, wishing he could run his lips over that marvelous skin.

"*Damn it!*" The popping of hands as they clapped to together brought him back.

"You here? Hello! Food's getting cold." Talina snapped, shattering the image. "That's almost five minutes, Dek. Figured the next thing I'd try was a punch to your jaw."

He clenched his hands to stop the trembling in his arms. "Why's he so obsessed with her?"

"Who?"

"Demon. He keeps triggering memories of Kalay. What's he want with her?"

"Who's Kalay?"

Dek rubbed his sore eyes, wondered at the way his sense of smell had his mouth watering at the odor of squash, garlic, and poblano. At least it wasn't pus-sucking peppermint.

Dek picked up his fork, speared some of the thick, yellow meat, lifted it, froze as he almost offered it to Talina as he just had to Kalay.

"Stop fucking with my mind!" he shouted. Fought to control the trembling in his hand, got the fork to his mouth and let the flavor of squash roll over his tongue.

Eat. Just make myself eat, he thought. *That's it. One forkful after another. Chew. Enjoy. Swallow.*

From the look Talina was giving him, she wasn't going to let the question drop. "Kalay? Part of my training to be a young man. All of us. We're groomed, educated, prepared in all ways. In politics, history, economics, technology, social engineering, political science, resource allotment, the arts, etiquette, and pretty much every skill we should be masters of. I had just turned fifteen. Kalay was nineteen and recently confirmed in the Eros guild. The family chose her to be my introduction to the erotic arts and refined social behavior. A young Taglioni must be totally competent, familiar, and comfortable with all the intricacies of sex."

Dek smiled wistfully. "It's common for a boy to fall in love with his first courtesan. I just fell harder than most. Problem was, so did she."

"How'd it end?"

"We tried to run. No one gets far in The Corporation. Father was furious. So much so that he bought her contract from the Eros guild. Made me sign the transfer order that shipped her off to Okeus 1-7 out in the Van Oort Cloud."

"Okeus? Series of survey and mining bases, right?" Talina asked. "Number 1-7, that would have been one of the stations waaaay out there."

"Yeah. The farthest one from Transluna." Dek studied his thumbnail. "Three years transit time just to get there, and her contract was for twenty years. Assuming she's still alive."

Talina cocked her head, considering. "Guess there's worse things in the universe than quetzals and TriNA."

"The part that still haunts me is that when my father told me to sign the order, I didn't even argue. Didn't try to bargain. I just signed the damn thing without so much as a peep."

"You were fifteen."

"I was a Taglioni."

elix jerked awake in the dark room, pulled rudely from the peculiar dream when his leg began to spasm so hard it shook his whole body. Just as he started to slip off to sleep, his leg jumped again. Hard. Like he was kicking something. And whatever it was, he sure hadn't ordered his leg to do it.

Anything but. He'd been in open turquoise water, bobbing and riding the waves while sunlight filtered down around him. Not only that, he'd been listening to music—an eerie singing sound of rising and falling melodies unlike anything he'd heard the adults play from their pads or recorders. Remarkable sound had filled the water, a high symphonic humming augmented by thumps, low booms, and something that might have been called squealing mixed with a yodel.

Outside of the magic of it, he was slightly frustrated because he knew it was telling him something. That understanding was so close, just barely out of his grasp. Like the times when adults were talking, using words that sounded sort of like words he knew.

His leg continued to quiver like it had a mind of its own.

He glanced around in the darkness, aware that Kim Yee snored softly where he slept with Mother in the big bed. They always slept better after sex. The faint hiss of the air conditioning was reassuring. The room still felt strange after *Ashanti*. But Felix had to admit he so enjoyed having his own bed on the other side of the room.

Like tonight, it was easier to ignore Mother and Yee. After the lights were out, they'd whispered just soft enough that Felix couldn't make out the words but could still hear the concern. Only when they thought Felix was asleep had Yee hushed mother and shifted his body onto hers.

They had tried to be quiet. Felix couldn't help but sense that tonight was different. Almost desperate, right up to the intensity of the sounds they tried so hard to stifle. Then their panting slowed, and the rustle of the blankets finally went still.

Desperate. Yes, he'd felt that way as he finally drifted off to sleep. Only to dream that wondrous dream.

Felix closed his eyes again, floating in the sea as the sunlight glowed blue and gleaming in the water around him. He had never floated, never been in water. But now he lived it, rocking, carried by the waves in a universe of movement.

His fingers tingled, and he extended his arms, reaching out for the sunlight on the water. As he did, his fingers expanded, growing slick, and when he could see them in the sunlight, they were slippery and green-blue and had become the algae.

And that was all right. If he turned into algae, he could float forever in the golden sunlight and remarkable blue waves . . .

33

Supper that night in the Pod cafeteria was subdued. Michaela struggled with shock and disbelief. Lara Sanz had been forty-three, with a PhD in crustal geology. Her expertise had been in seismology, hydrophonics, and mapping. She had only begun to collect data from the few buoys that had been deployed. Her work would have provided the overview, the framework into which the rest of the Maritime Unit's research would fit.

Lara had always sat at the back table with Dik Dharman. They'd never officially married, but during the last couple of years in *Ashanti*, the two had formed a monogamous bond. Now Lara's chair next to Dik was achingly empty. The man looked on the verge of emotional collapse, his face working, hands knotting and twisting his coveralls. His eyes puffed out, red and swollen from weeping.

Who could blame him? They were all reeling. Michaela might have allowed herself to topple into the endless pool of grief but for the hard-blue stare in Kalico Aguila's eyes.

What the hell was the woman made of, anyway? Sialon? But that look in her eyes couldn't be mistaken, it practically screamed, *Don't you dare.*

Jym Odinga, the ichthyologist, had been sobbing off and on through the meal. For a while, back in the early years aboard *Ashanti*, he and Lara had cohabited in their upper bunk in the rear of the Maritime quarters. Maybe he'd never fully gotten over his fondness for Lara, even though he'd moved on to the curious relationship he had with Casey Stoner and Tobi Ruto.

First Shinwua and now Lara Sanz. Both without warning.

Michaela figured that enough of them were finished with the evening meal that she should speak. She took a deep breath and stood, calling, "If I could have your attention. I know it's a horrible shock. Lara was, in many ways, the best of us. Her loss is a terrible blow, not only to us personally, but to the project itself."

"How did it happen?" Dik cried out, as if her telling of it this time would be any different than the last.

Aguila stood. "She didn't obey orders."

"What orders?" Bryan Atumbo asked. "As I hear it, she was right beside you."

Mumbles of assent filtered through the room. The children were staring wide-eyed, looking, well, somehow strange. Even little Toni, normally a self-absorbed three-year-old boy, was watching her with the most peculiar focus. The eerie, half-possessed-and-almost-alien stare sent an uneasy shiver through her.

Kalico rose from the table and stood at ease, hands behind her, rocking back and forth on her feet as she said, "Dr. Sanz was told to go no farther than a couple of paces from the seatruck. The spot where she was taken was a good fifty meters away, less than ten meters from the edge of the pad. Whatever grabbed her was most likely hidden in the tumble of trees and overburden. No clue as to what it was, and being on freshly scraped bedrock, there were no tracks. Best guess as to the predator? Step Allenovich and I suspect a quetzal."

"How come you didn't see it?" Varina Tam demanded. "It had to be right there! It grabbed her out in the open!"

"Could have been there the whole time, watching, camouflaged to match the piled rock, soil, and trees." Kalico raised her hands to stifle any protest. "People, this is Donovan. It plays for keeps. Get it through your heads that you have to think differently. Act differently."

"We're not trained for this!" Anna Gabarron snapped from her chair by the door. "I'm an aquatic chemist, not a space marine. I'm here to do science, not bundle about carrying a big gun and looking to shoot things before they eat me. You're the Supervisor. It's your responsibility to ensure that we can do our work without danger. So instead of standing up there lecturing us about rules, why don't you call your Corporate Mine and dispatch some people out here who can take care of us? That's *your* responsibility to us as citizens."

To Michaela's disquiet, her people began to applaud, nodding in affirmation.

Kalico fixed her steely glare on Gabarron, who, as usual, was too socially incompetent to understand the ramifications. "My people have enough on their hands as it is. Corporate Mine is not here to provide services that you yourselves can perform. My responsibility is *not* to keep you safe. It is to manage Corporate ventures on Donovan, not play nursemaid to people who can't adapt to Donovan's challenges."

"Then perhaps we'd be better off on our own," Gabarron declared stiffly. "We did well enough on *Ashanti* by relying on ourselves. And here we have a better hydroponics system that we can recharge. Not to mention an ocean full of resources. So, if The Corporation refuses to honor its responsibilities to its citizens, then perhaps cutting ties, as Port Authority did, will be in our better interests."

"Wait!" Michaela cried, raising her hands before Aguila came unglued. She stepped forward, calling, "Since her arrival, the Supervisor has gone out of her way to—"

"She's been present at each death!" Gabarron cried, pointing a finger at the smoldering Aguila. "That's the constant! She was standing right there when Shinwua was taken, the same for Lara. If she's so smart about Donovan and danger, why is she always a little too late, and more than a little short when it comes to saving our people?"

Mutterings came from around the room. All but the children, who seemed to be watching with those new eerily wide-eyed and emotionless expressions. What the hell was it about them?

"Fine!" Aguila snapped, eyes gone fierce. "If you want, I can shut this whole thing down."

"Supervisor, please," Michaela turned. "We're just a little upset. To have so many losses, so quickly. It's emotion talking, not—"

"Is it?" Bill Martin asked from where he stood in the kitchen door. He looked at the now-sobbing Dik Dharman. "I hate agreeing with Anna, but how many of us are going to lose loved ones if we keep doing things the Supervisor's way? I understand her responsibilities, but we're the Maritime Unit. We're the ones trained in oceanography, marine biology, and the functioning of the Pod and its equipment."

"Supervisor Aguila is an administrator," Kevina Schwantz stated as she stood and looked around the room. "Key word: Administrator. The role of a Supervisor is to oversee the big picture. She might know what's best when it comes to Corporate Mine and digging holes, but we are the experts when it comes to the oceans. Will we make mistakes? Sure. But I think we're better equipped to adapt our methodologies and equipment to Donovan's maritime environment."

Yoshimura rose even before Kevina stopped speaking, and said, "Let's not be too hasty. I was out there the day the scimitar grabbed Shin. The Supervisor's instincts were correct. We just didn't know what a scimitar was. What it was capable of."

"And Shin's dead!" Bill Martin cried passionately. "The person I loved more than life was needlessly and cruelly taken from me. In my nightmares do you know what I see? It's his body in those jaws. That's my partner. The man I loved with all my heart."

To Michaela's surprise, Aguila hadn't exploded. Instead she stood with one hand on her pistol butt, a flint-like hardness in her half-slitted eyes.

"Supervisor," Michaela told her, stepping close. "They're just . . ."

"I say we go it on our own," Dharman interjected. The man's jaw trembled, his cheeks tear-damp and shining in the light. "It worked on *Ashanti*, it's best for us now."

Gabarron cried, "Who says we do it as we did on *Ashanti*? We've always functioned the best when we did so as a family. I'm with Kevina. Let the Supervisor supervise from Corporate Mine, but we need to run things the way we think they need to be run. Who's with me? Raise your hands."

Michaela's chest went tight, seeing the growing determination in the expressions, in the defiant looks and thin-set lips. She knew them well enough to mark that instant when they had reached a consensus. One by one, the hands went up. The last to lift his was Yoshimura, who was plainly conflicted.

Maybe, if Shinwua had been there to back her, she might have persuaded them to give the Supervisor another chance.

Michaela shot a desperate glance at Aguila, saw the ghost of a deadly smile flicker across the woman's lips.

Michaela told her. "I don't know where this came from, but

maybe after we can come to terms with what's happened to Shin and Lara . . ."

Aguila's stare might have been a laser the way it burned through Michaela. "Director, I hope you and your people know what they're doing. They remind me of a flock of sheep. The last time The Corporation brought sheep to Donovan it didn't work out well."

"Supervisor, don't close us down. Give us a little time to come to grips with our loss, work some things out."

"You still don't get it, do you?" Aguila still had her hand propped on her pistol. "Sure, I could close you down. Bring a couple of my marines in armor and load you all up to go work in Corporate Mine. Cut the Pod loose from the reef and haul it to the mainland."

"Please, don't."

The room had gone deathly quiet, people straining to hear.

Aguila took a quick measure of the room. Said, "Once, I would have done just that. Ordered this place evacuated. Shot Gabarron for mutiny and stuck the rest of you in the most menial jobs I could find for the rest of your contracts." She paused to let the import of her words sink in. "I'm not the same person I was back in those early days. Since then, Donovan has provided me with a macabre sense of humor. I'll give you my final decision in the morning."

So saying, she turned on her heel, boots rapping on the sialon as she strode from the room.

Michaela felt her guts turn to sand, sank into the chair, and closed her eyes. What the hell had just happened? How had this day gone so wrong?

When she finally looked up, it was to see her people talking, looking nervous as they stood in clusters, many laying reassuring hands on Bill Martin and Dik Dharman. Sharing their sympathy.

Gabarron had a self-satisfied smile on her face—as if she'd just achieved some remarkable victory.

Where they were scattered around the room, the children were still watching with that unnerving and blank-eyed stare.

Aguila can close us down. What the hell am I going to do?

34

Kalico awakened to a stiff pounding on her door. Dragging herself from a troubled sleep, she threw back the covers, calling, "I'm coming."

Memory of last night returned, and with it the fact that she'd just been present at a mutiny. The Maritime Unit had tossed her out. They hadn't quite gone as far as the Donovanians at Port Authority after they'd killed Clemenceau, but this was just a step short of that.

Or is it? Kalico wondered as she pulled on her coveralls and secured the utility belt at her waist. She pulled her hair back, pinned it, and loosened her pistol in its holster. Stepping to the door, she flicked on the camera, and to her relief, found only Michaela Hailwood on the other side. Not an armed mob with assassination on their minds.

Kalico opened the door, greeting, "Director. I'm hoping that cooler heads have reassessed the situation and retracted that bit of theater we witnessed."

Michaela's face reflected anything but relief. "Dik couldn't sleep. Checked the radio. Corporate Mine is calling. Desch Ituri is desperate to talk to you. There's been a cave-in the Number Three. People are missing, and they've evacuated the mine shaft. Ituri says it's bad."

Kalico's stomach sank. "People missing? Who?"

"I don't know. Ituri just told Dik that he needed to—"

"Get the seatruck ready. I mean now! Tell your good friend Dik to tell Desch I'm on the way. And he needs to tell Makarov to have my A-7 at the beach pad, waiting, when I get there."

"Of course, Supervisor. I'll have some food prepared and ready for you to—"

"After last night, I'm not sure I want to trust my health to anything Bill Martin might fix."

Michaela's eyes widened, her lips parting. "Certainly you don't think he'd—"

"Director, I don't know what the hell to think. Now, I'm packing my bag, and I'm going to want that seatruck waiting on the deck by the time I get there. So move!"

Kalico slammed the door in the woman's face. Not that she had a lot to pack. She washed, threw her few things into the bag, and all the while was picturing the Number Three. That miserable hole through crumbling and dripping rock.

It's cost me people? Who? How many?

More familiar faces, human beings with whom she had joked, eaten, and shared. Companions who had given their all in the effort to make Corporate Mine into a miracle.

When she stepped out onto the dock where the seatrucks were stored, a stiff wind blew in from the east. Given the looks of the white-capped swells, it was pushing a two-meter sea. Where she waited beside the seatruck, a stiff gust tried to push Michaela Hailwood off balance and ruffled the woman's coveralls. Up in the seatruck's cab, Bryan Atumbo sat at the wheel, his dark face a mixture of excitement and apprehension.

Kalico Aguila let her gaze shift from one to the other of them.

"I'm so sorry for all of this," Hailwood told her. "I don't know where all that anger came from. Shin dying the way he did, it sort of acted like a catalyst. Then, to have Lara go like that? It's like they have lost all of their direction. When Anna said we should go it alone, they just all jumped on it, as if they'd found something to cling to even if it was wrong."

Kalico grabbed her hair as the breeze tried to whip it around her face. "You have something to ponder here, Michaela. If your people are so lost, if they're looking for something, it's your job to find it for them. If there's a failure here, it's yours."

The woman's dark brown eyes widened, then hardened. "Don't lay this on me, Supervisor. I did everything I was supposed to. I got my people out of Deck Three, kept them unified. I got them to Donovan. No one prepared me for what we'd find here. It's The

Corporation's fault. They should have given me the tools I'd need to keep my people safe."

Kalico chuckled. "Shig Mosadek once told me that if I could overcome my cultural baggage, look past who I used to be back in the Solar System, I could accomplish great things on Donovan. Maybe you can, too."

"Are you going to shut us down?" Michaela asked. "I saw how mad you were last night. Are you going to take it out on us?"

Kalico staggered under a gust that flapped her pants against her legs. "I thought about it. On the other hand, when people have made up their minds and won't listen to reason, sometimes you just have to let them run headlong off the cliff. Maybe I've been spending too much time around these damned libertarians. Tell your people I said they've got their chance. Welcome to Donovan."

With that, Kalico tossed her bag into the seatruck, grabbed the handrail, and hauled herself up into the cab. Without a look back, she dropped into the seat, telling Atumbo, "Now, get me to the beach. Fast as this thing can go . . . and remember that I'm in one hell of a bad mood."

"Yes, Supervisor." Atumbo powered up the fans, lifted them off, and eased out over the water. As he circled, and the tail wind sent them flying across the waves, Kalico got one last look back at the Pod.

Michaela Hailwood stood there, braced against the wind, looking small and defeated.

35

S ince she had watched the seatruck vanish over the horizon, Michaela Hailwood had passed the morning in stunned relief. She had fully anticipated Kalico Aguila to give the order that would shut down the Maritime Unit. A Board Supervisor with marines to back her up, Aguila could enforce any decision she made. And she'd do it without remorse.

"She personally shot a couple of deserters," Michaela reminded herself as she crossed the landing in level one and worked the upper hatch that let her descend the tube to the Undersea Bay. The story had been recounted several times during the Maritime Unit's short stay in Port Authority. According to the Donovanians, Kalico Aguila was a woman that no one with sense messed with. And that included beasts like mobbers and quetzals.

A woman like that? Last night Michaela's own people had figuratively given the Supervisor a slap across the face.

Michaela entered the pressure lock, cycled it, and stepped through into the brightly lit Underwater Bay with its gleaming submarines, equipment, workbenches, and cabinets. The open pool of water was perfectly still, reflecting the lights and walls above its translucence. She crossed the deck, aware of the small spots of teal-colored stuff on the floor. Yoshimura was crouched at the edge of the water, staring down at the coating of what looked like green-blue slime that clung to every surface at the waterline.

"What have you got, Yosh?"

Yoshimura used a glass rod to scoop some of the slime up, stood and studied it in the light. "Well, I wanted a word alone with you. I thought you did a pretty good job with that speech at breakfast. You got everyone charged up and gave us all a boost. Okay, so the Supervisor's off to deal with a disaster at Corporate Mine, but Michaela, ultimately we're going to pay for what we did."

"Yosh, what could I do? I keep thinking that maybe, if Shin was just here, we could have sidestepped this whole calamity."

"You were trapped. Had to side with the vote." He chuckled as he studied the goo on the glass rod. "A vote, can you imagine? When did we start doing that?"

"On *Ashanti*. Once it was apparent what kind of trouble we were in, we had to have community consensus. It was that or we'd have started murdering each other when things got tense. Survival hinged on group harmony being more important than interpersonal differences, grudges, and jealousies." She gestured her futility. "What I didn't get was how frightened and anxious our people are. That they could rally around surly old Anna, of all people, shows how deep the problem lies. But how could they blame Aguila?"

"Because Aguila's an outsider. And she's the face of The Corporation that sent us here, had us locked in *Ashanti*, and landed us in this little Pod out in the middle of an ocean full of nasty creatures that can kill us. If you've got to have a scapegoat, she's made for it. She comes across as hard and uncaring. Not one drop of empathy for an individual's suffering or feelings. She's as tough as the scars on her face, hands, and arms."

"Our fate hangs by a thread, Yosh. This disaster at Corporate Mine might have been the only thing that saved us. Bottom line, up front? Whatever happens out here, we are on our own. Get it?"

"Yeah, you stressed that at breakfast. But saying it and understanding it might be two different things."

"Help me get it through people's heads. Back home, The Corporation was always there. Rescue was always just a call away. On *Ashanti*, it was the crew. For a while, here, it was Aguila, and what little she had to offer. But that just flew east with the seatruck."

Michaela paced back and forth, knotting and unknotting her fists. "If we call on Aguila to bail us out. For any reason. She's coming back with her marines and shuttles. She's loading us all up and packing us off to Corporate Mine to scrub floors and carry rocks. The Pod will be picked up in its constituent pieces and hauled off to the mainland to be recycled into things Corporate Mine can use.

Or maybe it will be sold to Port Authority in this insane market economy they've created."

Yosh walked over, carefully tilted his glass rod so the teal-colored goo ran into a sample jar; then he capped it. The rod he washed in one of the sinks, then inserted it into a sterilizer. Bearing his prize, he turned to face her.

"Michaela, here's the thing: I was out there with Aguila when Shin was taken. If the Supervisor hadn't been with us, we would have lost both UUVs. We would have gone together to collect the samples, as a team. Not individually, let alone in a hurry like Aguila had us do. We'd have both been standing there, side by side in the surf when that scimitar burst out of the water. It wouldn't have just been Shin. Both of us would have been dead."

He pointed a finger. "And from the reports, Lara was told to stay next to the seatruck. She wandered off, right? To the edge of the pad. And she did it after Aguila told her not to."

"That's right."

"Michaela, it's our fault. If Shin had run out, taken his sample, and hurried back like he was told, he'd be alive. Instead he just stood there, staring out at the surf. Same with Lara, she disobeyed. We just turned on a woman who did everything she could to help us. From here on out, we can't fail. We can't give her reason to shut us down."

"I'm way ahead of you. I've ordered Dik to cut all communications with Corporate Mine. Aguila says we're going to lose more people. If we do, and if we have other failures, I don't want it getting back to Aguila. If she calls us, I'll tell her that everything is fine, and research is progressing."

"And the trips to Port Authority? Anything that happens, she'll hear it through PA and be doubly pissed off that we didn't tell her."

"Let's postpone those rotations until things settle down. After losing Lara, we can make a case for putting them on hold." She indicated the sample jar. "What is that?"

"Don't know. But it's all over the pilings and the bottom of the Pod. I thought I'd get Vik to take a look at it under the scope. See if she can figure out what this stuff is. Probably some sort of Dono-vanian algae or the like."

"Good thinking." She started for the hatch, lost in thought. Stopped as she opened the pressure door. "Yosh, you and I are thinking along the same lines. Aguila won't forget this. We really are on our own. If you think of anything, and I mean anything, that I might need to know to keep us alive out here, you will tell me, won't you?"

He gave her a smile, nodded. "I can't be Shin. He was a one of a kind. But yeah. We've been though too much to lose it all now."

36

The tooth flower, in all of its glorious colors, hung low over the trail as Dek slowed, cocked his head, and studied the predator. In the twilight, he backed a step, feeling the roots under his foot squirm. Better to go around. With a bunching of his legs, he leapt the two meters to the top of a thick tangle of chabacho roots, ran the five meters along the top root, and dropped with a thump onto the trail beyond the tooth flower. Not that it was a trail in the Earthly sense, just an opening in the forest floor that allowed passage between the massed snarls of intertwined roots.

As he lowered his body parallel to the ground, mouth open, and sprinted down the winding way, he was aware of the sidewinder that jetted back out of sight. The bem he passed didn't so much as shift its camouflage, despite the intensifying of its odor. A sure indication of fear.

Better yet, Dek's vision gave him added confidence as he shot through the mazework of vines, root bundles, and occasional dips and rises. Nothing had prepared him to see the world with such clarity. Human stereoscopic vision was so limited. With three widely spaced eyes, his depth perception was perfect, even at the speed he ran. Never had he been so surefooted, able to run so fast without a bobble or a misstep. His body might have been one with the terrain, each step perfectly placed.

Dek paused at the base of a vertical tumble of black rock, the stone cloaked in a fine tracery of roots. A leap took him to the top of a fallen boulder, and dodging vines, he scampered his way up to the flat meadow above. There, on the black bedrock, he stopped short, scenting for danger, and used the air funneling into his lungs to expel excess body heat from the vents beside his tail. The sensation of air sucking through his mouth, compressing for oxygen, and jetting out behind him, filled him with exultation.

He thrived on the intensity. A totality of existence. Experienced the sense of "Eternal Now" with such clarity. Color, depth, the complexity of sound, the movement of air on his expanded collar, the scents of plants and prey, immersed him in a celebration of what it meant to be alive.

I am free.

Filling his lungs, he expelled a harmonic blast of sound from his vents, chittering at the same time in an exploration of quetzal expression.

Around him, the chime changed, its pitch rising.

Through the gap in the trees, he could see the sheer mountain wall rising to the clouds, its colorful and patterned rock broken and craggy along the fault lines, the stone radiating in different shades of infrared where Capella's rays warmed the cliffs. Lines of waterfalls, shadowed cracks and crevices gave off a duller shade, almost blue.

Dek reveled at the vista, taken by the grandeur of the place. He had seen Earth's most spectacular scenery, and nothing compared. As the human inside him marveled, the quetzal became confused and then amazed. How could the creatures not have a sense of aesthetic beauty? But here it was, as if in illumination.

"That's Demon. It never accessed that part of Talina's brain." Rocket whispered from his shoulder. *"He was too intent on just killing her."*

"But Kylee knew. You shared with her."

"Grew up with it. So much to explore now. Like the miracle you experience seeing through quetzal eyes, we feel seeing through yours. A remarkable—"

A blast of pain exploded in Dek's gut. Bent him double. The agony of it left him wheezing for breath and clutching his middle.

"What that . . . ?"

"Not to be heard." The voice had a hissing quality now, coming from inside.

"Demon," Dek gritted, made himself straighten and breathe. "So, you can just blast Rocket out of my head with a jolt of pain. Talina warned me."

"Yesss. Stronger."

Dek blinked, the world coming back in focus. The mountain wall remained before him, more stunning than he remembered as it rose in sheer cliffs to the cloud-wrapped peaks so high above, but the image wasn't quite the same. Flatter now, and the IR shading had lost its vibrancy. His breath was labored, sucking and expelling out of his lungs. The sounds not as rich to his ears as the chime rose, seemed to catch a melody, and then disintegrated into atonality.

He looked down, surprised to find his body, not quetzal, but human. He wore only a set of coveralls, belted at the waist, and his boots. But looking around, he was on that block of stone, only to gaze up at the same mountain he'd seen as a quetzal.

"What the hell?" he demanded, turning. Capella hung over the treetops above the eastern horizon.

"Brought you out here to die, human." Demon's voice seemed to chortle down inside Dek's gut.

"Where's my rifle? My pistol?"

"Just you. Time to die."

Dek rubbed hard at his face. Blinked. This was no dream. He was here—atop a block of toppled gneiss—surrounded by forest at the very foot of the titanic up-thrust of the mountain wall. Worse, he had no clue how he had come to this place.

"So, which way is Two Falls Gap?" he wondered, staring wistfully off to the east. Had to be that way. But which trail did he take? How could he keep his orientation once he was back in the trees?

Instead of an answer, all he got in return was the rising and falling of the chime.

"Think, Dek. Think."

Try as he might, cudgel his brain all he could, the only image was of a mazework of trees and a torturous path that he'd run at high speed. The forest floor had been a jumble of giant roots, all knotted and intertwined, of ups and downs, twists and turns.

No clue remained as to where he'd been, how he had managed to get here.

"Talina!" he bellowed.

The only answer was the monotonous shifting of the chime.

And, damn it, as loud as the invertebrates were, if Tal wasn't within a hundred meters or so, she'd never hear his call. Not even with her quetzal-augmented senses.

Dek knotted a fist, turned as several buzzing flying things whisked past his ear like slow bullets. Creatures like he'd never seen before. They paid him no heed.

"How the hell did I get here?"

"*I brought you.*"

"Yeah, yeah, I know. You brought me here to die, you piece of shit. Why?"

"*Talina. What she calls 'payback.'*"

"The problem with learning about humans? You're starting to think like one."

"*Talina is a blunt tool. Your way is much more cruel.*"

"My way? What the hell is that supposed to mean?"

"*As you did to Kalay.*"

"Go fuck yourself, Demon."

Demon didn't reply, just uttered that infuriating chittering.

Dek kept turning, searching desperately to discover some sign, some clue that would lead him back to Two Falls Gap. All he could see was trees, their leaves and branches slowly moving as they shifted and jockeyed for a better exposure to the morning light.

"Think, Dek." He swallowed hard, realized that his mouth was dry. Where the hell was he going to find a drink? He didn't even have a knife to cut a hole in an aquajade to tap one of the veins for water, toxic though it might be.

Glancing to the west, he studied the closest of the waterfalls tumbling down the mountain. That was maybe a hundred meters to the south across impossibly piled chunks of colluvial rock intertwined with trees and vines. Not even a quetzal could cross that.

But water? Wherever it collected at the base of the slope, there lay his drink. As to the knot in his stomach? It came as the first pang of hunger. The thing about having survived starvation was that he knew how far he could go on empty.

Walking to the edge of the tumbled block, he looked back down the drop. He had climbed up that, could see the last of the fine roots he'd scrambled across as they relaxed into their usual slow, sinuous motion. By now, any trail he'd left had faded back into the normal rhythms of forest life.

"Pus in a bucket, I don't even know how long I've been gone, let alone how far."

The miracle was that he'd made it. That some chokeya vine, biteya bush, you're screwed vine, sidewinder, spike, or skewer hadn't grabbed him and killed him.

"So, if being a quetzal got me this far . . . ?" Dek cocked an eyebrow, tried to imagine himself back into a quetzal's body. Tried harder. Still didn't happen. So, how had Demon done that? Taken over all of his consciousness, essentially stolen his body and turned off his mind?

He was staring up at the mountain wall again, the futility of his circumstances beginning to take hold, when he saw movement. A lot of movement, like a thousand sparkles of color against the craggy rock wall no more than a couple hundred meters to the south.

The jinking flight—fluttering and uniform patterns of movement—was familiar. Like a nightmare come to life.

He knew that shape as the closest of the flying beasts rose up above the trees. The four wings, the keel-shaped breast, the furry tail and gleaming knife-like claws on the beast's wrists.

Mobbers.

And they were headed his way.

37

Talina hadn't slept well. She awakened late, blinked the rheum out of her eyes, and sat up in her makeshift bed. Light spilled in through the film-covered window. Not that window washing was one of her preferred occupations, but she'd have to attend to some cleaning today. Maybe get Dek to help her. The man liked to brag about how he'd scrubbed toilets, so she'd let him take a whack at the scum on the . . .

She glanced across, saw that his bedding was thrown back. Empty.

Didn't make sense. Normally, she'd have awakened at the crackling of the plastic emergency bedding the guy was sleeping in. And she should have heard him dress. Dek's boots were gone, too. Surely she should have heard him clumping across the duraplast floor. What had he done? Tiptoed out in his sock feet to put his boots on in the front room?

Whatever. Maybe he had breakfast ready. She'd found mint plants in the wet areas the day before. Be nice if Dek had a cup steaming for her.

She dressed, rolled her shoulders to loosen the muscles, pulled on her boots, and made her way into the bathroom. No way she'd walk barefoot on that kind of filth. As she inspected the floor, she figured that here was a better way for Dek to demonstrate his prowess when it came to cleaning. The place needed to be sprayed with disinfectant followed by a thorough scrubbing, and then to be hosed down.

When she'd finished her morning constitutional, she walked out into the main room. Only to find it empty.

On the rack beside the door, her rifle rested next to Dek's fancy Holland & Holland. His cloak and hat were hanging on the back of the couch. The door gaped open a crack, allowing easy access for any passing sidewinder, bem, or quetzal.

What the hell? Dek was smarter than this.

"Or is he?" she asked, slinging her utility belt and pistol around her hips before grabbing up her own hat and cloak. Pulling her rifle from the rack, she stepped out, locking the door behind her. The morning was beautiful, crystal clear in Capella's slanting light. Dew glistened on her aircar and beaded in drops on the large-leafed plants. Mist was rising in a gray haze from the garden, and the morning chime kept rising and falling in half-symphonic regularity.

"Dek!" Talina slowly scoured the area. And in the golden light, she noticed where the dew had been knocked off the leaves by Dek's passage.

"Dek! Damn it, where are you?"

Nothing came in answer but the mocking sound of the chime.

Slinging her rifle, Talina started off in Dek's footsteps. As soon as Capella's implacable rays had a chance to do their thing, any semblance of a dew trail would be gone.

She crossed the garden at a trot, slowing at the edge of the trees. Behind the outlying aquajade and chabacho, the forest rose in an impenetrable mass of vines, branches, and leaves. But Dek's trail headed straight into the shadowed depths.

"Well, shit, you stupid fool." Talina unslung her rifle. She'd find him all right. Probably hanging half-devoured from a tooth flower, or maybe wrapped up in a sidewinder's embrace. Worst would be if a nightmare had caught him and hauled him up into a mundo tree's dim recesses to digest for a couple of months.

"Please, Dek, if it's a nightmare, be dead already." The last time she'd shot anyone in a nightmare's embrace it had been Clemenceau. She'd hated Clemenceau, and it had still been one of the hardest things she'd ever done. Pulling the trigger on Dek? That would break her heart.

"*Good,*" Demon whispered.

"Oh, go fuck yourself."

"*Can't. Takes three.*"

"Piece of shit."

Irritated, Talina started forward, her vision adjusting to the darkness as she slipped into the forest's shadowed depths. Here, beneath the thick overstory, the visibility was little better than in starlight;

Capella's angle remained too low to shoot even refracted rays through the higher branches. Thick root mat squirmed slowly under Talina's weight as she scented the air, her wary gaze taking in the surrounding vines, looking for the lethal predators.

Dek's track had been in a straight line from the dome. West. Toward the mountain wall. But once he was in the trees? Picking and holding a direction was nigh on impossible without a compass or global positioning aid, not that Donovan had anything like the latter.

She searched for any sign of Dek's passage, any difference in the movement of the roots. And saw nothing but the constant slow writhing normal to a forest floor.

How much lead did he have? And more to the point, why in hell had he wandered off into the forest? Soft meat he might be, but it just didn't make sense. He was smarter than this. Nothing would have been tempting enough to lure him into the bush without his rifle or his . . .

"He's not in his right mind," Rocket told her from her shoulder.

"Demon's got him locked in a hallucination," she agreed, her hopes dropping.

Had to be.

"So, Demon, you piece of shit, what's your game? If you wanted him dead, you could have just hallucinated him into shooting himself." A pause. "Or could you?"

No answer came from down behind her stomach where her hated quetzal seemed to crouch in anticipation.

"This is a game, isn't it? There's no fun or payback in killing Dek fast. That's too easy. I'd just grieve for a bit, load up, and head back to my life. No, you're going to try and make the two of us suffer. To do that, you need to keep him alive. Make it a challenge."

She could feel the quetzal shift in her gut, as if delighted that she'd caught on so quickly.

"West."

How in the hell would her Demon know what Dek's Demon was planning? But then, it was the same intelligence. And who knew how that worked?

Toward the mountains? Where the forest was thicker, the land more rugged and broken as it rose toward the sheer cliffs?

Talina checked her wrist compass, and—focusing on her surroundings—started forward into the hidden depths. It came to her in a curious revelation that she did so with an uncanny ease. Almost a feeling of being at home, moving with a surefooted speed. She sidestepped the biteya bush and thorncactus, gave wide berth to the pincushion thing, and instinctively leapt from root to root, secure in her understanding of which roots would support her weight with the least amount of disturbance.

This was a far cry from that hesitant, start and falter, forever-on-the-edge-of-disaster trip she'd made with Cap Taggart all those years ago. Not that anything about her passage was cavalier. Death lurked on all sides. Not just in the predatory plants, but in the ever-questing roots, in the hidden hunters that prowled the shadows.

"So how did Dek get past all this without being turned into a skeleton?"

"Made him quetzal?" Rocket suggested.

That scared, more than reassured, her. If Demon's TriNA had that much control over Dek's brain, was it even worth finding him?

Worst case, Demon would use the guy to toss her into a nightmare's tentacles or shove her down in slug-filled mud so that she'd die horribly and in agony.

Best case? She'd find him a blithering idiot, or zombie-like under Demon's control. And it would be her responsibility to put a bullet in his head.

"Either way sucks toilet water," she growled as she slipped around a black hole in the roots that reeked of slightly different vinegar smell than she was used to. Something down there that she was unfamiliar with, not a skewer or bem. Her quetzal sense formed an image of a two-sword-clawed, blue, three-eyed thing in a hard shell. Weird how the image came clear with just the smell.

Skipping across a series of roots, she startled a collection of invertebrates on a fallen chabacho trunk. They scattered in an explosion of multicolored shells and buzzing wings.

By the numbers on her wrist unit, she'd been traveling west for twenty minutes when she picked up the first trace of Dek's passage: a slight agitation in the roots off to her left. No telling if it was Demon's influence or Dek's previous experience, but he'd made a wide circuit around the stand of brown caps.

Then which way?

She frowned, couldn't pick out any unusual activity in the roots beyond the brown caps, but a fallen aquajade trunk served as a ramp that led up to a bench on her left. Talina took it, racing to the stony outcrop's top. Here she could see the thin root mat's agitation where Dek's booted feet had bruised them. Talina raced along in pursuit, and into the dense forest beyond where deeper soil allowed the trees to grow into towering specimens. Some of the boles were a good five meters in diameter, the roots snaking out beneath them like supple pillars.

Dek's trail through the jumble let her make good time, proceeding almost at a run. Breath came easily to her lungs, the familiar weight of her rifle acting as a balance as she leapt from root to root, heedless of the disturbance she left by her rapid passage.

"Come on, Dek. Where the hell are you?"

For the first time, a spear of hope began to build. The guy was still alive. Protected either by incredible luck—or more likely, Demon's guiding hand—Dek had crossed almost a kilometer of virgin forest. Unarmed.

"So, seriously, Tal," she mused as she climbed up a three-meter-high knot of interlaced roots, "you like the guy. If he's a blank-gazed automaton possessed by a demented quetzal, can you really make yourself walk up and shoot him in the head?"

Damn it, why the hell did these things always happen to her? Why was it she who had to make the choice? Chock it up to some cosmic injustice? Bad karma on her part? Or was Shig right, and her young soul had to pay a weird penance for sins committed in one of her earlier and even younger existences?

"Screw the Hindus. Or Buddhists. Or who the hell ever," she muttered.

In her memory she could hear her half-Maya mother telling her,

"The universe wouldn't pick you if you weren't strong enough to do what you had to."

The way was steeper now, and she had to dig in with her toes to find purchase on the already irritated roots. She was gaining. Just minutes behind her prey if she were any judge of the roots' activity. The light was brighter, indicating a break in the trees, probably a rock outcrop or one of the jumbled ridges abutting the mountain wall. She could hear the faint roar of whitewater tumbling down a defile somewhere beyond the steep incline just ahead.

Talina fought for footing in the roiling roots as she scrambled up the abuttal. She was on the verge of crashing through the screen of leaves and into the open when she heard the chittering, the tweeting whistles and harmonics. She didn't need the panicked quetzals inside to bring her to a hard stop. Her own heart might have leapt from her chest.

Mobbers!

Talina immediately dropped to a knee, every muscle frozen.

The sound grew, ever louder.

And Dek had to be just on the other side of those leaves, out in the open.

"Think, Tal," she managed through gritted teeth.

Dropping onto her stomach, she wiggled across the roots to peer through a gap in the leaves.

A wheeling, fluttering chaos of laser-flashing colors met her gaze. Mostly crimsons, stunning oranges, vermillion yellows, blinding greens, and pulsing blues, a riot of color in a whirlwind column that descended from above. For the briefest of instants, Tal fixed on the image of Dek Taglioni, lying flat, face-down and motionless on the bare stone.

Within seconds, Talina was going to bear witness as the beasts stripped Dek's body down to bloody bones.

The scream of the quetzals inside her, the momentary paralysis they imposed, froze every muscle.

Dek is going to die!

She choked off the stone-cold fear. A scream tore from her lips, causing the mobbers to hesitate just as the four-winged terrors descended on Dek. Talina had a momentary vision of the triangular heads turning her way amid the flapping of a thousand rainbow-patterned wings. Of the three-eyed gazes fixing on hers. The curved claws, like thin razors, flashed in the light.

She didn't consciously flip the safety to automatic as she rose. The rifle in her hands might have pointed itself, erupted on its own. Automatic fire spewed into the center of the twisting vortex of flying bodies. Muzzle blast shredded the leaves around her, blowing bits and fragments into the air.

She would remember it like a vision: the multicolored bodies exploding as the rounds tore through them at three thousand feet per second. Bits of cad-yellow, aqua, violet, and turquoise pelage, the spraying haze of blood and body parts. Fragments of bone, strings of guts, furry tails, heads, and severed wings cartwheeled in the air. As tightly packed as they were for the kill, each bullet tore three or four of the flying horrors into pieces.

Talina screamed as she charged out, raising the rifle, stitching her way up through the dense column of flying bodies. She could follow the path of her bullets by the exploding bodies, the haze of blood and fluids and burst, tumbling, wheeling body parts. It might have been a perverted and hellish vision. Shreds of tissue, heads, guts, ripped apart, half obscured by a red and watery mist. The flying bits and pieces blotted the sky with chaos.

And then silence. Only the ringing in her ears.

Talina stood, trembling, rifle lifted, bolt open after the last round, a curl of smoke rising from the elevated barrel.

From out of the whirling, contorting, vortex above came a rain of blood, tissue, bones and wings. She crouched, covered her head as the gore came cascading down. Bits and pieces were falling like a mad bombardment, to batter, splat, and thump on the stone around her and Dek. Mingled in the body parts were wounded and dying mobbers, shrieking as they fell and slammed into the hard rock. Most died when they smacked into the stone; some flapped broken wings, crying piteously.

And in the midst of it came an eerie shriek that grew into a deafening squeal born of a hundred lungs as what remained of the column broke into a panicked confusion, colors flashing to black and orange throughout what was left of the shattered flock.

Maybe a hundred of the wheeling, milling beasts remained, and there Talina was, crouched over Dek's body, out in the open, with an empty rifle.

The deafening squeal grew louder, painful enough to make her wince.

Dropping her rifle, Talina clawed for her pistol, prepared to take as many of the little bastards with her as she could before they cut her to ribbons. As she lifted it, the lowest mobbers jinked sideways in flight, their squeal like an icepick through her ears.

With incomprehensible agility—the deafening squeal spreading up the column—the horde broke, jinked a couple meters to the left, and within seconds, fled into the trees.

As the chime began to rise again, Talina and Dek—spattered and dripping with blood and bits—were left alone beneath an open sky; offal, fluids, and pieces of dead and dying mobbers colored the patterned gneiss.

When Talina finally caught her breath, got her heart rate back to normal, and stopped the shaking in her arms and fingers, she dropped to a knee in the gore.

Placing a hand on Dek's shoulder, she rolled him over, asking, "Hey, Dek. You all right?"

When she stared into his eyes, it was to meet a terror-locked stare. The man might have been catatonic.

"Dek? *Dek!* You okay?"

He blinked. Seemed to focus. As his eyes widened in terror, a bloodcurdling scream tore from his throat.

38

Kalico stared out the side window as her A-7 dropped from the sky toward Corporate Mine. As it lost altitude, she had a perfect view of her empire. Corporate Mine perched on a metal-rich ridge jutting out on the southeast side of the Corporate Range. Part of the crater's rim, Corporate Range composed the southern arc of the Wind Mountains where they curved eastward toward the Gulf. On a resistant outcrop below the high peaks, Kalico had blasted a flat pad, built a fenced compound around a large dome and equipment yard, and erected two headstocks over the Number One and Number Two mines.

A tramline carried ore down the mountain and across the forested lowlands to the smelter where it had been built on the floodplain beside a bend in the river. Contiguous to it lay the small plot of farmland and the lower shuttle landing field. *Landing field* might have been a stretch; the thing consisted of nothing more than a thruster-baked red-dirt field. The faint scar of the slowly proceeding haul road could be seen where the trees had been held at bay by the struggling line of immature pines.

When she'd stepped out of the seatruck back on the beach pad and climbed into the A-7, Makarov had told her that her missing miners were Alia Fey and Stana Viola. The two had just driven the mucking machine into place and began removing ore when the roof goafed less than a hundred meters behind them. Meanwhile, Jin and Masters were servicing the drill back at the portal. The framing crew had been in the adit, preparing to haul timbers up to the working face. The miracle was that the cave-in hadn't killed the entire crew.

Be that as it may, two of her people remained trapped by—or dead under—tons of rock.

Everything on Donovan is a fight, Kalico thought, her chin propped on her knotted fist as she contemplated her small settlement. Didn't matter if it was the mine, the forest, the geology, the climate, the ancient and forever-breaking equipment . . . or the fucking Maritime Unit.

Now she faced her first cave-in. Worse, this time it wasn't just statistics, but names, women she knew: Alia and Stana. In her hurried communications with Aurobindo Ghosh, she'd learned that any chance that they might be alive was either little, slim, or most likely, none.

"Supervisor, we're still at the beginning of this. We're just getting an idea of the extent of the roof fall. Since we talked to you last, we've had more rock come down one hundred and fifty meters back from the face. The shoring just keeps giving way."

One hundred and fifty meters.

She could see it in her mind's eye: The rotten and cracked rock, the water dripping through the elaborate wood shoring, the timbers giving way. See—as if in slow motion—the cascade of splintered wood, the falling tons of broken and cracked rock . . . crushing the very light out of existence.

The notion was mind-and-soul-numbing.

What if Alia and Stana were still trapped in there? Clinging desperately to a small pocket of air? Crouched in the darkest of black and soundless eternity? Knowing that with each breath, they were exhausting the last of the air?

Kalico ground her teeth, wondering if she was a monster to hope that they'd been crushed instantly.

"Coming in," Makarov called as he banked hard, g-force pressing Kalico down into her conforming seat. She watched the forest rise to meet her as Makarov eased up on the thrusters at exactly the right moment to settle them with a feather-lightness onto the red soil of the smelter landing pad.

"Give me a moment to spool down, Supervisor," Makarov called as Kalico unbuckled from her seat, grabbed her small bag, and made her way to the hatch.

As the ramp dropped, she called, "Thanks, Juri. Superb job, as usual."

"Hope it turns out well, ma'am." Makarov called back. "I'm

going to sit tight with the shuttle until, one way or another, this thing is over. You need me and the bird for anything, we'll be ready to lift within five minutes."

"Appreciate that. It won't be forgotten." And she was out the door, smelling the stink of exhaust mixed with dust.

Overhead, Capella burned down with glaring white intensity. She could see the heat waves rising over the packed crowns of the trees where they towered on all sides. A constant reminder that her little settlement with its fragile perimeter of pines, walnuts, and other terrestrial trees held but the most precarious of toeholds.

Beside the square and featureless walls of the smelter, an aircar waited at the edge of the landing pad. The top was up as a sunshade, and as she approached, Fenn Bogarten, her structural engineer, stepped out. Fenn's expression betrayed his anger, pain, and worry, but a question, almost a hope, lay behind his brown eyes. As if just the sight of her meant things might turn out all right.

"Any news, Fenn?" she asked as she tossed her bag in the back and slipped into the passenger seat.

"No, ma'am." Fenn told her as he climbed behind the wheel and spun up the fans. "People heard a loud bang. Like one of the timbers just snapped. Then the roof let go with a crackling as more timbers broke. It all came down so fast it compressed the air, blew Jones, Master, and O'Leary off their feet and a couple of meters down hole. They're pretty banged up, but outside of bruises and having to clean out the seats of their overalls, they're feeling damned lucky."

Kalico pursed her lips, knotted her fists as Bogarten shot them along the new haul road—as far as it went—and then lifted them over the forest on a line paralleling the tram.

As they cleared the last of the trees, the works at the tunnel mouth came into view. The waste dump and spoils to one side created a flat next to where the portal entered the foot of the mountain. She could see the ditch where the water-make trickled out of the tunnel mouth to glitter in the hot light. A couple of aircars, two haulers, and a line of ore cars waited where the rails curved onto the dump. Even as they approached, people were emerging from the mine to shade their eyes at her approach.

Bogarten settled them next to one of the other aircars, letting the fans spin down. Even as they did, Kalico was out, nodding in response to the subdued greetings from her people.

In front, Aurobindo Ghosh and Desch Ituri stood, their overalls stained and smudged; haggard looks rode both of their faces. Behind them, Talovich had a stricken expression—the sort a tortured saint might wear on the way to the Inquisition. But then, Kalico could imagine his guilt. Talovich was her best structural engineer. He was the one who'd designed and overseen the installation of the shoring.

"What have we got?" she demanded. "Tell me that there is word from Stana and Alia. Maybe tapping. Some hint that they're alive."

"Supervisor," Ghosh told her, hands spread, "About fifteen minutes ago, we felt another collapse. Shook the whole mountain. Came from deep inside. I immediately ordered everyone out of the tunnel. Not that I had to say it twice."

Ituri wiped at his eyes as he said, "Can't tell if it was void migration or more goaf deeper in the mine."

"What are the chances that our friends are alive back there?"

Ghosh pointed at the trickle of murky yellow water now running in the ricket. "The water-make is down to almost nothing. Supervisor, if they are alive, if they are holed up, depending upon the amount of space they have . . ." He swallowed hard. "You know how much water was running out of that head rock. Given the little that we have running now, it means the collapse is acting like a dam, backing it up."

Ituri couldn't meet her eyes. "Most likely, if they're still back there, they'll drown before they suffocate, ma'am."

Fists knotted at her sides, eyes squinted, Kalico snapped. "Well, what are you standing here for? Those are our people in there. Why isn't the mucking machine from the Number Two already down here? That's all loose cave-in. Let's get the tunnel mucked out and . . ."

Ghosh—also unable to look her in the eyes—was shaking his head. "Can't, ma'am. We're talking tons of rockfall. The more we pull out, the larger the void migration. As it is, the falling rock is loose, so it has more volume. Eventually it will slow, the loose stuff taking up the space. The bigger the hole we make, the more room the rock has to fall as the void is enlarged. Eventually it will bring down the whole mountain. What they call a glory hole. You get that, right?"

But to just do nothing? Those were two of her people in there. A yawning emptiness began to grow in her gut.

Ituri added, "And the tremors we're feeling? If they are not void migration, they're the tunnel collapsing that last couple of meters to the working face."

"I don't care! I want every effort made. Even if we have to go in and haul that rock out by hand."

She started for the portal. All her imagination could do was fix itself on the women trapped behind all those thousands of metric tons of rock. On their desperation, entombed as they were in the silent midnight black. Terrified as cold water rose up around their legs. Kalico could feel their fear, the knowledge that they were going to die.

She was just inside the portal when the ground shook, a muffled thump sounding from the rock around her. She felt it—hard through her feet—terrifying in its own promise of finality.

Kalico stopped, staring at the darkness. "Where are the lights?"

"Shorted out, ma'am," Ituri called from behind her shoulder. "If we're going in, we need head lights and . . . ."

She jumped as another thump sounded ominously from above. Not two heartbeats later, a loud bang, sort of like a muffled lightning strike, preceded a rumble. The floor twitched under her as a puff of air blew past.

"That's on this side," Talovich whispered. "Supervisor, please, I beg you, don't go in there. We don't want to lose you, too."

Kalico staggered sideways, braced herself on the portal shoring. "I see. It's just . . . Just . . ."

"Yeah," Ghosh told her. "We know. We're as heartbroken as you are."

"What did I do wrong?"

Talovich stepped up. "Nothing, ma'am. The math was right, the design was right. If it's anyone's fault, it's mine. That's my shoring in there."

"We double-checked everything," Ghosh declared. "Wasn't anything about Talovich's design or construction that wasn't top notch. I'm in charge, if there's a fault, it's on my head."

"Mine, too," Ituri told her. "We knew it was tricky once we got into the shocked zone." He glanced away. "We were the ones who told you we could do it."

"No," she rubbed her tired eyes, staring back into the tunnel's stygian maw. "I'm the one who sent people into that mess. Hell, it scared me that last time I was in there. It's my responsibility for not pulling the plug. I was just . . ." She couldn't allow herself to finish the sentence out loud. *I was too damned cocky. I wanted a quick fix to the drainage in the Number One.*

First the Maritime Unit, and now this? What the hell else could go wrong?

As if to feed on her gloom, another tremor rumbled through the mountain.

39

"I need some help here," Yoshimura's voice echoed up the stairs as Michaela braced herself against the communications room door. The room, little more than a closet on the second level, was too tight for two. Inside, Dik Dharman sat with one hand on the desk. To Michaela's disgust, the photonic com and the hyperlink, along with the other fancy communications equipment, had been set to the side to make a place for the primitive radio. Radio? A person couldn't even see who he or she was talking to. This was the twenty-second century, for God's sake. How primitive could it get?

Yeah? Welcome to Donovan, my ass!

Michaela had come up to learn if Dik had overheard any communications between Port Authority and Corporate Mine about the cave-in. Not that it was any of her concern, but she did have a vested interest in knowing what preoccupied Supervisor Aguila. Disaster at Corporate Mine meant the woman wasn't conjuring up terrible things to do to the Maritime Unit.

"Yosh?" she called, hearing the man's frantic steps as he pounded up the stairway. Coming into sight, she could see his terrified expression, and in his arms lay Toni. The three-year-old boy was rigid as a board, his arms and legs straight and stiff, his face a strained rictus. The wide-eyed stare in the boy's paralyzed face looked almost monstrous. The kid was breathing hard, each breath forced, and a sheen of perspiration coated his face.

"Yosh? What happened?"

"Don't know," the man almost choked. "Mikoru asked me to get him ready for breakfast. We let him sleep late. I found him like this. I need Anna up here now! She has the medical implant."

Michaela leaned into the communications room, grabbed for the mic, and keyed it. "Attention. Anna, we have a medical emergency on level two. Please report to the clinic. Repeat: Medical emergency."

"Come on." Michaela led the way down the hall that separated the labs and to the small clinic located just below the landing pad. She opened the door to the room, and Yosh pushed past her to lay the comatose Toni on the examining table. The little boy looked catatonic, with his eyes fixed and mouth pulled out of shape.

"My, God." Michaela placed a hand to her throat. "What did this?"

"No clue." Yosh was massaging the boy's hand. "Come on, Toni. Wake up. *Toni!* Do you hear me? Toni, it's Yosh. Hey, son. Come back! *Toni!* Please, son. Wake up!"

Michaela stepped back, watching as the man massaged his son's body, stripped off the boy's shirt and began rubbing his sweaty chest.

"Weird." Yosh lifted his hands, studied them as he rubbed his thumb and fingers together. "It's like . . . greasy. Slick."

Michaela started to lean forward, only to have Anna Gabarron burst in, demanding, "What's wrong?"

Yosh cried, "Something's wrong with Toni. He's like, paralyzed."

She elbowed her way in. "Give me room."

Yosh and Michaela stepped back, watched as Gabarron reached down the scope from its holder, used it to peer into the boy's eyes. "Pupils react," she noted, "Toni? Can you hear me?"

She snapped her fingers next to the boy's ears, used the little rubber hammer to tap his elbows and knees. Got nothing. Pulled down the stethoscope, listened. "Heart's racing." Taking down the monitor, she ran it over the boy's body. "Hundred and five beats a minute, blood pressure is one-sixty over one hundred. Not good."

Then she began pressing on his board-stiff body, carefully watching the boy's face for any reaction. In the end, she pinched the child's arm, hard. Toni did nothing.

Gabarron, too, rubbed her fingers together, made a face. "Did he get into something? Is this some chemical? A lubricant that he might have found somewhere?"

"As far as I know," Yosh told her, "Toni hasn't been off the first level. There's cleaning supplies in the closet, but I know that Iso keeps them locked. And then there's the kitchen. But even then, none of the cleansers would leave an oily feel. And Bill's cooking oils wouldn't cause this kind of a paralysis."

Gabarron stepped to the sink, washed her hands. Dried them. Rubbed her fingers and scowled as she washed them again with a more stringent soap. Again she dried them. "This stuff doesn't wash off. Until I know what I'm dealing with, I don't know what to give him besides an antihistamine to ameliorate any allergic reaction. If that's what's causing this paralysis."

Pounding steps in the hallway preceded Mikoru's arrival. The woman's panic was plain to see, her lips trembling. Anxiously she pushed past Michaela, crowding forward as she demanded, "Toni? What's wrong with my boy?"

Michaela eased out into the hallway just as Kevina Schwantz thundered up the stairs, asking, "What's the emergency. Jaim said it was a boy. Tell me it's not Felix."

"It's Toni. He got into something. Some oily chemical. It's all over his body."

"He did it this morning?"

"Yosh says he found him in bed after he slept late. Must have got into it last night. But do me a favor. Go down and check Iso's storeroom. She keeps it locked. Maybe it was left open by mistake."

Kevina whirled, thundering back down the stairs as others started up. She was calling, "It's Toni. He's poisoned. Some kind of reaction."

Michaela hurried to the head of the stairs, stopping Kel, Jaim, and Casey as they climbed. "Go back, everyone. Have breakfast. There's no sense filling the hallway and making things worse. Yes, it's Toni. I'll be down with a report as soon as there's anything to know. Casey, I need you to check with Tomaya and the rest of the children. See if they know about Toni getting into any kind of oil."

"Got, it!" Casey said, wheeling on the stairs and heading back down.

"You need anything," Kel told her, "you call."

"Thanks. Anna will probably figure it out. She's giving him antihistamines. But I need the rest of you to go eat. We've got a busy day. We're taking the subs out under the new protocol."

She gave them a "go back" wave before retreating to the clinic door. Inside, Yosh and Mikoru bent over the table. Mikoru clung to the boy's hand while Yosh stroked his son's hair.

Gabarron was bent over the med com, having inserted a blood sample, and was studying the analysis as it came up on the screen.

Michaela slipped past the parents, crowding into the space beside Gabarron to ask, "What have you got?"

"The kid's immune system is running on overdrive. T-cells, antibodies, histamine, white blood cell count, C reactive protein, it's all elevated. The kicker is that the machine hasn't identified any known bacterium, virus, spirochete, or protozoan, but it does register a high percentage of proteins that it can't tag. What I'm not getting is any signature for the usual poisons." She gave the machine a pat. "But, Michaela, this beast only has limited diagnostic functions for specific toxins. If it's not in the machine's catalog, it can't tag it. For sophisticated analyses, you need a hospital-grade unit."

"We don't have one."

Gabarron cocked an eyebrow, glanced back at the boy. "I'm pretty limited myself. I'm trained to render initial aid, evaluate and stabilize the patient, administer pharma, deal with immediate trauma, and give out bandages. Anything beyond that, I'm supposed to load the patient up and ship them off to The Corporation's closest hospital for advanced care."

"Which is Port Authority."

"What do we do? Call them up, ask them to send their A-7? Try and get Toni aboard as they hover like the Supervisor did when she got here? Or send a seatruck to the beach pad and transfer the boy there?"

"They'll want money, Anna. Those miserable SDRs they're so fond of." This would have been a wonderful time to remind Gabarron that she'd been the one to piss on the Supervisor's shoe and incite the rest to sever relations.

Instead, Michaela told her, "Get on the radio. Have Dik patch you through to Raya Turnienko at the PA hospital. Use the hospital frequency and *only* the hospital frequency. Then, when you get Turnienko, agree on a specific frequency for our use so we can talk privately. We don't want Aguila listening in. See if Raya has seen anything like this, and if she knows how to treat it. Maybe it's something simple that we can handle here, on our own."

"Call now!" Mikoru snapped. "Whatever it takes, we are going to save my son's life."

"I don't care what we have to do," Yosh insisted, panic and desperation in his dark eyes. "Mikoru and I have already lost three to miscarriage and stillbirth. Three. My son is going to live!"

If passion could heal, Yosh certainly had it nailed.

"We'll do everything," Michaela told them. Glanced at Gabarron. "Let's go talk to PA."

As she led the way out into the hall, Michaela wondered what this was ultimately going to cost them. How did you pay people for saving other people's lives? How did anyone put a price on that?

Problem was, after a fifteen-minute conversation where Anna Gabarron read off the diagnosis from the printout, Raya Turnienko told them, *"I'm sorry, Director. We have nothing similar to your patient's symptoms in our experience. I don't know what we could do if you sent him here. But, if I could make a suggestion? You have labs on the Pod. Test the boy for Donovanian TriNA."*

"And if he tests positive?" Gabarron asked.

"You'll just have to monitor him, keep him hydrated. So far we have no way of purging the blood and tissues once they are infected. We're all off the map when it comes to this stuff."

40

Dek came awake, staring up at the seeming eternity of his familiar bedroom ceiling. He lay flat on his back in his great bed in Taglioni Tower high in Transluna. The intricately laid layers of crystalline glass gave the illusion of staring up through a cascade of prismatic light. That it seemed to rise to a translucent infinity was an illusion created by refraction through elongated bars of cut glass; the effect was mesmerizing. With a mental command through his implants, he could change the colors, shift the patterns into an endless display of hues and visual spectacle.

His giant antigrav bed dominated the middle of the room where it rose from the shimmering interactive floor with its programmable imaging. Gossamer sheets, like a caress of air, fell away as he moved. On the bed beside him, the woman stirred, groaned, and reached up to flip thick red hair back from her face. Klea Morena. Dek started, wondering if this was real . . . and then, through the fading drug haze, he remembered.

He grinned, flopping back onto the shimmering sheets as colors of red, blue, and gold ran through the hollow-fiber's sheen. And Dek didn't need to see the stains on the sheets to remind him; they'd had quite the night.

Amazing what a good dose of eros would do for a man and woman.

Even at the thought a tingle formed at the root of his penis.

"What am I . . . ?" Klea's horrified green eyes fixed on Dek's, a moment of shock registering before a weary acceptance blanked her expression. "Good morning, Dek." The words were bright, springy. The woman was an actress after all. Didn't matter that she was one of the hottest women on holovid, or that her current dramatic adventure show was streamed by billions, here she was in Dek's bed.

"You're better in person, you know," he told her. "I always thought you and Tiggerson weren't right for each other."

"Tiggerson's a character," she told him. "So's Eunice Iverson. What you see on the show? That's just acting. I can't stand the guy in real life."

Dek chuckled, slapping his naked thigh. "Bet, despite all those scenes, Tig never gave it to you as good as I did last night."

"No." He could see the effort it took her to smile. "You were . . . um . . . I guess *wow* is the only word." For a moment, she might have been on the verge of tears, then that bright smile flashed back across her face. "Yeah . . . really, um . . . wow."

Dek had noticed that about her. Klea Morena wasn't nearly as smart, quick-witted, or cunningly competent as the Eunice Iverson she played in the holovid. So what? As far as he was concerned, it had been Eunice that he'd brought to one orgasm after another last night. That, after all, was the magic of it. Half the males and a quarter of the females in Solar System fantasized about sex with Eunice Iverson, the same kind of sex he'd enjoyed last night.

Hardening at the thought, he was about to reach for her when she slipped off the bed, walked naked to his bathroom, and disappeared inside.

Let her empty her bladder. He need only beckon with his little finger, and he'd be sliding his erection back into the most coveted vagina in all of Solar System. He lay back, remembering the widening of her eyes, her intake of breath, those happy moans coming from deep in her throat.

What the hell? He shot a hard look at the bathroom entrance. What was she doing in there? Not like they had an entire morning to spend with her sitting on the . . .

The door opened from the hall, his father striding in. Claudio walked like a man with a purpose, his heels clicking on the translucent floor, the elegant lines of his Dumont-tailored suit flashing in the room's refracted light.

"Klea?" Claudio called. "You are no longer needed. Consider yourself free to go. If you'd like, stop by the breakfast suite. I recommend the quail eggs over caviar on thin-sliced salmon. A car will take you wherever you need to be."

At his words, Klea emerged from the bathroom, a flash of relief quickly covered by that radiant smile that she seemed to produce upon demand. With a slight skip, the woman snagged her Clementine Saffrom evening dress from the floor where it had floated down the night before. She demonstrated remarkable skill and rapidity the way she slipped it on and sealed it around her perfect body. Never even missing a stride when doing it. Then she was out the door.

Claudio stopped at the foot of Dek's bed, stared disdainfully at his fading erection, and said, "Conference room in fifteen minutes. The topic is molybdenum. Projections are that our mining operations in the Hilda Zone are going to be seven percent lower than our target figure. We need to—"

"Wait!" Dek threw himself off the bed, stalking up to his father. "You just dismissed the woman I was—"

"By all that's scintillating, I did just that." Claudio's wicked smile bent his thin lips. "You are my eldest son. Did you think the lessons stopped when you shipped that courtesan whore off to the far reaches of the Solar System?"

"That woman you just dismissed like she was some household servant is Klea Morena! Last night I managed what no other man in this—"

"*You* managed?" Claudio laughed, head thrown back. "Oh, that is rich."

Then his father's designer-gold eyes narrowed. "How naïve are you? You think your charm brought her to your bed?" A hard finger poked into Dek's face. "I won't have you playing Hamlet over your puerile broken heart. So, this is a lesson. Learn it. You are a Taglioni." Claudio pointed at the door. "That woman is one of the most desired in all of human space. And, at my request, she was in your bed last night."

"Your request?" Dek cried incredulously, images of his flirting, of her resistance melting, of his insistence that she . . .

"All these years in this household and you still have no conception of power, do you?"

"Father, you don't get it. She can say no to any man. Klea Morena is no one's courtesan. She's the most celebrated—"

"Of course she is. Why the hell else would I put her in your bed?

You think you dazzled her? You're barely seventeen. And a spoiled prig at that. No, boy, the lesson is that *being* a Taglioni, you can have anything you want. Any woman you desire. Own any person you want. Do you get it? In concert with the other families and the few individuals who have managed to win seats on the Board, we control it all. Everything. And, if it belongs to one of the other families, we can usually barter, buy, or otherwise find a way to obtain our heart's desire." He paused. "Even Klea Morena."

Dek stared at the door where Morena had just vanished like a dream. "You *paid* her to meet me last night?" It still seemed too fantastic to believe, but then, this was Claudio. No doubt it had been orchestrated with the full approval of Malissa, his mother. In fact, he could almost feel her touch in the whole thing: "Darling, let's put Klea Morena in his bed. Slap this foolishness out of his head for once and for all."

Father's smile dripped satisfaction. "Paid? Good heavens, no. I asked. As a favor."

"You just asked? And she came?"

"Boy, I am Claudio Taglioni. When I ask, whatever I ask, it always . . ."

The hiss of quetzal laughter sent a shiver through Dek's gut.

In his mind's eye, Claudio's classically sculpted face began to morph, the beautiful blond hair turning yellow and then blood red. Father's designer-gold eyes merged into a cyclopean sphere that flattened, split into three, and the wide lips stretched into a quetzal's serrated jaws.

"Yeah, figures," Dek whispered dryly. "If ever there was a quetzal in human form, it would be my father." The man who'd snapped his fingers, and with a word, sent one of the most coveted women alive to his son's bed. And, despite all that Klea Morena had been, she'd nevertheless had to comply. Because it was Claudio Taglioni's command.

Dek's gut burned with the injustice of it.

"Hate. Feel it."

At the words, a burning, loathing fire burst through Dek's chest. As it did he reached out, grabbed his despicable wretch of a father by the throat. He chortled with glee, fingers tightening on the man's skin. Claudio's throat collapsed under Dek's iron grip as he crushed the windpipe and larynx. His father's golden eyes began to bulge from their sockets, the man's tongue protruding beyond his teeth as Dek made him suffer for every indignity he'd ever inflicted.

Through gritted teeth, he told his panicked father, "Whatever it takes to rid the world of you, you foul bit of human trash!"

"Dek! Damn it! Wake up."

The words battered their way through the burning hatred. Claudio's purpling face widened, became one with Demon's, frantic and desperate as Dek choked the very life from it.

He felt his body shake, his head jerking back and forth. That implacable voice demanded, "Dek! Wake the fuck up! It's Talina."

He blinked, saw the quetzal image fade into Talina's. Could see the similarity, the differences. "What the . . . ?"

"Who's Klea?"

Dek shook the fragments of images, clinging like cobwebs, from his mind; his body was still riding the adrenaline high of choking his father to death. Burning in hatred and rage. God, he wanted to kill. To burn his father's bones on a pyre of . . .

"Hey! Where are you?"

Dek, fought, managed to clear his head. His hands were knotted so tight the joints ached. Looked around in disbelief as he whispered, "I was in my bedroom. In Taglioni Tower. In Transluna. But I'm . . . in a clearing? What the hell happened? How did you get here? Where are we? What happened to my father? What's happening to me?" He made a face. "And worse, what is that horrible smell?"

Talina hunched over him, her rifle slung across her back. Beyond was Donovan's turquoise sky, dotted with clouds. He could hear the chime. Hard rock ate into his back. Rock? Where the hell was he, anyway?

As Talina plucked a long string of something bloody from her matted hair and tossed it to the side, she said, "Demon's fingering his way through your memories. Experimenting with different ways to stimulate your limbic system. He's learning how to trigger whichever emotional response he thinks might be advantageous when the time comes to turn you into a weapon."

"Shit on a shoe," Dek rubbed his face. Struggled to clear his head. It was true. They were somewhere in the forest, on a hard patch of dark and mineral-speckled gneiss. He could look up at the sheer face of the mountain, see the endless crags, the cracked and implacable rock that rose to towering heights against the morning sky. All in all, a damn stunning view. But how had he gotten here?

"So, who's Klea?"

"Klea Morena."

"The actor? The one who played Priss Talahan? Eunice Iverson? Seela Fitch? That one?"

"That's her."

"No wonder your flagpole was at full mast and you were sweating pheromones like an elephant in must. And that's just for the fantasy version."

"Nothing fantasy about it."

Talina's gaze narrowed. "You're kidding. You mean to tell me—"

"You *don't* want to know." He struggled to sit up. "Where the hell are we? I have a vague memory of mobbers. That shit of a quetzal must have picked them from my memory. From when I was . . ." He stopped, staring at the bits and pieces of gore that were scattered about, at the bloody spatters and chunks of tissue that clung to his coveralls. A red string of guts hung down from his shoulders. A severed mobber's head, the three eyes staring, lay next to his boot.

And then the stench began to make sense.

Talina flicked a chunk of bloody tissue from her shoulder as she stood. "That was real. And they were dropping down to turn you into a thin-sliced meal when I finally caught up with you."

"That's why he let me go," Dek realized. "Demon was scared of the mobbers."

"Yeah. Find something that terrifies him. It's one of the few ways you can learn to kick the miserable shit out of your head." She helped him to his feet. "Come on. We have to get back to the dome. Wash the mobber guts out of my hair and clothes. It's about a kilometer.

How you made it this far is beyond my understanding. You should have been a meal five times over."

"I was a quetzal." Dek let her lead the way, appalled by the carnage littering the rock. Invertebrates were already flocking to the bits and chunks, swarming the still-dying mobbers that flopped on the unforgiving rock. "Where's my rifle?"

"Back at the dome. The last place it should be. I burned up a whole magazine on that flock. I'm empty. Out of rounds. And covered in blood and guts like we are, who knows what kind of predator we'll attract. Which is why we need to beat feet back to the barn before one of those flying freaks gets the bright idea to come back and finish what they were starting."

"On Donovan," Dek quoted, "a full magazine trumps all the mystical teachings in the universe."

"Been hanging around Shig, huh?" She stomped a bleating mobber dead with a hard heel, led the way to the north edge of the outcrop, parted the still-agitated leaves, and started down the steep slope.

"I don't want to live like this. It's reliving hell."

"I don't know what your version of hell is."

"That rage you shook me out of? I was strangling my father with my bare hands."

"Must be fun to be at your house for family time at Christmas."

"We don't celebrate Christmas. Holidays are for lesser beings who are in need of occasional relief from the drudgery of their normal lives." He felt a sense of relief to be back in the forest, away from the ruination of blasted wings, guts, and blown-apart bodies.

"If that's how your dad feels, I'll strangle him for you."

"Trade you my Christmas for yours," he told her as he ducked a vine and willed his feet to find the same purchase she'd used to descend the squirming roots onto the dim root mat at the bottom of the slope. As he did, he let the memory come. "I can smell it. See the steam rising off that pot on the stove. The one with the dent. There are big red tiles on the floor, and the table is a ponderous wooden thing. You are putting some kind of stoneware plates on the—"

"Hey." She turned, an angry frown marring the smooth lines of her forehead. "You have that? In your head? In that kind of detail?"

"Yeah. But this time the bowl isn't there. I see your mother. A tall woman, thin, her hair in a ponytail that hangs down her back. She's wearing a white cotton dress with a floral pattern. Stops at her knees. Muscular brown calves. She's wearing sandals. And her smile. . . . I like that about her. How she—"

"Stop." Talina started off again, moving fast, the set of her shoulders reflecting her irritation. "How much more of me is inside that head of yours?"

"Makes me jealous."

"What? Sharing my memories?"

"No. That your mother loved you like that."

onovanian TriNA. If the stories were true, the molecules were a
nightmare turned real, an insidious presence that crept into the
blood and took over a person's body. Especially children. They had
all heard the stories about Kylee Simonov, who was so wild she'd
never set foot in Port Authority.

Michaela had met Talina Perez, looked into the woman's inhuman eyes, tried not to stare at her peculiar cheekbones or the alien
shape of her face. She'd felt as if Perez was something "other." Just
being in her presence had been upsetting. That she'd almost murdered other human beings while under the influence of alien TriNA
made her even more disturbing.

Now they were afraid of it here? Among one of the children?
Was little Toni, too, going to become a half-human monster like
the Perez woman?

"I don't even know what I'm looking for," Vik Lawrence muttered in a harried voice as she peered into her microscope's imaging
screen.

Michaela had followed the microbiologist into the lab after the
breakfast dishes had been cleared. Not that anyone was getting
much done, most of her people finding ways to stand around in
little groups with like-minded friends, all trying to figure out what
Toni's paralysis meant. Discussing whether they should or shouldn't
fly the little boy to Port Authority. Periodically checking on their
own children, alarmed to find that most had a slight fever, muscle
aches, and sore joints.

Iso was giving Felicity aspirin and had confined her to bed. She
said that she was sweating enough to stain the sheets. Anna had
checked her and could find no sign of fever or incipient paralysis like
Toni exhibited. But her sweat remained curiously slick, almost oily.

Gabarron—never anyone's favorite given her usually sour

disposition—was now on call, going from kid to kid, taking temperatures and blood samples, peering into eyes with her scope, and tapping on chests and bellies.

For their part, the children were adamantly maintaining that none of them had ever, ever, taken anything from Iso's storage closet. They all swore that not one of them had seen Toni playing with any detergent bottles or cans of any kind of oil or lubricant. And that was probably true. Not only were the toxic chemicals all accounted for, but the children were constantly underfoot, always within sight of an adult. The only time they were ever unsupervised was when they were in "science club" in the observation blister. Whatever science club was.

Nothing that resembled oil had been in the observation blister. The place consisted of a transparent dome with cushioned benches. Period. The safest place on the Pod for a kid to be.

Toni's exposure remained a mystery.

The bio lab where Michaela watched over Vik's shoulder was on the Pod's west side, second level, directly over the living quarters. Scientific and diagnostic equipment packed the room, everything necessary for a preliminary cataloging and study of Donovanian marine life. It had microscopes, FTIR, genetic sequencers, its own dedicated quantum computer, centrifuges, racks of test tubes and sample jars, imaging equipment, spectrometry, freezers, a Level 5 biohazard unit and incinerator, hood, and vent, as well as a myriad of other tools and chemicals.

"So, here's what I've done," Vik said. "I've used the centrifuge to precipitate some of those seawater samples that Kevina collected. I've siphoned off the liquid, leaving a sludge consisting of microorganisms. This, I've placed on the slide and stained. And wow. It's a whole wild and incredible biota the likes of which I've never seen. But, that said, the plankton morphology could almost be terrestrial. I stress the word *almost*. I mean, there's claws, cilia, eyes, scales, limbs. First thing that's readily different? Trilateral symmetry in all the multicellular organisms. The stuff we might equate with plankton. Second thing that pops? When you increase the magnification, all of these lifeforms are composed of prokaryotic cells. That means no nucleus."

"Same as the land-based organisms."

"Right. But it's still early in the cataloging process." She pointed to a row of sample jars. "I still have a backlog of thirty samples that Yosh, Kevina, and Odinga want analyzed. The memorials have me three days behind on running them. Maybe when I can get to them we will find eukaryotes in one of the more complex and advanced marine organisms. Maybe an order that hasn't transitioned to land."

Vik glanced sidelong at Michaela. "Our job is to check the boy for TriNA. To do that, we've got to isolate some TriNA and feed the data into the scope. I've chosen a single-celled specimen from one of Kevina's original water samples as the easiest source for locating TriNA. Keep your eyes on the screen."

Michaela crowded close, watching as the tube-shaped image of a microorganism resolved. "Do we still call it a cell?"

"Might as well. The gross morphology I'm seeing here is no different than a bacterium on Earth." She used a pointer. "Here's the cell wall." She checked a readout as she used her pointer to delineate a section of the wall and clicked. "Got the same polysaccharides and peptides, which we expected from the original survey research. The theory is that organic chemistry—being the same all across the universe—will have the same structure and function on Donovan as it does on Earth. Carbon, hydrogen, oxygen, and nitrogen only fit together in so many ways. At the atomic level, chemistry has to follow the rules of covalence and bonding. Can only form so many shapes of molecules here or back home. The simplest organic molecules to do the job will be the most likely molecules that life will use."

Vik dialed up the magnification, used her pointer to mark another small box inside the cellular wall, and clicked. Again, she studied the readout. "That's the plasma membrane. Again, no surprises. Could be terrestrial chemistry with a few oddities. I'm seeing a bilayer composed of phospholipids and proteins."

Vik outlined a box in the cytoplasm and clicked. "Okay, this is a little different. These structures here? Essentially they serve as the ribosomes. The architecture is almost the same with some variations in morphology compared to what we see on Earth. Fits the model. If you are making proteins with RNA, how many different ways can nature engineer that factory? In fact, mix ribosomal proteins and rRNAs together in vitro and they'll reform into a functional ribosome. That's just chemistry."

Now Vik stared thoughtfully. "Here's a big difference, Michaela. I should see what we call a nucleoid where the DNA is. I'm not getting one." Vik increased the magnification, searching through the granular image, and stopped. As she enlarged the image, what looked like a traditional S-twist, tightly wrapped and knotty rope seemed to emerge in the cytoplasm.

"What's that?"

"I think that's our mysterious TriNA. Let me get a better perspective." Vik blocked it, clicked, and stared at her screen. "The scope tags its chemical signature as deoxyribonucleic acid." A pause. "But we know it isn't. Structure's wrong. It's not a double helix. It's a rope-shaped, three-strand molecule." She smiled. "Wow! It's like, real, you know?"

"Glad you're so thrilled."

"Hey, Michaela, I'm looking at three-strand DNA that I just resolved on my own scope. This is life on another planet. Proof. What I came here to see. And this is just the first step."

"Okay, so jazz over it later. Record it so we know what we're looking for."

"Just like the reports from PA, it's a lot stiffer, bent around more like a wad of wire than the way DNA's double helix can be compacted into chromatids. Wow. This is going to be a whole new world of polymerases, histones, helicases, and binding proteins. Let me get some more images."

Michaela waited while Vik changed the angle and clicked, all the while building a three-dimensional model on the screen. When she was finished, she cycled the slide and slipped in one that she had precipitated from Toni's blood sample.

Vik wiggled her fingers, as if tuning them like a maestro at the keyboard. "All right, if Dr. Turnienko suspects TriNA, our first task is to see if it's what we call cell-free. That means it would be circulating in Toni's bloodstream. Or, at least, that's what we're going to test for to start with. Recovering cfDNA is a relatively easy procedure using centrifugation. I've processed Toni's blood, and it should be ready."

She slipped from the chair, stepped to the centrifuge, and recovered a tube. Placing it in one of her machines, she monitored a screen as the supernatant was removed. Then the sample was automatically transferred to the slide, stained, and presented behind a transparent door.

Vik carefully removed the slide, carried it over, and placed it in her scope.

"Truth time," she murmured. "Let's see if anything is running around in Toni's blood."

Michaela watched the microscope adjust magnification, its programming searching the slide for anything that might have resembled the TriNA molecule they'd recorded in the prokaryote cell.

The haze on the screen refined, the image firming up.

Michaela, of course, recognized the intertwined spaghetti of DNA, which was what the centrifugation protocol and methodology was designed to recover. And there, right in the middle of the tangle of DNA, like a bent-up and coiled wire, was the now-familiar form.

"What the hell?" Michaela wondered. "TriNA. But, where did he get it?"

"And more to the point," Vik noted as she began to scan the slide, picking up the twisted-wire form again and again, "Where did Toni get so much of it?"

"Go back a couple of steps," Michaela suggested. "Do you still have the pellet you recovered from Toni's blood after centrifugation?"

"Of course."

"Check it. See if you can recover anything larger. Maybe a cell."

"Got it."

Vik stepped over to her centrifuge, gave it a command for a sample reference. Again, the drawer popped open, a slide prepared. This she brought back to the microscope and inserted.

The scope searched the slide, changing magnifications, and the first thing that popped was the familiar image of red blood cells, the occasional, much larger white blood cells, and there, in the plasma, something that appeared as a blanket-like honeycomb of cells.

"What's that?" Michaela pointed.

Vik boxed it, clicked, and the image expanded to fill the screen. "I'll be damned. But wait. Let me get a three-dimensional look with X-ray and resonance." The woman's competent fingers clicked several of the keys, and the image seemed to pop from the screen, to fix on one of the hexagonally shaped cells, its internal structure in eerie relief.

"So, it has a different morphology from that first reference prokaryote we recovered from seawater." Michaela pointed. "What are these structures?"

Vik again boxed and clicked, looked at the internally folded organelles, and clicked on the FTIR function. "I'd call them the Donovanian equivalent of a terrestrial chloroplast. Whatever this is, it's capable of photosynthesis."

"Some sort of plant cells? In the kid's blood?"

Vik's jaw had tensed. "Not a plant, Michaela. I'm not reading cellulose. The structural support is some kind of polymer. This is nothing from Earth. Besides, terrestrial plant cells have a nucleus. This thing is a combination of weird organelles the likes of which I've never seen."

Vik boxed a section of cytoplasm, clicked, and enlarged. "Got you, you toilet-sucker." She glanced sidelong at Michaela. "Recognize that?"

"Yep. TriNA." A cold shiver ran through her. "Toni's got some kind of colony living inside of him that's made up of photosynthesizing cells. And his blood is full of cell-free TriNA."

"So, what do we do now, Director?"

"Vik, I don't have a fricking clue. I can't even imagine what kind of etiology we're talking about. But however Toni was exposed, it's all through the kid's body."

"Doesn't make sense!" Vik cried. "That little boy has never been outside the Pod. This is a photosynthesizing cellular organism. How is it living inside the child's body? There is no way it could have infected him. The kid's three!"

"No clue," Michaela told her. "But one thing we'd better figure out bottom-line up-front: Is this stuff contagious?"

Vik didn't answer; she just stared at the screen.

Thinking of her daughter, Sheena, no doubt.

42

Felix hated being scared. And now he was really, really scared. One by one he and the rest of the children had been marched up the now-threatening stairs to the second level. A forbidden place of mystery and wonder with its labs and specimen rooms, everything up there reeked of danger and threat. Like it had been back on *Ashanti* where cannibals were down on Deck Three. Living there. Just under that thin layer of sialon beneath his feet. Everyone was afraid that they might get past the sealed hatch, creep up the stairs at night, and kidnap people to be hauled back down into that dark and terrible place to be horribly killed, cut up into bloody pieces, and eaten.

The Pod had been free of monsters. The first safe place Felix had ever known. There were no cannibals, no terrifying monsters that would drag a kid away from his parents and, in this case, up dark stairs to some awful fate.

That had all changed. Some creepy alien thing had sneaked into Toni's body and made him sick. Word was Toni couldn't move. That he was still trapped inside, alive, but that creatures were running around in his blood. Doing evil things.

What would that feel like? To have aliens crawling around inside his veins and swimming in his blood? The whole idea made Felix's skin crawl. Made him want to go stand in the shower where anything that might get on him would be washed away before it could eat a hole into his skin and crawl inside him.

But the worst part was that Toni had been put inside something called an isolation tent. He was now living inside a big plastic bag. The air he breathed was cycled in from outside, and then sent out through a vent pipe that heated it really hot before blowing it outside again. So hot that nothing could live.

Felix now sat in his room, his skin itching. It had been itching for days, but nothing like this. Had to be because he was afraid of itty-bitty aliens creeping around, looking for a place that they could crawl inside him.

He shook himself all over, pulled off his shirt, was looking for any sign of crawly . . .

The door opened, Mother stepping in. She had that look on her face. The one she got when things were really bad.

"Why is your shirt off?"

"Nothing. I was just looking at it." He tried to frown studiously at the fabric.

"How do you feel, Felix?"

"I'm fine," he lied. He didn't dare tell Mother his skin itched, or that it felt slightly greasy. Just like his fingers always felt ever since he and Mother had taken the boat ride out to drop the buoy. The itch and greasy feeling had been getting a lot worse ever since Toni had spilled the algae all over.

Then Mother was bent down, her gray-blue eyes serious. "Baby, you have to promise me. If you start feeling sick, you let me know. Let me know right away, okay, sweetie?"

Felix nodded. He hated it when she called him *baby*. He was eight, after all. "I will."

Did he tell her about the way his body jerked all by itself? Or how, on occasion, his vision would get funny, runny, and full of colors? And there was something going on that he couldn't quite understand. Sometimes he'd think about reaching for something. Just think about it. And his arm would do it. All by itself. Even if he kept willing his arm to stay put.

Mother was staring hard at him now. "I know that look. Is something wrong? Are you feeling sick? Hiding it from me?"

"No, Mama." He felt better and gave her a relieved smile. Things like feeling oily and his arms doing stuff he didn't ask them to, that was different. He'd been sick before and thrown up, and his guts had hurt. What he was going through was really different from being sick.

Mother clamped a hand to his forehead, feeling for fever. Then, relieved, she straightened. "I've got to go. We're taking the subs out today, and with Shin gone, I have to monitor the control board. I want you to go to the cafeteria. The other children will be there. Bill can keep an eye on you, and Iso will be in and out checking."

"What about Toni?"

"Sweetie, Toni's really sick. We can't figure out where he could have come in contact with TriNA. We've been so careful about the sample collection. And Toni has never been out of the Pod. He couldn't have touched the subs or the UUVs. We're doing everything we can to trace the etiology of the contamination."

Felix wondered what *etiology of contamination* meant.

She gave him a relieved smile. "Okay, I'm off for the tube. You trot yourself down to the cafeteria, and you don't leave until either Father or I come to get you. Got that?"

"Yes, Mother."

"Then, off you go." She pointed at the door.

Felix led the way. After she turned off and worked the pressure hatch for the tube that would take her down to the Underwater Bay, Felix stopped at the cafeteria door. Willed himself to stand still. Then he lifted his right arm, extended his hand to the door latch. Didn't touch it.

Lowering his arm, he willed himself to keep his arm still. Focusing on the latch—but ordering his arm to stay put—he nevertheless watched it rise, felt the touch of the latch as his arm opened the door.

How weird was that?

43

Dressed in a chamois-hide shirt, claw-shrub-fiber pants belted at the waist, and her quetzal-hide boots, Kalico straight-armed the door to the conference room in the big dome. She wasn't sure how this was going to go. Her crew chiefs, engineers, and head techs were all seated around the table, some standing in the rear.

She had thought to hold this in the cafeteria, with all of her one hundred and thirteen people. But not after that debacle back in the Pod. Not that her people were anything like the Maritime Unit, but fact was, Kalico felt gun-shy after the lambasting she'd taken. Far better that she limit this to her administrative staff. She'd still get a feel for the mood her people were in.

"Where are we? Any news?" she demanded as she took the sole open seat at the head of the table.

Desch shook his head, eyes lowered. "No news, Supervisor. Jin and Masters volunteered to stay at the portal. Last I talked to them, maybe fifteen minutes ago, they said that but for a couple of rumbles, the tunnel's quiet. They've wired geophones into the rock. Clever of them, actually. But even with the extra sensitivity, there's nothing resembling a human sound. No tapping, nothing rhythmic. Most of what they're hearing sounds like fill settling. If they're interpreting the sounds right, the void migration has slowed. The fill has probably about used up the volume."

Kalico looked around, going from face to face. "Where're Bogarten and Talovich? They should be here."

Ghosh leaned forward at the table, rubbing his tired face with dirty hands. "They're down at the river with a couple of aquajade beams that had been laying around. Talovich has taken this hard, Supervisor. He thinks it's somehow his fault. That he didn't figure the load-bearing design right. He's trying—"

"Excuse me? You're telling me that my structural engineer and my top chemist and fabricator are down at the river? Alone? That while we're sitting here, some quetzal or flock of mobbers might be chowing down on two of my most important people? I gave them *an order*! They trying to get themselves eaten? Or shot?"

Ghosh gave her a bleary-eyed stare, a trace of a smile on his lips. "Talovich said you'd say that. Neither, ma'am. They took two of the marines, Abu Sassi and Dina Michegan, in armor and with tech, to watch their backs. That should keep them from being eaten. And Talovich said if he couldn't figure out what he'd done wrong, he deserved to be shot."

Kalico narrowed an eye, felt the building rage shift into a macabre sense of amusement. Piss in a pot, she'd been on Donovan for too long. That, and her people knew her too well.

"All right. They get a break this time. Unless this goes sideways, and we lose somebody else." She considered as they watched her, their expressions running the gamut from worry to outright grief. "No one ever said that any of this would be easy. And I think we were getting too cocky. Think about it. We've won every battle. Built the smelter, beat back the forest, exterminated the local mobbers, learned how to mine the Number One and Number Two, made ourselves richer than half the Boardmembers in Transluna. We're growing our own food. We've figured out how to build whatever we need, almost from scratch. We've got eleven families with kids."

"The Number Three shouldn't have collapsed," Desch insisted doggedly. "We weren't cocky, Supervisor. Sure, it was a risky business, shooting our way through that shocked-rock zone. But Ghosh, Bogarten, me, Talovich . . . all of us . . . we figured out how to do it. We all double-checked the math, tested the shoring. The geometry was right. The shoring should have taken the load. That's just physics and solid engineering. We've been beating our heads against the wall 'cause what happened shouldn't have."

Ghosh added, "And we need the Number Three, ma'am. As deep as we are in the mountain with the Number One and Two, we can't pump out the water make. Our pumps, running round the clock, can barely keep up. Any deeper and we either need more or bigger pumps."

Kalico leaned back, ran a finger along the scar on her cheek. "Hell of a thing, to be stopped by water after all we've been through. Can we make a bigger pump?"

Ghosh nodded. "Bogarten, Stryski, and I can draw up the plans. We'll need Lawson and Montoya to help fabricate, along with Mac Hanson to cast the housing up at PA. That's just for the pump. Problem comes with the hose. We'll need to fabricate that. The larger the diameter, the stronger it has to be to keep it from collapsing under vacuum. And then there's the power. We're going to have to figure how much the water weighs, friction in the line, what the load is, and how much horsepower we're going to need. That means we're going to have to see if we can generate that kind of electrical power."

Ituri tapped an index finger on the table as he asked, "Or do we want to use hydrocarbons? See if we can broker something with Ollie Throlson for a supply of diesel? Might be easier to run it on internal combustion than build the electric motor and generate the power."

"We've got a slew of electric motors in old equipment that's just laying around outside PA's landing field." Stryski reminded them as he joined the conversation. "Most of the motors are essentially new. The equipment was abandoned in the first place because of a lack of spare parts that had nothing to do with the engines."

"Easier than building a diesel from scratch," Ghosh agree. "But that leaves us back with the generator. Maybe one of the reactors from *Freelander*?"

Kalico said, "We've had this conversation before, gentlemen. If you'll recall, we figured it was easier to make holes and let gravity drain water from below than to pump water uphill from above."

"Got an idea?"

"No," Kalico said with a sigh. The notion that Alia and Stana's corpses were lying down there in the waterlogged blackness, under tons of broken rock, kept haunting her. "My call? We refocus on the

Number Two. Maybe run a couple of lateral drifts off the main stope that follow the uplift's strike northwest. That will keep the crews busy while we figure out what the hell went wrong in the Number Three."

"We don't know what's in the mountain in that direction," Ghosh reminded. "Let alone what cutting through that rock will contribute to the water make. We might drift that way and find nothing worth the cost of the magtex."

Kalico arched an eyebrow. "Bet you didn't know it, but there's a mining term for what we're going to be doing."

Ghosh glanced nervously back and forth. "Yes, Supervisor?"

"It's called prospecting."

Ghosh almost hid his flinch.

"So . . . ?" Ituri asked, "We're just giving up on the Number Three?"

Kalico traced her index finger down the scar on the line of her jaw. "We de-boarded *Turalon* with a little over three hundred people. Some spaced back to Solar System on *Turalon*. Some ran off to the bush or otherwise took their own fate in their hands. Some killed themselves. We came down here to Corporate Mine with one hundred and ninety-seven. A handful of us spaced back on *Ashanti*. I shot a couple. A few were deserters. Three were murdered. Most of the rest were taken by quetzals, mobbers, a couple by slugs, and some of the other wildlife. After the cave-in, we're down to one hundred and thirteen of us."

Every eye in the room was watching her.

"We're a tight bunch here. We've made this our home. This mine is ours. Each and every one of us pitches in and does more than his or her share. Not a one of us is the same person who first set foot here. What you will earn by fulfilling your contracts will make you all rich back in Solar System. Think about it. That's a lot of credit in the system. You'll have the finest apartments, health care, pretty much anything you requisition through The Corporation. You'd never want for anything again."

Heads were nodding around the table.

She added, "And compared to the plunder you're taking back

home, everything you've earned through Contract is like a pit-
tance." She paused. "When you go back, it will be to a different
Corporation. Just by showing up, wealthy as you will be, nothing
will ever be the same. The reason I bring this up is because I want
you all to have the chance. I want you to make it home and show
those white-assed Corporate bastards what it means to take a risk
and have it pay off. I want you all to stick it to them."

Ghosh leaned back, straight-armed, from the table. "You sound
like you're not going."

Kalico shrugged. "I don't know if I can. Shig doesn't think so.
Neither does Derek Taglioni. They think I belong to Donovan
now. That somehow I wouldn't fit into Transluna high society with
my scars, pistol, and quetzal-hide cloak."

That brought a round of laughter.

"So, hell, Ghosh. I don't know what I'll decide in the end, but it
will be a while before I make the trip back to Transluna." Assuming
she ever did. "Meanwhile, I want us all to stand down for the next
couple of days. We need to figure this thing out. Determine what
went wrong. We owe it to Alia and Stana to make sure it never
happens again."

44

Three different times Talina had had to slap Dek Taglioni free of Demon's hold. The miracle was that—smelling like a tasty Donovanian meal of blood and raw meat—they'd made it back across that kilometer of forest to the Two Falls Gap dome. She'd fretted the entire trip, driven by the gnawing realization that she was traveling with an empty rifle. Didn't matter that nine times out of ten when she crossed forest, she'd never fired a shot. Just the knowledge that her gun was empty left her feeling as vulnerable and exposed as parading naked down the central avenue in Port Authority.

They were back in the dome, her rifle safely reloaded and racked beside the door. Tal had used a hose to rinse off their gore-covered clothes, and they'd both showered. She'd needed most of a half hour to get the blood and guts out of her hair. Still didn't feel wholly clean, but it had a glossy feel and sleek sheen as she dragged her comb through it.

Dek had insisted on cooking. Said it kept Demon from taking over his thoughts. She had finished eating first, washed her plate. Now she leaned against the wall, crossed her arms, and watched Dek finish off the last of his breakfast of sautéed vegetables. What the hell was she going to do with the guy?

Klea Morena? Seriously?

She'd pried the story out of him on the way back as they dodged tooth flower, claw shrub, three sidewinders, and a bem trying to imitate a boulder on an outcrop. She tried to get her head around the notion that Dek's father could just ask a woman like Klea to hop into bed with his spoiled teenage son, and the poor woman couldn't afford to say no. What kind of power was that? What did it say about the kind of system The Corporation had become?

"So, who is the real Derek Taglioni?" Talina wondered under her breath.

"You're not the only one wondering that," Dek said after he swallowed a last forkful of broccoli.

"Forgot you've got quetzal hearing now. I'm going to have to bite my tongue."

"Don't. It hurts too much . . . and the scabs get in the way of tasting a good wine." Dek used a sleeve to wipe his mouth.

Talina figured old Claudio would have burst a vein if he could have seen his son do that.

Dek took his plate, walked over to the sink, and washed it. Placing it on the rack next to Talina's, he turned, thoughtful yellow-green eyes on hers. "So, let me help you with your little problem. I told you, you're getting glimpses of my hell. I grew up as a Taglioni."

"You grew up like a sadistic Roman emperor. So, tell me, given all that, what makes you worth my time?"

He turned, giving her a thoughtful stare. "You and Kalico thought I had a death wish when I got here. After my family, after the horror of surviving *Ashanti*, it was more of a life wish. It didn't matter how long I lived. Hours, days, weeks, or months. I just needed to live. Free. On my own terms. I needed to be respected for being the kind of man I am, not who I was."

Dek smiled, paused, then said, "I was there, Tal. I made it. And then this damn quetzal comes along and starts dragging me right back down that same damn wormhole. Back into a universe I'd mostly come to think of as a bad dream. And I can't shake it. Like right now, I can feel Demon inside my brain. Like he's hovering over my memories, peering down into them, figuring out which one he's going to pull from the bin and replay for my own personal humiliation and self-loathing."

"Sorry about that. But, given what you just told me, would you rather I had let you die that day out at your claim?"

"For that kiss? I guess, win, lose, or draw, it was worth it."

"You've got to be kidding."

"Marry me."

"What?"

He gave her a wistful smile. "Ah, there, see? That hesitation, the instant disbelief. That's the same response you'd give Stepan

Allenovich if he asked you. And, yes, you respect Step for his abilities as a man on Donovan. But he's not worthy of you. I plan to be. In spite of my past and who I was."

She threw her hands up. "Pay attention here. Step's a philandering, whoring, drinking gambler. He's not my kind of man."

"Damn straight he's not. But I intend to be when I get this *thing* out of my head."

"Thought you understood the biology. It's all through you. And it's not going away."

He seemed to sober. "Yeah. Guess I'm not sure who or what I'm going to be when this is finished." His eyes started to lose focus, and with effort, he got control again. "I'd die for you, you know."

"Why?"

"Because that's what love's all about, Talina."

45

Michaela and her team had chosen the Pod's location based on the original Donovanian surveys conducted by ships like *Tempest* and the ill-fated *Impala* before she vanished on her second spacing to Donovan.

The reef where *Ashanti*'s shuttles had dropped the Pod registered as being particularly high in metals during the remote-sensor planetary scans. If the models were correct, the strata had been pushed up from the mantle, first by the impact, and subsequently by the quakes and altered tectonic pressures left in the impact's wake.

The Maritime Unit should be sitting on some of Donovan's oldest rocks. Perhaps strata that dated back to just after the formation of the planet. From comparisons against baseline data derived from *Impala*'s initial survey, Michaela hoped that Varina Tam—their expert in planetary evolution and physical oceanography—could begin to assemble a tectonic model for Donovan. Tam hoped to identify, date, and track the movement of the crustal plates and how they interacted to form Donovanian seas. From there—working in tandem with Lara Sanz—it had been hoped that they would start the process of piecing together a history and theory of the planet's oceans and marine phenomena. Now Kevina Schwantz would step into Lara's shoes as the backup marine geologist.

Today Michaela and her team would take both submarines, working in tandem, with Michaela and Casey in the second sub providing cover as Jaim Elvridge piloted the first sub in accordance with Varina's instructions. As Varina began her mapping and sample collection transect from the surface down to two thousand meters, Michaela and Casey—armed with the new compressed-air-driven torpedo—would stand guard and keep watch for any threats appearing out of the deep.

In the event that any large predators like the BMT approached,

it would be Michaela and Casey's job to first threaten, and finally—
if no other option presented—to shoot the thing with the explosive
torpedo Kel and Tobi had cobbled together.

If the torpedo had no effect, the two subs would link up with the
grapples, blow ballast, and retreat together to the safety of the Pod's
Underwater Bay.

At least, that was the plan. The agreement was that anyone per-
ceiving a threat—be it from some leviathan down to jellyfish—
could call off the mission. On that they had total unanimity.

Michaela, however, didn't anticipate trouble. Fact was, unlike the
circumstances where they'd lost Shin and Lara, no one was exposed.
She could think of no place safer than being inside one of the subs.
The vessels were Seascape Model 15s. They weighed tons and were
constructed of steel, graphite fiber, sialon, and thick vacuum-formed
drop-forged glass. Not exactly the savory mouthful of organic
goodness that would appeal to any denizen of Donovan's deep.

Michaela sat in the elevated commander's chair behind the glass
transparency in the nose, while Casey Stoner sat in the driver's seat
ahead and below. The controls were situated so that the commander
was sort of piggyback with the driver's head between the commander's feet. Both had a complete one hundred-and-eighty-degree
view. Call it the next best thing to being in open ocean.

Using her implants, Michaela interfaced directly with the submarine's lights, diving controls, remote mechanical arms, and ballast.
With a simple command, she could aim and fire the torpedo.

The main cabin behind her had additional view ports as well as
workstations and seating that would accommodate an additional
two occupants. For this initial run, Michaela had made the decision
that it would only be the two of them. Assured as she was that this
initial voyage was low-risk, she was nevertheless unwilling to place
any additional personnel in jeopardy.

The others would be watching from the monitors aboard the
Pod, and those with research interests would be able to make requests of the subs' occupants if they saw anything through either of
the Seascapes' cameras that piqued their interests. Michaela suspected that group participation would be anything but limited. In

fact, she suspected that once they got in position, the requests would be coming so fast and furious that she'd have to referee, or they'd never get past twenty meters.

"Ready to go?" Casey called up from the driver's seat.

"We're tight and charged," Michaela told the woman as she checked the heads-up display where the sub's systems were displayed. "Varina? Are you a 'go' for submersion?"

"Roger that, Director. Tight and charged."

"Kevina, how do you read?"

"My readouts for both subs are all green. I read tight and fully charged. Telemetry is at one hundred percent. Every system on my board is a go. You're a go for launch."

"Let's do this, people. Tobi, put us in the water."

Michaela felt the vehicle shove forward on its track. Through the sub's transparency she watched the Underwater Bay's interior slide past. Then, at the edge of the pool, the sub's nose dropped and Michaela felt herself tilt forward.

She saw the thick blue-green scum clinging to the side of the pool. The stuff that looked like algae. Yosh's sample was still in Vik Lawrence's backlog of specimens, waiting to be put under the scope and catalogued. In the days since they'd set the Pod, the pilings and the entire underbelly had collected a coating. In places it looked like it was ten centimeters thick and had started to climb up the Pod walls.

Not that it would be a problem. Ruto said he'd been able to dislodge entire colonies with a power washer where they were creeping out onto the Underwater Bay floor.

Then Michaela watched water rise around the sub's nose as they slipped into the crystalline depths. A few bubbles trickled up around the transparency as Casey released the grapples, kicked on the motors, and sent them down and right to clear the way for Varina's sub. As they passed from under the Pod's shadow, the view was stunning.

Capella's rays danced in shafts as they refracted down through the swells to illuminate a wondrous aquatic world. Here was a wealth of fascinating biota. Michaela didn't know what else to call it. Sure, it was easy to bias the nomenclature and call the blue-green growths sprouting from the sea floor plants, but were they? Falling into terrestrial terminology and classification before actually studying the specimens, was—if Donovanian land-based life was any guide—nothing more than a spurious exercise in futility.

What she saw here was a wonderland of strange life-forms, some of it stemmed and sporting paddles, some a collection of waving green tendrils, others like a corona of stalks and pods, many of them incredibly colorful as they opened and closed. Here and there, taller specimens sent spears up that were covered with leaves or tentacles, sometimes with fan-like appendages, and even what looked like flexible arms with multi-fingered hands that fished around and tried to grab the zipping tubes as they squirted past. No matter how bizarrely different this was from Earth's oceans, what was rapidly apparent was trilateral symmetry.

"Holy wow!" Casey gasped as a school of paper-thin creatures flashed past the transparency in a full spectrum of color. In an instant, they flipped sideways, so thin they vanished into seeming nothingness.

"*We're right behind you,*" Jaim's voice came through Michaela's com. "*We're passing to your right and above. We're going to start taking samples at the five-meter mark on the transect.*"

"Roger that," Michaela told her. "We're flipping on the instruments. We'll take station ten meters off your stern and match depth." In her monitors she kept track of the second sub as it passed above, turned into the reef, and nosed close to the bottom so that Varina could begin taking samples with the sub's extendable arms. Even as she did, the observers in the Pod began chattering. Michaela deleted the distraction, setting her com to react if a request was directed to her.

To Casey, she said, "Point us out toward deepwater. I'm turning on the sonar."

"Got it. And I've got Jaim and Varina's location on my instruments. They're nosing into position now."

Michaela watched as the sub's orientation shifted, swinging them around to the open water where it shone in a marvelous turquoise that seemed to fade into infinity. Beams of light danced from the waves above, reminding her of the magic of being underwater. The heads-up display reflected sonar hits on tubes and other creatures as tiny blips of yellow on the screen.

"Michaela?" Varina's voice came through the com, *"Try the hydrophones. You've got to hear this. You'll need to use the program to mask the mechanical sound of the subs, but this is amazing."*

"Roger that." Michaela accessed her implants to turn on the hydrophones, overwhelmed at first by the wealth of sound. Then, from memory, she used the program to remove the hum from the electric motors on the two subs.

"How do you describe that?" Casey asked as she established neutral buoyancy at a depth of five meters, her eyes on the instruments.

"Like that sound you hear when an orchestra is tuning up before playing a symphony." Michaela made a face. "But not really. There's so much more range here above and below our hearing. I'm getting readings from four hertz to two hundred and twenty kilohertz. It's the tremolo, the harmony, almost a rhythm. Then there's the bumping bass. Deep thrumming. A chorus of sound. Like nothing I've ever heard. Even more complex than the chime we heard outside Port Authority."

"You ask me," Casey told her, "the whole ocean is singing."

For long moments, they just sat there listening. Fascinated and not a little awed as tubes darted past the transparency and occasionally hit it hard enough to give off soft thumps.

Michaela got a ping on sonar, watching the Doppler that marked the creature's approach from off to the left. Given the signal return, it measured close to four meters, but seeing it appear out of the blue, first as a shadow, only to solidify into a four-flippered . . . No, that was wrong. These were like four underwater wings that shot the organism forward, then, at sight of the sub, flashed to spin the creature into an impossible right-angled flight where it disappeared into the distance.

"Nothing can move like that," Michaela whispered her awe. She pulled up the visual recorded by the camera, studied the beast closely. Got a really good look at the head with its meter-long, needle-like beak that parted into three jaws, an eye behind each. The body was covered by what looked like pelage rather than scales or skin. It changed from blue to red and then bright yellow as the organism spun and fled. The mobility came from the four wings. They allowed the creature to turn in its own length. To Michaela's eye, the wings might have been feathered, or rather, some morphological feature that might have served a similar function. She ached to have a sample so that she could work out the physics of how the structures would function in a liquid rather than gaseous medium. What kind of drag would they have? Did they achieve lamellar flow, or maybe serve as compressors to shoot water back as they contracted with each stroke? Or did they function like an anhinga's wing back on Earth?

"Did you catch the sound?" Casey asked. "How it changed when that thing fled?"

"Yeah. Like it let out a squeal and the background mimicked it. And did you notice? The tubes all disappeared. Like so many things down here, they went invisible. Makes you think that four-winged flyer was a predator."

"Pretty magical," Casey said, her voice filled with wonder.

Before Michaela could respond, Jaim's voice came through com. *"We're done with samples, descending ten meters."*

"Roger that, We're on station."

Michaela kept an eye on the monitor as Casey dropped them down, carefully keeping her position ten meters off the other sub's stern. As they descended, the light began to change, the color seeming to wash out of the tubes as they flicked past the transparency. What had been a light-blue turquoise in the distance had taken on a bluer tint.

"Not so many hits on the sonar," Michaela noted. "And the background singing is deeper, as if the higher frequency creatures are getting fewer."

"Yeah, but look at this. Appearing just on our right as we descend."

Michaela watched a thick spear of something lance up beside the sub's transparency. As they dropped past the organism, arms that

had been folded close to the central trunk detached, reaching out
with remarkable dexterity; the ends seemed to explode with wispy
fingers that stroked along the transparency's glass surface.

"Ten meters," Casey announced. "Neutral buoyancy. Holding
steady."

Michaela shot a quick glance at the monitor where Varina's sub
was nose-first in a profusion of pale blue and green biota. She had
to reach through the growth with the mechanical arm in an attempt
to obtain her geological samples. The mass of living material apparently didn't like it. Michaela watched a ripple move outward as the
massed biota shifted, shoved, and tried to get out of the way. This
was accompanied by a bursting dispersion of colorful shelled creatures from where they'd been hidden in the biomass. Sand puffed
and squirted, leaves, paddles, and tentacles all waving in the disturbance.

A thump on the side of the sub brought Michaela's attention back
to the transparency where the armed spear was now leaning toward
them, more of the wispy fingers tracing the sub's sides and transpar-
encies as the long green stem bent toward them.

"How tall is this thing?" Michaela wondered, checking her depth
meter. The bottom was a good nine meters below them, and the top
of the spear had to be another meter and half above.

"So, it's like a tree?" Casey wondered.

"You tell me, you're the expert on the kelp forests."

"This thing doesn't have leaves like kelp, and kelp doesn't have
arms and feelers. Being blue-green, it can probably photosynthesize,
but I'm betting that with the arms and these feather-like feelers?
This is a predator."

"Yeah, well, there's a slew more of them around us. Pretty much
all along the bottom for as far as we can see." Michaela glanced
beyond the delicate feelers to see spears of various sizes poking up.
Sonar pinged, and one of the mysterious torpedoes appeared out of
the blue haze to drift their direction. This was Michaela's first good
look at the creature, and she made sure the camera caught its entire
passage. *Torpedo* wasn't a bad name. Three large eyes were placed
equidistantly around the head, the tripartite mouth open as it

approached. The long length could barely be seen to pulse along the scintillating patterns of color that ran down its sides. Three fins gave it a rocket-like appearance, and as it streamed past, Michaela was able to see three vents surrounding a short stinger-thin tail.

"Jet propulsion," Casey announced, her head slightly cocked. "Like the tubes, but bigger."

"Michaela?" Varina's voice came through the com. *"We're done here. We've got the samples stowed. We're ready to descend."*

"Roger that," Casey told her, easing the controls forward. "Wait, what's this?"

Past where the spear was feeling its way along the side of the transparency, Michaela could see that some of the other arms had wrapped around some of the light mounting hardware. It seemed to be hanging on, unwilling to let go.

"I'm on it." Michaela said.

She maneuvered the mechanical arm to reach around. Grasping the spear's restraining arm, she used the hydraulics to crush it next to the stalk, and actually severed the clinging arm. Suddenly freed, the sub rocked, sank, and ripped away from the feeling tendrils.

Immediately, the spear reacted, striking viciously at the sub as it sank along the thing's tall stem, the lower arms reaching out. As it did, the hydrophone erupted in what sounded like a ululating scream. Michaela could see the spear's trunk vibrating in the water.

"Get us away from this," Michaela called, as the spear began to bend toward them. "Full speed."

Casey accelerated out beyond the spear's reach. Michaela watched it drop behind in the rear cameras. The spine-chilling scream began to recede, morphing into a plaintive kind of *peuwww peuwww* call that dwarfed the musical background she'd grown used to.

"Jaim? You might want to steer clear of the spears. Uh, these really tall tree-like things. They have arms that shoot out from the trunk to grab hold of you. That's the sound that is overloading your hydrophones."

"Roger that. We had the same problem with the bottom growth. Several of the life-forms kept grabbing the remote arm, and others tried to attack the

mechanical hand. When I pulled us back, we ripped a couple of plants out of the bottom. They're still refusing to let go."

"Varina? What's your call?"

"Let's go for another fifty meters. Give it a look-see."

"Roger that. We're on descent, but we're out about twenty meters after our escape from the spear. Once you establish a position, we'll maneuver in as closely as we can to cover you."

"Roger that, Michaela," Varina replied. *"We're giving it a once-over. Trying to see where there's an opening that won't disturb the plants so much. Okay, so plants might be the wrong word. These things are way too interactive. And it's so weird the way they scamper along the bottom on their roots."*

"Yeah, welcome to a whole new world."

Michaela heard the first ping from the sonar. She watched the signal grow. The thing was rising up along the sloping bottom, ascending from one hundred fifty meters. Maybe attracted by the "tree's" distress call? Perhaps like a coyote reacted to a wounded rabbit's vocalizations?

"We've got a hard contact," Michaela said. "Coming up. One hundred twenty-five meters and rising."

"What do you want me to do?" Casey asked.

"Position us right behind Varina's sub," Michaela said thoughtfully. "We'll just go neutral buoyant, hold position, and let the thing pass. Maybe it will just ignore us if we play dead."

"Good plan," Casey agreed, looking at monitors as she maneuvered around, keeping a careful distance from the closest spear as she backed in toward Varina's sub.

"Fifty meters. Everyone hold your positions. Freeze, now."

"Roger," came Jaim's voice. *"Wow. Big sucker! Would you look at that!"*

Michaela craned her neck to peer down the irregular slope as the bottom dropped off into the indigo depths below. The creature rose from the shadowy deep, body elongated, but thicker in front. As it came near, she could finally make out its form. If she had to draw an analogy to a terrestrial creature, the three giant claws made her think of a lobster—but one without legs and made up of three armored backs conjoined along the ventral axis. Three eyes, each on a stalk behind its claw, nasty tripartite mandibles that clicked and gnashed around the central mouth. More to the point, the creature had to be a good forty meters in length, the claws measuring a meter and half from tip to hinge.

"Pus-sucking son of a bitch," Casey whispered as the thing floated up to within a couple meters of the transparency.

Michaela's mouth had gone dry, her heart hammering in her chest. She fixed on the closest of the eyes, a dark and gleaming orb. It might have been peering right through her soul. She ignored the frantic calls from the Pod, like everyone was yelling over everyone else.

"If that thing attacks . . ." Casey said hoarsely. "Shoot it, Michaela. Right now. While you've got the chance."

"I . . ." She swallowed hard. Damn it, the thing was as big around as the sub. If the torpedo didn't kill it . . . She accessed the firing control through her implant, her breath coming in hard pants. What the hell should she do? Some part of her brain was screaming: *Too close! The detonation will destroy the sub!*

"We're leaving!" Varina's panicked voice came through com. *"Surface! Surface now!"*

"Varina! No, wait!"

But it was too late. To Michaela's dismay, through the hydrophones she could hear Varina's sub blowing ballast.

Before Michaela could react to the movement, the thing shot past with incredible speed; its passage knocked the sub sideways with enough force to slam her viciously in the seat restraints. The last she remembered was the bang, lightning shooting through her head as it hit the monitor beside her. And a descending gray mist that . . .

46

Varina gasped when the great three-clawed apparition hit Michaela and Casey's sub. From the way both monster and yellow sub bounced off each other—not mention the audible bang—it had to be quite a bump. Just the sight of the thing defied belief. Three claws, three carapaces that faded into segmented rows of armored plates running down the length of the tail. But most of all, those outlandish eyes on their stalks and the central mouth with its three triskelion-oriented mandibles.

After hitting Michaela's sub, the creature collected itself, the three eyes still on Varina and Jaim, as though it was focused on them through the transparency. Then the mouth opened, and the monster shot toward their rising sub. Impossibly fast. Like something propelled by a jet.

Varina gaped in stunned disbelief as it loomed. In just a matter of a heartbeat, the three claws extended, the mouth yawning as the mandibles clicked together and parted.

Huge! So . . . huge!

It filled her vision.

Jaim was screaming, crying out, "No! God's sake, no!"

With a resounding crack it hit the transparency. Varina was slammed forward against her seat restraints. Her arms, head, and feet whipped forward and back. Pain shot along her nerves, the world blurring. She barely heard herself scream. Everything loose was bouncing around the cabin, coffee cups, the logbook, her personal pad, Jaim's graphite-fiber bag, the lunch tray as it lost its cover and flung food across the glass and soaked her short hair.

The whine of the pumps, the hiss of air flooding the ballast tanks, along with the bang and clatter of cascading cans and personal items, mingled with an intense warbling that rose into a pulsating, almost painful squeal. The creature shook the sub as it uttered a series of crescendos and vented its rage.

Clearing her vision, Varina wiped at the soup trickling down her face, felt her heart battering against her sternum. The three mandibles were sliding across the glass less than an arm's length from her face. Wicked things, each reminded her of a brown-freckled scythe a half meter in length. They parted, widened to encompass the submarine's nose, and slid back together as they slipped across the glass.

"Michaela? Do you copy us? Michaela. Hello?"

Nothing.

"Kevina? Anyone in the Pod. Hello? Do you copy?"

More silence. Not even a crackle on the com. She glanced at the readout. Dead.

"Oh, God . . . Oh, God . . ." Jaim kept whimpering from the driver's seat.

Varina felt, as well as heard, metal buckle and snap, the submarine shaking as something outside collapsed under the power of the claws. She whimpered. Grasped the chair arms in a death grip, as the sub lurched sideways, spilling the loose items along the transparency's concave surface.

Jaim's terror-laced scream matched Varina's own.

One of the forward-facing lights screeched as it was slammed against the sub's hull to shine in from the right side of the transparency. It served to better illuminate those three terrible speckled mandibles. In the light, Varina could see additional knife-shaped denticles that sliced back and forth like self-honing shears behind the scythe-like mandibles.

"We're gonna die . . . We're gonna die . . ." Jaim kept sobbing.

"No!" Varina screamed. "We've blown the ballast! Hear it? We're going to pop up to the surface. Any second, now, babe. We're gonna pop like a breaching whale."

"Gonna die," Jaim insisted through trembling lips. "Thing's . . . gonna kill us. Crush us and eat us."

"It *can't!*" Varina insisted. "We're gonna surface. Hear the air hissing in the tanks, babe? That's positive buoyancy. We're gonna go up." She swallowed hard as the sub jerked sideways, something on the hull giving way with a bang. "Gonna . . . go . . ."

The sub twisted her off balance as it was rotated sideways and more of the loose items clattered around.

Damn it! If she just didn't have to stare at those clamping and chopping mandibles.

"Let us the fuck go!" she screamed, hearing her own building terror.

The beast shook the sub with a vengeance, the mandibles clicking and banging as they bounced off the transparency, but the thick vacuum-molded glass held.

Varina's fear broke free, a sob catching in her throat as she hung upside down in her restraints. A stream of bubbles began to trace their way upward across the glass, mixing with the mandibles, sucking into the clicking and clacking denticles, and vanishing down that dark throat.

That was the worst part, that she could hear those damn teeth through the thick glass.

"Gotta be close. Gonna surface any second," she promised herself, unable to tear her gaze away from those shit-sucking teeth.

In the seat below, Jaim had gone apoplectic, her arms shaking as she gripped the controls. "Please, God. Please," she barely managed to whisper.

"Where's the surface?" Varina demanded, staring out at what little she could see past the flailing mandibles.

What the hell? If anything, it looked darker out there. They should be rising into the sun-dappled light, just beneath the waves.

Even as she thought it, the creature shifted, gave the sub a hard wrench, and with a bang, air whooshed, water gurgling. What the hell could that have been? But the air . . . it just kept venting, as if the entire tank had let go.

But what the . . . ?

The valve! It snapped the valve off the tank.

Hot tears began to stream down her cheeks. They silvered her sight, blurring the flicking and flashing mandibles ever so close to her face. There would be no surface. No positive buoyancy.

Out beyond the mandibles, where they clattered against the glass, the light seemed to be fading.

Glancing at the depth gauge, Varina watched in disbelief as they passed two hundred meters. The thing was taking them down. Ever deeper.

"Tam?" Jaim asked, her voice hoarse with fear.

"Yeah, babe?"

"Tell me it's not going to eat us."

Panic built. Varina wanted to throw up, to scream, to shriek at the fucking injustice of it all.

Can't. Got to be there for Jaim.

"It can't eat us, babe. It can't crush the sub."

As if that was any consolation.

The sound of grinding came through the hull. Then a bang.

One of the alarms went off.

Oh, great. The thing had somehow managed to short one of the batteries.

More grinding, the sound of metal being bent, scraping on the hull.

What the hell was it doing with those monster claws, picking the outside apart? First the light struts, then the pressure tanks, and now one of the two batteries?

So, it wouldn't take long. Not if the battery was really shorted. The electrical system would drain, the lights growing dim. The pumps would stop, the motors would slow, the heaters would fail, and within hours, they would be hanging sideways, or upside down in the dark, getting colder, and each breath would be using up what little oxygen remained.

She glanced up. They'd just passed three hundred meters.

Outside the pressure was building, tons of water pressing down on all sides.

"Tam?" Jaim called. She'd always called her Tam. Hated to refer to her as Varina.

"Yeah, babe?"

"Think the kids will be all right?"

"Yeah. They've got good people to take care of them. Love them."

"Like family," Jaim whispered. Then shrieked as the sub was jerked this way and that as the great beast squealed and thrashed back and forth, as if trying the shake its prey apart. More metal could be heard as it parted with pinging sound. The hull groaned as the pressure built.

According to the depth gauge, they were passing five hundred meters.

With another bang, the lights went out, the hum of the pumps and fans stopped. Only the faintest hiss of air remained as their captor uttered another of those ear-grating squeals of frustration.

The hull groaned again, the sound of several thousand atmospheres of pressure squeezing them like a giant vice. Outside, beyond the transparency and the monster, everything was black.

47

The pain brought Michaela back. Terrible. Head splitting. Her stomach pumped, body bucking forward as she threw up. Then her gut contorted again, the agony like someone had driven an ax into her skull.

"Easy." Casey's voice came from beyond the misery.

"What the hell?" Michaela wiped her bile-filled mouth, blinked, aware of bright light, of a slow bobbing. She struggled with the image, trying to understand the water slapping on the transparency. Water? Where was . . . ? And it came to her. She was in the sub, strapped into the command chair. Casey was behind her, pressing something cold and stinging to the side of her head. They were floating? What . . . ?

"We're all right," Casey said. "Kel is preparing the launch. He's going to tow us back to the Pod."

"What happened?"

"That fucking lobster thing hit the starboard prop when it went past us to get at Varina and Jaim's sub. Bent the guard into the propeller blades. We've got maneuverability . . . as long as we want to go in circles and listen to the sound of tortured metal."

"What are you doing?" Michaela's wheeling thoughts tried to make sense as she leaned away from Casey's cold pack. That's when she saw the blood and vomit staining her jacket.

"You hit your head. It's still bleeding. You know how scalp wounds are."

"Shit on a shoe," she murmured against the throb in her skull. "What happened to that lobster thing?"

"I guess it's still down there," Casey told her. "I pretty much had my hands full. Not to mention that the impact had me a bit pie-eyed and stunned. We were sinking at a forty-degree list, bleeding air from the number two tank, so I blew the ballast. Never prayed so hard in all my life as I watched the depth gauge."

"Where's Varina and Jaim?"

"No clue. They blew ballast before we did. Pissed the beast off if you ask me. There's nothing on com. I've looked around, not that I can see much as deep as this thing drafts. Com was breaking up. Like the antennae is only directional. Haven't heard a peep since Kel said he was coming to get us."

Michaela shifted, felt a whole new pain run up her left arm. "Damn, that hurts. Help me out of this seat." Her left arm didn't want to move. Was really smarting, which really sucked toilet water given her world-class headache. It was all she could do to keep from throwing up again.

With Casey's help, she got unbuckled, gasped, and winced with each jolt to her arm. She made it back to one of the passenger seats when the side of the launch appeared through the transparency at the sub's nose.

Just to sit, gasp for breath, and wish her head would clear was like a small victory.

Casey undogged the hatch, pulled out the ladder, and called, "Michaela's hurt. Hit her head, and I think her arm's broken."

Kel's voice could be heard over the waves slapping on the hull. "Hang on. Let us get a line on the sub. Are you taking any water?"

"No. We're tight. Where's Varina and Jaim?"

"Deal with that later." Kel's voice had an unusual tension. "Let's get Michaela out. Can she climb?"

Casey ducked back, her ash-blond hair swinging. The look in her gray eyes betrayed a deep-seated worry. "Can you make it up the ladder?"

"Guess I have to, huh? God, if my head would just stop hurting." Michaela stood, wavered, had to have Casey prop her against the pitch and sway as the sub rolled with the swells. She got hold of the ladder with her right hand, put a foot on the bottom rung, and levered herself up, her left arm hanging in agony. With Casey pushing on her butt, she made the climb, stuck her head out to find Kel waiting. The man bent over, half-pulling her from the hatch.

Michaela uttered a piteous cry as her arm slammed the hatch rim. Then she was out, on her feet on the wet and pitching hull. Kel helped her make it to where the launch was tied alongside. Kevina, who'd been standing at the wheel, reached out as Michaela braced her butt on the gunwale and swung her legs over into the launch. From there, with Kevina's help, it was a quick drop to the cushions on the back seat.

"That's a lot of blood," Kevina said darkly as she pulled the first-aid kit from its bracket and began scrubbing at the matted blood on the side of Michaela's head. She could feel the cloth pull in the co-agulated mess on her cheek.

"Where's Jaim and Varina?" Michaela squinted against Capella's light as she glanced around. There should be another bright yellow submarine bobbing in the blinding light. They'd blown ballast first. Should have beaten Michaela's craft to the surface. The second sub should have surfaced within meters of theirs. But there was nothing but rising and falling waves in any direction. Just the big white Pod a couple hundred meters away.

"That thing took them," Kevina said bitterly.

"Took them?"

"We lost any kind of telemetry when it grabbed their sub. We're still waiting. Yosh is watching the instruments. When that *thing* gets finished doing whatever it's doing, they'll pop up. Jaim blew the ballast. The sub's got positive buoyancy, so it's just a matter of time. That creature can't hold them underwater forever."

"How can it hold them underwater? They're in a submarine, for God's sake." Michaela tried to make her wounded brain work. Thoughts kept slipping away.

"Despite as mean and strong as that thing looked," Kevina told her shortly, "it can't crush the hull. Given the possible biomechanics, Odinga figured out the theoretical crush capacity of those claws. He thinks the beast can mangle the mounting hardware for the cameras and mechanical arm, but those pincers can't come close to putting a dent in the sub. They just have to wait it out."

Wait it out?

At the hatch, Kel helped Casey out, walked the woman to the side of the launch, and steadied her as she climbed aboard. Then he closed and dogged the sub's hatch. He paused for a moment, taking in the damage to the ballast tank where a valve had been bent and broken. Next Kel tried to get a glimpse of the trashed propeller guard before giving it up as a lost cause until they could get the vehicle out of the water.

He swung over the launch's side and took charge of the line tied to the sub as Kevina cast off and throttled up, easing the launch out as the tow line came taut.

"That thing can't crush the sub," Michaela repeated to herself, hope stirring. As long as it had compressed air in the tanks, it could inflate the ballast tanks.

That's when she straightened. Holding her broken arm, she made herself climb up on the transom and stare at the submarine bobbing in their wake. She could see spots of algae clinging to the hull. The mounting hardware for the port camera had been folded back, the forward mounting strut torn from its mount. She could see the damage to the number two tank. The valve was bent at an angle, the crack in the pipe visible even from where she perched.

The valve.

Casey had said they were at a forty-degree list, losing air.

The tank had been fine, it was built for pressure. But the valve? Nothing in the design parameters would have kept it from breaking off if something big hit it.

Michaela stumbled back to her seat. Casey was giving her a worried stare, maybe thinking the same thing. That they'd barely made it.

No monster lobster-clawed creature had been trying to break into their sub.

They'd only been bumped.

48

At a shallow slant, morning light shone through the dome window. Talina blinked awake from dreams filled with Dek Taglioni. Funny thing was, she knew which parts had been stimulated by Rocket's TriNA, the parts that Demon had concocted, and which were inspired by her own desires.

Face it, woman. You like the guy.

Didn't mean that Talina wasn't wary. Kalico had always said that leopards didn't change their spots, and Dek, in his own words, had been "a shit-sucking piece of work." A monster. All that power and privilege, being trained to believe that the entire rest of humanity existed only to serve the wants and needs of the family. Didn't matter who they hurt, who they abused, or who they destroyed in the process of their self-fulfillment.

No wonder Demon was so taken with him.

"Yesss. He's perfect for you."

"Eat shit and die, asshole."

Demon chuckled in response.

"He's worth fighting to save," Rocket said from beside her pillow.

She glanced sidelong to Dek's bed. The man slept with his head cocked, looking uncomfortable where she'd strapped him to the mattress.

Hard to believe he'd assented to the indignity, but not even Demon wanted to repeat the trip into the forest, only to wake up in some unknown place as a flock of mobbers descended out of the sky.

"Yeah, tie me." Dek had given her a wink that flexed the scar on his cheek. "Not only will I awaken alive, but I'll have the sexiest of dreams thinking about the woman I love and bondage."

"You have got to be kidding."

"Okay, two out of the three. I'm not so big on the bondage thing. I'm more of a give-and-take kind of guy. But, yeah, strap me in.

The last time was too damn close for comfort, and my clothes still smell like mobber guts."

So she'd tied him down with cargo straps. Couldn't have been comfortable. The good news was that he was still here.

And Talina's problem was as vexing as ever. More and more, the man kept saying he loved her. But was that Dek or the quetzal? Did he truly feel that way? Or was that Demon's TriNA slipping little bits of tRNA into Dek's limbic system to give his hormones a romantic rush?

"How the hell do I tell the difference?"

"When do humans ever know?" Rocket wondered.

"Yeah, well, little buddy, there's truth in that." She pulled her blanket back and swung out of the bed. Standing, she stretched, yawned, and pulled on her overalls.

When she had returned from the bathroom, Dek was watching her through half-lidded eyes, as if he weren't really seeing her.

"Hey, you okay?"

Dek responded with a mocking laugh, voice slurred as he said, "Miko, you are such a blood-sucking spineless parasite. You think you're a spider? A spider needs to have a grip on each thread of its web. Be ready to pull the prey in and strike. You're pathetic . . . don't have the discipline necessary to be completely ruthless. Now, me . . . if I were going to take your father down . . . I'd make sure he knew in those last instants that it was me. You get it? Grind him with my heel . . . so he knows he has nothing left but the extent of his own failure. Call it . . . Call it . . . a parting gift, like a poison kiss . . ."

Talina made a face. "Hey! Wake up. Dek, you in there? Or is it just the monster today?"

She reached down, shook him. Didn't get a reaction.

Dek's words dropped into a mumble, kept repeating, " . . . Such a pus-licking piece of shit . . ." over and over.

"Demon is winning," Rocket told her from her shoulder.

Down in Talina's gut, Demon chortled in delight.

49

*W*hy didn't I shoot? The thought kept repeating in Michaela's head. She kept reliving that moment when the lobster monster had been face-to-face with the sub. If she'd shot? If the torpedo had driven into the thing's mouth, blown it up? Would the detonation, so close, still have destroyed the sub?

If, if, if. Such a little word with huge implications.

The nightmare she now lived was insidious, eating at her, consuming in its horror and impossibility: Jaim and Varina had to be alive. Somewhere a couple hundred meters down, trapped inside a dark and broken submarine. Their ballast tanks punctured, or the valves broken off, or otherwise disabled as the creature tried this hold and that in an attempt to crack its prize open.

The worst part was knowing that if the sub had been functional, it should have surfaced. Should have sent a distress beacon. It wouldn't have mattered that the creature couldn't have crushed it; eventually the monster would have tired of the constant battle against the craft's buoyancy. The struggle to keep it submerged would have eventually worn the thing out. When it let go, the sub would have risen.

Physics were physics.

That had been hours ago.

Kel and Tobi Ruto had been flying circles in the seatruck, glassing the ocean in all directions for a bobbing yellow submarine.

Which means that Jaim and Varina are down there. Fully aware that they are encased in their tomb.

Sitting at her desk, her broken-and-aching arm in a sling, Michaela ran the figures. Assuming that Jaim and Varina still had power and directional maneuverability—but with their ballast fully compromised—with a full charge in the batteries they should be able to elevate the submarine's nose and power their way to the surface from a maximum depth of around a thousand meters. Having its own power supply, the emergency transponder would broadcast their location even if the sub's powerpacks were totally depleted.

But they didn't have full power. Given elapsed time since submerging, and the draw on the batteries, the sub could still surface from three hundred meters. As the clock ran out, the depth from which the sub would be able to power its way to the surface grew shallower and shallower.

Much more concerning was the oxygen supply. With two people—assuming full power—the sub was capable of reprocessing oxygen through the scrubbers for a little over twenty-four hours. Without power to run the fans and reprocessing filters and scrubbers, Varina and Jaim had about six hours. Maybe seven.

Michaela glanced at the clock. "This isn't happening. Not after all that we've been through. They've got two kids, a daughter and an infant son." She raised her eyes, as if toward the heavens. "Come on. Give us a break! Don't put us through this shit!"

The white ceiling overhead remained featureless, blank, and as unfeeling as the distant stars.

If the lobster monster had compromised the sub's power, Varina and Jaim would be down there, somewhere, on the verge of losing consciousness as CO_2 saturated the air.

She looked up as Yosh walked into the office. "Anything?"

"Nothing. Director, it's dark. I took the liberty of calling in the seatrucks. Kim Yee is up on the landing pad with the fifty-power scope. He says he'll stay out there until midnight. He keeps sweeping a circle, looking in all directions for any sign of a light."

"Will he be all right up there alone?"

"Kevina said she'll go up and keep him company as soon as she gets Felix and Breez put to bed. She and Yee have set up another bed in their quarters for Breez. So far, all we've told the girl is that her mothers are still underwater in the submarine. She's not old enough to figure out just what that means."

"And Tam's little boy?"

"Kayle's with Mikoru tonight while Toni's in the isolation tent."

He rubbed his weary eyes. "I just stopped by the clinic to see if there was any change."

"And?"

"Gabarron's out of her league. She's been on the radio with Raya Turnienko. Toni's limbs have started to twitch and move. But not with any kind of coordination. Turnienko thinks we ought to fly him to Port Authority. Mikoru and I . . ." Yosh hunched his shoulders in a defeated shrug. "We don't know what to do."

"Shit on a shoe, Yosh. I'm at wit's end, too." She tried desperately not to think about Varina and Jaim, who might even now be gasping for air. How did that feel? How did a person live with the panic, the fear, and the awfulness of slowly suffocating in a compartment so many meters under all that water?

"Shit on a shoe?" Yosh lifted an eyebrow.

"I never cursed much until I came to Donovan. I guess now I'm starting to figure out why they do it here. Sometimes words . . . well, they just don't seem adequate sometimes."

"How's the arm?"

"Aches. According to the X-ray, it's a linear fracture of the proximal ulna. Could have been worse. Anna says it's a miracle I didn't snap it in two."

Her gaze went back to the screen. If the sub's power remained undamaged, it could barely ascend from two hundred and fifty meters. But as the seconds ticked by, the curve was growing steeper. In another hour and five minutes, that sub had better be on the surface, blinking its location.

"Maybe the lobster monster, as you call it, has them wound up in a bunch of those spear trees or something. It's just taking them time to cut their way loose with the robotic arm."

"I can live with that, Yosh." She rubbed her eyes with her good hand, careful of the bandaged wound on the side of her head. Gabarron had given her a steroid for the concussion. Nevertheless, it made her brain foggy.

"How did we read this place so wrong?" Michaela glanced up at him. "Are we that stupid? These submarines are state of the art. Seascapes are used on every ocean on Earth."

"We were watching on telemetry." Yosh pulled over a chair and dropped into it, his eyes on her countdown to disaster where it flashed on her monitor. "That . . . *thing* just rose up out of the depths. We couldn't believe the way it looked, I mean, wow, what a fantastic evolutionary solution to aquatic design."

"But what the hell set it off? Why'd it go for the second sub instead of mine?"

"Best guess? The scream that 'spear-tree' made when you wounded it attracted the tri-lobster. Varina and Jaim panicked." Yosh's brown eyes softened. "From the telemetry, the thing went for them when they went positive buoyancy. Maybe it was the pumps, maybe the sound of the compressed air driving the ballast from the tanks. It could have been the movement. Did the creature think they were fleeing, so it was a predatory response? Like running from a lion?"

"As hard as it hit us, the impact should have stunned it, slowed it down."

"Didn't. We had a clear view through Varina's cameras. It bounced off your sub, and just kept right on coming. Didn't matter that it bent up a lot of metal, the collision just put scratches in that thing's armor. And it hit Varina's sub like a ram." A pause. "That's when the telemetry cut off."

"So you had nothing after that?"

"The feed went totally dead." He shifted on the chair. "Listen, Michaela, maybe that's a godsend. Just between the two of us? Given what the alternatives are? Let's hope that thing hit them so hard it killed them on impact."

"Yosh?"

His gaze hardened. "You know as well as I do that if something wasn't horribly wrong, they'd have surfaced by now. Since they haven't, I think it's pretty obvious they can't."

She pursed her lips, struggled to come up with anything reasonable. Fact was that yes, the subs couldn't be crushed, but if that accursed lobster thing had mauled the tanks, battery packs, lights, and propeller modules, it could very well have damaged the sub beyond any chance of survival.

"The Seascape is the best," she admitted painfully. "But it's not designed for this. Who would have thought? Where the hell was the engineering that would anticipate creatures like we're seeing here?"

"Makes sharks, moray eels, and sea snakes almost warm and cuddly, doesn't it?" Yosh said thoughtfully. "But there's something else we need to be considering." At her raised eyebrow, his tone dropped. "That thing was armored, Michaela. Like I said, when it bumped your sub, it hit it hard. So, if the lights, ballast tanks, and propeller cage didn't even scratch that armor, what did evolution design it to be protection against? That suggests that there is some even bigger and badder predator lurking out there."

Michaela swallowed hard. "If there is, are we sure we even want to try and find it? I mean, damn it, we've lost one sub, and it's going to take a week to repair the one we have. How do we armor it against something like the lobster monster, let alone whatever might be out there that preys on lobster monsters? Like, let's say, that Big Mouth Thing that Kevina said she saw."

On the monitor, the graph showed that the missing sub could only power its way to the surface from two hundred meters.

Michaela reached over with her good arm and turned it off. Unwilling to watch any longer.

"These are our friends," she whispered. "And they're dying, one by one. We are family. All of us, we held each other together aboard *Ashanti*. We made it work, loved each other, forgave each other, became brothers and sisters. And now we're being whittled away."

"Michaela, it's just a string of bad luck. We'll figure it out."

"Will we?" she asked hollowly. "If they didn't die in the impact, they're down there, Yosh. We can't contact them. We can't find them. And if we could, with my sub damaged, we can't even attempt a rescue."

Kevina burst in the door, her frantic eyes searching the room. "Did you pull Kim off the watch upstairs? Order him down for any reason?"

"No," Michaela told her, shifting her broken arm as she swiveled in the chair. "He said he'd stay up there until midnight."

"Well, I just came from the landing pad. Kim's gone. The glasses are still there, on their stand. Kim's coat is hanging on the chair he took up. His cup is spilled, rolling around as the wind blows. He'd never leave that cup."

"He's got to be here somewhere," Yosh said bluffly, rising. "Come on. Let's go run him down. Probably stopped by the cafeteria to see what Bill had left over from supper."

As they hurried out, Michaela fixed on the panicked expression on Kevina's face.

Please. Not Kim Yee. Not today.

When Yosh got up to the landing pad, he accessed com, said the tea in Yee's cup was still hot.

Michaela immediately called up the landing-pad video—the images recorded by the camera that constantly monitored the pad. Once they'd watched Kalico Aguila barely survive her departure from that hovering A-7 shuttle.

Michaela ran the feed backward to replay the last half hour, watching as first Yosh, and then Kevina appeared and hurried around in reverse, leaving the pad empty but for the rolling cup as the wind played with it. The binoculars stood on their tripod as a solitary reminder of Yee's mission. After fast-reversing through twenty minutes, Michaela watched Kim Yee drop magically from the night sky.

She stopped, forwarded at normal speed. And there, to her disbelief, she caught the image as something big swooped down from the night. It might have been a four-winged pterodactyl, little more than a dark image, spectral in the darkness. A sort of night-flying terror beyond belief.

Little more than a black silhouette, it came winging in, coasting into the wind like a macabre glider. The thing impaled the unsuspecting Yee from behind, driving claws through the man's back. Yee's zero-g cup dropped from nerveless fingers. Then, with all four wings beating, the night creature lifted, bearing the kicking and screaming man away into the night.

All that remained were the tripod-mounted binoculars, and the zero-g cup rolling around on the pad.

50

Only the faint hiss of the air conditioning could be heard in the darkness. Outside of the clock on the wall that glowed with the time—a little after two in the morning—the only illumination came from Felix's pad. It provided just enough light to see Mother's body. She lay on her back, the bed coverings thrown off in the warm night. Her long, thin left leg crooked at an angle. He had watched her take a pill, one that she had told him would make her sleep. She'd said it was better than crying all night. Especially since Breez was staying with them. Mother often took pills when she couldn't sleep.

Father was dead. Taken into the sky by some flying thing. Felix should have been sad. Instead, it just felt distant. Somehow far away. Like he was sad way down inside himself.

He had wanted to cry, but a weird voice inside told him, *"It's all right not to."* And it was.

He didn't hear the Voice like a real voice. But it seemed to know things. Kind of like Mother and Father did, but it was inside, and it had started to tell him things. Like to get out of bed, and take the pad, and turn it on. When he did, he watched his fingers tap in commands that brought up images of something called anatomy.

Breez had climbed out of bed, too. She just stared at him, and then Mother, with wide and waiting eyes.

Felix used the pad's glowing screen to call up the medical records about Mother's body. Breez came over to stand beside him. She said nothing. Just looked at the pictures, and then over at Mother's body.

As he learned, the melody repeated in his head:

"*London bridge is broken down, broken down.*
"*Namby Pamby is a clown, my fair lady.*
"*Now he courts the lady fair, lady fair.*
"*My fair lady.*"

The song lulled him. Felix thought he might be asleep. Maybe he was dreaming? It was all so clear. He stood at the side of the bed, but when his hands moved on the pad, it wasn't him. His hands just moved on the screen by themselves. Like most of him was shut off, just watching from someplace else while his body did things he didn't understand.

All the parts of Mother's body could be seen. Like looking down through the skin. He could see muscles, blood vessels, bones. Then an overlay of nerves. One by one, the organs came up: brain, lungs, heart, stomach, intestines, kidneys, liver, spleen, colon, uterus, bladder. Some remote part of his brain cataloged these things.

Felix's head turned, Breez's moving the same way his did, mimicking him as she looked at the pad, and then compared it to Mother. His eyes fixed on Mother's head. Compared it with the image on the pad. It seemed to take a long time, looking at Mother's closed eyes, her thin nose, the way the mouth was. Then came the rounded top of her head. Like figuring out a puzzle, pieces began to fit together. Brain: Surrounded by skull. Vital and armored.

Then Felix watched the pad shift to Mother's pale throat. Neck: Blood vessels, air tube, and spinal cord. Vital and vulnerable. He glanced at Breez, and they both nodded in some understanding.

And the process went on. Chest: Heart, lungs, and spinal cord. Vital and armored.

Torso: Stomach, liver, kidneys, intestines, and bladder. Digestion. Vulnerable but not immediately vital.

Legs: Bone and muscle. Movement. Not vital.

Arms: Defense. Manipulation. Not vital.

Felix wondered at the words. Sometimes the Voice said strange things.

So was he dreaming? Was that what looking so hard at Mother's body was all about? What was really weird was that the Voice wanted to know what was inside her. Was it because the Voice was worried about her now that Father was dead? But as he started to wonder, felt the worry and grief build, the Voice made it go away. And it was better. Really, it was a relief not to have to cry, or be scared, or be sad.

He and Breez froze as Mother made a whimpering sound and shifted, rolling onto her side. Then her breathing deepened again.

Felix dream-watched as his eyes compared the drawing on the pad against mother's new position. How the Voice looked closely, twisting this way and that, bending down to stare at the round top of her head. Then how it carefully inspected her neck, fixing on the faint pulse visible at the side. Blood vessels: Vulnerable, the larger ones vital.

Mother's back seemed particularly fascinating as Felix's eyes compared the glowing image on the pad. Spinal cord: Motor function. Vital. Armored.

He watched the rising and falling as Mother breathed, could imagine how the heart was beating under the breastbone, where the lungs lay under the ribs.

The same with her stomach. And then the legs, comparing the image on the screen with Mother's long legs, particularly the joints of the knees. How the muscles attached to the bone, the tendons, nerves, and blood vessels, all so close to the surface.

Breez shifted, reached for Felix's hand. The one that didn't hold the pad. At her grip, he felt that slick feeling as if his palms were damp and sweaty.

We know now.

Breez let loose of his hand, walked carefully over to the bed Mother had made up for her. She lay down, closed her eyes, and was immediately asleep.

Felix, his body still on automatic, walked over to his bed, shut down the pad, and laid himself on the mattress.

"Go to sleep now, Felix. Forget everything that happened."

And he did.

51

No way could Kalico get the Number Three out of her mind. Her wild imagination kept playing with her, kept intruding into her thoughts. Out of nowhere fragments of images would flit into her head: visions of Alia and Stana sitting hunched, waist-deep in cold water. Shivering. The blackness beyond pitch, so thick and impenetrable that it felt like a viscous substance. The only sound outside of their chattering teeth and gasping for fading breath was the echoing drip of water from above.

Didn't matter that Kalico knew they had to be dead, that not even tough old Stana Viola could have lasted this long immersed in cold water.

Her imagination wouldn't allow her to admit reality. It kept insisting on seeing them alive. Communicating their fear, the evaporating hope, and the sick realization that they were going to die without a single attempt to save them.

"That's the worst fucking part," Kalico muttered as she skimmed her aircar through Capella's first morning light and across the treetops on the descent from the Corporate Mine compound down to the Number Three portal. The need to go down to the Number Three had been like an itch; it had filled her dreams, left her too restless to sleep. So, first thing, after breakfast and her morning briefing on the Numbers One and Two, she'd walked out, climbed into her aircar, and spooled it up.

As she settled onto the waste dump to one side, it was to see that another aircar had beaten her to it. Must have been that one of the crews had already arrived to check the adit.

Spooling down, she double-checked the sky out of habit. Mobbers had almost killed her once; she never took the sky for granted. Stepping out, she left her hat and cloak in the aircar, walked past the line of ore cars, and followed the rails to the black maw of the portal.

She stepped inside, not exactly sure why she was here. The cool air in the black shaft smelled of wet rock, seemed to cling damply to her skin. As her eyes adjusted, she pulled the flashlight from her hip and flicked it on.

"This is fart-sucking crazy, Kalico," she muttered to herself as she started down the rails toward the collapse. Damn it, she just had to see it for herself. So much had been wagered on the Number Three. Completing it would have solved so many problems. For all she, Ghosh, and Ituri knew, it might have dewatered the entire lower part of the mountain. Who knew what kind of wealth that might have freed up?

Her steps echoed in the darkness, hollow-sounding as her soles grated on the broken gravel under the tracks. The light played on the shining steel rails, reflected from irregular pools of water to glow on the surrounding rock. Plopping drips of water could be heard splashing into puddles.

She reached the first of the shoring, let her light play across the squared timbers. This was the leading edge of the shattered rock zone. Overhead, the dark lights and conduit had a forlorn appearance, as if abandoned to eternal darkness.

Kalico chewed thoughtfully on her lips as she stepped close, studied the thick beams of chabacho. Each had been precisely milled. Fitted. Additionally, the ceiling was carefully supported by crosspieces, and in places of greater potential instability, even heavier beams reinforced any fractured head rock.

Damn it, it all looked good. Overengineered if anything. She'd come to associate that with Talovich's work. Since the man had looked up into the muzzle of her pistol that long-ago morning when Kalico had been ready to shoot him in the head for desertion, Sula Talovich had never, not once, cut a corner. Immaculate craftsmanship might have become a matter of honor with him. Time after time, he'd halted progress because he considered something the others thought adequate to be substandard. Kalico had always backed him on that.

"So why did this fail?" she wondered.

Ahead of her, she heard the characteristic clatter of rock being shifted, the rattle and hollow clack of one angular stone striking another. Someone cursed, a faint whimper following.

Didn't sound like a crew. Sounded like a lone person.

She stepped forward, saw the light where it had been placed atop an inverted bucket to shine onto the slanting spill of rock that poured down from the cave-in. Splintered and broken timbers jutted out from the chaos of angular yellow-brown stone. The broken shoring, now-jagged wood, shone pale in the light with toothpick-thin splinters protruding.

And there, a lone figure worked, tossing one chunk of stone after another as he labored futilely to remove the pile. The man wore grubby overalls, his feet clad in quetzal-hide boots. Black collarlength hair swayed as he reached out with muck-covered-and-bleeding fingers and tried to wrestle a trapezoidal block of stone from the fall.

"What are you doing?" Kalico demanded.

The man froze, startled. Then he wheeled around, the loose stone shifting under his feet. He windmilled his arms for balance, slid a couple of feet lower on the unstable slope.

Tadeki Ozawa shot her stricken look, blinded by the light. He raised a hand, tried to shield his eyes. Squinting. "Who's there?"

"Supervisor Aguila, Tadeki. I said, what are you doing?"

He sniffed, rubbed a damp and grit-cover sleeve under his flat nose. "No one else is trying. That's my Stana in there. She's back there. I know it. She called to me."

"Tadeki, I'm so sorry. Listen, we're doing everything we can. We're—"

"Then why aren't you digging Stana out! She's alive. Can't you hear her?"

Kalico stepped forward, keeping her light on him. "You need to get off that rubble. It's loose, unstable. You pull out the wrong piece, and it's all going to come cascading down. You'll be as buried and crushed as Stana and Alia are."

"No! I tell you, she's alive back there."

"Damn it, Tadeki! You fucking listen to me. You keep up this insanity, you're going to pull the whole mountain down on top of you. There are tons of loose rock piled up, and all it will take is pulling the wrong stone loose. You do that, and you'll end up just as dead as Stana."

Madness in his eyes, lips twitching, he glared into the light. Said, "She's carrying our baby. Three months now. She needs me. More than she's ever needed me. She's my life. I have to get her out."

"Yeah, okay."

"Why aren't you digging? Why isn't the whole crew digging? We need everyone. All of us. We have to get to her!"

"Tadeki, come down from there. I don't want to lose you, too."

He seemed to struggle, as if having trouble understanding what she was saying.

"Tadeki, that's an order. Climb down now . . . and do it carefully." When he still didn't move, she snapped, "Now!"

That finally penetrated his fog, and he carefully began to pick his way down the shifting scree of stone. At the same time, his expression had grown confused. He slowly shook his head, flicked it, as if at something buzzing by his ear. His worried brown gaze fixed on hers. "You need to call down everyone. We have to get her out."

Kalico watched his eyes; they kept shifting, as if a flurry of conflicting thoughts filled his head. "Call them," he insisted. "Access com. We have to get her out. She's in there. Just behind that rock. She's pregnant. I told you that, right?"

Kalico raised a soothing hand. "Easy, Tadeki. I'm stunned by this as well. Stana wasn't as close to me as she was to you, and I'm so sorry. For you. For her. For the baby, too. I didn't know she was pregnant."

"Our secret," he whispered miserably. "Going to be a family. That's why we've got to get her out."

"Tadeki, you're not even supposed to be here. Does Stryski know you're down here? Did he give you permission?"

"I have to save Stana," he continued to plead. "She's all I've got. Do you understand? She's my life. We're going to have a baby." He jabbed a thumb over his shoulder. "I have to get her out of there."

"Come on. Let's get you outside. We'll figure out what to do with Stana and Alia when we can determine why the shoring let go."

Tadeki's cheek twitched, his gaze thinning. "You're not going to save her, are you?"

"Did you hear a word I said? She and Alia are dead, Tadeki. There's nothing to save. They're back there under tons of rock. Like you're going to be if you go back to destabilizing that roof fall. Now, come on. Something tells me you're absent without leave."

He turned, staring back at the slope of tumbled rock. "I have to save her."

"Yeah, I know. And I share your loss. Stana and Alia, both of them, were remarkable women. So, listen. Go back to work. I'll tell Stryski to cut you a break. Hell, I might have done the same thing if it was someone I loved. Come on."

Tadeki was sniffing, a trembling in his hands, his shoulders bowed. Head down, he kept knotting and unknotting his fingers. The man looked completely undone. Kept repeating, "You're not going to dig her out. Just leave her there to rot."

"Nothing we can do." Kalico tried to keep her voice even. "Just had to come down and take one last look."

In the gleam of the lights, she could see his lips quivering, how his eyes were blinking.

"Pick up your stuff. Come on."

She saw Tadeki reach for an iron bar, pick it up in his knotted hands; the weird gleam in his eyes seemed to intensify. Gripping the bar as if it were a bat he took a step toward her, saying, "If you won't save her, I don't have any other choice but to . . ."

A voice called, "Supervisor?"

"Here!" She turned, hearing the pattering and grating of footsteps as several people approached. Lights were bobbing, beams gleaming off the rails and water puddles.

Kalico glanced back; tears streaked Tadeki's smudged cheeks. Feet braced, he gripped the iron bar as if to crush it. Good thing he hadn't taken it up with him to pry out that big trapezoidal stone. She might have arrived just in time to see him vanish under a cascade of rock that might have destabilized the whole mountain.

Tadeki stood as if frozen, breath laboring in and out of his lungs. Head hanging. Then his body began to tremble.

"Supervisor?" Sula Talovich called as he held up a hand against the shine of her light. He led the way, Ghosh and Ituri behind him.

"Mr. Talovich," she told him. "Where have you been?"

"I know what happened," he told her.

"Tadeki?" Ituri asked. "Aren't you supposed to be up top working on a hauler?"

"Tadeki was just leaving," Kalico told them. Turning to the man, she said, "Go on. Tell Stryski I said it was all right. Go back to work."

The man's muscles tensed, the iron bar wavering in his knotted grip. Glancing up, he shot a half-glazed look at Ghosh and then Ituri. The iron bar clanged musically on the rock floor as it slipped from his suddenly nerveless fingers. Lips working soundlessly, he awkwardly stumbled past them, caught his stride, and broke into a run. Fleeing as if the furies of hell were behind him.

"What's that all about?" Ghosh asked.

"He and Stana were expecting a child." Kalico rubbed the back of her neck where it had suddenly gone tight. "She was three months pregnant. The damn fool thought he could dig her out. That she was still alive back there. Said he could hear her calling to him." She paused. "Is there any possible way he could be right?"

"There is not," Talovich told her. "It's not our fault. I mean, it is, but it isn't."

"You want to be a bit more concise in your wording?"

Talovich shot a look around him, pointing to the shoring. "That's chabacho."

"Very good, Mr. Talovich." She crossed her arms, making sure not to blind them with her light.

"Back in the addit, we switched off. Chabacho and aquajade. It just depended on what we had cut as we built the haul road. We've used aquajade for years in the Number One and Number Two. It's a good structural wood . . . right up until you put it in water."

"What do you mean, put it in water?"

He pointed to the ricket where it ran a stream of yellow-brown water, then to the puddles where they dotted the tunnel floor. "We had places where the aquajade was constantly in standing water. You know about the veins in the wood, right? The ones you can tap? Drink from if you're lost in the forest?"

"Uh, yeah. But it's not a healthy practice because of the heavy metals that accumulate in the tree."

Talovich ran a weary hand over his short-cut hair. "Those same veins suck up the water, ma'am. Act like suction tubes and saturate the wood. In that environment, it accelerates the bacterial action, which denatures the cells and weakens the polymer bonds in the cell walls. In short, it takes a seasoned timber and, over a couple of months, turns it into a sort of sponge."

Kalico experienced a sick feeling deep in her gut. "How did we miss this?"

"We're still learning, ma'am. But I swear on Alia and Stana's graves, we're never going to make this mistake again."

52

Talina sat on a low basalt outcrop and studied the clear waters where the South River spilled over boulders in a set of Class III rapids. She had come here to make a decision about her "Dek problem." It was a good place for soul-searching. Below the outcrop and crashing white water, the gradient flattened, the current still whirling and welling. To either side, the forest rose to varied heights, the trees moving slowly, their branches and leaves following Capella as the primary traced its way across the afternoon sky. The chime rose and fell, mocking in its predictable search for a nonexistent harmony.

Talina cradled her rifle across her lap, her hair pulled back, butt half-asleep from sitting on the angular basalt. She'd opened the fastening on the front of her coveralls, allowing the breeze to cool her chest as she baked in the sun.

She kept scanning the skies, looking for any sign of the mobbers. Her hope was that after she'd blasted the column, the survivors had been scared enough to flee the area. But then, no one had data on how the fearsome predators thought or behaved. Some dim part of her memory recalled that the more biologically efficient a predator was, the less intelligence it needed. That, back on Earth, that explained why ravens and crows were so much smarter than eagles or owls, or why wolves had to be smarter than cheetahs.

But who knew if any of that held true on Donovan?

She needed only look at the surrounding forest. From the height of the trees, she could tell where the soil was deepest. There, the largest and most powerful of the forest giants stood; it was only as the soils shallowed that the smaller trees were jostling for space, wrestling, trying to topple each other.

Maybe that was the legacy of organic-based life. It was bound to be in conflict with itself, a system built on predators and prey moving energy up the trophic levels, only to recycle it back to the lowest.

"Then which level am I on when it comes to Dek?" she wondered.

The guy had been out of his head for most of the morning, and nothing Talina had been able to do could reach him. She'd even tried a series of hard slaps to the face. Enough to raise a red welt on the guy's already-scarred cheek. But his eyes had remained half-lidded. Whatever insane rush of memories and consciousness currently possessed him had him mumbling in poorly articulated syllables and periodically breaking out in bitter and derisive laughter—the kind that had nothing to do with delight.

"Should I have really hurt him?"

That's when she'd had to leave.

If it meant having to break his arm to bring him back to sanity, what would it take next time? Shocking him with electrodes?

No, face it. Somewhere along the line, Dek was going to have to win this fight by himself. Or lose to Demon.

She felt so damned helpless. It hurt too much to watch. And where had that come from?

"Face it, Talina," she told herself, "you don't even know who Dek is anymore."

Was he the charming fellow who'd once helped Chaco Briggs fix a broken water pump? Or the wide-eyed and sunburned Dek who'd beamed over having picked a bucket of peppers in Reuben Miranda's fields? Or was he the Dek she'd carried up the cliff at Tyson Station after he'd pushed himself to the limits of his endurance? That Dek would never be muttering about being a spider and destroying his father in the most painful way possible.

Or would he?

She rubbed her tired eyes, futility building inside. The old Dek—the one who was willing to risk it all to make it or break on Donovan—had charmed her. She'd found herself daydreaming about his smile, the dimple in his chin, and the animation in those yellow-green eyes of his. Something about the fact that he'd been so willing, desperate even, to meet Donovan's challenges had appealed to something in her psyche.

What had he said? "Hours, days, weeks, or months. I just needed to live. Free. On my own terms." She pursed her lips. That was a man to respect.

"He's been a weight around your neck," Demon chimed in from down inside. *"Can't take care of himself."*

"He survived a mobber attack, climbed out of the canyon with a leg full of thorns, you piece of shit."

"And you condemned him. Should have let him die."

Talina ground her jaws, refusing to rise to the bait.

"Be a mercy, you know." Demon continued to twist the barb. *"Put him down now. Save him the agony of living in despair and misery."*

"Yeah? If I do, you win."

"I already have."

She squinted against the sun, letting the heat punish her. Problem was, the evil little shit might be right. What if it had figured out a way to shut off the part of Dek's brain that controlled his post-*Ashanti* personality? What if it had excluded Rocket's and Flute's various lines of more beneficial TriNA? Somehow figured out a way to sequester itself in Dek's head?

"What do you do then, Talina?"

She didn't have to put a bullet in his brain. She could simply leave what was left of Dek here, at Two Falls. He'd have to live with what he'd become. Eventually, Donovan would kill him. Until then maybe Demon would keep him alive to torture and drive insane. Dek would have food, shelter, a fighting chance if Demon allowed.

"But I wouldn't have to watch it play out," she told herself, eyes drawn to a couple of scarlet fliers that rose from the treetops to chase a rising column of invertebrates.

"You owe him nothing."

"Sorry, but I'm the one who put you inside him. Hell, but for me, by now Dek might be working out a compromise with Flute's TriNA. See, Flute's line has Tip and Kylee and me in it. All your line has is hatred."

"We learned from you, human."

"Then you didn't learn very well. But that's history." She wiped at the sweat beading on her brow. Time to be moving on, find some shade, cool off. "Face it, girl, the man you were falling in love with as good as died that day on the canyon rim."

The smart money was to cut her losses, save herself the pain. Dek was on his own.

She rose to her feet, took one last look around. The river looked so cool and inviting, the sound of the water pulsing as it poured over the rocks, the rapids flexing and bulging like muscles to churn into whitewater. Where it slowed in the channel below, she could look down into the clear green depths, see the rocks that lined the bottom. Sleek shapes moved there, but she couldn't make out the details, just that they were long and cylindrical.

Movement at the corner of her vision caused her to turn.

"What the hell? How did you get loose?"

Dek was downstream from the rapids and below Talina's outcrop, his path paralleling the river. The man wore his coveralls and boots, but this time, lucid or not, he'd remembered to arm himself, though only with his pistol. He carried it in his right hand; Capella's light glinted off the fancy gold inlay and gleamed on the polished wood.

"Dek!"

He didn't seem to hear, weaving his way around the boles of aquajade beside the river and ducking wide of the tooth flower and bluelinda that grew down next to the riverbank.

How had he gotten down there? Somehow he'd found a path that led around the outcrop, circled wide, and made his way back to the water.

"Shit on a shoe," Talina muttered, fastening the open front of her coveralls. "Idiot's going to get himself killed."

And, fact was, he clearly wasn't in his right mind.

"My fault," she reminded herself as she slung her rifle and studied on how to find a way down the outcrop. There, but it was dicey. She'd have to use the cracks and crevices, hope that nothing lethal was hiding in them, and work her way down.

Cursing and worried, she lowered herself over the edge, feeling the way with her feet, clinging with her fingers. Once upon a time, she'd never have had the strength or agility. TriNA might have ruined her life—and maybe Dek's, too—but it did have its advantages.

Halfway down, she almost reached into a slug's hiding place, saw it at the last instant, and swung sideways to grasp a different handhold.

Getting her heart to slow, she took a deep breath and, looking down, dared to drop the last two meters to a flat-topped boulder. But for a wild swing of her arms, she'd have fallen. As it was, she leaped, dropped, and hit the ground hard. At the impact, the rifle's sling liked to have dislocated her shoulder. The roots underfoot went berserk, and she skipped quickly to a rock and jumped away from the questing tendrils. Looking back up the rock face, she shook her head and turned.

It took longer than she thought it would to wind through the predatory vines, avoid a skewer, and figure a way past a shallow pool where the outlines of slugs could be seen under a thin layer of mud.

What had it been? Fifteen minutes? Twenty? But she caught sight of Dek's boot print in a small gravel bar beside the river.

"What the hell are you up to this time?" she groused as she unslung her rifle and hurried in pursuit. She'd left the guy half-comatose, strapped to the bed. If he was coming to and had enough of his faculties to extricate himself, dress, and charge off into the wilderness with a pistol, her containment strategy was going to have to be re-thought. Or was it?

"Didn't I just decide to leave?" She made a face.

"Can't," she shot back before Rocket could get the satisfaction of playing angel-on-her-shoulder.

But damn it, she couldn't spend the rest of her life being nurse-maid, chasing Demon Dek around the Two Falls Gap wilderness.

"Not that it will be the rest of my life," she muttered, skipping wide around one of the black meter-in-diameter pincushions with its hundreds of deadly spines.

As good as Demon was at making Dek think he was a quetzal during these jaunts, just like the other day, mobbers, brown caps, a sidewinder, slugs, or one of the predatory vines was going to kill the guy. Hell, for all she knew, she'd round the next bend of the river and see him speared through by a bem and being engulfed. Not to mention that this was nightmare country. And though the mundo trees grew back from the river on better-drained soils, odds were that one or two of the local trees had to have a fricking nightmare living in it.

The sound of the waterfall had grown louder; now it almost drowned out the chime.

Talina clambered over a two-meter-tall knot of roots that followed a cleft in the underlying gabbro and broke out onto bare rock. Not more than ten meters beyond, the rock ended in a cliff. The river beside her flowed over the edge, curled, and the clear water vanished into the depths below to roar and thunder, mist rising from the thirty-meter drop.

To her right, bare bedrock extended some fifteen or so meters before a low growth of something resembling ferngrass clung to the thin soils. Behind it, a kind of brush Talina had never seen slowly gave way to a tangle of vines with huge scarlet flowers sprouting long whip-like tendrils. The stuff just looked deadly, which, on Donovan, meant it was.

More to the point, however, Dek was standing at the edge of the falls. His head tilted back, and Talina could see his face, sweaty, expression pained. The veins in the man's neck were sticking out. His left hand knotted into a fist, the tendons hard under his skin.

"Dek?" she called softly, stepping carefully onto the bare rock.

He didn't answer, but as she came closer, she could see tears streaking down his face.

"Dek?"

A hard swallow ran down his throat. Soundlessly, Dek's lips worked, as though he was in dialog with himself.

Only as she stepped wide did she see that he had his pistol up, the three rails braced on the side of his head.

"Dek, you don't want to do this."

"Can't."

She barely heard his whisper over the thunder of the falls. "Can't what, Dek? Hey, listen, we'll find a way through this." She lowered her rifle to the stone, hands out in a gesture of surrender.

For the first time, his eyes flicked her direction. "It just keeps pulling horrible things out of my memory, Tal. I won't live that shit. I *won't* be that man!"

"If you shoot yourself, Demon wins," she told him in her best calm-the-situation voice. "Dek, there's got to be another way."

"Yeah," he told her. "There is."

"Okay, then let's put the pistol down." She was closer now. Just another couple of meters.

"Can't. Not my call. That son of a bitch knows what I'm trying to do."

"And what's that?" She made another step.

"Something you told me. Something Demon remembers."

"I've told you a lot of things."

A shattered smile crossed his lips. "Got me at an impasse, he does. I do this, or I'll pull the trigger."

"He? Demon will make you shoot yourself?"

"Says he won't lose." A dry swallow. "And I won't let him win."

"Lose how?" Talina was a step away. "You're sounding crazy."

She charged her muscles, had to move quetzal-fast to make this work. If she didn't . . .

"I won't live like this," Dek insisted, a trickle of sweat breaking from his hairline. "Not . . . your . . . fault . . . Tal."

She leaped, levered the pistol away from his head as it discharged into the air with a loud crack. She pulled his arm down, hammered it to stun the nerve, and pried the pistol from his fingers. Let it drop beside her rifle. As she did, to her horror, Dek pivoted on his heel. She grabbed for him as he started to fall. Tried to pull him back.

As he overbalanced, he reached out, ripped her hand free of his sleeve.

That instant fixed in her memory: Dek's face, eyes alight with triumph, a victorious smile on his lips. The expression was jubilant as he toppled into the abyss. And then he was gone.

Talina fought for balance, only to have one of the broken and cracked stones beneath her foot give way.

And then she was falling, tumbling, twisting. The world spun, water oddly frozen in motion beside her. Paralyzed she watched the boiling water come close as she fell headfirst . . .

53

Michaela had barely slept. Kept reliving the horror of the entire day: from Toni's paralysis, the fateful deployment of the submarines, the lobster monster, the loss of Varina Tam and Jaim Elvridge, and finally Kim Yee's unnerving fate.

How much more can we take? Michaela fought tears, wanted nothing more than to lock herself in her quarters and scream into the silence of her room. And, damn it, her fractured arm kept aching.

My people need me.

That one baseline had kept her sane through all those years aboard *Ashanti*. Now, like festering acid, it ate at her. Forced her to dress despite her broken arm, to gird herself, and open the door. She checked the monitors in her office. Still no sign of the second sub, no distress signal, no bobbing hull visible out among the swells. Even with full power, the sub's oxygen regeneration was long depleted. Varina and Jaim were dead. No hope remained.

Calling up all the dignity of a prisoner facing the gallows, she made herself enter the cafeteria.

With the exception of Vik Lawrence, who was working in her lab, the older children who were doing "science club" in the observation dome, and Gabarron—the surly woman was up keeping an eye on Toni in the clinic—everyone who remained was seated behind the tables. At the sight of the empty chairs—so damn many of them—Michaela's nerve almost broke. And then she had to meet their eyes, see the reflected confusion, grief, anger, and disbelief.

Shinwua, Lara, Jaim and Varina, and now Kim Yee, all dead. Five of her people, killed in the most horrible of ways. And no telling what was wrong with little Toni, filled as he was with Donovanian TriNA.

What do I tell them?

"We had a tough day yesterday." She tried to feel her way, the words sounding so hollow.

"Tough doesn't begin to cover it," Jym Odinga called from where he was sitting beside Casey Stoner. "Any news about Varina and Jaim?"

"Nothing on the scanners."

Yosh said, "I sent one of the drones up at first light. Flew all along the reef. Nothing's floating. No wreckage from the sub. No sign of Kim's body. There's just . . . nothing."

"I say we leave," Tobi Ruto muttered where he sat on Casey's other side. "Get out while we still can."

"And do what?" Kel asked from across the room. "Remember what Supervisor Aguila said? There's no way off this planet. We're here for keeps."

"Then we go to Port Authority." Odinga glanced at Casey, who was breastfeeding little Saleen. "Casey, Tobi, and I have two kids to think of. At Port Authority, they've got a school. Other kids. We've been asking ourselves, what it if had been Casey's sub that was destroyed by the lobster monster yesterday? And then Kim's grabbed up from behind? He never saw it coming. For our part, my family doesn't want either of our kids to grow up without a parent."

"And what are you going to do at Port Authority?" Kel asked. "You were there, you saw. You're an ichthyologist, Casey's a marine botanist with a specialization in kelp-forest ecology and trophic systems. Given what I saw walking around that sorry collection of houses, the only one of you with skills is Tobi."

The guy was a Pod Technician Class I. He could fix things.

Where they sat side-by-side, Iso Suzuki and Bryan Atumbo were nodding. Like Casey's family, they, too, had their kids, Felicity and Vetch, to think about.

"Where do you stand, Yosh?" Michaela asked. Might as well get all the parents on the record.

"Mikoru and I think we ought to stay for the time being." He glanced around. "As long as we're inside the Pod, we're safe. Nothing can get to us. And the Pod provides us with everything we need to survive. We've got the hydroponics, and we can import anything else from the mainland. Surely, if the animals on land are edible, we can supplement from the sea. We just need to do the necessary research in the lab to see what's poisonous before we put it on the plate. I think we can survive here just fine. And when we begin to figure this place out, we can even thrive."

"We've got five dead!" Bill Martin almost exploded where he stood in the kitchen door. "What part of *dead* don't you get? And that's your boy up in the isolation tent."

"He's going to be infected here or at Port Authority," Mikoru shot back. "Anna says he's starting to get some of his motor control back. Vik's working on it. Yosh and I, we think there's a better chance of us figuring out the infection here, with our lab equipment, than back at Port Authority, where they don't even have a scanning electron microscope that still works."

Yosh added, "Come on, people. Think it through. We're scientists. Our biggest assets don't lie in the subs and UUVs, they lie in our brains. I have to believe that we're smarter than Donovan."

Dik slapped a hand to the table. "I don't want to piss on your pride, Yosh, but Donovan's winning. What part of 'we're being picked off one by one' don't you get?'"

Kevina, her eyes puffy from crying, flatly said, "If he were here, Kim would tell you to stay. Damn it all, I don't believe this. He and I, we just had this conversation yesterday. 'Kev,' he said, 'so, if something happens to me, don't let this place beat you. Nothing comes for free, and this place is the future.'"

"And what if Felix turns out to be infected like Toni?" Bill Martin asked. "You still think that he's—"

"He is," Vik Lawrence called as she walked into the room. "They all are." She stopped by Michaela at the front table. "Every one of the children test positive for TriNA and prokaryotes in their blood and cells. And there's a lot of it. Don't ask me what it means, I still don't have a clue. Neither does Raya Turnienko at the PA hospital. According to her, however, it's highly unlikely that it's life-threatening. So, I know this was a meeting to figure out what we're going to do next, but if you're thinking about leaving as a way to protect the kids from what Toni got, you're too late."

"What about the infants?" Iso cried. "Vetch, Kayle, and Saleen?"

"They've got it as well," Vik admitted. "The reason, I'm guessing, is that it's spread by contact. If I'm right it's from an oily secretion generated by Donovanian bacteria in the skin and sebaceous glands."

"That means that the parents would have been exposed as well," Michaela said, as a cold wave ran through her.

"That's next on my list," Vik agreed. "I want each and every one of you upstairs. Now. I want a blood sample from everyone. We need to see how far this has gone."

"Any of you been feeling sick?" Michaela asked. "Fever? Nausea? Sweats? Vertigo?"

Around the room, heads shook, another layer of anxiety brewing atop their previous discord. Bodies were shifting uncomfortably in the chairs.

"Felix has been strange," Kevina blurted. "I set my alarm for early. When it went off, he was sleepwalking." She shook her head, as if to rid it of some unpleasant memory. "I couldn't sleep. Just kept seeing that thing grabbing Kim off the landing pad . . . I took a pill. So, I don't know if he was up all night." She winced. "I was just lying there in bed, feeling miserable. And Felix gets up. Walks to the door. He reaches up and unlocks it."

She rubbed her grief-swollen eyes. "I asked where he was going. But Felix just froze in place with his hand on the door. I told him I knew what he was feeling. That I was just as horrified at Kim's death. That Daddy would want us to go on. He never answered me. Like he wasn't there. His eyes vacant."

Kevina stared emptily at her hands, as if there was some answer hidden there. "I got up and physically turned him around and marched him back to bed. It was as if he was putty. I just sort of bent him back onto the mattress, covered him up.

"But the weirder thing was that when he got up again, he didn't remember it. Wasn't even concerned when I told him. Said it had nothing to do with his father's death. He and Breez just sat there holding hands. Their faces . . . um, sort of blank."

Michaela walked over, stared down at Kevina. "The boy lost

his father last night. It's shock." She took a breath, looked around at the room, at the jumble of expressions. Some with weary acceptance, others broken, some scared, all of them desperate.

Michaela declared, "As far as deciding whether to stay or leave, let's table that for now. Give it a couple of days to settle. In the meantime, everyone stays in. Nothing can get to us as long as we are protected by the Pod's walls. Let's see if we can get a handle on how the kids got infected, see if it's spread to the adults."

And what if it has? she asked herself. *What are we going to do if we're all infected?*

At least—if Raya Turnienko was correct—it wasn't deadly.

Her thoughts returned to the image of Kim Yee being speared from behind and lifted into the night sky.

There were far more dangerous threats on Donovan than just a sick little boy.

54

The adults said science club was a way to keep the children's minds off the terrible things that kept happening. For Felix, it was a relief. The notion that his father had been carried off in the night still wasn't real. Didn't matter that Mother just kept weeping, that she wanted to lay in bed and clutch Daddy's pillow to her stomach. Kim had always been there. His smile, the delight in Kim's brown gaze, filled Felix's memory. He only had to close his eyes, and Father wasn't gone; he'd be bent down on one knee to be on Felix's level. Mostly the memories were on Crew Deck on *Ashanti*. Father was just always there. Telling Felix things, making him better when he fell, or got in trouble.

Or the times Father had taken him to Astrogation Control, or the hydroponics where they had to pass the horrifying hatch that kept the cannibals from eating people. Father had always made things better. More than Mother, he'd been a friend.

"Don't be sad." The Voice came every time Felix wanted to cry. And it was like a warm rush would fill his body. Even when he wanted to bawl like Mother was doing, the warm rush would dry his tears. The terror would just go away. In its place, Felix would feel blank. Not hurt. Not happy. Just blank.

Blank was okay. It was better than hurting, better than crying and feeling sorry that Father had been carried away by some flying thing in the night. Better than knowing he would never see Father again. Ever. Better than knowing Father was dead.

Sheena, of course, was delighted as Vik Lawrence led Felix, Felicity, Tomaya, and Breez up the forbidden stairs to the upper floor with its laboratories, com, clinic, and offices. Like downstairs, a central hallway ran the length of the building. At the far end was Michaela's office, then the radio room as they now called communications. After that came the various labs, specimen rooms, the clinic, and the shops.

Vik led the way down the white hallway, the soles of her slippers tapping on the hard floor.

The woman wore a lab coat with a pocket that held her pad. Underneath she had on common coveralls.

Sheena walked proudly behind her mother, almost strutting, because, after all, science club was her idea. And now, just like she had said, they were going to actually do science. Not on the algae—that was a secret after Toni had spilled it all over—but on something the adults called a "tube."

Felix had overheard Michaela telling Vik Lawrence, "Can you take the kids up to your lab? Give them something to do except dwell on the situation?"

"Sure. I've got one of the tubes Cascy netted. Been meaning to dissect it, get a first look at the anatomy. Maybe it will take Breez and Felix's mind off their parents." A pause. "And I think Kevina needs time alone."

"Odd that Felix isn't as torn up over his father's death."

"He's a kid. It's probably still not real," Vik had answered.

Was that it? It still wasn't real?

Felix made a face. Something in the night had taken Father, flown off and eaten him. Something terrible like the cannibals on Deck Three. As the welling grief had started, the Voice just made it go away. That was all.

And then they got to do science club.

Vik led them to a door, tapped in a code too fast for Felix to see, and ushered them into the lab. The room was large, dominated by a central island full of all kinds of equipment, scopes, boxy-looking machines, lots of glass jars and test tubes, stuff made of pretty glass piping, and shiny metal gizmos. Each wall was packed with cabinets, desks, counters, monitors, and all kinds of fascinating things.

"This is the most zambo room I've ever seen," Felix whispered, feeling the Voice's assent.

"It's my mom's lab," Sheena told him with authority. "It's where microbiologists work."

"Yes, it is," Vik told them, turning and lacing her fingers together before her. "The first rule in microbiology lab is that you don't touch anything. Do you understand? If you want to see a piece of equipment or a specimen, I will explain it. All you have to do is ask. But first rule is keep your fingers to yourselves."

Felix and the rest all nodded. That wasn't a hard rule to follow. They'd had to live that way the entire time on *Ashanti*.

"Good. The second rule we have to follow is that we all stay together. No wandering around the lab by yourselves."

They nodded.

"Good. Now, we're going to have a very special day today. We're going to do the very first dissection of a creature out of the ocean here. We call it a tube, because, well, that's what it most reminds us of. It appears to be the most common organism to live in the water around us. Kel caught this one, and I have put it in a jar with pre-servative to keep it just like it was when it was alive."

Sheena put up her hand. "That's to keep it like it was fresh forever."

"That's right. Now, are we ready to begin?"

At their eagerly nodding heads, she said, "Follow me" and walked over to one of the counters that folded down. This she lowered until even Breez could see.

A large glass jar rested on the lowered countertop, and inside it held a blue, red, yellow, and silver creature that looked like a piece of hose with lines of fins on three sides. Felix could see the gaping, three-jawed mouth with teeth and lifeless gray eyes equally spaced around the head.

"Let's take it out," Vik told them, removing the jar lid.

With tongs she lifted the dripping specimen from the jar, let it drain, and laid it on an absorptive sheet on the counter. With long skewers she pinned it in place.

"Zambo!" Felix whispered, amazed to see the thing up close.

"Zambo twice!" Sheena agreed.

Felicity just stared, but Felicity was never much fun.

"What is it?" Breez wondered, lifting a finger to suck on it, her eyes big.

"This," Vik told her, "is the tube I told you about, but maybe today we'll give it another name. One that you all think up. So, as you grow up, you'll always think back to this day."

"What's wrong with *tube*?" Felix asked.

Vik shot him a glance. "Felix, if what we're seeing in the films is correct, most of the life in Donovan's oceans is tubular. We have to have a way to name them that allows us to keep all the kinds of tubes separate in a classificatory system."

He nodded, not sure what a classificatory system was, but if Vik said so, it had to be.

"Like calling all boys Felix," Sheena told him crossly. "You'd never know you from Toni or Kayle, if you were all called Felix."

He waited until Vik couldn't see and stuck his tongue out at Sheena. She just giggled and lifted her chin to show him she didn't care.

Vik was pulling on gloves. "All right, let's take a look. We have the cameras on to record everything we do. Why is that important, Felicity?"

"So everyone can see how it's done?"

"Well, yes, but also so that everyone can see the same anatomy we do. Scientists will look at this recording for years and learn what we do. So to begin with, I'm going to describe what we're seeing."

Felix and the rest listened and watched while Vik described the tube's head, the jaws and teeth, measured it, inspected the lines of triangular fins and the three holes in the tail that she said were vents.

But the real fun came when Vik used a scalpel and sliced down the length of the thing.

"Zambo!" Felix whispered as Vik used metal probes and laid the tube open so that its insides were exposed.

Felicity said, "Ohh" and made a face.

Breez asked, "What's it made of?" She stood to the side, eyes still wide. Periodically, she would press at the bottom of her jaw and the sides of her throat as if it hurt.

"Fascinating," Vik said. The woman carefully splayed the creature across the blotter, exposing all kinds of linear "organs" that ran the length of the creature. Pointing at this piece and that, Vik rattled off a lot of terms that Felix couldn't understand as she made the official record. For long moments Felix lost himself, suddenly frozen when the Voice took over. It used Felix's eyes to stare at the exposed pieces of the tube. The Voice was listening, watching, and totally absorbed as Vik picked through the tube's separated guts with a probe.

Felix might not have been in his body, as if the Voice was running it, learning. Weird. Felix was there . . . and he wasn't. Sort of like he was in a dream.

From a great distance, Felix heard Vik say, "What all that scientific jargon says is that this creature has three sides, see. People, like you and me, have two. Right and Left. That's bilateral symmetry. Donovanian life is three-sided. Like the tube. So, look. There is a central, shared digestive system that runs through a kind of web. When you look closely you can see the little bugs it ate for dinner being digested in different places around the net."

"Ohh!" Felicity took a step back.

"Grow up," Sheena told her. "This is zambo."

"But here"—Vik used her probe to separate out one of the three light-brown strands that ran from the root of one of the jaws clear to the vent—"we have the most fascinating organ. See the thick places with all the blood vessels? Those are the gills, our equivalent of lungs, and then we have these bands of muscles running all the way to the vent at the rear. I'm betting they work like our esophagus does, through something called peristalsis. They expel water out the back and shoot the tube forward like a jet. This organ serves to both aerate the blood and propel the creature. Call it a gill jet."

"What's wrong with lungs?" Sheena asked and made her point by breathing hard.

Vik considered, her brow furrowed. "Nothing. We do fine with them. But, like fish, life on Donovan has found a more efficient solution than either the vertebrate or arthropod versions of lungs."

"What's a arthro-what's-its?" Felix asked, coming back into possession of his body. In an instant it was like the Voice had never been there. Felix could move his arms and legs again.

"Like spiders and scorpions. Being born on *Ashanti*, you've never seen one."

The Voice made him ask, "Are humans better designed?"

"Not necessarily better," Vik told him. "We're just adapted to a different environment. The nervous system, our organs, and bones are made for walking and living on land. The tube is designed to live in the sea. Feel the bones in your arms, and then look at the tube. Notice how the bone structure is?" She prodded a line of hard structures that the gill jet was attached to. "It's not the same as bones, but more like a plastic."

Off to the side, Felicity had gone blank, her eyes unfocused. She kept humming the melody to "London Bridge Is Falling Down" under her breath. It was all he could do to keep from singing with her.

Felix felt it when the Voice took control of his eyes, seemed to be directing them to different parts of the splayed creature.

"This is how we know how things work," he told the Voice.

"Yes. I see."

55

Her first thought was that she was smothering, only to have a blast of air inflate her lungs. With a start, Talina jerked, coughed. Felt something shift her body, lowering it onto a painful surface as she gasped for air and coughed. And coughed. She grew aware of the powerful roar; it seemed to fill the world. In addition, Talina's back ached. She shouldn't be this cold. This uncomfortable.

A racking bout of coughing sent spasms through her body. Caused her to sit up on the hard gravel.

Gravel? Shit on a shoe, the stuff was eating into her backside and butt.

But, where the hell . . . ?

Talina tried to understand. The little angular stones under her butt were part of a lenticular gravel bar in the middle of a river. On either side, the water was bounded by the vertical walls of a high gorge. Bits of greenery—some of them with gorgeous blooms—clung to cracks and fissures in the black canyon's sheer sides. Colorful four-winged flying creatures wheeled overhead in flight. Smaller than mobbers, these were apparently a cliff-dwelling species. To Talina's instant relief, none seemed to pay her the least bit of attention. Maybe they didn't have human on the menu.

From long habit, she checked. Her pistol, knife, and survival pouch were on her belt, but her overalls were soaked, as was her hair, and she could feel the water squish in her boots.

Craning her neck, she stared back upstream to the twin cascading waterfalls for which Two Falls Gap was named. The gravel bar had to be four hundred meters downstream from the thundering falls. She stared across the roiling water, gaped at the dizzying heights; how the hell could she have survived that plummet?

Another fit of coughing left her breathless.

To her right, a soggy Dek Taglioni sat with his butt on a driftwood log, his feet at the lapping water's edge. The man had his forearms braced on his knees, limp fingers dripping water where it drained out of his soaked overalls. He had a crooked smile on his lips, a daredevil twinkle in his designer-yellow eyes that she hadn't seen for some time now. The pink scar contrasted with his pale skin. And what was it about his eyes? The pupils seemed larger, darker, with an uncanny depth.

"What the hell?" Talina shifted, groaned. Her body felt like it had been pulled sideways through a singularity. "Did I just fall off a cliff? Am I remembering that right? Like, I was moving at the same speed as the water falling next to me?"

"Remember hitting the bottom?" he asked.

"No."

"Probably because the way you hit, it should have broken your back." He paused. "It wasn't supposed to happen this way."

"Excuse me?"

"I tore loose of your hold, so you wouldn't fall. What happened?"

"Rock came loose under my foot as I was careening for balance. What do you mean you tore loose? You did this on purpose? You leaped off the cliff and went over a waterfall? That's a fricking thirty-meter drop! You trying to kill yourself?"

"Yeah, well, I figured it was worth the risk. Had to do something to get that little shit out of my brain. That stuff, that TriNA was picking through my head, playing with my emotions. Making me hate myself. Turned me into a fucking lab rat. I was losing, Tal." Again the crooked grin. "Maybe you've been too busy to notice, but I don't like losing."

She shook her head, which did nothing but slap wet hair around. Gasping, she made herself stand. Her whole body felt like a bruise. Every joint ached. Cocking her head, she used a finger to squeegee the water out of her ears. "So, maybe it's you who haven't noticed, but we're on a gravel bar in the middle of the river. How did we get here?"

"I was treading water at the bottom of the falls when I saw you pop up a couple of meters away. I swam over, got your head out of the water, and towed you downstream. Pulled you up on the gravel.

Got the water out of your mouth and throat and as much of your lungs as I could. Repaid you a favor. Gave you mouth-to-mouth until you coughed your way back to consciousness."

That sense of smothering and the burst of air? Mouth-to-mouth?

"I don't taste peppermint."

He frowned, worked his tongue. "Me either." A laugh. "The bastards were too panicked by the near-drowning. I can feel them cowering inside. Is that weird, or what? I mean, they're just molecules, right? From the moment I hit the water, I've just been me. After the last couple of weeks? I can't tell you what a relief this is."

"This is what your plan was? Throw yourself into the river?"

"I remember what you told me about quetzals hating water." His shoulders jerked in a halfhearted "Oh-well" shrug. "The waterfall wasn't in the original plan. Just dive into the river below the dome. Submerge myself and play like I was drowning. Easy, right? Get control, and wade back on shore. Repeat as necessary until I could figure a way to keep Demon at bay."

He winced. "The molecules wouldn't let me. We just kept struggling, me trying to get into the water, the quetzals trying to keep me out. Might have gotten it done my way, but Flute and Rocket's bunch were just as afraid as Demon's. We seesawed back and forth, and just kept battling our way downstream until there was nowhere to go. By then I was desperate enough to shoot myself rather than let Demon win."

He worked his right index finger as if pulling a trigger, staring at it thoughtfully. "I was going to get him out of my head, even if it meant blowing him out with a bullet. Weird thing. I had the distinct feeling he couldn't comprehend what I was doing. That somehow, given quetzal sensibilities, the fact that I'd kill myself confused him. Sort of like it was so far beyond any rational action it defied reality."

"Quetzals don't understand suicide? Makes sense. It would be a dead end for TriNA, which is essentially immortal. Quetzals eat their elders, pass the TriNA along down the generations. The idea of just letting all that information go to waste would be a nonstarter. An act of incomprehensible futility."

He gave her a soft look. "When I saw you floating, I had a moment of complete panic. I was afraid you were dead. That it was my fault."

"Nope. It was the quetzals'." She looked around at the roiling water as it swirled and sucked its way on both sides. The closest bank was a good thirty meters away, but the basalt walls were sheer. The other shore, maybe sixty meters distant, was wooded back for a distance of ten meters or so before the vertical wall of stone rose to the tree-topped heights so far above. "But, more to the point, how are we going to get out of here and back to the dome?"

Dek made a face as he glanced around. "Okay, now there's a question. And we've got another problem."

"What's that?"

"After I dragged you out and got you breathing, I pulled a number of soft tube-shaped sucker things from where they were chewing on our overalls." He pointed to a frayed spot on his sleeve and then to a couple more on his and her pant legs. "See? None of them had latched onto flesh, but if they could do that kind of damage to fabric, I'd bet skin wouldn't even slow them down."

Talina fingered one of the frayed spots in her right coverall thigh. "Well that sucks snot, doesn't it?"

"Yeah." Dek was staring back up at the falls, at the high cliff from which they'd fallen. "Got my pistol and your rifle up there. That pistol on your hip still functional after a soaking like we just had?"

"Military model. It will take a lot more than a dunking to disable it. But it's a short-range weapon. Only carries ten rounds of explosive tip. We run into a Tyson-type treetop terror, we're gone. If what's left of those mobbers find us, we're going to end up sliced finer than sandwich cuts. If we come face-to-face with a quetzal, I can put him down if we're up-close and personal. The good news is that it will make sausage out of sidewinders, bems, and skewers. But that's assuming we can get back to land."

"Yeah." Dek glanced around, fixed on something large that passed just under the water's surface and made a splash. "That was a whole lot bigger than one of those tube things. Think it's dangerous?"

"Just what planet do you think you're on?"

Talina turned her attention down-canyon. The distance was perhaps another four hundred yards, and she couldn't be certain, but it looked like an alluvial fan spread out from under a crack in gorge's sheer walls.

She pointed, saying, "That might be our way out."

"How are we going to get there? I consider it a miracle that I was able to tow you to this gravel bar without being eaten. After seeing that big thing swim by, getting in the water is about as exciting as letting quetzals back into my mind."

She studied the chabacho log he sat on, took in the couple of pieces of aquajade that had had the misfortune of being tossed into the river by their fellows. Definitely not enough to make a raft out of.

She unsealed her pouch, poured the water out, and found what she was looking for. A tube of adhesive and a roll of cord.

Raising an eyebrow, she told Dek, "Time for us to get naked."

He grinned. "I thought you'd never ask. But shouldn't we be putting our energy into getting off this gravel bar first?"

"What if I told you I have a plan?"

56

Michaela had come at a fast trot when Anna Gabarron had paged her through com, saying, *"Director, we've got trouble."*

Michaela took the stairs to the lab level two at a time. She had been in her quarters, at her sink, preparing for bed. Now, a robe wrapped around her, her broken arm in a sling, she rushed through the quiet Pod.

The only sound was the soft purr of the HVAC system and the distant splashing of water on the pilings. She'd seen the latest view from the external cameras. The once-white pilings were now blue-green, covered with a thick and slimy coating of algae. The stuff had worked its way up to cover the bottom of the Pod. In places it looked like it might have been a couple of centimeters thick and was now creeping up in dendritic patterns that almost reminded her of veins.

She wasn't sure why that was surprising; she'd seen algae and moss growths back on Earth that were twice the size.

Turned out that not everything on Donovan was terrifying. Some things, like the algae, were a constant. Right down to the ever-present patches that Tobi Ruto kept blasting off the deck and more particularly out of the Underwater Bay. The good news was that the power washer removed the stuff in mats that just peeled free and sluiced back into the sea.

At the top of the stairs, she made the left, hurrying to the clinic. Ducking inside, she closed the door behind her, asking, "What have we got?"

Anna turned from the isolation tent—a clear, plastic bio-container with its own oxygen and ventilation system. The intravenous drip fed a needle in little Toni Yoshimura's arm to keep him hydrated and fed; a catheter ran from the little boy's penis to the collection bag on the isolation tent's wall. Samples could be drawn through the plastic by means of a syringe for analysis.

"Got a problem," Anna told her. "Sorry to bother you, especially with everything that's going on, but I thought you should know. Toni's got some kind of growth in his neck. I saw the swelling under the corners of his jaw. Didn't think much of it, but it's creeping down the sides of his throat. Take a look."

Michaela stepped close, looked down through the plastic to where Toni lay on his back. The IV in his arm looked incongruous, too large for a such a little boy. The half-lidded eyes remained vacant, the kid's breathing oddly automatic, more like a machine's than a person's.

And yes, there, at the corner of the jaw, Michaela could see the swelling. It looked linear, running down on either side of the child's trachea to just above the collarbones.

"Mumps?" Michaela asked, searching for anything in memory that might be similar.

"Mumps has been extinct on Earth for the last hundred years. Thought it might be an infection, maybe from a molar that was draining through a cloaca into the soft tissue. I've got a negative on any kind of titer or elevated white blood cell count. No sign of infection. If it was a swollen salivary gland, it wouldn't be running down the neck that way. So, with nothing else left to try, I used a needle and aspirated the edema."

Anna turned away, tapped a finger to the wall monitor, flipping through images to the one she wanted. "That's what I got."

"What am I seeing here?"

"Those are cells, Director. Donovanian cells interacting with human cells. The invaders are the ones without a nucleus. But look at the structure. This is ordered. Not random like cancer cells. These are forming a specific . . . God, what do I call it? I'm not sure that it's an organ and not sure that it isn't a tumor. It's something new. Half-human, half-Donovanian."

"What does Raya Turnienko say?"

"I don't know. I've got a call in, but Two Spot said she was in surgery. Fixing some guy's foot who got it run over at the mine.

Said she could get back to me, but it would be late. I told him that I'd call back in the morning." Anna ran a hand over the back of her neck, a soul-deep weariness in her eyes. "I thought I'd show you before we called Yosh and Mikoru."

"Thanks." Michaela stared down at the swelling. Shit on a stick, couldn't the little guy get a break? What the hell was this going to turn out to be?

"If it's a tumor, can we surgically remove it?"

Anna crossed her arms. "I can't. I don't have the implants or the experience. We're going to have to fly Toni to PA. Turnienko's the only person on the planet who can deal with this. Especially if it turns out to be malignant."

"Malignant?"

"Hey, Michaela, we're way off the map here. Whatever these things growing down the side of the kid's neck are, it's like nothing recorded so far on Donovan. It's something new. And I don't have a clue about how to reverse this, let alone get this kid out of his coma."

"What about an antihistamine? Something to reduce inflammation? A steroid or something that would make the swelling go down?"

"You're assuming it's glandular, maybe—"

"Hell, I *don't* know. I'm grasping at straws here. But, screw me with an ion, it's worth a try."

"Okay, you got it." A pause. "Call Yosh and Mikoru?"

"They just put Breez to bed. Given Kevina and Felix's problems, they took her. The little girl still hasn't realized that her moms are gone forever. Let the kid sleep. Hell, maybe by morning the swelling will be down, and we'll have all caught a lucky break."

"Yeah . . . maybe." But Gabarron didn't look like she believed it for a minute.

57

F elix came awake. Or it seemed like he did. He should have been asleep. In his bed. That was the last thing he remembered: Mother, that sad look in her eyes, the quivering of her lips, as she tucked him in.

She had undressed, laying her clothes out on the chest of drawers as she always did, pants and shirt folded neatly. She had pinned her golden hair up. On the ship, where most shaved their heads, she'd kept her hair long. Said it was an "affectation." Whatever that was. She used to leave it down when she and Yee were going to do the sex thing.

Felix had watched as she pulled her blanket back and folded her long legs into the bedding. Her face working, she'd turned off the light. For a while it was quiet and dark. Then Felix had heard Mother crying softly.

He had thought about slipping out of bed, of climbing in with her, holding her. That maybe that would have made things all right. But he missed Father, too. Wondered if crawling in where Father had slept would be wrong. Like he was trying to take Father's place. And doing so might hurt Mother even worse than she was.

He'd been thinking that when he fell asleep. And he should have been in his bed. That was the last thing he remembered.

But now, as his mind began to work, he was standing in the Pod's kitchen. And he could hear things. Things he'd never heard before, like the waves washing against the pilings down below. And deep thrumming, an almost musical sound. Then he realized the slight whisper was the wind around the landing pad two floors up.

Weird. He'd never heard those things before.

"You will hear a great many things, even more than you can now."

The Voice was right.

The kitchen's refrigeration unit was really loud with its fan and pumps. He had no idea how he had gotten to be here. He'd been asleep. That's all he remembered.

Now, here he was. The lights were on. He was standing by the door, his back to the cafeteria. Something wasn't right with his hands, and when he looked down, it was to see them covered with sticky blood. Lots and lots of sticky blood. So much that it was thick on his fingers, clotted on his nails, and rolled like little balls when he rubbed his hands to try and get it off.

For a moment he was terrified, a thrill of fear making him cry out.

"It's all right," the Voice told him.

As it did, the fear faded, and to Felix's surprise, it was all right. Like being afraid just drained out of him.

Next he looked to see if he was hurt. But there was no cut anywhere. He was standing in his underwear, his legs, arms, and chest naked, but blood smeared.

So if he wasn't hurt, who was?

Felix turned around, followed his bloody footprints back around the kitchen island. He should have been afraid. That's what he told himself. But he wasn't. The way Bill Martin was laid out on the floor was just wrong. Instead of running like good sense said he should, Felix stepped closer, heedless of the pooled and drying blood that tried to stick his feet to the floor.

Bill Martin was flat on his back. His clothes had been cut off and spread out like a sheet under him. Felix stared in fascination at the way the man's skin had been slit up the front of his thighs to a place at the root of his penis, and then up through the man's chest, up his throat, and through his head. Then the skin had been peeled back to expose the guts.

There they all were. Looking shiny. Mother had shown him pictures of human guts on her pad. Felix couldn't remember what went where, but Bill Martin's guts looked like they'd been moved around, and one, a dark-red oblong organ, had even been left out.

So, who had opened Bill Martin up like this? And why?

"Now we know how humans work."

Again, the fear started down in Felix's stomach. Started to make him panic. He wanted to cry, afraid like he'd never been.

But the Voice brought reassurance, and the icy-scared feeling went away.

For that, Felix was ever so thankful. He hated being afraid. This other feeling of being reassured, calm, was so much better. He understood that he should be sad for Bill Martin. Bill Martin had always been good to him. Smiled and winked. And since they'd come to the Pod, Bill Martin had slipped Felix and the rest of the children special treats when the other grownups weren't looking.

Funny how he wasn't sad. Wasn't tempted to cry. He was just normal. And what had happened to Bill Martin was normal.

Felix looked down at the blood on his skin. Then up at the clock. People would be getting up soon. Martin always came to the kitchen to start breakfast at 4:00. The time now was 5:35.

"I should go take a shower now," he told himself. If Mother saw him all covered with blood, it would scare her. And Felix didn't want to scare her. She was already sad enough about Father being taken by the thing in the night.

If he hurried, he could be back in bed before Mother even woke up.

58

The sheer brassy ingenuity of it had to be admired. Dek would have marveled over it had he not been so busy huffing and puffing as he blew into the sleeve of his overalls. It was a constant battle, and he was getting light-headed. But the fact was, he and Talina were out of the water. Mostly.

Talina's plan was simple: Build a frame out of the chabacho log and the smaller aquajade poles that had beached on the gravel bar. By themselves they were nowhere near buoyant enough to float two people. But with the overalls placed beneath an ad hoc netting made of knotted cord, the contraption made a sort of inflatable raft. The inflatable part being the variable as the once-close-knit fabric over their overalls wasn't nearly airtight. The more egregious leaks—like where the tube things had chewed—had been sealed with Talina's adhesive. The rest had been smeared on places like elbows, knees, and the seats where wear had loosened the weave. After that, the wrists and ankles had been double knotted, the fasteners closed, and they'd blow the things up, then cast out, adrift.

And blow. And blow. And continued to blow. The overalls deflated as fast as Talina and Dek could huff and puff in a frantic effort to keep the things afloat.

But they were almost to the alluvial fan as the current wheeled them around and seemed to play with them. When Dek looked down through the clear water, he could see things moving down there. Nothing he could discern, just shapes. And periodically invertebrates would break from the surface to fly a short distance before hitting the water again and disappearing. Like they were being chased from below.

He barely had time to marvel at the canyon's beauty. Let alone fantasize about the woman beside him, her thick hair pulled back as she lay partially submerged, head up, blowing into a sleeve for all she was worth.

They had to make that shore, but a quirk of the current wheeled them around and tried to dance them closer to the river's thread where it curled away from the alluvial fan.

"Legs over the side. Kick!" Dek called from breathless lungs. "We've got to get to that beach!"

Talina, sharp as ever, shifted, half supported by the chabacho log as she slipped her muscular legs into water and began kicking. Dek—almost capsizing them—did the same. Kicking like mad as he propelled their sinking raft toward the beach.

And all the while, he expected to feel that sudden sharp pain as some riverine leviathan rose from below and sank its teeth into his pumping calves or feet.

They were making it.

Closer.

Just another thirty meters. Twenty.

The sinking raft was more a hindrance to progress, the deflating coveralls acting like sea anchors. But the contraption was keeping their chests and stomachs above water.

Ten meters.

That's when he glanced sideways, saw the shape headed toward them. Something big and coming fast enough that the water flowed smoothly up and over its back. Dek watched with growing unease. Whatever this was, fast as it was, it came to attack. Drawn to their kicking as they pushed the raft.

Do I stop? Ask Talina for her pistol?

Too late. It was on them. Through the clear water Dek had a momentary glimpse of eyes, a greenish-brown shark-like head. He could see the mouth, three jaws, lined with teeth as they parted. He braced for the . . .

Something big caught the predator from beneath, bursting up from below. Water erupted, showered Dek with spray as the two creatures battled. Dek got a fast glimpse of the shark-like attacker, its three-jawed mouth open in agony as it thrashed back and forth. Whatever had it from beneath had sunk long teeth into the thing's sides. Blood streaked and smeared on a silver-shiny hide beneath a speckled and green-brown back. Thick muscle bulged, as the creature tried to tear free of those hideous jaws.

And with a massive flip of its body, whatever had the shark wrenched its victim down into the depths. Another fountain of spray cascaded down, and the wave it left behind came within a whisker of capsizing Dek and Talina's sinking raft.

"What the hell?" Talina asked, having missed the entire show.

"Just get us to shore!"

Dek kicked for all he was worth, heart in his throat. He could feel the stress in his lungs, the chafing in his throat, and the burn in his legs as he gave all to the effort.

Five meters to go, and the current was carrying them past, rushing them.

Come on! Dek willed everything he had into making that fast-vanishing beach.

Which was when Talina rolled off the raft, dove, and appeared on the shoreward side. She was standing, having obviously found bottom. Head and shoulders out of the water, she pulled, dragging them against the current. The image of her straining face, the passion in her eyes, would stick with him.

Then it hit him, and he, too, rolled into the water, thrashed for footing, and struggled to pull their unwieldy vessel to the shore. Barely beached, Talina shouted, "Back on the raft. We're barefoot. Get your boots on first thing. I don't want to dig a slug out of your foot."

Dek didn't think, just tumbled onto the wet mat of their half-submerged raft. He reached for his quetzal-hide boots—stopped long enough to painfully rip one to the tube things from his left calf and sling it into the river. As it hit, something broke the surface, snapping it between tooth-filled jaws and vanishing beneath the roiling waters.

"So help me, if I never see another river . . ." A shiver ran down his spine. Looking back, the sucking and welling currents showed no trace of the shark-thing or its bigger and much scarier killer.

Heedless of the blood streaming from the wound, Dek pulled on his boots, and in his underwear, helped Talina drag the craft higher on the beach.

Dek bent at the waist, hands propped on his knees as he sucked for breath. "God, that was close. You have no idea. That big splash? That was a predator killing a predator that was going to kill us. And the beach. It never looked so far away. We'd have missed it . . . but for you."

She shot him a weary grin, her own lungs heaving.

Dek decided he liked the view; he'd keep that image of her: half naked, her toned body at the river's edge, the fantastic beauty of the sheer-walled canyon and vegetation for background. She exuded something primal—the essence of a healthy female in a state of nature, untamed, incredibly competent, and reeking of sensuality.

"My God, I love you," he told her. "Promise me you'll stay at my side for the rest of my life."

The way she laughed and slung her wet hair back, sent a tingle through him. "Dek, gotta tell you, that's the best offer I've had since . . . Well, for years." She looked around, took in the narrow beach of mixed sand, gravel, and small rocks. Then she turned her attention to the narrow fissure in the gorge wall. Vegetation choked the narrow cleft. "But, looking up at where we have to go, the rest of your life might be a matter of minutes. No telling what's waiting for us up in that crack."

He pulled himself straight, letting his gaze roam the dark recesses in the cleft. The crack was bare meters across, packed with trees, vines, and brush. "No way past if there's a chokepoint full of predatory vines, brown caps, or a tangle of fast roots, huh?"

"Not unless we can climb around them. You any better at climbing than you were outside of Tyson Station?"

"Thankfully, for once I can say that I am." He allowed himself a triumphant smile. "A couple of months on Donovan, not to mention the quetzal in my blood, has worked wonders."

She studied the angle of light on the canyon walls, the packed tufts of cloud rolling in from the east. "We've got maybe three or four hours before dark. And you know what happens at dark."

"Welcome to Donovan?"

"Correct. Let's get dressed and get the hell up and out of here."

After all, Talina only had ten rounds in that pistol of hers. If there was any bright lining to their situation, it was that whatever they came face-to-face with in that narrow slit in the rock, it would be up close and personal.

Made him wonder. What was the point of being madly in love with a woman if he was going to be dead in a matter of hours?

Seemed universally unfair.

59

The way Bill Martin was positioned on the kitchen floor, skin peeled back, guts exposed, blood everywhere, the single kidney left outside his body in the puddled gore . . . could it be real? Michaela stumbled sideways against the kitchen island to brace herself. Tried to understand what she was seeing: blood—smeared and pooled—the colors of the exposed organs, the dark red-brown of the liver, the pink lungs, intestines tan-gray, the stomach rose-pink. And then there was the head, split in two like a . . . a . . .

She turned away, the image of the brain sagging and bloody in that transected skull nightmarish. Beyond belief. The kitchen seemed to reel, spin, and she clutched the counter to steady herself. This couldn't be. It just couldn't.

Iso Suzuki's frantic call had brought Michaela at a run, her bathrobe wrapped around her, her skin still dripping from her shower. Now she wished she'd taken the time to at least put on shoes.

Iso stood back by the door, her round face slack with disbelief, her eyes large and stunned. The woman was shivering, her entire body wracked. "This is how I found him," Iso kept protesting. "I was going to get a cup of tea for Bryan. So when he got out of the shower, he'd have it. I . . . I . . ."

Michaela stepped back, still unable to process what she was seeing. Bill Martin's clothes had been sliced up the front, laid flat like some macabre sheet before whoever or whatever had cut him open. The whole scene was so bizarre, so unbelievable, she was having trouble finding her thoughts. Part of her insisted this was some creepy joke, perhaps a dummy placed there for shock value.

This couldn't be Bill Martin. Kind, suffering Bill Martin, who'd loved Shinwua, dealt with his lover's peccadillos, and always took him back.

Yosh burst through the kitchen door, pulling to a stop as he got his first look at the gruesome corpse behind the island.

"What the fuck?"

"This is . . ." Michaela fought for words. "What the hell happened here, Yosh? Who did this?"

People were calling, steps pounding outside in the cafeteria.

Michaela turned, ordering, "Stay back! Everyone. Stay back! Keep your asses out of the kitchen."

At the door, Anna, Kevina, Odinga, and Ruto all crowded together, expressions anxious.

"Yosh. This is insane," Michaela managed as she forced her brain to work. "Who'd do this?"

"No one!" Yosh cried. "This is Bill, for God's sake!"

Yosh started forward, Michaela grabbing the fabric on his shoulder. "Wait. Think. We've got to use our heads. Look around. What do you see?"

"Blood. Bill's body. It's like it was dissected. The organs are jumbled. Not put back in anatomical order. I mean, the skin's like it was flayed open. The way his clothes were cut up the front . . . autopsy style"

"Vibraknife there," Michaela pointed. "That's what cut through his pubis and sternum, then up through the jaw and laid the skull open."

"Yeah, well, it's covered with blood." Yosh bent down, staring at the floor. "Shit on a shoe, Michaela, these tracks? Look! Barefoot. It's a fucking kid. One of the children was here."

Michaela vaguely heard the uttered speculation running from lip to lip among the people clogging the doorway. Iso was telling them exactly what was hidden by the kitchen island.

"A kid?" Michaela stumbled over the notion. When she really fixed on the tracks—and there were a lot of them—it sank in. "This can't be happening."

Yosh carefully picked his way around the body, trying unsuccessfully to stay out of the mostly dried blood. He used two fingers to pick up the vibraknife. Squinted as he studied the handle. "I'm no expert, but these prints in the blood. It's a child's hand."

Yosh laid the vibraknife on the counter, fixed on Martin's right leg. "This is the only cut that isn't surgical and precise. Here, on the back of Bill's knee. Like it sliced right through the back of the joint. See? Severed the tendons and ligaments, transected the femoral arteries and veins. Bill couldn't have stayed on his feet. Would have fallen. Bled out within minutes."

"How could that happen?"

"He was cut from behind. Never saw it coming," Yosh told her, straightening. "Down low like that? And with a child's fingerprints on the vibraknife? You thinking what I'm thinking?"

"No! And neither should you. None of our kids would do something like this. It's totally . . . I mean, do you hear what you're saying?"

"How could they? Felix is only eight, for God's sake. Sheena and Felicity are seven. Breez was with us last night. This is freaking impossible." Yosh's face worked; he swallowed hard. "None of our kids would do this. Not to Bill."

Michaela fought for air. "This is a nightmare. An impossible fucking nightmare."

Yosh had tears streaking his face when he turned to face her. "What's happening to us?"

60

Dek had ducked beneath the first of the vines and was crossing a shallow root mat when the quetzals began to insert their presence into his mind. At first it came as a subtle warning to step right, to avoid putting a foot on a particular greenish root as he followed Talina. What left him unsettled was a feeling of turmoil, once removed. A realization that something seethed and flexed just below the surface, that it was locked in conflict. But inexplicably, recognition hovered just below his consciousness. Like it teetered on the edge of breaking free—and if it did, it would consume him. If he had to put it into words, it might be likened to having an unfelt inferno in his core, nothing he could physically experience, but he sure as hell knew that his gut was twisting itself into a knot.

It's all of them. Locked in milling, moiling, and mayhem.

The determination to end it all, the plunge over the falls—the river—had reshuffled the deck. All that TriNA intelligence, Flute's, Rocket's, and Demon's, was resorting.

Talk about toilet-sucking weird. A battle was going on inside him, and he couldn't even act as spectator. Those competing, replicating molecules were deciding his future. Realization engendered a queasiness in his muscles, bones, and nerves.

What if Demon's side wins?

And all the while, he had to remain focused on the bush. Everything he'd gained could be lost in an instant with a single wrong move. For the moment, brown caps, a pincushion, or some unknown creature, not to mention thorncactus, claw shrub, or purple burst flower, could kill him dead.

Unsure what he could do to influence the molecular conflict in his blood, he tried to focus on Talina. On the root mat, the hanging vegetation, and any scent of vinegar that would warn of a bem or skewer. He followed her, mimicking her steps, echoing every move her supple body made. He stepped wide where she did, seemed to share her awareness of the dark holes, the curious and new vines that hinted of danger. Periodically she'd glance back, and he'd see the flash in her now-familiar eyes. And most of all, a new intimacy in the way she shared his glances.

He'd always had an attraction toward her, but after this day, he was falling hard. Dealing with feelings he hadn't known since his youthful fling with Kalay. But Kalay had been about the heart-pounding passion of first love. That total commitment of raging hormones and all-consuming obsession driven by sexual novelty and the belief that their bond was unbreakable and eternal.

"What are you thinking?" Talina called over her shoulder as she skipped from one head-sized stone to the next where they protruded from the root mat.

"That it's different this time."

"What is?"

"Until I met you . . . No, wait. How do I say this? I've known a lot of women."

"No shit? How'd I miss that?"

"Hey, cut the caustic. You never had to live as a pampered and frustrated Taglioni first-born son. That's a lot to overcome in an entire lifetime, let alone a measly decade."

"So? Have you?" Talina flipped out her knife. Like a blur, she severed a thick stem where a biteya bush that blocked the way grew from a crack in the rock. The vine immediately began to contort, fluids spattering this way and that. "Don't get any of that on you. I think if we go back around that boulder, the rest of the vine is going to be so busy dying it will ignore us."

"Dying does that," Dek agreed, stepping back, leading the way around the boulder, making sure in the process that nothing hid on the stone's opposite side. He got no quetzal warning as he winced and scurried beneath an outlying tendril of the contorting biteya bush. The air was ripe with its peppery odor.

Dek picked his way, taking his time before each step as he climbed. Through the thin branches of an aquajade, he could see the cleft toward which they ascended. The root mat was thinner here; the stuff squirmed under his weight and the grinding rock that shifted underfoot.

He said, "Going back to the subject, let's just say that becoming a human being after having been a Taglioni is a brutal and sobering ordeal. One I've had to relive in too-intimate a detail over the last month as Demon picked through the disgusting flotsam that makes up my memory. The man I am now really hates that guy who swaggered his way onto *Ashanti*. Not only that, I'm ashamed of him. The stuff you heard about? As the old saying goes: tip of the iceberg."

"That's not winning you a whole lot of points." She scrambled when rock rolled under her feet. As it did, a flurry of invertebrates exploded, only to vanish into cracks and crevices. "But I will say this, it's nice to have Dek back and Demon at bay. How's that going, by the way?"

"I think we're on the way to solving something. That fall into the river, it broke the impasse. I've got a war going on inside me. Nothing I can put my finger on. A feeling of desperation and conflict, and the fact that one way or another, I'm going to be different when it's all settled."

"Different, how?"

"One way, I'm a new Dek. The other way, Demon triumphs and I either drown myself or put a bullet in my head. The lines are drawn, Tal. I won't be what Demon wants me to be. Nor will I be the heartless-and-amoral tool that my dear father was so desperate to mold me into. I will be the man I want to be—one worthy of what I think you might come to love in a man."

"You think I'm that kind of a prize? Me?"

"That's what I was getting at when I said I'd known a lot of women. Even loved a few. You, however, make me whole." He smiled to himself. "And that is something I've never known."

She remained silent as they climbed through a steep cone of talus. Little multi-legged creatures kept scattering this way and that. Most had sharp horns, stingers, or things that looked like spears protruding from their backs. Not the kind of creatures to grab with a bare hand. At the head of the talus, the narrow-walled crevice loomed dark in shadow, the aquajade, stonewood, and some big-leafed overhanging . . . "Tal? That's a mundo tree right there in the open-ing to the crevice."

He stopped, let her climb up next to him. On either side, weird thorn-covered two-meter-tall plants with waving hair-covered leaves ensured they didn't venture too near.

"Mundo tree all right," she agreed, avoiding his eyes. "See the detritus beneath? That's bones and bits of body parts. If you look closely you'll see tentacles hanging down in the lowest leaves."

"Uh-huh. If I was an old Donovan pro, I'd say that might be a real honest-to-God nightmare up in those big leaves." He didn't need her assent. He could feel it through quetzal sense. It still sur-prised him, that weird way of knowing without knowing how he knew it.

"You'd be right."

"What are we going to do? The damn thing's right across the trail."

Talina glanced to each side, staring thoughtfully at the rock walls where they rose in angular blocks. "Thank God it's basalt. Dek, time to show that gnarly old nightmare what primates are all about."

Dek chewed his lips, nodded. "Still, it's a hell of a good location. That nightmare tags anything climbing up or down the chute."

This time she gave him the intimate look again. "I think you'll do, Dek. That is, assuming that the right band of quetzal molecules comes out the winner. I'm starting to think I'd really hate it if Demon won. I like you a lot better when you're you."

"Yeah, me, too."

So, come on Flute, Rocket, and clan. I'll get us past this shit-sucking nightmare if you can keep a lid on Demon. And maybe we can all convince Talina to fall in love with us.

61

The psychic trauma just got worse. Michaela cradled her aching arm and sat at the front table in the cafeteria. Bill's body had been wrapped in plastic and carried out to the dock where the seatrucks and launch were parked. As she looked out at her people, the horror of it kept crashing down on her.

Did she really believe that a child murdered Bill Martin? Then cut him up like he was a frog in a science lab? That dissection could *not* have been a child's work. Kids didn't think like that, have that kind of motor control. The cuts had been so precise. A child wasn't capable of that kind of lab-perfect efficiency.

People were shouting at each other, some crying, others pacing between the tables, expressions dark and brooding. Like them, Michaela had no idea what to do.

"My son didn't do it!" Kevina thundered as she faced Yosh. "He was asleep in bed when I left the room. If you think he's the murderer, where's the blood? I just got him out of bed. Looked at his hands. They're clean! He didn't do it."

"Then who did?" Yosh roared back, his face red, fists knotted. "You saw that knife, the tracks in the floor. It was a child's, and you're telling me it was Felicity or Sheena? They were in bed, too. And they have no clue about any of this. The tracks on the floor are too big for Breez, even if she hadn't been in the same room as Mikoru and me."

"My son didn't do this: He's a kid. He's only *eight*, for God's sake!"

Michaela took a deep breath; all of it kept spiraling out of control. "Hey! Stop it! All of you. Sit down and be quiet. We have to think. Figure this thing out." They just stared at her, eyes reflecting anger, fear, disbelief, and confusion.

"I said, *sit down!*" She jabbed a no-nonsense index finger to emphasize the point.

One by one they dropped into the nearest seats, glancing back toward the kitchen as the room went quiet enough that they could hear Iso where she was cleaning up the dried blood. If anything, that sobered them more than any demand Michaela might have made.

And damn it, who was going to cook? Which one of them could stand to be alone in that kitchen, taking Bill's place?

Solve that later, she told herself.

"Stop the recriminations," Michaela shouted, feeling herself on the verge of panic. "We're scientists, for God's sake. We'll find who did this. Yosh is right. We've got the prints on that knife, and only one set of feet will match that blood trail. When we do—"

"My son didn't do this." Kevina cried. "He was in bed, I tell you."

"And he's locked up with the other children in the observation dome," Michaela shot back. "Anna's keeping an eye on all of the children as we figure this out."

"And what if Felix attacks one of the girls?" Mikoru asked.

"Don't you *dare!*" Kevina half-shrieked, leaping from her chair. "Felix would no more hurt one of those girls than he'd hurt a fly."

"Or Bill Martin?" Mikoru cried, arms spread wide.

Kevina started for her, only to have Kel Carruthers rise to block her way, saying calmly, "It's all right, Kev. We'll figure this out. Now, sit down. You have my word."

"That's right." Michaela tried to use a reassuring tone. "There's got to be an explanation. We're going to find it. Now, I've got Casey doing a little research with the UV light. She's taking a look at the hallway. If the person who walked in all that blood walked down the hallway, Casey will find traces of it."

"And what happens when she does?" Kel asked, sharing glances with the others. "Let's say it is one of the kids. What do we do next?"

"No one lays a finger on my kid," Kevina promised, her face like a mask.

Piss in a pot, what if it really was one of the children? Michaela used her good hand and rubbed the back of her neck, images of Bill's dissected body making a horrific vision behind her eyes.

"How could a child do what we saw done to Bill?" Vik asked, shooting a frantic glance at her husband. "Sheena, Felix, Felicity, they're *children*. It would have taken a man to do what was done to Bill."

"Or a woman," Atumbo declared.

"Hey," Michaela barked. "The killer used a vibraknife. Cut Bill across the back of the knee. A vibraknife will cut through bone, as Bill's skull more than proves. He was taken down from behind. Probably had no idea what was happening. One second he's getting ready to start breakfast, the next he was on the floor, bleeding out."

Yosh added, "And the angle of the wound? It's low, at a slight slant. The outside of the stroke runs lateral to the femoral condyles. Then the blade was run medially and down. A man or woman would have had to be on their knees to make that same cut."

"That's crazy!" Tobi Ruto slapped his hands to the table. "That's saying one of the kids . . . Hey, I know these kids. We all do. Come on, seriously, you're going to tell me that Felix, Sheena, or Felicity just decided to get up early and wander down to the kitchen to murder Bill? Are you hearing how pus-sucking *insane* that sounds?"

"All of this is insane," Mikoru half-whispered as she broke into tears and dropped her head into her hands. Yosh laid a reassuring arm across her back.

"Got that right," Odinga muttered, arms crossed. "Nightmare on the ocean, and it doesn't seem to be letting up."

"It doesn't make any sense." Kevina's voice actually came across as half-rational for once. "These kids aren't crazy. Seriously, any of you, have you ever seen any of the children acting irrationally? Violently? Making threats?"

"Does that include going catatonic like Toni?" Vik asked. "Let's be honest. Sheena's my daughter. I haven't been watching her like a hawk. I've had other concerns. We all have. Yes, she's seemed reserved, introspective. I caught her walking in a daze yesterday. Like she wasn't home inside her head. But when I touched her, she was back. Looking up at me like she hadn't seen me in a week. But to think that that same girl might have murdered Bill?"

Michaela added, "Think about this from the children's perspectives. They only knew *Ashanti*. That was their world, and lord help us, with the Unreconciled down on Deck Three, it wasn't the most stable of environments in which to raise kids. Then, magically, they're here. Like an entire frame and paradigm shift. And no sooner are we moved into the Pod than people start dying in horrible ways. Sometimes it's their parents, but everyone who was killed is like an aunt or uncle. Shin, Lara, Jaim and Varina, Lee, these are people these kids have lived with and counted on for their entire lives. And we're all afraid . . . all of us grieving and scared. Then we tell the kids they've been infected. That there are alien molecules *living* inside them. Think of the psychic shock to those developing brains and personalities. It's a miracle they aren't screaming in the hallways."

"Tomaya was just staring into space," Odinga agreed. "I mean, sitting there on her bed, her arm raising and lowering, hand pronating and supinating. I asked her, 'What are you doing?' Took me three tries to get through. Like Vik said with Sheena, I finally touched her, and she came back. When I asked her what she was doing, she said, 'I'm not doing anything. It's just my arm. It's learning.'"

"Learning?" Ruto had a strained look on his face. "She told me the same thing about her leg the other day. Said it was learning how to walk. I told her that was interesting, because she'd been walking since she was two. She told me it was 'learning by itself.'" He shrugged. "You know how kids are at that age."

Kel said, "Hey, well, an arm or leg 'learning by itself' is harmless compared to what happened to Bill."

Michaela raised a hand for their attention. "No matter what we find out, people, we've got to start keeping a better eye on our children. We may be carried away with our own tragedies and loss, but at least we can process them. For the kids? Raised as they were on a single deck in a starship? This whole experience has to be terrifying. We owe it to them to be . . ."

Michaela stopped as Casey came striding into the room, her face ashen, cheeks tear-damp as if she'd wiped them before entering.

The woman's mouth was working, her gray eyes as terrified as Michaela had ever seen them. The UV blacklight was still clutched in Casey's right hand, a child's underwear in her left.

First Casey fixed on Kevina, then she glanced around the room, her gaze ending with Michaela.

"What have you got?" Michaela placed her hand to her suddenly pounding heart. Her breath seemed to have vanished.

The moment was caught in her memory, crystalline, every detail so precise.

Casey lifted the underwear, shined the UV on it. In the room light, it could barely be made out. The black splotches where blood absorbed the spectrum. "Found the child," Casey said woodenly.

"Those are Felix's!" Kevina cried, standing. "I made those for him."

"Yeah," Casey told her. "And he's got blood under his fingernails. I didn't run the fingerprints yet, but you can bet they're going to match the ones on the vibraknife. And none of the other children fluoresced. Only Felix." A pause. "When I asked him about it, Felix said, 'I wasn't there till the end.' When I pursued it, he told me, 'The Voice said it was all right.'"

The Voice?

62

Years ago, when Kalico's father had finished a tough day, he had used the expression, "I feel like I've been beaten with supple sticks." The saying seemed particularly apropos that evening when Kalico stepped into Inga's, crossed the foyer, and paused at the head of the stairs that led down into the tavern. Damn. She had a lot of history in this place.

At the long tables, her people—along with PA's residents and a handful of Wild Ones—sat behind mugs and glasses or bent over plates as they chowed down on whatever Inga's special was. The sight of all those wide-brimmed hats, the quetzal-hide cloaks, propped rifles, and tough-looking people, brought a smile her face.

God, it was good to be back. Especially after her disastrous visit to the Maritime Unit and then the pain of the cave-in and all that came spiraling out of that. For the first time since the collapse in the Number Three, she'd reinstated the weekly rotations to PA. During the disaster, she'd wanted all hands available for rescue, support, or who knew what? Not that any of her people would have wanted to be anywhere but Corporate Mine.

At the bottom of the steps, she strode down the central aisle, waving and answering greetings called by the locals as she passed.

She could imagine the reaction back in Transluna. She was a fricking Board Supervisor, one of the most powerful women alive. The very notion that a woman of that stature would deign to share greetings, let alone riposte to ribald and insolently familiar salutations, would have left her old boss Miko Taglioni apoplectic.

Calls of "Sorry to hear about the cave-in," "Anything we can do to help, you call," "Our prayers are with you, Supervisor," and "You need anything, let me know" warmed her heart. Doubly because had she asked, each and every one of the crusty Donovanians would have sprung to. Not because she was a vacuum-sucking Board Supervisor, but because she was one of them.

When did these become my people?

Kalico found her way to her old stool beside Talina Perez's where it stood on the far-right side of the bar. To her surprise, Shig Mosadek was seated at his accustomed place. He had a half-full glass of red wine, was staring thoughtfully at the back bar with its mirror and bottles, jars, and jugs. The man's unruly thatch of hair reminded her of a stiff mop gone gray at the sides. Shig's expression looked pinched around his blob of a nose. He'd taken his quetzal cape off and hung it from the back of his chair.

"I hear you've had a rather tough time of it down at Corporate Mine."

"Lost the Number Three. When it went, it took two of us with it." She caught Inga's eye. The woman was stretched up to write a charge on the big board where she kept her accounts. Inga jerked her a nod as she scribbled with her chalk.

"Anything Yvette or I can do?"

"Turn back time?"

"Been to *Freelander* recently?"

The reminder of the ghost ship up in orbit sent a shiver down her back. "If I could figure a way to go up there and warn myself, I would. Problem is, you never know what you're going to get. That creep-freaked wreck isn't exactly reliable when it comes to messages from the future."

"I heard it was the aquajade."

"Yeah." She propped her elbows on the bar. "Don't let it get saturated." A pause. "Talovich is going through the Number One right now. Checking every single piece of aquajade for potential failure. Soon as we landed, I ran down Lee Halston. Bought up every chabacho timber he had that might be used to replace a compromised aquajade. Until Talovich finishes his survey, Corporate Mine is officially on standby."

"Businesses here will welcome that. Gives your people time to come spend money." He shot her a sidelong glance. "What about

Maritime Unit? Two Spot tells me that your parting of the ways wasn't amicable."

"My presence wasn't welcome."

Inga came lumbering down the bar, two fingers of whiskey, neat, in a glass. Inga flipped the bar towel from her shoulder and took a couple of swipes before she set the glass on the battered chabacho-wood bar. "Heard it's been a tough time down at Corporate Mine," Inga told her. "That one's on the house. From all of us. Anything else I can get you?"

"On behalf of my people, the drink is deeply appreciated. Whatever's on special, I'll have it. Haven't eaten since breakfast. Way I feel now? I could eat a bucket of slugs. Raw."

"No slugs on the menu." Inga turned, headed back down toward her taps, bellowing, "One special for the Supervisor. Extra portion. The lady's hungry!"

Shig grinned. "Wouldn't the Board love to have seen that?"

She jerked a thumb toward the rest of the patrons. "Funny thing, Shig. After the last couple of weeks, I was feeling right at home walking down those stairs. Come a long way since we held that sham of a show trial here. I was just marveling that each and every one of these people have my back."

"They know you've got theirs. You've put your life on the line for them too many times. Pity the Corporation if they ever show up and try and bring you to heel."

"You saying I'm totally corrupted by you libertarian bastards?"

"Totally." Shig picked up his wine, looked at the color, and set it back down. "What happened with the Maritime Unit? Anything Yvette and I need to know about? Anything you need us to do?"

Kalico lifted the whiskey. Tasted it. "What is this? Inga tapped all the right keys this time around."

"After her last disastrous attempt, she dug out the last barrel of the good stuff. It's going fast. If you like it, get a bottle while you still can."

Kalico let the rye sit on her tongue in order to savor it, swallowed, and said, "Maritime Unit decided that they were better able to run their affairs without my advice. They didn't trust me. Thought I was getting them killed. Asked me to leave."

"That's Corporate property. You are a Supervisor. And, as I still like to remind you, you have marines. With armor. Not to mention tech. Essentially you are not only the law, but there's nothing they could do to stop you."

"I've been here too long." Kalico pointed a finger Shig's way. "You're right. There's nothing they could do to stop me. But worse, I've sucked up so much of your libertarian insanity, I am unwilling to expend the effort to try and save them from themselves. Why the hell should I? Stupidity is just Darwin in action."

"They do have a nice Pod out there, I'm told."

"The survivors will be calling one of these days soon. They can choose Corporate Mine or PA. They'll be broke." Kalico gave Shig a poke with that same finger. "The Pod and the equipment are Corporate. I would take it badly if someone were to take any of it in trade."

"They have a sick kid."

"They do?"

"You didn't hear?"

"They don't talk to Corporate Mine. Must have been on the hospital frequency?"

"They set up their own frequency. Maybe they didn't want you to know? They're talking to Raya about it. A little boy. I guess there's some sort of infection. A bacterium or something. Two Spot says they've lost a submarine. You've heard none of this?"

"Not a word." *Lost a submarine? Shit!*

"Guess that parting really was acrimonious."

"Maybe I shouldn't hold it against them. Like my arrival here tonight reminded me, I was pretty arrogant, self-assured, brash, and righteous when I got here. They're suffering from the same Corporate delusion that life is a fairy tale. I won't put up with it. Which makes me ask: Why the hell did you put up with me?"

"You were surrounded by twenty armored marines with tech that could have flattened PA and murdered every man, woman, and child in the compound."

"I suppose that does elicit a modicum of tolerance."

"A small modicum, I suppose. Ultimately, you know that Director Hailwood's people are going to need relief of some kind or another."

"Yeah, Shig." Kalico sighed as Inga approached with a heaping plate of enchiladas drowned in red chili sauce surrounded by stuffed poblanos. The smell was heavenly.

"Two-fifty, Supervisor," Inga told her. "You're up ten on the board, so I'll just subtract." And she was gone, bellowing, "Yeah, yeah, Hofer, I hear you. Give me a second to scratch my achin' ass, and then I'll get you your damn whiskey."

"Transluna never had it so good," Shig observed mildly. "Are you sure you want to call these your people?"

"Damn straight." Kalico picked up the fork and dove into the steaming delight. Chewing, she asked, "Where's Tal?"

"She's still out at Two Falls Gap with Dek." Shig shot her a mild look. "Dek, it seems, is dealing with the ramifications of being awash in quetzal TriNA. Given the creative and violent nature of his hallucinations, Talina rightly figured that he—not to mention the rest of us—was a great deal safer with him out in the bush."

Kalico stopped cold, a curious unease in her gut. "Tal and Dek? Alone at Two Falls Gap? For how long now?"

"Long enough." Shig arched a bushy eyebrow. "Talina radios in every couple of days to keep tabs on things. I do know that Tal is worried that Demon might be getting the upper hand."

"And what is Tal going to do if he does?"

Shig gave her a fatherly smile. "She will do what she has to, even if it breaks her heart."

Yeah? Kalico thought, *and what about mine?*

63

Fire popped and snapped, sparks shooting up toward the night sky as the flames flickered yellow on the closest aquajade trunks and danced across the thick leaves the trees pointed in their direction. Camp was made on the canyon rim—on bedrock where no roots or slugs could wiggle their way close. Overhead, a column of invertebrates swarmed, chittered, hummed, and chimed, as well as occasionally roasted and fell into the fire to blacken and crackle, adding to the sandalwood scent from the burning aquajade, chabacho, and mundo stem.

Talina studied Dek where he sat in the firelight and used her knife to sharpen the end of an aquajade sapling. The poor aquajade had been a youngster a little over three meters tall when it was uprooted by its neighbors and tossed out onto the bedrock. There it had withered, desiccated, and died. Dek had claimed it for a spear and was whittling the end into a lethal point that he occasionally fire-hardened in the flames.

Maybe it wasn't the perfect weapon for Donovan, but it beat nothing. After the trip up the cleft, anything was an improvement. The miracle was that they had made it.

Talina sat cross-legged, studying her scabbed and raw hands. Some of the places she'd scaled defied description, let alone belief. Then she'd glance at Dek. All through that hard and dangerous climb, he'd been a perfect companion. Not quite as adept at spotting danger as she, he'd nevertheless saved her from disaster more than once. Asserted to by the fact that her pistol was now three rounds shy of a full mag. And that last shot had been made by a hair's breadth. She had no clue what to call the snake-like creature that had shot out of a dark crack in the basalt canyon wall. It had been big, three-eyed, and had a lot of teeth in a triskelion-jointed jaw.

Dek's warning had barely been in time.

The thing would have killed me, and I'd never have seen it coming.

Nor would she have been able to make that climb without a second person to lend a hand, to lift her up, and to steady her as she eased her way across the treacherous gaps. A couple of times, she'd been scared to the core; he'd given her that reassuring smile, his odd Taglioni eyes looked even more odd as the quetzal TriNA continued to modify the receptors in his retina.

"He's never going back," Rocket told her from his perch on her shoulder.

She chewed on her lip, realizing that with Rocket's declaration, she felt a curious sense of relief. Some part of her had expected him to eventually leave. The man was a Taglioni. One of the elite ruling class. And, from the perspective of a woman raised in Chiapas, almost an Olympian god. A sort of magical and mythical being who would ultimately be called back into the clouds.

Or Transluna. Essentially just as unreachable.

Fact was: Rocket was right. Donovan had taken Derek Taglioni for its own.

She asked, "What do you want, Dek? Assuming that is that Demon doesn't win, and you don't kill yourself."

"Nothing like sugarcoating a question, is there?" He sliced off another long shaving of white wood with the gleaming blade.

"I mean it. Oh, I know, there's the claim out west, your rigged poker game at The Jewel on those rare nights when you can get there. But be real. The claim will make you rich, granted, but it's small-time. Just gold, some silver, a little platinum. To really make it pay, you need equipment. Some way to transport the ore to Kalico's smelter. That's where the real money can be made. In the beginning, I thought the claim was a way to kill time. Get your feet under you. I figured that eventually you were going to hook up with Kalico. Broker some partnership with her that would get you an interest in Corporate Mine, but now, after being with you out here, I'm not sure."

A flicker of a smile crossed his lips. "Kalico? She and I will always be confidants. It's a measure of the kind of woman she is that she could look beyond the man I was back in Solar System. And I'll always owe her for that."

Dek frowned into the flames as some night creature screamed out in the trees. The night chime answered, and back in the forest a ululating call carried on the still air.

"So, you didn't plan to make a play for Corporate Mine?"

"I might have. But it was a fleeting notion that died within days of leaving Port Authority that first time. Kalico Aguila is never, ever, under any circumstance, going to surrender so much as a share of Corporate Mine to anyone. Not ever her old sponsor, Miko. She's bled too much, sacrificed too much. And if Miko should show up and try to claim it out from under her?" He gave Talina a conspiratorial wink. "God and the universe help the man. She'll gut him."

"So, back to the question. What do you want?"

"Right now? To keep a lid on these quetzals."

"Wish you'd never shared Flute's TriNA?"

He shook his head, looking perplexed. "You and me, we're alive today because of this TriNA. Without it, you'd have died when you hit the bottom of the waterfall. Impact would have killed you. But for quetzal sense, I'd have died a horrible death four or five times climbing up out of that dark fissure. I'm soft meat, Talina. I could not have known about that nightmare, the three-eyed snake in the crack, those green-shelled invertebrates, or that creepy white-thorn vine. After ten years of atrophy in *Ashanti* there's no way I could have clung to that cliff as we climbed around that patch of tentacle bushes."

"Hence my original question. What do you want, Dek?"

He lifted his spear, tested its point with the ball of his thumb. Then he gave her an eerily intent stare. "I want to be with you. Do what we're doing. I want to join my life to yours."

"*Good man.*" Rocket whispered into her ear as the intensity of his declaration warmed her.

"It's a lonely life, Dek. And years ago, when I shot Clemenceau, I made my choice. I have responsibilities to my people. To protect them, do what I can to keep them safe." She rubbed her forehead, aware of the weight of it all. "These days, Whitey is using what he learned from me to threaten Port Authority. With all the advantages this TriNA gives me, keeping my people safe may be even more important than in the past."

"I understand." His gaze narrowed as he considered her. "You like doing it alone? Being different? Never having anyone to confide in, to share the load?"

"I . . ." Shit, what did she tell him?

"I've been honest with you, Tal. How about reciprocity?"

"All right, it's like this. I have Shig, and Yvette, and Kalico, and Kylee. That's it. Kylee's been in my head. She's got a lot of TriNA with my memories. We're bonded that way. The others? Shig is more like a priest and father, but I love him anyway. Yvette and I have shared blood, history, and loss. Kalico? She's an equal, but were we not thrown together on Donovan, I doubt we'd socialize much."

"What about you and Trish?"

"She was the daughter I never had. I counted on her. Even though things had been strained, when she went, it tore a hole in me."

"And Cap Taggart?"

"That tore me up, too. He and I never got a chance before he was . . . dead." She gave him a half-lidded stare. Did she tell him? Could she trust him? "You heard that he was murdered?"

"Uh-huh. Someone slipped in and overdosed him on pain meds. They never found the killer."

"Trish."

He started, frowned. "But everything I've ever heard about her . . . That doesn't make sense."

"It does when you know Trish. Donovan is a tough place to grow up. Trish had a hard life filled with loss. When Cap was crippled and paralyzed, Trish knew I'd spend the rest of my life caring for him. She did it to free me, and maybe Cap, too. She called it an act of love." She arched an eyebrow. "Shig, Yvette, and I know. And now there is you. Please don't let me down."

He gave the fire a thoughtful appraisal. "Of course not. That's between us." A pause. "Makes you even more amazing."

"How's that?"

"Is there anything you can't withstand? You come across as invincible . . . but there must be moments when you wonder if it's even worth getting out of bed, let alone continuing to be a pillar of strength for the rest of us."

She laughed at that. "Yeah. There are those days."

"My turn to ask. What do you want from me?"

Now, there was a twist. She let her gaze melt into his, was reassured that it was unflinching, honest. "I had fun today."

"You didn't see how close we came to being a meal on the river when the big monster was eaten at the last moment by the bigger monster."

"You didn't see how close that sidewinder came to grabbing your boot when I swung you up over that last ledge."

"Okay, so we had fun. Seriously, Tal, what do you want in a man?"

"I guess I want today. Well, all but the fall off that cliff. I still hurt all over from that." Again she met his earnest gaze. "I mean it. After you got your wits back from Demon possession, I had fun. You and I were a team, getting off the gravel bar, getting up the cleft in the basalt, figuring our way around danger. I enjoyed a sense of exhilaration I haven't had . . . well, since the academy I guess."

"Explain that. You've been in the bush plenty. You've had close calls up the yazoo. What made today different?"

It hit her like thrown rock. "I wasn't taking care of anyone."

He read her amazement. A slow smile spread across his lips.

She verbalized her thoughts: "I mean, yes. I was taking care of you, but you were just as involved in taking care of me. I sort of had that with Trish back before the quetzal TriNA started screwing with my life. The difference was, I was always the lead, and Trish had my back. You and I today, we switched off. With the exception of Kylee and Tip, there's no other human being on the planet that could have done what we did today."

The realization was like magic.

The look in Dek's yellow-green eyes added to her revelation. The man was practically beaming. "Victory," he whispered in self-satisfaction.

"That's not all there is to a relationship," she told him.

"No," he agreed. "But predator-filled rivers and clefts thick with deadly man-eaters is a start. There's also holding someone's heart in one's hands and realizing it's the most precious thing in the universe."

His gaze was now boring into hers. Firelight shone on the pink scar tissue on his cheek.

"And you think you're the one to hold my heart?"

"I was convinced of it as early as Tyson Station, but after today, I know it more than ever."

She tossed another section of mundo branch on the fire to keep the blaze up and predators away. "That's you, right now. In possession of yourself. You told me earlier today that the different strains of TriNA were still working it out. What if Demon starts pulling out the old Derek Taglioni? The one who trolled courtesans through Corporate high society as a way to show off? That guy worries me. Before I let you get close enough to see, let alone hold any heart of mine, I have to know that guy's dead."

Dek pursed his lips, chewed on them for moment as a frown lined his forehead. Finally, he nodded as if to himself. "Yeah, that makes two of us."

"That's giving in pretty quickly. Why no dying protestation of love?"

His eyes gleamed in the firelight. "Because I've come across the stars to find a woman I love more than life itself. Having done that, I don't want a bunch of alien chemicals to screw it up. And I don't know what's going on with the quetzal stuff inside me. I can sense rather than feel it, like a churning, and it's been fingering around the edges of my mind, as if trying to judge me."

"Judge you how?"

Dek frowned again, deeper, eyes narrowing in concentration. As if to something inside, he said, "Because I'm back on the rim again. And before I let you ruin my life, I'll toss us all off the edge. And this time, there won't be any water at the bottom. Just hard and unforgiving rocks."

64

The look in Michaela Hailwood's eyes should have frightened Felix. Instead, he was more worried about the deep-seated ache just down below the corners of his jaw. He hadn't been able to figure out what it meant. Just that the sides of his mouth hurt, and if he pushed on either side of his neck, he could trace the pain down to just above his collarbone.

And the sound had changed. Like the Voice had promised, he could hear more now. A faint singing, like a changing, fluttering harmony that surrounded the Pod. It sort of sounded like Shin's symphony music that he used to play on *Ashanti*, but different. And there were deep bass sounds, like a reassuring thrumming that crept up from the sea and through the pilings.

"Felix?" Michaela asked, leaning her dark face down to stare into his eyes. The woman looked scared. That, more than anything, had him slightly unsettled.

"Do you hear the music?" he asked, head cocked. "It's coming from the water."

"I don't hear anything. And we're way above the water."

Well, maybe she couldn't. Used to be that he couldn't either, and they had him locked in the containment room on the second floor. This was supposed to be for lab specimens, and now he was in here. There was nothing to do but look at the walls, hear the music, and he was hungry.

"Felix? Do you hear me?"

"Yes."

"Why did you kill Bill Martin?"

"I didn't. I wasn't there until the last."

"What do you mean, you weren't there until the last?"

"It was already done. Someone had done a study on Bill. You

know, dissected. Like we did with the tube in science club. But that wasn't me. I wasn't there until after it was all over."

Michaela's expression pinched, her eyes going hard. "Listen to me, Felix. Your fingerprints are on the vibraknife. In Bill's blood. You know what fingerprints are? Those are the little lines on the pads of your fingers and palms. Yours are distinct. No one anywhere has the same little ridges. That was your hand on the vibraknife."

"Okay. But it wasn't me."

"Then who was it?"

"I guess it must have been the Voice."

"Whose voice? Someone on the Pod? Your mother's, maybe Yee's?"

"No, it's a different Voice."

"Do you hear it now?"

"No. It's just listening. Wondering."

"The Voice listens and wonders?"

"Yes. It's learning."

At the word, Michaela seemed to start, her forehead lining. She studied him for a moment, then asked, "Do you feel bad about what happened to Bill?"

"I liked him a lot. All of us kids did. He was always nice."

"Then why did you cut open the back of his leg?"

"I didn't."

"Who did, Felix?"

"I don't know. Maybe it was the Voice."

He saw the flash of fear behind Michaela's dark eyes. She seemed to swell as she drew a deep breath. Took a moment, like Mother did when she was finding the right words. "What made you go to the kitchen in the first place?"

"I didn't. I was asleep in bed. And then I was there. And there was all this blood. But the Voice said it was okay. And it was. I could feel it."

"You don't remember going to the kitchen?"

"No!" Felix cried. "Don't you get it? I didn't cut Bill up. I was asleep. And then I was there. The Voice was learning. Like we did with the tube. It's how science is done."

"And you don't feel bad about Bill? My God, Felix, you were covered with his blood."

He could see that Michaela was getting upset. "I didn't get bloody. I was already that way. And I knew it would make Mother mad, so I went to the shower and washed it all off. Then I went to bed."

"You went to bed?"

Why did grownups always repeat things? "Yes. The Voice said it was okay. And I didn't want Mother to worry. She and me, we're already sad. That thing grabbed Father and took him away to eat him. People are dying. Everyone is scared. Sheena and me, we're just trying to figure it out. It's just got to be science."

"Wait, easy. I'm sorry. I didn't want to make you scared. I know you miss your father. I just need to know. We all do. Why did you kill Bill?"

He felt the welling tears. "I didn't! I wasn't there!"

Michaela's gaze went vacant, which was when Felix realized someone was talking to her on her com. She shifted uneasily, cradling her broken arm in its sling.

She asked, "Does the Voice ever do other things? Things you don't know it's doing?"

Feeling better, he said, "Sure. It does all kinds of things."

"Like what?"

He lifted his arm. Twisted his hand back and forth. "Like that. I can tell my hand, say, 'Don't move.' And the Voice will make it move anyway. Or open doors and things. It's like I'm me, but not me. Like I'm not driving my body. Pretty zambo."

"Pretty zambo?" she whispered under her breath, gaze vacant as something was said into her ear com. "Felix, what do you think the Voice is? Where does it come from?"

He shrugged. "I don't know. It's just there. In my head. It's not really a voice. More of a feeling, I guess. Sort of there and not there, except when it's moving me around."

"And how long have you felt this 'there and not there' feeling?"

"Since science club? Maybe before. Sometimes it's hard to tell."

"Does the Voice ever tell you to do things you don't want to?"

How did he answer that? "It kind of just does things."

"Like with Bill?"

"I *didn't* hurt Bill! I swear."

Michaela's worry-hard eyes seemed to bore into him. They were terrible eyes. Eyes that burned right through him. Made him squirm in the chair until tears started to well in his vision.

"I want my mother!"

"You'll see her in a bit," Michaela told him in that short, "I'm angry" adult voice.

"I didn't do it! The Voice said it would be okay. I was in bed, and then I was there. Don't you see?"

But Michaela stood, her face gone hard, cold.

"Yes, I see. I almost pray it's TriNA instead of psychosis," she muttered as she walked out of the room and closed the door.

As Felix wondered what psychosis was and stared at the door, he rubbed the sore places on the side of his throat. They had started to feel puffy now, as well as tender. On top of everything, they kept hurting worse and worse.

The Voice told him, *"It won't be long now."*

65

The shift in the chime brought Dek awake from crazy and tumultuous dreams. Quetzal dreams where he hunted silently in dim forest shadows mixed with human images, memories of his past, as well as bits of pieces of Kylee through Rocket's eyes. Then he'd be in Talina's mother's kitchen, or some insane Mayan ballcourt in Mexico. Once he was at a military-style graduation ceremony; another time a dark-haired, sloe-eyed young man was saying, "Hey, I don't want to see you again. I'm with Beth now," and his heart was breaking as he called, "Bucky? Hey, don't do this to me!" But the guy only stalked away.

Bucky? Beth? Who the hell?

Something screamed in agony out in the trees.

Dek blinked his eyes open. Crap! Capella's light was burning red on the undersides of the clouds drifting in from the Gulf. The eastern sky glowed—a rumpled-looking silhouette of black treetops in the distant lowlands marking the horizon.

A pop from the fireplace reminded him of where they were: exposed on weathered bedrock. At the lip of a sheer dropoff into Two Falls River Gorge. The aches in his body—in addition to the bruises and tortured muscles from his river adventures the day before—proved just how unforgiving basalt could be. When he looked at his fingers, they were scabbed, scuffed, and abused from the hard climb. A warm weight on his stomach made him glance down. Talina's wealth of black hair spilled across his chest; her head lay full on his belly. Dek savored how Tal's shoulder pressed against his side, and her arm draped across his crotch. The woman had drawn her knees up against his hip.

Okay, maybe sleeping on hard basalt had its positive points. That, or was this just his dreams come true?

The deal had been that they'd sit back-to-back in order to keep watch through the night and toss wood on the fire. After all, given the number of diurnal predators, who knew what kind of nocturnal beasts might come creeping or flying in out of the darkness. Tal's infrared sight was excellent, and Dek, to his amazement, found that he had night vision in a way he'd never had. But after the climb, they'd been exhausted. Needed the rest. And a fire was safety when they didn't know the local predators.

So, how had Talina's head come to be on his stomach? When had he fallen asleep?

He let his memory drift back to the gravel bar the day before. He replayed Talina's every move as she stripped off her overalls, baring that remarkable body. How the sun had played on her skin as she stood beside the crystalline river and shot him a conspiratorial smile.

At the thought, another of those anonymous memories appeared in his head: Talina, naked as she bathed in a pool of water beside a river. A camp on a gravel bar. A stormy and dark night. Thunder booming. Rain lashed the dark river, pattered on a broadleaf-vine shelter overhead. A fire crackled just beyond the shelter where the remains of a crest cooked. Lightning flashed to illuminate the clouds like giant white lanterns and silvered the rain-stippled river.

Dek could see the guy, ruggedly handsome, head shaved. Realized he lived the memory as Talina, who curled into the crook of the man's arm. Heard the guy say, "Talina Perez, I'd cross a thousand galaxies just to sit here and share your company."

She shifted, reached up to pull the man's lips to hers.

The tingle grew down in his pelvis; he felt the longing, the need for another human being. Talina's desperate fingers were pulling at the man's jacket, peeling it from his shoulders as the . . .

The image burst when one of the four-winged canyon fliers rose above the edge of the cliff, gave him a surprised three-eyed stare, and squawked.

Dek jerked. Talina started, instantly awake, and rolled off his stomach to pull at her pistol.

"It's all right," Dek told her. "I was having a dream."

"Oh?" Talina tossed her hair back, rubbed her eyes, and climbed wearily to her feet.

"Gravel bar. Different from the one we were on. Lightning and rain, a broadleaf-vine shelter. I was you. Weird. There was a man there. Said something about crossing a thousand galaxies . . ."

He stopped at the startled and panicked flash of her eyes.

"That was real, wasn't it?" he asked softly. "You lived that."

She took a deep breath, walked over to stare down into the morning-dark depths of the canyon. "Wow. Well, I guess it's not all that unexpected." She turned, fixing him with a hostile stare. "Just how far did that memory go?"

"You were pulling at the guy's jacket when I jerked you awake. I can guess where it was going. That was Cap, wasn't it? The guy looked like a marine."

She closed her eyes, obviously upset. Jerked a brief nod.

"It's all right, Tal." He stood, walked over, and put his hands on her shoulders. "Look at me." When her uncertain eyes fixed on his, he added, "Remember the part from last night about holding a person's heart in my hands? You see, this is the part of love that I never understood. Never would have if I hadn't survived *Ashanti,* hadn't come to you."

"Want to get to the point?"

"That's quetzal TriNA sharing your memory, and there's probably going to be a lot more as I come to grips with this stuff. But the thing that I understand now? It's how far I will go to protect you. I promise to respect your memories. I will not pass judgement. That's part of your heart, and I will honor and cherish it. I give you my word."

He saw the welling of her tears and pulled her close, reveling in the feel of her firm body against his.

In the end, she pushed back, wiping the wetness from her eyes, and gave him a wary smile. "I'll take that promise. Listen. I did things. Stuff I'm not proud of. Like Pak and Paolo. That Talina? That woman? She's not necessarily who I am today."

"Way ahead of you. I, uh, sort of have the same problem, as you're now well aware. God help me if you ever get memories of the man I was. You'd puke and put a bullet in my head just out of principle. Humans live messy lives. Some of us learn, and while we can't change the sins of the past, we can learn from them. Use what shames us to make us better people."

She gave him a halfhearted nod. "Yeah, well I was falling in love with Cap. That night on the river? That was special for the both of us."

"I know. I could only hope to be so lucky."

She gave him a wink. "Keep talking like you are, and you just might." A pause. "But, in the meantime, come on. It's light enough that we can see mobbers before they see us. Let's go find my rifle and your pistol. I'm half-starved, getting thirsty, and there's breakfast at the dome."

"You've got it." He reached down for his newly crafted spear.

As she started off along the canyon rim, she called back, "Thank God it was Cap. Could have been worse. Could have been good old Bucky Berkholtz."

Bucky? The guy who'd run off with Beth at that graduation?

Dek was smart enough to bite his tongue before he said anything that would have gotten him shot or tossed off the cliff.

66

The way Tobi Ruto saw it, things really couldn't get any worse. He passed the pressure hatch and started down the stairs in the tube, headed for the Underwater Bay. The UB was supposed to be on his daily inspection and maintenance routine. After Bill's gruesome murder, no one had done anything according to schedule. The situation was too appalling and incomprehensible. Tobi couldn't rid himself of the memory of Bill's body. Every time he thought of it, it made his skin creep. He'd loved Bill. Everyone had.

The notion that little Felix had murdered Bill—cut him apart and dissected him—defied any kind of credibility, but there it was. That cute little precocious eight-year-old child had committed bloody murder and then sliced Bill's body open to play with the man's guts?

Tobi slowed on the stairs, peering at the tube windows. They should have been crystal clear, allowing a visual experience as he descended beneath the waves, and then got a view of the underwater scape where the reef dropped off. Instead, each of the oval windows was covered with green-blue, leaving the tube so dark that the lights illuminated the steps.

Well, hell, that was just more of the shit that he was going to have to hose off. But what was it about that algae and the Pod? Last he'd seen it was coating every square centimeter of the pilings and water line. Worse than any moss or algae he'd ever seen on Earth's oceans.

Another thing to put on his endless list.

As his feet thumped off the stairs, he rubbed the back of his neck. During all those years in *Ashanti*, they'd grown into a tight-knit community. A sort of extended and sharing family. Like him, Jym, and Casey. Didn't matter that Tomaya was his daughter and little Saleen was Jym's, or that two men and a woman could be as good as married. Sure, Casey and Jym both had PhDs, and Tobi was a

lowly Pod Technician Level 1. They loved each other for one another's human qualities. Back in Solar System people would have
looked at them askance. In the Maritime Unit they were accepted
as who they were.

But it was all coming apart at the seams. So many beloved friends,
dead. The realization of how perilous their existence was, and now
Felix had used a vibraknife to murder Bill. Bill, of all people? For
God's sake why?

And little Toni was comatose, his neck swelling, and it appeared
to be nothing that Anna Gabarron could cure?

To his, Casey, and Jym's horror, that morning Tomaya had been
bleary-eyed. Said she wasn't feeling good. That her neck hurt.

Ruto, felt that nervous tension build in his stomach. Tomaya
hadn't been herself. Not for a couple of weeks. She'd been listless,
sometimes so vacuous it was like she was suddenly sleepwalking.
Then, after someone touched her, she'd be right back, as if unaware
that she'd ever gone blank.

"Give her a bit," Jym had told him. "She's under a huge amount
of stress. We're in a new place, an entirely new environment, and it
turns out that it's full of sea monsters. Bill is murdered, and her
friend Felix did it. Casey almost died in the sub that day. Tomaya
will figure it out. The miracle would be if she wasn't reacting to all
of this."

Still, the thing was, little Toni had a swollen throat. Whatever it
was, pray to God that Tomaya didn't end up like Toni. Or worse, turn
psychotic like Felix.

"How does that happen to a little boy?" Ruto wondered as he
tapped in the code for the pressure hatch that would let him into
the Underwater Bay. Especially to a boy he'd known from the time
the kid had been nothing more than a bump in his mother's belly?

Neither of Felix's parents had been crazy; if there had been a
history of mental illness in their families, they'd have never been
chosen for the Maritime Unit. Living as intimately as the Maritime
Unit did, any physical or mental abuse would have been known to
everyone. Felix had been loved and cherished his entire life.

"So where did this freaking murderer come from?" Ruto cycled the hatch, felt the pressure build, and undogged the interior door, stepping out into the Underwater Bay.

He stopped short as the hatch door closed behind him.

"What the hell?" The sight and the smell hit him at once. The bay reeked of . . . what did he say? Spicy? Musky? Pleasant and growy but alien and dank?

And the algae. The stuff was everywhere, lines like veins creeping across the bay floor, branching out, and thick where nodule-like growths emerged from the water. Ruto stepped over to the closest, stared down. He could see the trunk, if you could call it that. Thick at the base where it emerged from the water, it pulsed just the same as a pump. Ruto could see that it pushed water up through the trunk and along the stem on the floor. At each branch, the pulse of water was divided, the branches continuing to push the smaller and smaller pulse of water through additional branches to the ends where they radiated out like roots across the sialon.

And this was just one! Across the entire bay floor, the dendritically patterned veins of blue-green growth spread in a mazework across the sialon. At the nearest sub cradle, they traced up the track, onto the framework that supported the heavy craft. Here and there, the thin branches reached previous colonies, and now seemed to supply them with water. Those same colonies—that Ruto remembered as only being the size of a Port Authority 1 SDR coin—were now thick mats the size of a dinner plate.

The yellow submarine was splotched with them. Made it look oddly sick, as if a gleaming piece of equipment could.

Ruto stepped over the closest trunk, picked his way on tiptoe to the sub. Where Bryan Atumbo had been working to repair the bent propeller housing, a thick coat of the algae had grown around the disassembled parts.

"It's only been two days," Ruto cried.

His gaze traveled down the length of the bay. From one wall to the other, algae was growing out of the water, pumping, expanding.

Bending down to get a closer look, Ruto was amazed to see that the stuff was actually crawling. Moving slowly across the floor. Kind of like looking at the sun back on Earth. You never actually saw it move, but when you measured it against something like a scratch on the sialon, you could see an irregularity in the side of the trunk was actually creeping its way past.

So the stuff was growing out of the water; what the hell was it going to do? Take over the bay? What did it eat, anyway? It was supposed to be a bunch of single cells that would make up a sort of mat. Vik had said nothing about any tree-shaped madness growing to take over the UB.

"And it's only been two days? What if I hadn't made it down here in three?"

Maybe it would have been hanging from the ceiling, too?

Growling under his breath, Ruto heedlessly stomped his way across the bay floor. As he did, the trunks squished and splashed as they ruptured, pulses shooting along the various branches. Each of the stems convulsed—and the entire floor went apeshit, wiggling, jiggling and berserk.

"Crap. What a mess," he muttered as he reached the roll of hose on its spool and looked back.

How long was it going to take to shoot all this mess back into the water, and if it floated, how was he going to flush it back into the sea?

"I don't need this today," he cried as he began unspooling the hose. "My little girl's sick, and I gotta shoot a bunch of scum back into the ocean? Give me a fricking break!"

Ruto opened the valve, water shooting out from the nozzle. As he pulled out the hose and whipped pressurized streams back across the floor, clots of torn algae went with it.

That's when he saw where the stuff had made it across the floor and was climbing the UUVs in their hangers. Not just little threads of the blue-green, but whole thick mats were wound around the propellers, the camera stalks, and buoyancy tanks. Cleaning them was going to take hours.

His heart sank, irritation rising as he turned the nozzle on the closest mat of algae. Shit on a shoe, the stuff was a good three to four centimeters thick. Blast one spot loose and flap it back on top of itself, and it seemed to stick together, making a six-or-seven-centimeter-thick layer of ever-tougher-to-dislodge biomat. And the thicker it got, the more it resisted the blast of water. When that happened, instead of a jet blowing algae loose, it broke up the stream, shooting spray back in all directions. Within minutes Ruto was dripping, splotched by little patches of algae that had splattered back to land on him.

As he stomped back and forth, more algae was clinging to his boots. So, he figured he'd concentrate on the last in the line of UUVs. Shoot it clean, and slowly work his way back across the bay. Force the stuff into the water. Sort of like peeling a label off a smooth surface.

Bracing himself, he started shooting down the Aquaceptor's sleek hull, concentrating on blasting out the nooks and crannies. Which shot more water up onto the ceiling, with spray soaking the cabinets, toolboxes, benches, and underwater suits, as well as speckling them with algae.

Realizing what he was doing, Ruto groaned. That was just making more mess.

He shut the water down at that nozzle and stared glumly at the Aquaceptor. Patches of algae clung to the crevices around the camera stalks and tanks. Like it or not it was going to take a stiff brush to break the stuff loose. Then he could wash it away with the hose.

To Ruto's surprise, his feet were heavy where algae clung to his boots. Had to be a couple of centimeters thick where it stuck together on fastenings, around the soles, and conformed to the heels.

Nevertheless, he slogged across the floor, now awash with algae and water. Got the brush and slogged back to the Aquaceptor III. Brushing and scraping, he broke most of the goo loose. So what if little bits were left here and there? He'd get what remained tomorrow.

Well, assuming Felix didn't escape from his ad hoc prison and murder anyone else.

Ruto had been at the scraping and brushing for a good fifteen minutes. Shifting his feet, he'd barely noticed the drag. Now, when he tried to take a step, it felt like slogging his foot through wet concrete. To his surprise, the algae had thickened around his boots to become round masses. Looked more like elephant feet that extended up past his ankles.

"What the hell?"

Figuring he'd blast it off, he could see where the hose slithered down from the spool to disappear in the algae. The nozzle had vanished, buried in slime. Ruto tried to pull his right foot loose, but the thick mat of algae had sort of congealed.

"Oh, snot-sucking hell. This isn't happening." He bent down, used the brush to swipe at the goo, and actually managed to cut a couple of swaths before the bristles packed up solid.

Ruto straightened, feeling that first gut-deep stirring of unease. Looking back across the bay, the floor where he'd stomped his way across the trunks was now a mosaic of thick mats of algae joined by veins that continued to pump from the open water.

Ruto used all of his might, felt the muscles in his hip pull as he tried to break his right foot free. All he did was lift the thick mat a couple of centimeters. And when he gave up, and let it sink back down, his boot was that much deeper in the gunk. The blue-green jam just thickened around his upper ankle.

Now Ruto's heart was pounding.

"*Hey!*" he bellowed. "Anybody hear me? I've got a real problem here!"

He stared anxiously at the closest com terminal on the wall above the work bench. The blue icon blinked on the screen. All he had to do was touch it, and he'd be in contact with Michaela or Dharman up in communications. That fricking icon seemed to mock him: flash . . . flash . . . flash . . .

"Hey! Help!"

As if anyone would hear through the walls, all the water, or the heavy hatches that lay between the UB and the Pod.

"*Help me!*" Ruto screamed.

In a desperate panic, he threw himself against the thickening algae. Each time he pulled, it turned out that he was dragging more of the stuff across the floor to thicken around his boots.

Get out of the boots!

That was it. All he had to do was unfasten his boots, slip his feet out, and run like a striped-ass banshee before the stuff could cling to his bare feet. Make the hatch, cycle it, and he was golden. Michaela could figure out how to get her damn Underwater Bay back from the algae.

He reached down, flicked the fasteners at his boot tops free.

Heart hammering, breath coming hard in his lungs, Ruto slipped his fingers into the cold goo as he reached for the next set of fasteners. Felt the stuff, thick like an impossible jello, clinging. With all his might, Ruto managed to rip his hand free. A slick coating of blue green covered his fingers.

What the hell was this stuff? How was it sticking together like this?

"Help me!" he bellowed again.

The fear knot tightened deep down, running up from his anus, knotting his belly, and shivering his lungs. Twisting back and forth, he couldn't even manage to slide his feet.

"Oh, God. Somebody come! Please. Anybody. Help me!" The first of the tears silvered his vision. His heart quivered, blood electrified in his veins.

He tried to calm himself. Began to sob his fear. Just beyond the Aquaceptor's nose the thick trunk of algae was pulsing where it sucked water up from the open sea.

Ruto could feel it, the pulsing as algae contracted. Feel it through his boots, the rhythmic constrictions around his ankles. Looking down, to his horror, with each pulse the algae was creeping up his legs, having reached the tops of his boots.

"This isn't happening to me," he pleaded with the universe. Clenching his hands, the sticky algae squeezed between his fingers.

When he felt it top his boots and begin running down around his socks, Ruto screamed, thrashed this way and that, and in a fleeting instant of clarity, knew that instant when he lost his balance.

And then he was falling, the panic like a bright fire as he flopped into the cold goo, felt it closing around him, thick as it entombed his beating arms. Cold soaked in around his coveralls, eating into his skin.

For a moment, he whimpered, every muscle in his body quivering, the cold and wet running down his neck, seeping in around the back of his head and into his hair.

And through it all came the throbbing contractions as the algae slowly spread up around his body.

His glance—as the slick goo rose around his nostrils—fixed on the blinking blue icon on the com above the work bench.

The algae swallowed his last scream.

67

When the door to the dome burst open, Dek came staggering in with something long, shiny, and wet hanging over his shoulder. Talina did a double take as Dek duck-walked his way over to the small kitchen and flopped the heavy thing onto the counter there.

Talina rose from where she'd been on the radio with Two Spot, asking, "What the hell is that?"

"Supper," Dek told her proudly. "It's a fish. Er, uh, it's a snake. Well, maybe it's a . . . ? Who the hell knows what it is? I caught it out of the river. Made a lure out of a piece of chrome I took from one of the old engines out in the shed. Fashioned a hook from a bent bracket. For line I used some of that carbon-fiber twine. The pole I made out of old antennae. And, what do you know? Third cast and wham!" His gaze went slightly askance. "Of course, the thing came within a whisker of dragging me right into the water. If it had been one of the big ones, I might have ended up half drowned and going over the waterfall again."

"Yeah, well . . . you'd have been on your own. I'm not doing that again. Not even for you." She studied the sleek beast. The thing measured a meter and a half in length. Must have weighed in at around forty kilos. Brownish-green above shading into silver and finally a snowy white on what she thought was the bottom. Three lines of fins ran down the creature's muscular sides, eyes equidistant around the triple jaws with their long, in-curved teeth. A trio of tail vents must have been used for propulsion.

"You think it's edible?" she asked.

Dek sniffed his fingers. "Doesn't smell like fish, but we can test it for toxins. There's a spectrograph in the cabinet along with an FTIR that should give us an idea of what this thing's made of. That and Two Falls Gap was placed here because the water's good. The river's fed by surface water cascading down the cliffs. Doesn't have time to pick up much of a heavy-metal load. This guy," Dek indicated the creature, "might not be too terribly toxic, and I'm really tired of broccoli."

"I'd say order out next time."

"Inga's doesn't deliver." Dek reached over and plucked the long knife from Talina's belt. "Do you mind?"

"If I did, do think I'd tell you?" She gave him a nudge with an elbow. "Let's see what this guy's made of. If it turns out we can eat it, you might have found your calling."

Derek Taglioni, fisherman. Inga would pay a fortune if she could add something unique to her menu.

An hour later—the three-jawed fishsnake dissected, tested, and sort of filleted—the curious odor of frying fishsnake filled the air. Talina watched Dek carefully sear the pink meat while trying to decide what it smelled like. The closest she could come to the sweet aroma was paca meat—what the locals in Belize called "gibnut."

She crossed her arms, asking, "So, where did a mucky-muck Taglioni learn to cook? Or is that one of the skills, along with charming the fair sex, that your father taught you?"

"A Taglioni? Dare to foul his hands by preparing his own food? Not a chance in hell. Nope, this, like so many of my endearing traits, was learned aboard *Ashanti*. Not that we had much to prepare, but Gonzo really tried to do something with ration. I sat around for hours listening to him and Bill Martin talk about food. I mean, we were all starving, right? Those two guys could go on and on expounding about preparation, spices, temperatures, and recipes. Having eaten at the finest restaurants in Solar System, I was a rapt listener. Promised myself I'd learn to cook. A while back, Madison Briggs let me try it for real in her kitchen, and miracle of miracles, most of what Gonzo and Bill told me actually worked." He beamed a smile as he laid a fishsnake steak on her plate. "Now, if we only had a bottle of wine."

The last of the two bottles of wine had been finished off the night before.

She considered him. Arched a speculative eyebrow. Did she dare? "Got the next best thing. I'll get it while you dish up the rest."

Whirling on her heel, she stalked outside to her aircar, checked the charge out of habit—seeing it was up to ninety-two percent, which was about all the battery would take these days—and pulled the bottle of whiskey out from under the dash.

Back inside, Dek was setting the plates on the small table. He looked up, eyes widening at sight of the bottle. "Oh, my. Is that what I think it is?"

"One of Inga's outstanding bourbons from last year."

"This is a special treat indeed." With a flourish, Dek produced two duraplast glasses. "The first fried fishsnake ever, augmented by broccoli, mint, and cabbage, toasted with bourbon."

She seated herself, took a tentative bite of the fishsnake. "Oh, that is good. It's a softer meat than crest or chamois. Not sure what to compare it to."

"Be better with your red chili sauce," he said, "I think it's got the best texture on Donovan so far. Sort of reminds me of crab crossed with cod, having never had your gibnut for comparison."

"So, how's it going with the quetzal TriNA? You seem remarkably human today. Only seen a few of those disconnected looks." She cut another piece and forked it into her mouth.

"I took your advice. When Demon starts to fool with my memories, I close my eyes, imagine myself falling . . . that slam of impact as I hit the water. Then I'm down, under the surface, bubbles gurgling around me. I experience the pounding roar, that huge weight of the water beating me down into the darkness, and I imagine myself drowning. Feel the cold water rushing into my lungs . . ." A pause as he closed his eyes. "And my brain clears. I can almost feel him cowering down in the middle of my head."

"Middle of your head, huh? He hides behind my stomach most of the time. Funny where we imagine them inside us."

"Flute's starting to talk to me. At least, that's how I categorize the voice. Must be a combination of all the other quetzal TriNAs, but definitely an opponent of Demon's. And one equally terrified of drowning. Why is that?"

"Quetzals can't hold their breath," she told him. "Air in the mouth is piped through the lungs and out the vents behind. If they get in water over their heads, they drown. Period. Cheng thinks it's one of the reasons we're seeing vastly different TriNA haplotypes in quetzal populations. Rivers effectively isolate quetzal gene pools from each other. Quetzals might ford creeks and streams, but deep water makes an impenetrable barrier. Has implications for future settlement security when it comes to a lot of Donovanian wildlife."

"You know, you really are remarkable."

"How's that?"

"Because of what you know. Your pragmatism. That strength of character and the sacrifices you have made for people. Like . . . me. Bringing me out here to help me find myself. I think you are the most amazing woman alive."

"Oh, sure. Me and all my quetzals. I'm a friggin' mess, Dek. I'm not even sure I'm human anymore."

"You're more than human. I figure you are the beginning and end of my universe."

The look he gave her sent flutters through her core. Intimate, measuring, and compellingly erotic, it stirred something grown cold and lifeless within her. Damn, did she trust him? The guy was like a living contradiction. Charming and vulnerable, physically appealing with his smile, scar, and kind eyes, but she had only his word that the old Taglioni was dead and buried. Let alone that he had control of Demon.

"It's all right," he said softly. "I can wait."

"Read my mind, huh?"

He tossed off the last of his whiskey. "I've got a lot more of you inside me than you know. And, no, I can't give you a guarantee that I've got Demon forever whipped. But after the river? I know how to club him back into submission. I just haven't figured out how to do it with finesse or on demand."

"So . . ." She sipped her whiskey, having finished the last of the fishsnake. "Where do you see this going?" Damn, did he have to have such remarkable eyes?

He leaned forward, earnest gaze locked with hers. "It will go wherever you are comfortable going. Me, I want to hold you, cherish you, explore every last bit of you. I want to see if you and I fit together as seamlessly as I think we can."

"And if we can't?"

"Won't know until we try. I came alive after that escape from the river. That was you and me acting as a team. I want to see if we're heading to someplace fantastic."

Her heart was beginning to pound. She felt the quetzals stirring inside her, that rush of the limbic system.

Oh, Talina, do you dare do this?

She stood, reached for his hand and pulled him to his feet. For a long moment she stared into his no-longer-human eyes, looking into those yellow-ringed depths. His lips met hers as he pulled her close.

The tickle in her loins flickered into that familiar glow. Her breathing deepened, the rush building as she pressed against him. As his tongue delicately teased hers, she realized that she'd never been kissed like this. The way his mouth worked on hers, the faint taste of peppermint and whiskey, electrified her.

Breaking away, her body pounding, she could read his desire, see the rising and falling of his chest. Actually feel the blood throbbing through his body.

"Come on," she told him. "I've got nothing on my schedule for the rest of the day."

As she led him back to the bedroom, nothing remained but the moment.

68

Kalico Aguila, in a foul mood, ground her teeth and stared at the world through slitted eyes. She had been irritable ever since the last trip to PA. That rare moment of camaraderie she'd felt on the way into Inga's had slowly evaporated as she discovered that the Maritime Unit had lost a submarine with two people aboard, and then lost a man to some flying thing.

Well, Michaela, don't say you weren't warned.

But what really got under Kalico's skin and chafed was the notion that Dek and Talina were just over yonder, not more than a half-hour's flight to the southeast at Two Falls Gap. Not only was the knowledge maddening, but worse, Kalico wasn't sure what she wanted to do about it.

Talina was more than a trusted colleague and a woman to whom Kalico owed her life several times over; she was a friend. Granted, the path to that friendship had been rough, rocky, nearly fatal, and often acrimonious, but mutual admiration and shared values had triumphed in the end. In addition, no woman alive had earned more of Kalico's respect than Talina.

Kalico paced her office where it sat just off the main hallway in Corporate Mine's administration dome. Her desk seemed to mock her. As did the maps and mine schematics that were hung on the walls. Her mine. The richest diggings in the universe.

Shut down for the moment as all of her people spent time servicing machinery, inspecting shoring, conducting maintenance and cleaning, and otherwise essentially catching up and taking stock. Down at the smelter, Ituri had run that last load of ore, processing it down to elements. He had another two cargo containers that could be ferried up to orbit and placed into L5 storage at any time. The combined value of those two containers alone—based on prices when Kalico had left Solar System—was just shy of three million

SDRs. And there were a whole lot more containers already up there. Waiting. In hopes that either *Turalon* or *Ashanti* had successfully inverted symmetry and made the journey back to Solar System.

"Nothing is happening here," Kalico reminded herself. "Nor will it until Talovich finishes his inspection and they replace any suspect aquajade."

Which meant that nothing was keeping her from donning her bush clothing, strapping on her pistol belt, grabbing a rifle, and flying the aircar over to Two Falls Gap. You know, just to drop in and see how Dek and Talina were doing.

Under her breath, Kalico muttered, "Don't be an idiot. If Tal wanted you, she's got a radio. She knows damn well that you're only a half an hour away at cruising speed."

So why the hell was she so wound up about all of this? Imagining Dek and Talina, bodies locked together under a blanket. The very thought of it tripped her "now-I'm-really-pissed" trigger.

You jealous, bitch?

"Damn straight," she muttered under her breath.

Better ask yourself why.

Kalico growled to herself, stepped to the door, and prowled down the hall. At the arms locker she grabbed a rifle from the rack, checked the chamber and magazine, and stepped outside into Capella's bright light. Nodding to Dina Michegan, who stood in armor by the double doors, helmet slung on her belt, rifle at port arms, Kalico added, "Just going to walk the perimeter."

"You need an escort, ma'am?"

"God no. I'm trying to clear my head with a little exercise." She slapped her rifle. "If I see some quetzal climbing the fence, he'll be steaks and leather before you can call the alarm."

Michegan gave her a grin. "Yes, ma'am. But I think we'll keep you on telemetry . . . just in case."

Of course, they would. Only eleven of her original marines remained. They took their job seriously.

As Kalico walked out into Capella's heat, she asked herself: "So, woman, what does Dek mean to you?"

Back in Solar System, she'd hated the guy. Loathed having to breathe the same air. Derek Taglioni may have been the single most despicable human being she had ever met . . . well, right up until she crossed paths with Dan Wirth. The difference was that Dek didn't have the excuse of being a psychopath. He'd just been a purposefully hideous human being who had hated himself and everyone around him. Especially Miko, and by extension, Kalico, who was Miko's lover and subordinate. Foul-mouthed be he drunk or drugged, arrogant, hurtful, and condescending of anyone and everyone, Dek had been an unmitigated slime. Had she the power, she'd have damned him to the most excruciating of fates.

Right up to the moment he'd stepped down from *Ashanti*'s shuttle carrying what little luggage remained to him. The way he told it—and the records verified—that excruciating fate had landed full upon Taglioni's shoulders.

The man who'd emerged from *Ashanti* might have been an entirely different human being hidden away in a Dek Taglioni costume. A man who'd stooped to the most menial of duties in a desperate gamble to stay alive.

Once Kalico got over the shock—managed to separate "the odious beast from Transluna" with the humble man who now presented himself—she'd come to value his company.

At the fence, she glanced back. Saw that Abu Sassi had taken the station at the dome door, and Dina Michegan—Capella's light gleaming on her armor—was ambling along about twenty meters back. The woman was glancing this way and that, as if out for a sauntering stroll, admiring the scenery.

Nothing like being obvious.

Kalico allowed herself a smile. "All right, Private. Come walk with me. Not only will I be safer, but I could use the company."

"Ma'am?" Michegan called.

At Kalico's wave, the marine trotted up, eyes nervous.

"At ease, Private," Kalico told her. "You got a man in your life?"

After the surprised flicker died in her dark eyes, Michegan said, "Uh, yeah, Supervisor. He's a prospector working a claim out in the Blood Mountains west of PA."

"Must be tough getting together. You see him much?"

"We work it out." Dina kept shooting Kalico a wary glance.

"Relax, Private. I could give a hang and hoot about your personal life. In fact, just the opposite. You decide you need some time, let me know. That goes for the rest of you, too. There isn't a single marine left in this detail who hasn't carried more than his or her weight. Let's figure out a rotation for a little time off. What do you think?"

"It would be most appreciated, ma'am." Michegan smiled.

"I'm remiss for not thinking of it earlier. But, given what happened to Talbot, Shintzu, and Garcia, I think we'll have to have some ground rules."

"Yes ma'am. I'd hope we were a little smarter this time around, though I do know that Russ Tanner and Toni Nashala want to do some exploring." Again, the wary look. "Maybe there might be a way to make trips like those Corporate endorsed? Like for a percentage?"

Kalico gave the woman a thin-lidded look. "Damned creeping capitalistic libertarian crap is infiltrating all the best qualities of solid Corporate doctrine, if you ask me. Which means, fricking aye, we can go percentages." She paused. "As long as our people use their heads while they're out in the bush."

"Yes, ma'am. We know what's at stake." Michegan squinted up at the sun as they walked along the tall chain-link. On the other side, the fill dropped off to the forest below. The view through the wire was spectacular across the rumpled forest. Looking out, it was to see the trees in their constant movement, a bobbing sea of blues, greens, teal, and jade as the forest giants shuffled and struggled for position.

Nice distraction. What are you going to do about Dek?

Kalico thought back to the man who'd given her his last energy bar at the foot of the cliff below Tyson Station and lied about it. That bar had kept her going when she'd have played out. Maybe she wouldn't have died, but her collapse on that dangerous climb would have endangered them all.

Then came the memories of his dimple, of the twinkle in his green-ringed yellow eyes, that devilish smile. The scarred cheek he'd received saving her life. Just thinking of them warmed her heart.

Are you in love with him?

Good question.

"So," she asked Michegan, "I take it you're in love with this Wild One?"

"Uh, don't know, ma'am."

"What the hell is love?" Thinking back, she tried to dissect her relationships. She'd cared for some of the men she'd been involved with, enjoyed the company of others, but always in the background lurked the understanding that each had been temporary. And then there had been the other relationships. Like the one she'd shared with Miko. Purely mercenary on both of their parts. Emotion had nothing to do with it. She was using him for her own advancement as much as he was using her for sex and an arm ornament, and both of them had delivered in full measure.

Michegan hadn't answered the question about love. Maybe the marine was as uncertain about it as Kalico was.

"Private? Can we go off the record? Just you and me? In confidence?"

Michegan arched a dark brow. "Uh, as long as it's nothing that would compromise my oath or violate my honor."

"Nothing like that."

"All right, then we're off the record."

"What do you think about Dek Taglioni?"

"Ah," Michegan nodded. "I see."

"Do you?"

"Yeah." Michegan shifted her rifle, stared out across the forest as she considered her words. "You want this bottom line straight up?"

"That's why we're OTR." Kalico gestured her fluster. "I'm out of my league here. On the one hand, Dek and I have a not-so-savory history. On the other, since he's arrived on Donovan, he's a different guy. He comes from my world, my society. He's a piece of my world. And, I have to admit, I like this new Dek. I just don't know . . ." How did she put this?

"You don't know if you want him in your bed," Michegan finished.

"That's a little blunter than I would have phrased it."

"OTR, right? Our call? And that's all of us marines, we're the watchers. Security. Essentially invisible. Ignored when you and Dek are together. We keep this stuff to ourselves, don't talk to the rest of the folks out here, or, God forbid, let it slip when we're in PA. Your Mr. Taglioni isn't sure what to do with you, either. When he's around you, he's always on his best behavior, like he's got something to prove."

"Like he's still not the same toilet-sucking maggot he was back on Transluna."

"Could be. But the man genuinely likes you, admires you."

"But?"

"You said, OTR?"

"I did. Stop asking."

"As much as he likes you, watches you, you're not Talina Perez."

"And what's that supposed to mean?"

Michegan tilted her head, short black hair tossing in the morning breeze. Her dark eyes were prying, trying to see into Kalico's soul. "You in love with the man?"

"Hell, I . . . I . . . Tell me what the hell love is, Dina."

The marine's lips bent into an amused curl. "My call? You and I will walk around the compound. A Supervisor with her marine guard. Then you'll go back to your quarters, take a cold shower, and you'll go back to work."

"That simple, huh?"

"Oh, hell no. But a hell of a lot simpler than jumping in that aircar of yours and whizzing over to Two Falls Gap. If what you're telling me is true, you're not up to pouring reaction mass into a rocket you're not sure you want to ride."

"Wrong guy, huh?"

"Like I said. You're not Talina Perez. Those of us who watch, we know. That man looks at her in a whole different way."

69

Over the radio Raya Turnienko's voice said, *"The fact that all the children are suffering from the same painful edema, that it presents as a glandular swelling that starts under the angle of the jaw, suggests that it's some kind of contagious disease. Maybe something unique to the maritime environment you're in. But we're not going to know until we can isolate the pathogen responsible."*

"All right," Michaela agreed. "It's too late today. We're looking at flying little Toni into PA tomorrow morning at the earliest. If we're out of here at first light, can you have someone meet us at the shore landing pad at around ten tomorrow?"

"Roger that. That gives us time to prepare an isolation unit here. If the child is contagious with something new, we're going to want to treat it as a potential public health hazard."

"Roger that. We'll take precautions on our end, too."

"Director, we can only assume the worst. Chances are that this will turn out to be a novel virus. The fact that none of the adults has come down with it suggests that it's going to have a simple explanation and cure." A pause. *"Nevertheless, I'd like to limit the risk. Only bring the one little boy. Maybe I can figure out his coma at the same time and send him back with a vaccine or procedure that would cure the rest of the children."*

Michaela glanced sidelong at Dik Dharman. The man just shrugged his shoulders, looking worried. She said, "Doctor, before I commit to this let us all discuss this. These are other people's children. It's bigger than just my decision."

Dharman looked even more worried, if that were possible. Hell, they all looked worried anymore.

"All right. My preference, for quarantine purposes, is one child, but if you and your people feel differently, we can deal with it on this end."

"I really appreciate it, Doctor."

"You've got it. Call if you need anything. I'll have someone monitoring your special frequency all night."

"I suspect we'll see you tomorrow. And, from all of us, thank you."

"That's my job. And Director, one thing we never forget is that the children are all of our future on Donovan."

Michaela exhaled wearily.

"Instead of Toni, have you thought about sending Felix? People might sleep better. Word is, he's got the sore throat, too." As he spoke, Dharman tried to keep his expression neutral.

"Hell no." She met the man's eyes. Years back, Dharman and Kevina had had a fling back on *Ashanti*. But then, Kevina—the hot, Russian blond—had had a lot of flings. The way Michaela figured it, most of the men still carried a torch for her, even if it was mostly charred and only faintly smoldering these days.

To Dharman she confided, "Listen, my heart goes out to Kevina. She's lost her husband, and now her son turns out to have murdered Bill, of all people, and cut him into pieces. Kevina is torturing herself every second of the day, asking if it's her fault somehow. But, rationally, there's no way it can be. Nothing any of us could have foreseen would have saved Yee. And as to Felix? He belonged to all of us. Was a son to all of us, but I never saw this coming."

"Doesn't mean Kev isn't blaming herself."

"Yeah. Well, we'll do what we can for her. All of us."

"Right, I—"

Iso Suzuki stuck her head into the com center, worry shining from her dark eyes. "Michaela? You seen Bryan? Give him something to do since he went down to the UB? He's late. I've been all over the Pod. Even went down to the Underwater Bay, but the hatch isn't functioning."

"What do you mean, not functioning? And no. Last I saw of him was when Casey said Tobi didn't show up for lunch, so I sent Bryan down to check. That was around one."

Dharman bent over the com, asking, "Underwater Bay, check in please. Tobi? Bryan? Respond, please." He ran his fingers over the screen, adding, "Got visual coming up now."

Each of the com center monitors flashed on to show the UB from a different angle.

"What the hell?" Michaela tried to make sense of what she was seeing.

If she didn't know the UB, she'd have never recognized this. The familiar benches, the cabinets, equipment bins, the lines of UUVs, and the single remaining sub on its cradle, were at least familiar, but the entire floor pulsed in blue-green. Tendrils of the stuff were creeping up to cover the sub, UUVs, and other equipment.

The hatch door gaped open, a flood of green spilling over the threshold into the pressure hatch. No wonder it wouldn't open from the tube side. Until someone closed it from the UB, the hatch couldn't pressurize.

An odd, hump-shaped form could be seen midway between the hatch and the sub. Whatever it was, the blue-green goo covered it in a thick blanket.

"That's algae!" Dharman muttered. "But where the hell did it all come from?"

"The stuff that's been building up on the pilings and bottom of the Pod?" Iso asked. "What's it doing in the UB? And where are Bryan and Tobi?"

Dharman accessed his com. "Bryan? Tobi? Report to the com center. Bryan? Tobi? Report immediately."

Michaela struggled for breath as the seconds passed, the speakers silent.

"I don't understand," Iso cried. "Where's my husband?"

Dharman started playing with the Pod's cameras, checking inside and out as he flashed through different rooms and corridors, the landing pad, the seatruck deck.

Michaela, a wooden feeling in her breast, said, "They never left the UB."

"How do you know?" Dharman asked.

"The hatch is open." She swallowed hard, seeing the panic in Iso's eyes. "Go back to the UB cameras. We'll check the records to prove it, but think it through. Tobi hasn't checked in, missed his lunch. Doesn't answer com. Bryan goes down to check on him, cycles the hatch, and steps in. He sees the algae, something happens. He doesn't make it back to close and dog the UB side."

"Then where is he?" Iso demanded. "Where is my husband?"

"Dik," Michaela heard herself ask from someplace distant, "Can you get a close up of that hump between the sub and hatch? Yes. Right there, where that . . ."

She didn't need to finish. As the camera zoomed in, she could see the shape was humanoid, and that despite the thick covering of biomass, a protrusion had the distinct shape of a skeletal human hand. Whoever was under that lump was being devoured.

70

Eight of us are dead. The words kept repeating in Michaela's head as she took her place in the front of the cafeteria. Everyone was present with the exception of Gabarron, who remained upstairs to keep an eye on little Toni and the other sick infants and children, and to ensure that Felix didn't somehow escape from his room. Though, given that a code was necessary to open and close the door to his makeshift prison, that was a long shot.

Michaela had motioned her people forward, asked them to sit at the front tables. The sight of the empty chairs in their usual spots was too much to bear. Seeing only ten of her adults with the empty tables behind them was bad enough.

"We've lost the UB to the algae," Michaela told them dully. "As to how? Dik and I have reviewed the recordings. The algae, as we all know, has been building up on the underside of the Pod and Underwater Bay. Tobi had been hosing it back into the water as it crept up and onto the bay floor. None of us thought much of it. But, in the wake of Bill Martin's death, no one went down to wash it back into the sea. It managed to gain a foothold in the UB, and like a giant organism, it flowed down from the bottom of the Pod, down the pilings and tube, around the UB and into the bay itself."

She took a breath, willing herself to get through this. Trying to be cold and rational as a Director should. "When Tobi got back to the UB this morning, the algae was in the process of covering the bay floor. It had crept up onto the UUVs and sub. The hose wouldn't dislodge it. The stuff was thick. It . . ." She swallowed. "It sort of . . . I mean . . . Listen. He got stuck in the biomass, panicked. Fell . . ."

Every expression in the room had gone to flint. Casey Stoner's lips were trembling, tears welling in her eyes. Jym Odinga had wrapped his arm around her, his own demeanor on the verge of breaking.

"When Tobi didn't check in, Bryan went down to see if he was all right. When he stepped out of the hatch, he was so surprised, that he forgot to close it behind him. The slime was better this time, more efficient, as if it had learned from Tobi. It trapped him before he could get a body length from the hatch."

Iso was sobbing softly. Eyes down.

"So now what?" Yosh asked, his brown eyes casting from face to face. "I think we had better face it. We're running out of options here. Unless one of us swims down, braves the slime, and closes that hatch door, we've lost the Underwater Bay, the sub, the UUVs, and the equipment there. All we have left are two seatrucks and the launch."

"What if something happens to them?" Kel asked. "If it does, we're stuck here."

"The Supervisor can pull out us with her A-7," Michaela replied. "Wouldn't matter if the extraction damaged the landing pad in the process, not if we're abandoning the Pod."

"Scary," Kevina said from where she sat, partially isolated at the end of the table. "We'd have to rope the kids together with that down blast. Even then, I watched that day, it's a miracle the Supervisor wasn't blown off the pad."

"Hey, wait," Michaela told them. "Let's not get ahead of ourselves. We haven't lost the seatrucks yet. Haven't even seen anything that threatens them. If we pull the plug on the Pod, we can still evacuate. Even if it means flying to the beach pad, recharging for a day, and then flying on to either PA or Corporate Mine."

"Don't be too sure about Port Authority," Dik announced. "I was on the radio, too. Remember? Dr. Turnienko wasn't wild about us bringing a bunch of sick kids to PA while they had a communicable disease. Will they even allow any of us to land if we're infected with whatever's got the kids sick?"

"I don't know," Michaela told them. "And we might get the same answer if we tried for Corporate Mine. Supervisor Aguila might deny us the right to land or insist that we go into quarantine."

"We don't know that whatever is wrong with the kids is communicable," Yosh said. "None of the adults are sick, and we're sleeping in the same room with the kids, eating with them, touching the same surfaces. If they're infectious, why haven't any of us gotten it?"

"I don't have an answer for that, and neither does Anna." Michaela turned her attention to Vik Lawrence. "Do you have any idea?"

"No." Vik ran nervous fingers through her hair. "When this all started to go sideways this afternoon, I got a sample of the organism. If it's an organism. That's as good a name as any, I guess. We've had it logged in the system for weeks now. It's the same stuff that Kevina and Felix brought back from that first trip out to place that buoy. At its most basic, we're dealing with a single prokaryotic and photosynthesizing cell. Now that I have had time to really look at it, it's the same cell we recovered from all the children's blood and tissues. I cannot tell you why it's presenting as a disease in the kids and not the adults. It's present in the blood and tissues of everyone on this station."

"All of us?" Yosh demanded as everyone shifted uncomfortably, worried looks shooting back and forth.

"Everyone," Vik said in a hollow voice. "I don't know why it is worse in the children. I don't know why it started to cling to the Pod. I do know that when it starts attaching itself to other cells, it shares information. Slips TriNA back and forth, and maybe transferRNA, microRNAs, and some other molecules as well. Molecular intelligence."

"What does that mean?" Michaela asked.

Vik gestured her discomfort. "This stuff *thinks*. If I had to coin a name for it, I'd call it the ultimate intelligent organism. In one state it lives as independent cells that float around on the ocean. It is both omnivorous and photosynthetic, so it can live in a lot of different environments. When something stimulates it, the cells concentrate, form a sheet, that then forms a tube, which in turn allows it to grow as it accumulates additional cells. As it does, it begins adding other tubes, which allows it to form complex shapes. My take, in the wildest flight of imagination, is that while we're sitting here, it is studying the Underwater Bay, trying to figure out what we are, and why we are in its ocean."

Michaela winced. "But you said the same kind of cells are inside us, as well."

Vik nodded. "That's right. So far I've just isolated individual cells. I haven't seen any sign that they're joining together or accreting like they did in Toni's blood. But, that said, I can think of nothing that would stop them from coming together and forming an organism inside us. And if that doesn't frighten you right down to your bones, I don't know what will."

"You said it's in Toni?" Yosh asked.

"I think the algae is what's making him sick. Causing his paralysis." Vik crossed her arms.

Michaela's mouth had gone dry. Her whole body seemed to tingle. How the hell had the cells gotten inside her? How would she know if they started to accrete, grow, take over her heart, lungs, or liver? And the things were intelligent? Living inside her veins and arteries?

Are they in my brain as well? Listening? Observing?

Casey craned her neck so that she could better see Vik. "What did it do to Tobi? When it pulled him down and covered him? I saw. There was a lump after it sucked him in. Now, on the latest videos, there's nothing but his coveralls left."

That had been on the latest recording. Just Tobi's clothing, wadded, empty, and laying to one side.

Vik's gaze hardened. She pursed her lips. "There is no easy way to say this, Casey. I think the stuff digested him. Bryan, too. It's a giant living organism. It needs sustenance when it's not in direct light and able to photosynthesize."

"This is crazy," Jym cried passionately. "You're saying that stuff *ate* Tobi? And Bryan, too?"

"'Fraid so." Vik stared down at her hands. "And here's the kicker: They both had slime cells living in their bodies. Now those same cells are back with the organism, sharing everything they learned about what it's like to live inside a human host. That *creature* living down in the Underwater Bay, and inside us and our children, has the mathematical probability to be a whole lot smarter than we are, and it's considering what to do with us at this very moment."

71

What Anna Gabarron was seeing made no sense. Not that much of anything made sense now. Prior to the last couple of days, Anna would had told anyone who bothered to ask that it would be chemically impossible for two as distinctly different life forms as terrestrial humans and Donovanian algae to coexist within the same body. The human immune system functioned as a highly tuned early-warning and search-and-destroy identification system for foreign antigens. Such foreign "enemy" proteins caused a host of reactions throughout the body, stimulating B- and T-cells, white blood cells, titers, antibodies, you name it.

Now she stared through a small binocular scope at the skin sample she'd taken from Toni. When she'd walked into the clinic that morning to check on the boy, she'd been horrified to see that he'd turned a not-so-appealing shade of green. The first impulse had been that someone had painted the kid. But looking closely, she was seeing skin cells with a slight sheen. Definitely not normal, but certainly not painted or stained with any pigment.

Using a probe, she'd reached into the isolation tent and taken a scraping from the still-comatose boy's stomach. He continued to lay supine, locked away in that board-stiff paralysis that defied her ability to cure.

Placing her sample under the scope and dialing up the magnification, Anna saw the impossible: human skin cells living in a matrix with Donovanian prokaryotic "algae" cells. The prokaryotes had adapted, flattened, to interlock with Toni's skin cells at the molecular level. Like they were supposed to be there. Nor was the distribution of prokaryotes random or chaotic, but alternately patterned and uniform, as if by design.

She shouldn't be seeing this. Couldn't be seeing this. Somehow

Toni's immune system seemed to recognize the proteins and poly-saccharides in the algae cell walls as "friendly." She wasn't observing any immune response from the host cells: no inflammation, phago-cytes, or antibody response to algae antigens. The only explanation for that had to be that the algae had somehow reprogrammed the little boy's immune system at the genetic level.

"How can it do that?"

Anna sat back, frowning. It had taken human medicine thou-sands of years to learn how to manipulate immunogenetics and the use of quantum cubit computers to do it. And now they were ex-pected to believe that a bunch of solitary Donovanian prokaryotes had infected and completely reengineered little Toni's immune sys-tem within a week?

Apparently it had. She needed only to turn from the scope, look with her own eyes, and see the boy. Fact: He had turned green be-cause photosynthesizing algae cells now made up about forty per-cent of his integument. And it did so without inciting any kind of host response. Nor was it a random hodgepodge of infection, but well-orchestrated, as if by plan. And all of it smacked of the impos-sible.

So what was Toni? A hybrid? A chimera? A monster? Or just a little boy with an infection that had left him a vegetable?

Anna rubbed her temple and looked around her clinic with dull eyes. If she was seeing this in the boy's skin, what was happening inside? To his internal organs, his brain? If forty percent of the boy's integument was algae, then his brain might be just as compromised. And if it was? Skin was a pretty straightforward tissue. But the in-tricacy of the human brain? Compromised by all that infection?

She experienced a moment of sympathy for the kid. "Hell, Toni, your brain might be a total write-off. The miracle is that you still have autonomous functioning."

But if Toni was this compromised? What about the other kids?

And it hit her.

So much made sense now. The arms and legs "learning." Even Felix's inexplicable implication in Bill Martin's murder. It wasn't just immune systems that the algae was playing with. The stuff was trying to figure out the children's brains. All of which changed the entire equation when it came to Felix and his claims that he "wasn't there" when Bill was murdered. If the algae could rewrite a body's immune system to recognize its cells as friendly instead of foreign, what was to stop it from doing the same with the brain?

Whatever it was attempting, it must have gone wrong in Toni's brain to leave him comatose.

She stood, walked over, and stared down at Toni in his isolation tent. "What the hell are you? Why are you doing this?"

This was miles beyond quetzal TriNA floating around in humans. This was the planned and well-orchestrated remodeling of an entire organism. Take the edema at the side of the boy's throat. She could recognize the swellings now for what they were: gills. The perfect adaptation to an aquatic environment.

Anna shivered in spite of herself. Wondered for a moment if it wouldn't be to everyone's best interest if she were to slip a plastic bag over the little boy's head and simply let him die.

"Anna?"

She whirled. Almost jumped out of her skin.

Sheena and Felicity stood not more than a meter behind her.

How had they been so silent? Even with bare feet?

Both had that weirdly vacuous stare. Weirder, both girls were naked. And both, to Anna's horror, had the visible swellings of gill development along both sides of their throats. Felicity's ended in red slits above her collarbone. Sheena's swellings didn't look too far behind.

"What do you want?"

"My throat is sore." Sheena said, stepping forward.

"It's the algae." Anna couldn't help it. She backed up a step, her heart starting to pound. "Get away from me. You're not human. You're . . . things. Aliens."

"My throat hurts," Sheena insisted, stepping closer. "Help me."

Anna—fear turning her stomach runny—backed into the counter. She had to get past the girls. Get down to the meeting. Tell the rest what she'd found. But, after all, these were just girls, right? And, in this case, unlike poor Bill Martin, she understood the threat.

She nerved that old bitter snap into her voice. "You're going to let me pass. Time's come that the rest know what you are."

Felicity actually seemed to wilt, her right hand behind her back. Given the green tinge in her left hand, maybe she was embarrassed by her right? Was it further along in the transition?

"You didn't hear that, did you?" Felicity asked. "If you did, you'd know the message in the music."

"What music?"

"The music our friends are singing in the Underwater Bay. It's been changing ever since we digested Bryan and Tobi. Growing happier. It's almost time. Want to hear the music?"

A shiver ran up Anna's back when Felicity started humming the tune to "London Bridge Is Falling Down." Like the nursery rhyme was some innocent non sequitur given the fear she suddenly felt.

"Sheena, make way," Anna declared as she started forward.

At the last instant, Sheena stepped aside, her large blue eyes fixed on Anna's. Something about the girl—the incongruity of her red hair, the green tinge to her pale skin, and the swollen throat—to Anna it reeked of wrongness.

"What about Toni?" Sheena demanded as Anna made two steps, Felicity still humming that damn song, blocked her way.

Anna glanced back, seeing that Sheena had stepped over to stare into the clear plastic. Even as Anna paused, Sheena had reached out, was trying to pull the isolation tent from the countertop. The muscles swelled in the girl's arms, and incredibly, the heavy plastic tent moved. It stopped when the tube that evacuated air to the incinerator pulled tight.

"Hey!" Anna barked. "Leave that alone! Get your little alien fingers . . ." She stopped short. Not only should the isolation tent have been too heavy for seven-year-old Sheena to pull, but, damn, Sheena's fingers were leaf green.

Anna shook her head, panic let loose inside. "Let it go, Sheena.

You can't let him out. All of you, it's over. I know what you are. I'm going down to tell the rest."

Sheena gave the isolation tent's plastic one last tug.

Anna could barely hear Felicity singing, "*London bridge is broken down . . .*"

That's when Toni sat up. Stared around. His black eyes seemed oddly focused through the clear plastic as they fixed on Anna.

Sheena turned, head slightly cocked. "No. You're not telling."

"Not by a long shot. As soon as I tell them . . ."

The rustle came from behind. A fast patter of bare feet. In the polished stainless steel of the cabinet, Anna caught a shadowy reflection: thin, moving incredibly fast. It lifted something high, pulled it back, ready to swing.

Felicity!

Anna'd be damned if . . .

The sharp pain in the small of her back coupled with an impact surprised her. The effect was so strange. Instantaneous. Anna's hips, legs, feet. They just vanished. Went totally numb. She was falling, reached for the counter, snagged a tray of beakers. Her stunned brain couldn't process why as she collapsed, hit hard on the floor. Glass was smashing and crashing around her, fragments clattering. Her face smacked painfully into the sialon, blasting lights through her head. The hollow thump of the impact barely registered in the shock and surprise.

From behind, it made no sense as Felicity said, "Lumbar spinal column: Vital and armored."

Dazed, Anna stared at the base of the counters; the overhead lights gleamed like a thousand diamonds in the shattered glass that surrounded her.

Felicity sang, her girl's voice soft: "*Gabarron has fallen down, fallen down . . .*"

Anna tried to get up, managed to pull her hands under her shoulders. Pushed up.

"Got to do this right," Felicity said from behind.

Anna glanced up. Sheena stood over her, a scalpel in her hand.

The little girl's face was oddly blank as she said, "Neck: Blood vessels, windpipe, and spinal cord. Vulnerable and vital."

Anna tried to shove herself up again, but she couldn't feel her legs.

She filled her lungs to scream for help when Sheena leaned down with the scalpel.

72

The way Felix understood things, he was pretty much doomed.

That morning, Mother had come to see him, crying the entire time, sobbing, asking absolutely stupid questions. Why had he done this? Why had he done that? Was it her fault? Was it Yee's? Had Felix planned out Bill's murder?

That was stupid. Of course, Felix hadn't planned to go and murder Bill. He felt bad about Bill, really bad, and would have bawled his head off if the Voice hadn't told him that everything was fine. But it didn't matter what he said, Mother had just gotten more and more hysterical. In the end, shaking her head, she'd blubbered, "I have to go. I can't stand this."

"Mom?" he told her. "My throat hurts!"

"I know, baby. It's going around. All the children have it. Even the infants. Is that why you killed Bill?"

"I *wasn't* there. I only got there later. And the Voice said it was all right."

"The voice?" she asked. Felix had never seen such a panicked look in Mother's eyes as she said, "I don't know if you are my son, or some heartless monster that belongs to the algae."

"Mama? Please, I don't—"

"I can't stand this." Then, at the door, she'd raised her eyes and plaintively asked, "Please? Give me my little boy back."

She had closed the door behind her with finality.

That had been an eternity ago.

Since then, all Felix had for company was his cot, a can to pee in, and the sound of the air blowing softly from the vents.

And the song. Didn't matter that he was locked away on second level. He could hear it. Especially if he placed his ear against the wall or floor. The deep sounds came through the best. Low thrumming, clicks, a melodic rising and falling of vibrations. The higher sounds were harder to hear, hovering just at the edge of perception.

"You will hear it clearer . . . soon. You will live surrounded by the Song, floating within it," the Voice had told him.

Felix's throat really hurt, was swollen on the sides, but the Voice insisted this was normal. And when Felix started to worry—because it really did hurt—the Voice would show him images of underwater. Felix would be drifting along under the surface with the Song all around him, with mottled patterns of sunlight shooting beams through the aqua water. Being weightless, either floating or propelling himself ahead with light strokes of his hands and feet, filled Felix with a tingling sense of ecstasy.

All in all, the effect was magical. Until the Pod, his entire existence had been Crew Deck on *Ashanti*. As much a miracle as the Pod had been, the boat ride out to set the buoy had filled him with wonder. Now the visions in his head of endless freedom, of drifting where he would go, and never being contained within walls, intoxicated him.

But how was that going to happen?

"Soon," the Voice reassured him.

His stomach growled, and he wished he had something to drink.

At the thought a tickle ran through his fingers, and he lifted them. In the overhead light, they had a greenish hue. Sort of like they'd been stained with stuff from the hydroponics tank.

More than anything, though, he was lonely. All of his life had been spent with people. Either crowded into the quarters on Crew Deck, or here with Sheena, Felicity, Tomaya, and the rest of the children. When he wasn't with them, he was with Mother and Father, or one of the adults. Being alone was space scuz. It made him half-sad, half-desperate.

If it wasn't for the Voice, he'd have cried, kicked at the door, and screamed to be let out. Somehow, with the Voice's calm reassurance inside him, this wasn't so bad. As visions of drifting in water and light filled him, he could just let himself go.

Before his new hearing, he'd never have been able to discern the sound: tapping on the door pad as someone entered the code interrupted his dreamy eternity of water.

The lock clicked, and the handle turned before the door swung open.

Sheena and Felicity stood there. Both were naked, feet bare. The first thing Felix noticed was that Sheena was covered with blood spray. And he fixed on Felicity's swollen neck, and the two red streaks just up from her collarbone. Sheena, too, had the swelling, and only the faintest hint of a red line above her right collarbone. Somehow he knew that she'd get one on her left, too.

Felicity's eyes were vacant, and she was softly singing, *"Gabarron has fallen down, fallen down."*

"Come on," Sheena called. "The grownups are in the cafeteria trying to decide what to do."

"I'm in trouble. I'm supposed to stay locked in here."

"We know," Felicity told him as she broke off from the song, her voice slightly hoarse. "But the Song says we need you. You know which monitor controls the cameras in the com center."

"You're all bloody," Felix told Sheena.

She looked down, blinked, and with a shrug, started down the hall.

Felix climbed to his feet and stalked out into the hallway; he mechanically took Sheena's hand, feeling how sweaty it was. How his own began to perspire. Felicity took his other hand, their grips wet and clammy. Just holding hands, feeling the touch, was almost electric. Sheena and Felicity had joined hands. For long moments they stood there, the three of them, holding hands and just feeling . . . good.

And then better . . . and better.

The Song was louder now that he was out of the room. He could hear it, welling up from the stairs, rising from the Underwater Bay. Could feel the presence building, sending the Song through the very walls of the Pod.

"It's the Song," Felicity told him. "It tells us what to do."

Sheena and Felicity had closed their eyes, a happy look on their faces that matched the joy in his own chest. His blood pumping, running up his arms, sent a warmth spreading through his head. With the warmth came the knowledge that this was the way it should be. That, from here on out, it would always be like this.

Nothing in Felix's life had ever felt this wonderful, not even the boat ride. He, Sheena, and Felicity—all the children—they'd be blissful. Fulfilled. One and all.

An electric pulse flowed through him, sent a jolt of physical pleasure like he'd never known through his body. The magical tingle
burst through his hips, up his spine, and down to the souls of his
feet. He stiffened, gasped for breath, heart pounding as waves of
delight rolled through his body.

At the same time, Sheena and Felicity tensed, gasped in delighted
response. He could see the surprise in their eyes, and Sheena even
blushed pink in her neck.

Talk about zambo!

He had no clue how long they stood there, hands clasped in harmonic bliss. He shared Sheena's pulse, the excitement trembling up
her spine, and Felicity's electric joy as she took each quivering breath.

In that moment, he suddenly understood the Song: *We are one.*

Like they were seeping into him as he was seeping right back into
them.

Time to go.

Breaking contact caused him to almost cry out.

Sheena was blinking, stared at him as if she'd lost something
precious. Felicity reached up, traced the line of his cheek with a
blood-darkened green finger. All of their hands had turned a bright
blue-green.

"Come on," Sheena told him in her I'm-impatient voice. "We
have to let our friends out."

And with a frown, Felix understood that yes, they did. The Song
said so. Nothing would be right until all of the friends were out.
Only then could any of this make sense. Everything was a big question. All that mattered was solving the problem, making sense of the
Pod, of the Voice, and the people.

"Soon" Felix told them. He started down the hall and slowed
enough to glance into the clinic. Surrounded by broken glass, Anna
Gabarron lay on her stomach. Some kind of small ax had been buried in the small of her back. The woman's hand was stretched out, as
if asking for something, the fingers curled in a questing gesture. Her
normally hard dark eyes were vacant, oddly dull. The lips were bent,

crooked where they'd been pulled across the floor, and a pool of blood was still spreading from a gaping cut under the angle of the jaw.

Neck: Blood vessels, windpipe, spinal cord. Vulnerable and vital.

A bloody scalpel lay discarded in the pooled blood.

Funny, wasn't it? How fragile a human body was?

The isolation tent had been sliced into ribbons, and Felix could see Toni, his eyes blinking, sitting inside the ruin of slashed plastic.

Both Sheena and Felicity had that blank look in their eyes. Like they'd gone away. Neither moving except to breathe. He remembered how he had felt as he stood over Bill Martin's body. The Voice was probably telling them that it had to be done, as it had once told him.

Felicity, still blank-eyed, walked into the room, heedless of the broken glass, and reached around behind Gabarron's body. She gripped the ax handle with her bloody hands and wrenched it loose from the dead woman's spine. Then she turned and walked vacant-eyed to the hallway, stopped, and stood there.

From the remains of the isolation tent, Toni watched the entire event with large, dark eyes. He kept doing weird things with his face, twitching his lips, baring his teeth, scrunching his eyes. And he was making intricate gestures with his arms and hands. Felix caught a glimpse of the boy's throat, and finally got a good look. Tony had red slits at the base of his neck and over each delicate collarbone. His skin was a peculiar shade of green, as if he'd been dipped in dye.

The girls in the hallway stood there. Like they'd just turned off.

"Hey! Hello." Felix waved his hands in front of Sheena's and then Felicity's eyes. Neither reacted until he pushed Sheena, and she bumped Felicity.

"What are you doing?" Sheena asked, blinking, as if realizing where she was.

Felicity stared stupidly down at the ax where the blade still dripped blood. She seemed surprised to see it, confused even.

"Where did you get that?" Felix asked. "Was it in the clinic?"

"Mother's lab," Sheena said absently. "It's for chopping bones and stuff. Backbone. Spinal column. Vital and armored." Her eyes seemed to drift emptily. "The ax is for when we get to the com."

Felicity started forward, heedless of the bloody prints she left with her right foot.

Felix figured she must have cut it on some of the broken glass.

"What about Toni?" he called as Sheena started after Felicity.

"He's fine." Sheena told him. "He's all new."

"Can he get down?"

"When he's ready," Felicity called back. "You coming?"

Felix hurried after the girls, followed them into the com center. The various monitors were showing views of the landing pad, the deck, the cafeteria where the adults were all seated at the front table, Michaela at the head. Looked like the grownups were as serious as ever.

Felix did a double take when he saw the Underwater Bay in one of the monitors. The entire floor, the sub, the UUVs, and most of the workbenches were covered with algae. When had that happened?

Our friends. Something inside him began to glow with pleasure. Delight spread through Felix's stomach, sent a thrill of anticipation through him. His hands began to sweat and tickle. He really wanted to grab Sheena and Felicity's hands, share the explosive and remarkable surge of pleasure. Looking their way, they were smiling, staring at the monitor with as much excitement as he was.

Soon.

It all made so much sense. Of course. Just a few things to do now.

"Got to break the com," Felicity said with finality, and handed Felix the ax. "Then we can go turn the Song loose. Then we can be the Song."

73

"This is as good a time as any to bring this up," Kel called from his end of the table. "When it became apparent that the slime had flowed into the Underwater Bay, I figured maybe I ought to take a look at where it's been coating the pilings."

Michaela, face in her hands as she sat at the head table, looked at him through her spread fingers. Was there any good news? Anything that might give them a ray of hope? "And?"

The others shifted uncomfortably, expressions running from panicked to a sick-to-the-stomach countenance on Iso's face. Had to be hard knowing that her husband was in the last stages of being digested down in the UB.

God, when did I get so numb that I can't even share the horror?

The cafeteria might have been a morgue rather than a meeting room. Everywhere Michaela looked was a reminder of just how depressing their situation was.

Kel pulled up his pad, called up an image. He turned the screen so the rest of the team could see. "This what the piling should look like. Each of the supports is a duraplast pillar thirty centimeters in diameter, and it's sunk five meters into the bedrock. What you are seeing is a view of the piling before the slime."

Kel tapped the screen. "This is an image I took this afternoon. Notice any difference?"

Like a maestro, Kel tapped the screen, alternating the images back and forth.

Michaela gaped. "That *can't* be the same piling!"

"Yeah? Well, surprise, it is."

"How is this possible?" Michaela spoke for them all. "That's half the diameter, including however thick the slime is that's coating it."

"Let me help you with the math, Director." Kel looked around the table, a weary inevitableness in the set of his ruddy features. "As close as I can figure, about two thirds of the duraplast has been eaten away."

"Eaten away how?" Casey demanded, her fist clenched on the table before her. "That's goddamned duraplast! Not sialon, maybe, but it's still tough stuff!"

Kel pointed to the forlorn UUV where it rested on its cradle at the side of the room. "Remember the jellyfish that almost ate the UUV? I've got a theory about that after talking to Vik." He glanced at the microbiologist for assurance. "Donovanian life, like that tube the kids cut up in Vik's lab, has polymer structures that serve the same purpose bones do for life on Earth. Am I right?"

"You are. I haven't had the time to look into the histology, but polymer is just carbon chemistry." Vik glanced around. "I was telling Kel that I thought that Donovanian life had figured out a way to digest the polymer that makes up the internal structure of prey species. Or at least denature it to the point it will pass through the digestive net that serves advanced life-forms here for a stomach and intestines."

"So, the slime is either eating or denaturing our support pilings?" Michaela put the pieces together. "What the hell, people? Why didn't we see this coming?"

"Because we were looking the wrong way!" Kevina cried. "We were so fixated on BMTs, scimitars, lobster monsters, and flying terror, we sure as hell didn't care about a little algae!"

"It's not algae," Vik reminded. "That's the kind of thinking that got us in trouble in the first place." She paused. "And there's something else. I caught Sheena standing in front of the tube hatch, her head cocked and her eyes vacant. I asked what she was doing. When she came to, she said, 'Don't you hear it?' When I asked, 'Hear what?' she said, 'It's the Song. It's trying to tell me something.'"

"What does that mean?" Michaela wondered. "What Song?"

Vik rubbed a nervous hand over her face. "Call me paranoid, but anything happening with the children bears investigation. I used one of the high-sensitivity microphones. It's too faint for human hearing, but the entire Underwater Bay is, I guess you'd call it, singing. It's like a sounding chamber for low- and ultra-high-frequency sound. I got readings from thirty hertz up to almost one hundred and eighty kilohertz. Nor is it random, but patterned. Tonal. Who knows? But whatever it is, Sheena said she could hear it."

"That's impossible." Kel muttered.

"Is it?" Michaela asked. "TriNA changes human bodies. But it's easy enough to give Sheena a hearing test."

Kevina straightened. "Felix keeps talking about what he calls the Voice. Do you think that's it? He's hearing the slime? Thinks whatever this sound is, it's giving him orders?"

"How can slime give orders?" Kel crossed his arms, expression strained.

Vik slammed a fist into the table. "Damn it, don't you see? Our own semantics may have killed us. Algae? This life-form that we're calling slime is an intelligent organism like nothing we've ever conceptualized. It shares information through transferRNA, proteins, and entire strands of recombinant TriNA. It's made up of single prokaryotic cells that can assemble themselves at will into an organism that thinks, moves, plans, and inhabits our bodies. It's *infected* us. The mode of transmission is by physical contact. Through the skin. As long as it has light, it can survive."

"Can we kill it?" Yosh wondered.

Michaela felt like she was falling, like nothing was left. "What's to keep it from just disintegrating into single cells and floating away again? No, I suspect we'd have to kill every single cell, and do it all at once."

"Good luck!" Vik closed her eyes, paused to catch her breath, and said, "Do you begin to get it? This organism is everywhere, and we don't know what it wants. Let alone why it's doing what it's doing."

"Like with the kids," Mikoru barely whispered. "This stuff has taken my little boy from me. Maybe it's taken Felix and is about to do the same with Sheena."

"To do what?" Yosh demanded. "What does it want with Toni? Why infect him?"

"Or any of the children?" Michaela answered. And then it hit her. Like a big chunk of the puzzle falling into place. "Oh, dear God!"

"What?" Kel demanded.

"Felix!" Michaela cried. "What he calls the Voice. When he said that he wasn't there when Bill was killed."

"I don't understand." Kevina leaned forward, expression tight. "We found traces of Bill's blood on Felix's clothes, on his hands."

Yosh broke in. "You're saying the organism did this? Took over Felix's brain and murdered Bill? Turned the boy into an assassin? Why Bill, for God's sake?"

"Test run," Casey said bitterly. "See if the kid could really be turned into a weapon."

"Why a kid?" Casey asked. "Why not one of us?"

"Maybe adults aren't plastic enough? Or we're too hardwired?" Vik wondered.

Michaela felt a headache beginning to spin up from behind her right eye. Shit, she hadn't had a migraine since her university days. Or could it be the slime building some tumor in her brain? Was that it? Now that the creature was found out, it was going to kill her? Turn her into some sort of vegetable? Digest her body from the inside out in contrast to the way it had engulfed Tobi and Bryan?

Dear God, can it do that? Accrete and slowly digest me?

"People, wait. Think," Kel pleaded. "One thing at a time. Let's lay this out. Okay, as of now, the Underwater Bay belongs to the creature. Consider it gone for good. The pilings are two-thirds eaten through, so even though they were over-engineered, our structural integrity is compromised, and the stuff is still dissolving the duraplast. Final word: The Pod will eventually fail. Meanwhile, we're all infected. The algae—"

"Don't call it that!" Vik snapped. "It's a fucking intelligent organism, and we'd better start respecting it for what it is."

"Right," Kel agreed. "The organism has infected us all. It may be using . . . Scratch that. It is using the children for its own purposes. It's put Toni into a coma and may have taken control of Felix to kill Bill. We know that all the kids, even the infants, are sick with sore throats. We also know that being infected, we may not be allowed in PA or Corporate Mine. Lastly, we're being picked off one by one. Now, what are we going to do?"

Michaela stared around at her people. "They put the Unreconciled on an outlying research station. I know there are other abandoned bases out in the bush. We could ask for one. That's an option."

Yosh wore a miserable expression. "Isn't that exchanging bad for worse? We're still talking about Donovan. You heard the stories the Supervisor told when she was here. Three quarters of the cannibals who landed at Tyson are dead. Killed by Donovan's monsters. What makes us any safer on the mainland than out here?"

Casey added, "If the Pod collapses into the sea, as long as the upper tube hatch is closed, it's designed to float. And, while the supporting posts are duraplast, the Pod shell is sialon, that's a ceramic." She glanced at Kel. "Any sign the slime . . . er, organism eats sialon?"

"No. So far I can see no sign of corrosion or damage to the Pod's sialon shell. But we still have duraplast around the doors, hatches, and windows to be concerned about. Maybe we can figure out some way to protect them."

"And what does being adrift on open water get us?" Mikoru asked. "It puts us that much farther from any help from the Supervisor or PA. We're at the mercy of the winds, currents, and tides, and eventually we're going to wash up on some shore that might be a lot more hostile than what we have here."

"Assuming we can survive the organism," Vik noted. "Or defeat it somehow. Face it, people, we may not live long enough to make any of this even worth the debate. If Tobi and Bryan are any indication of its intentions, I'm not sure but that taking one of the seatrucks and hauling butt for shore wouldn't be the smartest route."

"What about the infection inside us?" Michaela asked. "Do we ever get rid of it? I mean, what if these cells start accreting inside us, creating an intelligence that lives in our muscles and brains?" She couldn't say *Takes us over like it did Felix?*

Could she stand that? To be a spectator while some alien intelligence used her body like a robot? Was there a more terrifying version of hell?

I won't let it happen. I promise!

"I don't know what to tell you," Vik said woodenly. "Last I

talked to Raya Turnienko, she wasn't very positive. Told me that Donovanian TriNA exists in most of the population on the planet. Some, like Talina Perez, show signs of the infection; in others the TriNA is just present in their blood. But that's just single molecules. Not cells that can accrete into an organism. As far as our situation is concerned, we're off the map."

"It's doing something to my little boy," Mikoru told them. "He has wounds at the base of his neck. Swelling. His skin is turning green. Anna has no clue what it means, and she said that Dr. Turnienko has never seen the like." A pause. "I want my little boy back."

Michaela massaged her brow. The headache was going to be a killer. "We all want the kids back. My bottom line—as Kel tells it—is that the supports under the Pod are going to fold. When that happens—assuming the drop into the sea doesn't compromise the Pod's integrity—we're going to just float away to whatever fate the organism has in store. Right?"

Kel nodded. "We could use cable, anchor the Pod to the reef, but the first big storm that comes along would probably tear us free. In the end, the result will be the same."

"Then I say we shoot for the mainland. See what the Supervisor has in the way of abandoned stations that we could inhabit."

"Die there as easily as we could here?" Casey asked caustically.

"Dead is dead," Yosh muttered. "As I understand it, we're talking no chance if we stick with the Pod, but a slim chance if we try the mainland. I vote slim chance."

"I second that," Kevina said. "I say that we pack up the seatrucks and abandon ship."

A nagging thought penetrated Michaela's growing headache. "Something to consider, people. To date we haven't lost a single child. Why is the organism keeping them alive?"

Vik—in that listless tone of voice—said, "I'd guess that it is planning something."

74

Danger! The quetzal in Dek's blood sent that jolt of adrenaline squirting into his arteries and veins. His heart rate increased, air charging his lungs. Around him, the dim forest floor pulsed with the chime, the sound of it filling the warm morning with a symphonic harmony. Invertebrates buzzed as a column of them swarmed past a blooming tooth flower. The vibrant colors attracted the little creatures, many of which landed, only to be trapped and ingested when the colorful bloom snapped shut, the teeth interlocking to preclude any escape by the surprised prey.

Dek calmed himself, stalking quietly forward over the root mat with his rifle at the ready. He could just detect the faint odor, a sort of balsamic scent mixing with the tang of vinegar. He had the ornate Holland & Holland set for a muzzle velocity of seven hundred meters per second with a one-hundred–eighty grain bullet.

"This thing will kill you," Rocket's voice seemed to sound from above.

"Die," Demon chided. *"Stupid human."* The knowledge that it was good riddance and fitting settled in Dek's mind like a misty net.

"Quetzals don't know everything," Dek whispered under his breath, trying to balance quetzal knowledge with his own. Damn it, he had to try this. See if he could integrate the two. He'd been working on this for two days now. Seesawing back and forth, battling to come to terms, to find that measure of control and fine balance.

He had Talina's image to rely on, memory of how she'd reassembled the Mayan pot. It helped, but that was Talina's solution. He could only use it as a sort of model, not a step-by-step guide. Maya mythology and tradition weren't in his worldview. Knowing that it was possible to integrate—if not how—was enough. He had to deal with this in a Taglioni fashion. That meant risk, cunning, and profiting from success.

"So you see," he told Demon, "we can die just as surely as drowning. I die, you die. Your TriNA never makes it back to your lineage. It dead-ends here."

"*Go back to Talina,*" Rocket pleaded.

"Can't," Dek muttered under his breath. "Understand, we're doing this. We're going to kill this thing. Together. Demon, you, me, we're all intelligent. So I'm gambling that Demon—hate humans as he does—is going to work with us when it comes that final moment."

"*Insane! Die.*"

"Sorry. I'm calling your bluff."

"*Why?*"

"It's a Taglioni thing. I won't live being half of what I could be. It's all or nothing."

"*You die, you lose Talina.*"

"And quetzals are supposed to be so smart? Come on. Share a little of that TriNA back and forth and think this through. It's my body, but all of our existences. Being my body, I get the final vote on how I'm going to live in it. What the rules are under which I will continue to live in it. So, Demon, the choice is yours. We can all survive together, or not at all."

Silence.

"Guess we find out how intelligent you really are." Dek carefully inspected the thick bundle of roots ahead of him. The twisted knot of them, many as big around as oil drums, was bounded on either side by monstrous boles of forest chabacho that rose majestically up into the soaring canopy, the trunks five or six meters in diameter. From the way the root mat squirmed, it indicated that something had passed this way not too long ago. Given the faint balsamic vinegar odor that remained, Dek figured he knew what it was.

Well, not exactly. He just had quetzal memory, nothing with a name. Just a hazy image of a creature. Long. With sleek sides and three sword-like pinchers. Something quetzals feared. Something that, like the treetop terror outside of Tyson, had rid this area around Two Falls Gap of quetzals.

Other than it was dangerous—and scared Demon and Rocket half to death—Dek only knew it came from the river. That this was the extent of its range.

What better way to take control of his body and mind than to bet it all on one roll of the dice? Either he'd win, or they'd all lose. Simple as that.

With a bound, Dek leapt onto the lowest of the thick roots, using his Holland & Holland for balance he scrambled his way up. Unlike outside Tyson, he had good wind now. His muscles, pushed during the months he'd been on the ground, were back. Not to mention that quetzal TriNA was working its transformation, improving the efficiency of each muscle fiber.

At the top of the slowly contorting pile, Dek peered over into the confusion of interlaced roots beyond. He could see the track of the thing, straight across the root mat.

"Let's go get it."

Demon tried to turn his limbs into lead. That weird feeling he used to get in dreams when he needed to run, only to find his legs grown impossibly heavy and slow to move. Where each step became a slow-motion struggle.

"Not a chance," Dek growled, jaw clenched. "A little help here, Rocket?"

He made the commitment, leaped off the root, trusting he'd have control when he thumped onto the next root down. He did. Demon wasn't as stupid as he'd let on. Spilling into the roots would have been just as lethal as being eaten by whatever lay at the end of the trail.

Victory. At least, a small one.

Dek smiled.

"Still no guarantee that we'll live through this." Rocket sounded unsure.

"Welcome to Donovan," Dek chided.

Rocket responded with that chittering that served for quetzal laughter.

Nothing from Demon. Dek imagined that all through his brain and blood, Demon's TriNA was separating, recombining, and spitting molecules back and forth.

Good, let the evil little son of a bitch think it through. It wasn't just Dek's resolve that he was betting on. Demon had been living inside Talina. It had experienced Talina's victory over one quetzal after another—ever since she'd killed the one that had infected her in that canyon in the Blood Mountains. Then there was the one she'd killed by dropping a front-end loader's bucket on its neck. And the one from Whitey's lineage she'd shot in PA. Not to mention that Demon had to have been affected by the TriNA from all those other lineages. The stuff learned from other molecules, right?

"That's right, boys. And I'm as dedicated to success as Talina."

Dek trotted across the root mat—heedless of the way it squirmed in protest—and tackled the next head-high tangle of barrel-thick roots. Scrambling to the top, he caught the faint scent of balsam as an eddy stirred.

"*Close,*" Rocket almost shrilled.

Dek stopped short just below the crest of interlocked roots. Flipped the safety off. His heart began to hammer in his chest, adrenaline charging his muscles. That full-body tingle—called buck fever—ran through his muscles and blood.

"Show time, boys," he said as forced himself to peer over the edge, the rifle at the ready.

The real thing was one hell of a lot more intimidating than that hazy image in quetzal memory. The monster might have been twenty meters in length. It didn't have legs as such but was propelled by double lines of paddles on either side of its belly. A third line—like fins—ran down the length of its back. A stalk-topped eye swiveled around, fixing full on Dek. The thing stopped halfway up the root ball across the flat.

"Pus in a bucket," Dek whispered. Made himself clamber over the top of the roots when every sensible nerve in his body was screaming, "*Shoot!*"

Trembling, his mouth dry, Dek carefully felt his way down the root tangle, rifle at the ready.

"Just like Tyson Station," he told himself. "If you can take out a drone with a snap shot, you can kill this thing."

That didn't mean that now, seeing the size of the beast, he forgot to flip up the velocity to a thousand meters a second and wish he'd loaded a two-hundred-fifty-grain bullet.

"Hey! Monster!" he yelled, more to assert his own flagging courage than to piss the beast off.

It whipped around, rainbow-bright colors flashing on its sides as it did. Damn, it was fast for its size. And Dek got a good look at the thing's front. Three broad inward-curving blades—each maybe a meter in length and topped with a hook—spread wide. The trio of stalk-like eyes were extended, the bottom one sticking straight out toward him from beneath the creature's belly. The mouth had three jaws that slid sideways, opening like some perverted iris, to expose a nightmare-fraught maw.

"Okay," Dek whispered to himself. "Bad idea."

Too late now. Dek pulled up the rifle and shot just as the thing charged.

75

Through that long and disturbing night, Kalico Aguila hadn't slept. She'd groused about the fact that when it came to Dek—as Michegan put it—she wasn't any Talina Perez. She obsessed that, for all intent and purpose, Corporate Mine was shut down, running at idle while make-work was attended to. And then, that morning, the shuttle had come in with the first rotation from PA after the cave-in. Corporal Abu Sassi had informed her that Tadeki Ozawa hadn't bothered to make the return trip, that Makarov had held the shuttle an additional fifteen minutes, and the man had failed to show.

A quick radio call to Two Spot had assured her that Tadeki hadn't been admitted to hospital, hadn't run afoul of PA security, or showed up in any way, manner, or form on their radar. That was either good or bad. Maybe the guy was dead in an alley, or he'd wandered out past the gate and been eaten by a quetzal, or maybe he'd deserted. No one had deserted Corporate Mine in years.

So, what am I going to do?

She had standing orders that deserters would be shot. Old orders that hadn't been needed in years.

"So, do I shoot Tadeki? The guy just lost his wife and unborn child." Shit on a shoe, that would make good press. "Supervisor murders grief-stricken man mourning the death of all that he loved."

Needing to get the hell out of Corporate Mine, she'd briefed Ghosh, accessed her com, and ordered, "Makarov, spool up the A-7. I need to go to PA."

"Roger that, Supervisor."

"Tadeki is missing," she'd told everyone. "I'm going to go find him."

It had made a hell of a good excuse.

So she'd had Makarov run her back to Port Authority. On the

way, she'd sat in the cockpit starboard-side passenger seat, one leg up, chewing on a thumbnail as she stared out at the thick carpet of forest and the curve of the Gulf off to the east. From this altitude, she could almost see as far as the Maritime Unit. Almost. As if that tiny dot of white would be visible to her naked eye.

Just thinking of it put her in an even fouler mood.

What the hell was I thinking of? Just walking away from it. Who the hell have I become?

The old Kalico Aguila—the one who'd schemed, scratched, plotted, and fought her way to the top of the heap back in Solar System—would have pulled out her pistol, shot that Gabarron woman dead on the spot, faced down the shocked scientists, and ordered, "Get your damned asses to work. This is not a democracy. And I'll shoot the next sorry pus-sucker who crosses me."

Now *that* was Kalico Aguila.

When, along the way, had that woman morphed into the one who had said, "Fine. Have it your way" and simply washed her hands of the matter?

Even if I'd shot them all, that's a huge Corporate investment. The equipment alone would refurbish half of PA's labs. She could trade for all the timbers and spare parts she needed to keep Corporate Mine running for another twenty years.

Mulling on that, she cocked an eyebrow and rubbed the scar running along the line of her jaw. Maybe that was the solution. She could fly out with Abu Sassi, Michegan, and Muldare. While they stood around in their armor, fingered their rifles, and looked mean, she could have Bogarten, Stryski, and their technicians strip the place of anything of value like the microscopes, PCRs, chromatographs, FTIRs, and other equipment.

Wasn't anything Michaela Hailwood or her people could do about it.

"I've been on this damned planet too long," Kalico grumbled.

"Ma'am?" Makarov asked.

"Juri, how did the shuttles from *Ashanti* place that Pod out on the reef?"

"Took four heavy-lift birds to lower the pieces from orbit. Pretty precise flying, ma'am. They had to settle the parts just so onto the pilings. A fancy bit of work with the lasers and all to measure distance as the four birds hovered, maneuvered, and put each piece into position."

"So, it would take four birds to lift it?"

"No, ma'am. They needed four to get it down from orbit. Lowering that much mass into a gravity well, that's a whole different story than just picking pieces up off the pilings. Once you had the landing pad removed, the UB disconnected. and the inside cleaned out, we could lift the main tube using the Corporate bird and PA's A-7. That is, if we're just picking the thing up and moving it somewhere where putting it down isn't tricky."

She narrowed an eye. That changed her entire calculus. She could pull the plug, blow the top off a mountain somewhere to expose bedrock, and use the Pod for a base of operations. Maybe on that mountain of palladium down south? And she had more shuttles mothballed up on *Freelander*.

Besides, who knew? Maybe, with a sick kid, one of the two subs lost, their UUVs vulnerable to the wildlife, and enough people dead, her rebellious Maritime Unit might be more than welcoming of a chance to step back into the fold. There was nothing like a good dose of Donovan to slap a bunch of soft meat back into line.

Time to take a trip back out there, and yes, she'd take a couple of marines with her. Michaela Hailwood's people would be ready to listen to reason, one way or another.

That solved, she felt better. That old killer instinct awake in her gut again.

Feeling that way, what did she do about Dek Taglioni?

And there, Kalico, is your real dilemma.

"Think, damn it." Her finger traced the slick scar along her jaw as she narrowed her eyes. Come on, where was the sly old Kalico? The one who'd played people like chess pieces, seduced, used, and discarded those who could help her on her rise to power? That Kalico should have been able to cunningly cut Talina's throat while at the same time beguiling Dek, dazzling him, and offering so much more than Tal could possibly . . .

"What the hell are you thinking?" she asked herself angrily.

Makarov said nothing this time, knowing well enough to keep his mouth shut.

This wasn't a Corporate game, and Dek wasn't a trophy like some notch on the butt of her pistol.

And that's the difference. She'd already won the grand prize. For once in her life, she could ask herself, what did Dek Taglioni mean *to* her? Not *for* her.

With no political advantage to be gained, no one to be compromised, no strategic value to the relationship, it didn't even matter that he was a Taglioni. Well, okay, it did. But that was, as Shig would say, cultural baggage. No one on Donovan gave a damn, and she didn't score any points by it.

Her gaze traveled out across the morning-bright forest, seeing the wealth of trees below; the tops of the various species of aquajade made a turquoise patchwork amidst the darker greens of the chabacho and stone wood. And there were other species down there, trees for which they had no name yet. So much of Donovan beckoned, unknown, unstudied, and uncatalogued.

Do I love the guy?

"Never had the freedom to ask a question like that," she murmured.

Do I love Derek? There it was. Laid out for her analytical mind to dissect. Fact: She did enjoy the man's company. He was the only person on the planet that she could talk to about the old days. Being a Taglioni, Dek understood her worldview, and shared that same cultural zeitgeist. They functioned under the same rules. And that proved comfortable for both of them.

But is that love? Fact: The lingering memory of that odious old Derek Taglioni remained fresh in her memory, constantly a reminder of who he had been. Who he might become again at any moment. Did a leopard ever change its spots? This Derek Taglioni wore the same skin as the drunken one in the Solar Elan Hotel ballroom who'd loudly and very publicly speculated on Kalico's lingual dexterity when it came to sucking Miko's cock.

Had that vile lout been entirely buried by the man who'd given her his last energy bar, and then struggled to get her up that forbidding cliff back at Tyson Station? The man who'd shot the drone that was diving to kill her? And who still had a healing scar in his cheek from a bit of shrapnel blown out of the bomb it carried?

She did look forward to seeing him. Enjoyed the meals they shared, the talks they engaged in at Inga's over a glass of whiskey. And she found amusement and appreciation in Dek's recounting of his adventures in the bush, his enthusiasm for Donovan's wilds, and the pride he derived from his claim and the wealth it produced.

But do I want him as my mate?

She was, after all, a healthy and long-too-celibate woman. Sexual relations had been a large part of her life back in Solar System. Since she'd set foot onto *Turalon* all those years ago, she had had no one of her station with whom to consort. Had Dek made the right overtures, she probably would have taken him to her bed. He was trained as all Taglionis were, so no doubt it would have been rewarding.

Occasional sex was a whole different thing than making a full-time commitment. Problem was, she did get lonely. Just like this morning. She needed to get the hell out of Corporate Mine. If Dek were around, he would offer the right encouragement. Help her keep things in perspective. A Board Supervisor and a Taglioni, they talked and thought the same.

"Be best if I could just file him away. Take him out when I needed him. Then put him back when I've finished with whatever," she whispered softly.

Ah, yes. Just have him on call.

That, my dearest Kalico, doesn't bode well for Dek as a mate.

So why her constant obsession over Dek and Talina? Together? Just over at Two Falls Gap? How the hell had Talina gotten the inside track? What exactly had happened that day at Dek's claim? Outside of a quetzal infection, what did the two of them possibly have in common? What did they have to talk about? Certainly not the menu at Tiboronne, or the view from Three Spires back in Transluna.

"*You're not Talina Perez,*" Dina Michegan's voice mocked.

Should she order Makarov to change course, drop her at Two Falls Gap? And . . . .what?

"Think," she told herself. "Be analytical. What you do now will be for high-value stakes." That old cold and calculating Kalico clicked into place. Laid out from a strategic perspective, was seducing Dek and making him hers worth alienating Talina? Love triangles were always tricky business. And, God knows, she'd used them with ruthless efficiency against adversaries back in Solar System. She knew exactly how to manipulate, exploit, and weaponize a sexual relationship. Unlike back in Solar System, there would be longterm consequences. In the aftermath, the ramifications of dumping Dek would be legion—assuming she tired of him or the loathsome Dek resurfaced. Hell, she might even have to assassinate him if he turned out to be a real pain in the ass.

Additionally, making an enemy out of Talina Perez would be sheer idiocy on so many levels.

Question: Is Dek worth more to me than my relationship with Talina?

Kalico laughed at herself. Cold analytics aside, Talina—for all of her differences with Kalico—had become a trusted friend. Friend? When had that ever mattered? Whatever trouble Kalico might ever get herself into, Talina would be there. Just as she'd been outside of Tyson Station.

"Just like I'd be there for her," Kalico whispered, seeing the horizon drop away as the shuttle began its bank toward Port Authority.

So much for the cold and analytical Kalico Aguila.

And Dek's infected with quetzal TriNA. I don't even know what or who he's going to be coming out of this.

That left Kalico facing the distinct reality that Dek and Tal might return from Two Falls Gap as an inseparable couple. If not as starryeyed lovers, at least sharing each other's bed, their lives inextricably joined.

So, how are you going to deal with that? Jealous as you feel now?

Deceleration pushed Kalico deeper into her seat as the shuttle descended toward Port Authority, the bush seeming to rise to meet her.

"This is nothing you can't handle," she told herself, locking that old analytic self into play. She was, after all, Kalico Aguila. The woman who'd made her way up to Board Supervisor by means of her wits, self-control, ultimate pragmatism, and sheer implacable intelligence.

She allowed herself a sigh of relief. The Dek problem taken care of, all she had to do was deal with the Maritime Unit, and then get her mine back on its feet.

Kalico congratulated herself as Makarov settled the big A-7 onto the heat-glazed dirt at Port Authority's field.

Before she looked up Shig to dicker over the rental of PA's A-7, she hoped Inga would have something savory for breakfast. Then she could tackle the next problem.

Too bad that not everything had as simple a solution as just denying one's heart.

76

Talina ducked wide around a gotcha vine. This was some lowland variety she'd never seen before. The thorns were longer, the leaves almost those of a succulent versus the thinner ones from inland and up north.

"Damn you, Dek," she whispered, following along the trail he'd left.

What the hell was she going to do with him? She'd awakened that morning to an empty bed when all she wanted to do was wrap herself around him and enjoy delicious sex. Instead of grabbing Dek and dragging him back to the mattress for refreshing bed play, she'd walked out to the kitchen to find breakfast simmering on the stove, a pot of tea steaming, and a note.

> *Tal:*
>
> *I've gone to the forest under the escarpment to deal with Demon. Since I can't put a Mayan bowl back together, I have to win or lose this as a Taglioni.*
>
> > *You are the love of my heart.*
> > *Dek.*

She'd panicked, turned off the stove, ran for her clothes, and was dressed and out of the dome in minutes.

She'd found his tracks in the trail that led to the edge of the falls and backtracked to the narrow gap. Didn't matter that she knew the route now; on the climb down she'd almost fallen to her death—and worse, ended up in the tangle of deadly vines that filled the bottom.

But there, beneath the falls, she'd found Dek's tracks. He'd been headed downriver.

As she hurried along at a trot, heedless of bruising the roots she trod on, Talina ground her teeth.

Dek, you idiot! You've got nothing to prove to me.

She'd been slowly but surely falling for the guy. And it wasn't just the remarkable sex. The man had a sense of humor, one sharpened and made wry by trial and testing. To her surprise, Dek Taglioni had turned out to be somewhat like Shig in that he'd seen all sides of life and had found peace with the vagaries of existence. She'd never spent time with a man who was as sure of himself when faced with his own ignorance, one who just accepted that he was going to have to learn in the most efficient way possible. And he did it with a complete lack of ego. Except when it counted. Like now. When whatever insanity had led him to charge out into the lowland forest—a place no one had even explored—to face who knew what kind of danger.

She had never known a man of such complexity—let alone one who seemed to deal with all of it in such a holistic way.

"I was a monster," he had told her. "Once I figured that out, I decided I didn't like myself. Since I'd been trained to be that way, I realized I could train myself to live another way."

"So, you can change personalities like some people change clothes?" she'd asked.

Expression pinching, he'd answered, "It's more of a philosophy of who you are. I don't believe in atonement. The hurt, damage, and pain you cause someone can't be taken back. It's real and permanent. Atonement is about making the perpetrator feel better about himself by making other people or their conditions better. Me? I live with the guilt. Through it, I am motived to never commit the same acts again."

He'd smiled. "Doesn't mean I'm a saint. I still have my petty side. I did, after all, send Dan Wirth back to Miko as payback. Sort of like lobbing a hand grenade into his well-manicured world."

For days now, her existence had been idyllic. Just her and Dek, fishing, taking walks, working in the garden, cooking together, sharing stories and laughter, and rationing out the last of the bourbon. Each of them lost in that first golden haze of exploring a human being they were attracted to.

And there was the sex.

Maybe there was something to this Taglioni "training." If Talina ever ran into this mysterious Kalay, she'd offer her personal thanks.

Everything going so well, and then Dek had to run off into the forest with this latest bullshit? Hell, he had been dealing: the episodes of blank looks, the sudden flashbacks had been fewer, of less impact.

"Clap-trapping hell, Dek! Couldn't you have just gone with the flow?"

It wasn't like they had to leave Two Falls Gap. For all Talina had started to care, they might just stay there. Become Wild Ones. The two of them. Hunting, fishing, telling stories by the fire. She loved it when Dek would listen, rapt, as she told stories of quetzal hunts, of taking down bad men, of rescues she'd made out in the bush. No man, not even Cap, had listened with such complete focus.

In turn, he'd recount stories about his youth, talking about people that Talina had thought of as some sort of gods. Names like Radcek, Montano, Suharto, Grunnels, and Xian Chan among others. He told of remarkable places, stunning residences, and opulent palaces. And then came the tales of intrigue, backstabbing, and the deadly games of the powerful and rabidly ambitious.

"All that," Talina groused, leaping to the top of a knot of roots and hopping surefooted down the other side. "And you're going to lose it all by getting yourself eaten out in the forest?"

That's when her nose caught the faint scent. A curious, almost balsamic vinegar kind of . . . The quetzal reaction was immediate: frightened, almost to the point of paralysis. Talina pushed it to the back of her mind, suddenly as wary as she'd ever been.

"Yeah, guys," she said softly, lifting her rifle, finger on the rest over the trigger, safety off. "I get the message."

The last time she'd felt like this, it had been out at Tyson. Then it had been the treetop terror. That same deep quetzal memory. By the time they'd dealt with that, at least three people, probably more, were dead, and they'd blown up half the forest. The treetop terror had still managed to escape.

I emptied an entire magazine into that thing. She remembered the explosive rounds hammering into the monster's wide belly. And it had absorbed the punishment, sort of folded in on itself, and kept right on fighting.

"Dek, for God's sake, tell me you smelled that, and you're backing off!"

Even as she said it, the bang of a rifle came from up ahead. Immediately it was followed by a soul-searing shriek the likes of which Talina had never heard.

77

As the Song flowed through him, Felix decided that he really liked the ax. It was a little shorter than the length of his arm, felt firmly heavy in his eight-year-old grasp, and was capable of marvelous things. Swinging it, he'd completely destroyed the com system, bashing the monitors. The quantum computer had split open with a satisfying clatter of broken ceramic matrix—fragments of which had spilled across the floor.

As it did, the Song spilling out from the stairway changed; the harmonics charged his nerves, and filled him with excitement. He could see Felicity and Sheena's reaction, like his own, almost glowing and energized.

They had finished with the com when Toni had appeared in the doorway; his shining eyes looked odd and totally black. Like, with no pupils or whites. And each time he breathed, the swellings in the side of his neck pulsed and the slits at his collar bones fluttered. When he opened his mouth, it wasn't to talk. Instead, his utterances carried the same notes and intonation as the Song rising from the UB. Even as Felix watched, Toni's already-green skin seemed to darken. What was that all about?

Then he looked at his own fingers; the deep-green color had spread through his hands and into his wrists.

The Song changed, seemed to vibrate in the air around them. Urgency, that was the message behind the changed harmony.

"Got to go now," Sheena told him absently. "Toni's ready."

"Got to go," Felix agreed. Definitely the right thing since Toni had joined them.

Weird how different Toni was. The vile little brat was gone. Toni didn't walk like a kid anymore but had a purposeful stride that got better with each step. He looked, well, somehow smarter, like he was someone Felix didn't want to know. The change made Felix uncomfortable. Like he was seeing some stranger inside Toni's body. Freaking spooky!

He hoped that would never happen to Sheena. She was his best friend, and he didn't want her to turn into some mean stranger.

Felicity led the way down the stairs, and Felix could remember when the second level had been off limits, a place where children couldn't go. Now, everything in the past seemed silly. His entire world was being made right.

At the bottom of the stairs, they rounded the landing to the hatch that opened to the tube.

Sheena, as usual, keyed in the code, and together, they undogged the watertight door. "Got to do this right," Sheena insisted. She looked at Felicity, seemed to fix on the sides of the girl's neck where the swellings had started to pulse. "Code is 6676. You feeling zambo?"

"Zambo," Felicity agreed, then turned to follow Toni down the stairs.

"Zambo," Felix chimed as he took the ax and smashed the code box that controlled the hatch. No one could lock them out. All it would take to open it would be to turn the handle.

It wouldn't be long now.

With the com broken, the safety overrides wouldn't work on the UB hatch lock. It would revert to manual, too.

They knew the moment Felicity entered the code to the pressurized hatch downstairs. Could hear the seawater surging into the Underwater Bay. Flooding the compartment. It came roaring as it poured through the open hatch and into the tube. A blast of air blew Felix and Sheena off their feet, tumbled them both onto their butts. The violence of it left Felix stunned and afraid. And then it was over, just as fast as it had come. The sound of water could be heard sloshing.

And the Song was joyous. It filled him, fit to burst his bones. Tears silvered his vision and spilled down his cheeks. *We are free!*

While Sheena was giggling like an idiot—apparently getting

knocked on her butt had been fun—Felix clambered to his feet, staring down where the algae-thick water lapped and splashed on the steps down at the water line. He extended a hand, could almost feel the Song rising, becoming one with his body.

Sheena's eyes were glittering with excitement. "This whole place, Felix! It's ours now!"

78

At the beast's nerve-chilling shriek, the quetzals were gone. As if they'd never existed. Dek almost fumbled as he dropped another bullet into the receiver. Around him, the forest went deathly quiet. Across the mat of squirming roots, the huge predator appeared shocked, frozen.

Dek, panting for breath, his heart pounding so hard it was fit to hammer through his sternum, pulled up the Holland & Holland. He fixed the sight, finger on the trigger.

The three sickle-like blades spread wide on the creature's head where they had flashed closed after the first shot. With a second scream, the monster started forward, mouth wide.

This is it!

Didn't remember triggering the gun. Barely felt the recoil, was faintly aware of the bang.

Only that fragmented visual: Charging beast, rifle rising in recoil, the creature jerking, stumbling. As the gun dropped back, the thing staggered sideways, roots gone crazy beneath it. Then it whirled. Colors like rainbow lasers of blaze-orange, translucent indigo, nacre-pink, and midnight-black dazzled along its smooth flanks to be followed by blinding crimson, searing yellows, streaks of blacks and deep purples, searing greens and violet.

Another of those mind-numbing shrieks, and the whole long length of it whipped around on the tortured root mat and seemed to squirt up the far tangle of thigh-thick roots, only to vanish over the top.

Dek was already running, trying to keep his footing on the roiling root mat. Managed, somehow, to make it across. The beast's trail was plain. The reddish fluid that passed for blood in most of Donovan's more advanced life had left smears across the tops of the roots. They were already reacting to the nutrients.

"Got to hurry." Dek threw himself up the thick tangle, barely found footing, and vaulted over the highest of the contorting roots.

The roots along the creature's path were a riot of motion, reacting not only to the weight of the animal's passing, but to the feast of rich blood.

Dek reloaded his rifle as he went, eyes warily taking in the pillar-like trunks of forest giants rising to either side. Vaguely he wondered if the blade beast could climb. If he needed to worry about being ambushed from above.

"Didn't look like it," he told himself. Those paddle-like flipper feet, they could sure move the beast across the flats and up over tall messes of the thick roots, but they'd be hard put to cling to anything.

At the top of the next mass of intertwined roots, Dek carefully peeked over. Saw nothing but more of the disturbed roots marking the creature's passage. It was all the same, endless masses of thickly entwined giant roots giving way to a hollow matted with smaller ones, all interwoven in the endless wrestling match that was the Donovanian forest floor.

The chime was back along with the usual forest sounds. In the trees he could hear hooting, unearthly chattering, and whooping countercalls.

And somewhere up ahead was a twenty-meter-long technicolor monster with slashing blades that would slice him into three pieces. Worse, the blade beast was wounded. Probably coming to the conclusion that it had nothing left to lose.

Maybe realizing that it could still get even.

What sobered Dek more than anything was the realization that if the monster had made it this far, it sure as hell wasn't disabled. Had it not been startled by the rifle, had it continued to charge, the blade beast would have already chopped him into butchered chunks, and he'd be ground to burger by those tooth-filled shearing jaws.

"Dek, old buddy, you might have just gotten lucky again."

He slowed, still treading wide of the excited roots on the creature's bloody trail. Should he go on? Take the chance that the beast might camouflage like a quetzal did? Maybe charge from the side after circling around to ambush its backtrail?

"I shot it," Dek muttered under his breath. "It's my responsibility."

If he was making a point—both to himself and to the quetzals—he had to finish this.

"Doesn't mean I ever have to do it again," he told himself sourly.

Heart hammering, ears pitched for the slightest sound, he kept padding as lightly as he could across the roots, climbed to the left of the blood trail at the next thick tangle, and peered over.

No dying blade beast met his searching gaze, just the roots doing their manic thing.

"Damn it, why couldn't it just be lying dead in the middle of that clearing while a thousand roots were climbing all over it ready for supper?"

The beast had taken two shots from no more than ten meters. Both of them right down the center. If the blade monster was anything like other Donovanian critters, those shots should have torn through lung, heart, and the net that made up the stomach.

"But not for the entire twenty-meter length of it." So what kind of penetration had his bullets made? Maybe a couple of meters?

"Should have dialed it up more."

Dek almost jumped out of his skin as something big flapped past his ear. Four-winged, the flying creature had to be two meters across. Covered with a sort of pelage, it flipped around on beating wings, stared at Dek with three eyes. The long, tooth-filled muzzle didn't strike Dek as warm and fuzzy. He raised the rifle, finger hovering over the trigger, and tried to get his muscles to stop shivering and his franticly pumping blood from making the rifle jump with each beat.

The flyer let out a squawk, turned from green to bright yellow before twisting in midair and flapping away.

"Shit on a shoe," Dek whispered, realized fear-sweat was beading on his face.

Where the hell was the blade monster?

He looked around at the twilight-dim forest. Seeing into the IR had real advantages. Hell, maybe it was worth the constant ache behind his eyes. Right now, all he wanted to do was get this over and get home to Talina. After that, he had nothing to prove to anyone.

Figured that was made even more probable by the fact that no quetzal was inserting itself into his thoughts or emotions. They really didn't want anything to do with the blade monster.

"Guess that makes it unanimous."

He slipped over the top root, made his way to the bottom, and picked a careful path around the clearing perimeter. Given the dark, cave-like arch of roots on the right, he chose the left side.

He was just on the verge of climbing the next tangle of ceiling-high roots when movement caught the corner of his eye. He wheeled, bringing the rifle up.

The blade monster came like a rocket: fast. As it did, it emitted a deafening squeal that might have been rage augmented by a bloody spray that misted around its three jaws.

Dek made a snap shot. Recoil hammered his shoulder. The impulse came out of nowhere; he pitched sideways at the last instant. As he did, he heard the sound of rapid gunshots, the meaty hollow pops of bullets spatting into flesh.

The closest blade hissed through the air less than an inch from Dek's face. He caught the blur of it—and then the bulk of the thing hurled past, knocking him off his feet as the barrel-thick body twisted. The impact tore the rifle from Dek's hands. Tossed him like an afterthought. His head hammered the thick root, hard.

And then everything was . . .

Kalico had demolished most of a chamois steak, beans simmered in red sauce, and roasted squash when Shig Mosadek appeared at her elbow and climbed up on the high barstool. This was midday; the lunch crowd—such as it was—had flocked in, calling boisterously for beer, bread, and the lunch special. The noise was louder than usual, speculation rampant over a quetzal sighting out at Rand Kope's claim. Quetzals—it had been learned—had no conception of trip wires tied to strings of tin cans. A big quetzal had run afoul of Kope's primitive but effective early warning system.

Kope had forted up, his rifle at the ready, and reported that the would-be raider had a scarred hip and a mangled left front arm.

Everyone in PA assumed it had been Whitey making another try at an isolated Wild One. Kope—who'd arrived fourth ship—was a grizzled old timer, and his diggings consistently turned up very nice pigeon's-blood rubies.

"I was surprised when I heard that you're here," Shig noted. "I just got the news that the shuttle dropped you off and lifted again for Corporate Mine. You heard about Whitey being sighted out at Kope's?"

"Too bad Kope didn't get a shot. A lot of us would enjoy a big, thick steak cut off that bastard's carcass." Kalico wiped her lips. "You heard about my missing man? Ozawa lost his woman in the cave-in. She was three months pregnant. He's been off his feed ever since. Didn't make the return trip this morning. Thought I'd come up and see if I could run him down. Inga says she hasn't heard a word." Kalico made a circular gesture. "Not a whole lot of places he could go. Someone's going to see him."

"Maybe he just needs time." Shig lifted a single finger when Inga glanced his direction. "Grief does funny things."

"Yeah," Kalico lifted her glass of whiskey, sipped.

"You've started early," Shig noted, leaning forward, his elbows on the scarred bar.

"It's a whiskey kind of day," Kalico retorted. "One of those times when you have to finally face realities and make decisions. So, I'm here. Making the damn decisions. And now I've got a missing man."

Shig's placid expression belied his keen eyes as he glanced her way. "Ah. Missing man. Dek or Ozawa?"

"Excuse me?"

At her hostile tone, Shig raised a hand. "At ease, Supervisor. That you are here, and not at Two Falls Gap, tells me that you are close to having found sattva when it comes to our mutual friend Dek. With regard to your possible deserter, I suspect you are shifting between *tamas* and *rajas*. But, there, too, you will find a solution."

"When did you get to know me so well?"

"By watching you get to know yourself."

"Talina says that when you were a baby you got dropped on your head a lot. The longer I know you, the more I think she was right."

Shig just gave her that benign, beaming smile as Inga placed a half-glass of wine on the chabacho bar, and asked, "Got an SDR on you, or is this credit?"

"He's on my tab today," Kalico told the woman. It was a well-known fact that Shig was one of the poorest if most prominent men on the planet.

Inga gave her a wink, slapped her bar towel over her shoulder, and stalked off.

"Thank you," Shig told her, lifting his wine to study the rich red color through the backbar lights.

"You're welcome. Like I said, it's decision day, and I'm hoping to get on your good side. So, drink up. I want your inhibitions to be befuddled by alcohol so I can get a better deal."

Shig's bushy brow lifted. "Befuddled by a half a glass of wine?"

"Shig, the way I figure it, the reason you only drink a half glass is because a full one would put you under the table. Anything that would make you blotto drunk would upset your hard-won moksha, so you compromise on a half-glass . . . that you normally don't finish anyway. So, bottoms up. Drink that and, in your stupefied state, say yes to my proposal."

Shig tilted his head, uttered a Buddha-esque chuckle, and took a full swig of the wine. This he swished around in his mouth and swallowed. All of which, Kalico decided was about as radical as Shig got when it came to a drink.

"What do you need?" Shig asked.

"What will you charge me to rent me your A-7? I'm thinking in terms of scientific equipment for compensation. Working microscopes, centrifuges, chromatographs, spectrometers, that sort of thing."

Shig pursed his lips, still working his mouth with the taste of the wine. Then he said, "I can only think of one place where those kinds of equipment might be found. I would assume that you have been in contact with the Maritime Unit? Is there something more than the sick children that's gone wrong out there?"

"Children? As in plural?"

"All of them, from my understanding. And then there was the murder."

Kalico stiffened. "What murder? I've had Tallia O'Hanley monitoring the PA and hospital bandwidths. She said there's been nothing broadcast, and they sure as hell haven't answered any query I've sent their way. So, spill it."

"Ah." Shig nodded. "As I understand it, they're using their own hospital frequency for privacy. You might wish to inquire more of Raya, but apparently all of the children are showing signs of infection from some sort of single-cell-based organism. Some of the children are turning green, some exhibit neck swellings, and most troubling of all, one little boy appears to have somehow murdered and then dissected one of the adults. Their clinician was wondering if it could be TriNA taking possession of the child's cognitive abilities."

"Pus in a bucket, why haven't I heard of any of this?" But she knew. She'd been too damned busy with the disaster at Corporate Mine. That and her insane obsession with Dek and Talina. As black as her mood had been before, she really wanted to kick herself now.

"There is more. According to Raya, some sort of slime has crept into the submerged bay and apparently eaten two people." Shig played with his wine. "I don't know any more than that."

"Slime?" Kalico asked.

Shig hunched his shoulders. "You now know as much as I do. Raya said she thought they were all coming apart out there, that the communications have been getting more and more strained."

Kalico accessed her com, asking, "Hospital please. Raya Turnienko."

"Roger that." Two Spot's voice answered.

Kalico waited, sharing glances with the curious Shig for close to thirty seconds.

"Turnienko here, Supervisor. What can I do for you?"

"You've been in contact with the Maritime Unit. Shig tells me that they've had a murder? A couple of people eaten by slime? Kids infected with TriNA? That it sounded like things were falling apart?"

"Roger that. I assumed you were in the loop. They asked for a secure frequency to protect patient privacy."

"Negative on the loop. But that's about to change. And this time they don't have a say in it. Anything you can add to that?"

"Just that they haven't answered my inquiries for the last couple of hours. Either no one's in the com center, they've decided not to respond, or they've shut down com for some reason."

"Thanks, Raya. I'll take it from here." To Two Spot, she said, "Patch me through to the Maritime Unit."

"Roger that." A pause. *"Patching. You have a clear channel, Supervisor."*

"This is Board Supervisor Aguila to the Maritime Unit. I have an urgent communication for Scientific Director Michaela Hailwood. Repeat: I have an urgent communication for Scientific Director Michaela Hailwood. Please respond that you have received this communication."

Nothing.

Kalico repeated it. And then again.

Nothing.

"Two Spot? Are they hearing this?"

"Yes, ma'am. Signal's fine. If there's a problem, it's on their end."

"Son of a bloody bitch," Kalico growled.

"What do you want to do?" Shig asked mildly. "Anything you need from us, is yours."

Kalico frowned down at her half-eaten lunch. "I'd say your A-7, but the last thing I ever want to do is make that run from the ramp to the Pod door." She cocked her head. "It's too far to fly out there in an airtruck. Not without a recharge at the beach pad. No, I need something small, light, that has the range . . ."

"Dek's airplane?" Shig suggested.

"That would work. It's light enough and has vertical take-off and landing." She frowned. "The only problem is that Dek is out at Two Falls Gap with Talina. And there's no telling if he's sane enough to fly it safely."

"Manny Bateman can fly it."

Did she dare? Tempting as it was, Kalico slowly shook her head. "It's Dek's plane, Shig. Even if this was a full-fledged emergency, which we can't be sure it is, I still wouldn't be brazen enough to commandeer a Taglioni's private property."

"Let me see what I can do," Shig said, sliding off his barstool. "If you need our A-7, it's yours on demand. We'll work out the rent later." He flicked fingers at the third-full glass of red wine. "See, how incredibly clever you are? A single swallow, and all my inhibitions are gone. Plied as I am with alcohol, I'm putty in your fingers."

As he walked away, Kalico muttered at his retreating back, "If I'm so fucking clever, Shig, why do I have the feeling that I caused whatever disaster is unfolding out at the Maritime Unit?"

80

Talina unlatched the door to the Two Falls Gap dome. Stepped wearily inside. Dek limped along behind her. He carried his rifle balanced with the weight of the barrel over his shoulder, his hand on the gun's high comb. They were both filthy, sweat-streaked, with their clothes smudged by roots and dirt.

Talina shot Dek another of her "you're an idiot" looks. Then gave him a weary smile. "You ever do that again, and I'm breaking your legs."

"Blade monster almost did. You hadn't made that last shot, he'd have hit me square instead of quartering. Even if the blades hadn't got me, a man with a broken leg won't last ten minutes among the roots."

"Wish we had another bottle of bourbon."

"Makes two of us." Dek waited for Talina to rack her rifle at the door, then placed his Holland & Holland beside it. "I'm ready for a hot shower. How's the food situation?"

"Whatever you left for breakfast the other morning is long cold, spoiled, and fit for the compost pile. Have to cook up something new."

Dek glanced across the dim room. "The light's blinking on the radio."

"I'll check it. You go start that shower. Then I'll join you."

"Got it," he told her.

Talina watched him limp his way across the room and exhaled a weary breath. They'd made it. Had a couple of close calls—not to mention having to sleep on a basalt outcrop at the foot of the cliff—but they were back to the dome.

As night had settled around them—and who knew what sort of flying people-eating creatures might come under the cover of darkness—she had asked, "So, Dek. Here we are, sitting out on top of a pile of unforgiving bedrock with empty bellies and no guarantee that we can make the climb up that cleft again. Let alone that either one of us will survive the night. Are you really going to look me in the eye and tell me you'd rather be here than back at the dome with a full stomach, enjoying slow sex in a soft bed?"

His forehead had lined. "Is that a trick question?" He had pointed up at the narrow band of night sky visible beyond the sheer gorge walls. "That should be obvious. You can't see the stars from our bed inside the dome."

She'd had to laugh. But then, that was Dek. What made him charming. Just as—on that return trip—she'd had to forgive him for his insane blade-monster hunt. Didn't matter that the thing would have killed him. She'd been there, was able to fire six rounds into the creature's body as it charged. The monster had turned and staggered sideways across the roots to collapse into a thrashing heap of flippers, gushing blood, and slashing blades. As it died, the hide had flashed all the colors in the spectrum, the stalk-mounted eyes going dim.

It had taken all of Talina's skill to get around the frenzied root mat and drag the half-stunned Dek up and over an intervening clump of knotting and bunching roots.

Then had come their stumbling retreat across an excited forest floor to make for the safety of the basalt bedrock.

But Dek was fully himself. And more.

"They know now," he'd told her. "And yes, woman-I-love, it was worth the risk. There at the last, it was the quetzals who saved me. I'm not certain if it was Rocket or Demon or maybe both, but I wasn't the one who threw myself sideways at the last instant. We have a workable compromise."

And he'd given her a wink. "One as good as making a new pot from a shattered one. And thank you. While you paved the way, I had to figure out a novel strategy that let me put your pavement on a different road."

On hearing that, Talina had grinned, feeling, for the first time since Cap died that she wasn't entirely on her own.

Hearing the shower water come on, she stepped over and grabbed up the mic. Keyed it. "What have you got, Two Spot?"

"Tal? That you?"

"As Kylee would say, well, duh."

Silence. Then: *"Oh, right. That's that girl out at Briggs's place. Dek there? I need to talk to him."*

"He's here. He's in the shower. Anything I can help you with?"

"Maritime Unit's offline. Kalico was wondering if she could get Dek to fly her out in his airplane. Can't set a shuttle down on the Pod, and it's too far for the airtrucks. Dek's airplane has vertical takeoff and landing capabilities, and it has the range."

"Got it. I'll go ask." She checked her watch. "It's too late to get back today. Ask Kalico if this can wait until morning. We've had a tough couple of days. Let us get a meal and a night's sleep."

"Roger that. I'll tell Kalico. Have a nice meal. Off."

Talina pulled her tangled and filthy hair back, arched an eyebrow at the now-silent radio. For a half second she wondered if she was right to have volunteered Dek's help and airplane, only to smile at herself for being a fool. Of course he'd fly Kalico out. Like he'd said. That was being the man he wanted to be.

And, besides, after the blade monster and two days in the forest, what the hell could a little trouble at Maritime Unit amount to?

81

The entire Pod shook as the Underwater Bay flooded.

Michaela—with a killer headache—clutched the table with her good hand, as if it would keep her from disaster. The entire cafeteria jolted, chairs rattling, the sound of cookware and utensils clattering in the kitchen. Might have been a quake the way the Pod rocked. Her people at the table tensed, grabbing on to steady themselves.

Her first thought: The supporting pilings had given way just as Kel said they would. But the Pod didn't drop, it stabilized after the first hard shake. As it did, a puff of air blew in from the central hallway. Michaela's ears reacted to the pressure spike.

"What the hell was that?" Kel demanded, leaping to his feet.

Michaela's headache was forgotten as chairs emptied and people rushed for the hallway. Cradling her broken arm, she hurried after them. The reaction by the parents was instinctive; they went pounding up the stairs to the second level, calling the children's names as they went.

Not that Michaela blamed them.

Kel, however, rounded the landing, staring at the open hatch to the tube. Walked forward and froze. From his posture, every muscle had gone tense.

"In the name of God, no!" he cried. "What have you done?"

Michaela crowded up behind him, stared over his shoulder. Through the hatch she could see down the stairs. Not more than a meter down, the tube was plugged with a blue-green mass. More to the point, it was already sending tendrils up the risers and treads where Felix and Sheena stood, eerie, beaming smiles on their faces. A hatchet hung from Felix's right hand.

At Kel's cry, the kids turned. Through her smile, Sheena said, "It's all right, Daddy. Our friends are coming now."

Michaela gaped, trying to understand. "How did this happen?"

"Sheena?" Kel cried. "Do you have any idea what this . . . ?" Kel couldn't finish, mouth working in stunned silence.

The little girl, her skin a sickly green in the light, stared up at her father. "It's the Song. Don't you hear it? Now it's free."

Free? What the hell did that mean. Michaela's brain seemed to stagger, unable to synthesize what she was seeing. Slime? How did it get past the hatch? It just . . . it couldn't be here!

A scream from up the stairs caused her to wheel around. Stumble back, her heart hammering.

"Michaela!" Casey's cry was filled with panic. "Get up here! Anna's murdered!"

Turning away from the senseless sight of Felix with his hatchet and Sheena and the slime, Michaela reeled on her feet, raced for the stairs. She took them two at a time, so charged that she barely noticed.

Murdered? Anna? God, don't let this be true.

At the head of the stairs, she turned toward the knot of people at the clinic door, pushed past Mikoru and Kevina to stare in horror at Anna Gabarron's body. The woman lay sprawled between the cabinets as if she'd been tossed face-first onto the floor. A tray full of beakers had been pulled down as she fell, broken glass everywhere. The blood that had pooled from Anna's severed throat remained wet enough to reflect the cabinet drawers beside the woman's head. Another bloody wound—a slit—marred the small of the woman's back.

"Where's my boy?" Mikoru demanded. "Where's Toni? Who has taken my son?"

Michaela raised her gaze to the shredded isolation tent. Saw blood smears on the slashed plastic, glanced back down to the scalpel that lay in Anna's blood. Noticed the child's footprints under her feet as they headed out the doorway and into the hall.

"They killed Anna to steal Toni?" Kevina sounded on the verge of hysteria. "Who'd do this?"

"No one stole him!" Michaela snapped, fighting for control. "Look at the fucking tracks! Barefoot. A big child's and a small one's. Toni walked out of here with one of the other children."

"He was *comatose!*" Mikoru had her fists knotted. "How could he?"

"You're saying one of the children killed Anna?" Kevina's eyes were slitted. "Don't you *dare* blame this on Felix!"

"He's not in his room," Casey declared hotly as she came pounding down the hall. "Someone let him out."

"Leave my son out of this." Kevina turned on the woman, started forward, hands out like claws, as if to rip Casey's eyes out.

"Hey! Stop it!" Michaela thrust herself between them. "Felix and Sheena are downstairs. The Underwater Bay is flooded, the pressure hatch was opened. The slime is pooling in the tube. Felix has a hatchet. And I don't fucking know how they got there! Think, damn it, this is all crazy!"

Yosh and Odinga came at a trot from where the rest of the children had been left, both looking worried.

"Felicity and Sheena are missing," Yosh announced. "Tomaya says the Song told them to 'set their friends free.' Whatever that means. And, it's like, well, the other kids have been drugged. They're listless, half-comatose, those swellings on their throats are worse, and I'd swear they're turning green. Maybe Anna gave them something for their swollen . . ."

"Anna's dead!" Mikoru shrilled. "Someone stole our son, damn you. We have to find him."

"Who stole Toni?" Yosh demanded, his face working. "What do you mean, Anna's—"

"Whoever stole Toni *murdered* her, you simple fool!"

Michaela raised her good hand, calling, "Hey, ease down. We'll find Toni. He walked out of here. Look, Mikoru. Look at the goddamned footprints. I tell you, those are Toni's. He was in here, and he walked out."

Michaela pushed past the trembling woman, pointing. "Then he walked down the hall with someone else. A girl, I'm betting. They were both barefoot."

Michaela led the way, pointing out track after track, as they got fainter. All but the girl's. Her right foot left a splotch of blood with each step. Right to the com center where . . .

In the doorway, Michaela stopped short, took in the damage, and sagged. "This can't be true."

Yosh shoved in beside her, broke out in a string of cursing the likes of which Michaela had never heard him utter.

As word of the damage to the com system spread, Odinga stuck his head in, face going ashen at sight of the fractured electronics. "It had to be Sheena and Felicity. Tomaya and Breez insist they left to 'free their friends.' They had to have let Felix out. Then Felix killed Anna and—"

"My son never hurt anyone!" Kevina shrieked the words. "He was locked up, you fucking lunatic."

"Sheena and Felix are downstairs in the tube," Michaela insisted. "Felix has a hatchet. Why aren't you listening to me?"

"In the tube?" Yosh asked, something stunned and broken behind his eyes. "What are they doing there?"

"Looking at the slime." Michaela grabbed him by his coat to get his attention. "Listen to me, damn it. Someone smashed the com to disable the safeties and opened the UB hatch."

"But where's my son?" Mikoru had a crazed look in her eyes.

"And where's Felicity?" Odinga couldn't tear his eyes from the smashed com. "We haven't even told her that her father's dead yet."

A wail started in Michaela's throat, only to be drowned by a flutter in her chest that turned into a sob.

"What are we going to do?" Iso asked as she came wandering down the hall. "Where's my daughter?" She fixed on Michaela's stricken face. "You're the pus-fucking Director. Do something!"

Michaela tried to answer, tried to think, but her chest felt like it was being squeezed. Try as she might, she couldn't catch her breath. All she could do was gasp for air that didn't come.

82

The Pod was no longer a sanctuary. The once-familiar halls, rooms, and ceiling had become a version of an impossible hell. Her people—the team she'd kept safe for all those years aboard *Ashanti*—were screaming at each other as if they'd gone insane. And maybe, with the slime cells in their brains, they had. And through the madness scampered the barefoot children, fleeing, giggling in joy as they skipped away from their parents. Chasing down the stairs after a naked and green-skinned Breez, Michaela had been horrified to see the little girl dart through the tube hatch. When Michaela pulled up at the top of the stairs, it was to see Breez dive headfirst into the slime and vanish without so much as a ripple.

At the point of despair, Michaela had fled to the safety of her personal quarters. Thankful to have the locked door between herself and whatever mayhem was breaking loose beyond, she lay in a fetal position on her bed, curled protectively around her aching left arm. Her bedside light shone on the white duraplast walls.

Duraplast. Not even that would save her.

The slime could denature it, dissolve it, and in the end it would seep through holes, pool around her bed, and inexorably ooze up to engulf her the way it had Tobi and Bryan. She could picture how the viscous blue-green mass would creep across the floor, deeper and deeper as it rose up the walls in tendrils. When it finally topped her bed, fingers of it would flow across the sheets to her skin. Cold, thick, like runny jelly it would trickle around her, soaking through her clothes, the chill of it slipping across her skin, sucking away her warmth.

Heavy, it would roll over her thighs, permeate the folds of her vulva and spill over her pubis onto her abdomen. At the same time the slippery mass would engulf her arms, ease along her biceps and into her armpits, chilling, and inevitable. As it rose around her head, she'd feel the cold running into her ears, around her chin and across her lips. In those final moments, as the slime pressed down around her, it would creep over her eyes and into her nostrils.

Sucking for breath, Michaela would draw it into her mouth, into her throat. Choking and coughing, panic would make her insane as she sucked more and more into her lungs.

I pray I am dead before it begins to eat me.

What did that feel like?

Did it hurt to be digested? Maybe burn like acid? Or was it nothing more than a gradual dissolution of proteins? Something numbing as the body disappeared molecule by molecule?

In the hallway beyond her door, someone shouted in anger, ranting.

A child's voice sang in a mocking tone, "*Now the Pod is falling down, falling down . . .*"

Michaela rolled over in her bed, used her good arm to jam her pillow down around her ears. Anything to shut out the sounds of her abject failure. She couldn't think, couldn't conceive. In the chaos, she'd staggered away, leaving Yosh and Mikoru face-to-face, each shouting and clawing at the other.

Kevina had been standing protectively in front of Felix, the boy's eyes having turned into weird black orbs, the swelling on the side of his neck pulsing with each breath.

Michaela had no idea where Casey Stoner was. The last she'd seen, the woman had infant Saleen in her arms, was hurrying down the hall. Jym Odinga had been following, gesturing frantically, demanding to know where Tomaya had vanished to.

Kel and Vik had locked themselves in the lab and barricaded the door. Supposedly, while Vik worked desperately to find some sort of poison or repellent that would force the slime back and let them take control of the Pod again.

Iso Suzuki was last seen locking herself, her three-month-old son Vetch, and some of the other children in her personal quarters. Tears had been streaking down the woman's face, and she'd been crying, "Why is my baby green? Where's my daughter? Where's Felicity?"

Michaela had no clue what had happened to Varina Tam's son, Kayle. For all she knew the little boy lay abandoned up in the infirmary room, forgotten in the small bed they'd made for him.

Up in the clinic—to Michaela's complete dismay—Anna Gabarron's body still lay sprawled in its own blood. No one had thought to try and do anything with it.

Madness. It's all gone insane.

She blinked at the hot tears that slipped past her eyelids.

Screams sounded from down the hallway, the terror barely muffled by the walls and door. Sounded like someone was being hacked to death. That kind of frantic screaming. Filled with disbelief and fear.

We were all one. Like some incredible family. This can't be us. Not the same people who survived Ashanti. *Not the people who endured all those years of deprivation. The ones who buoyed each other in the desperate moments. The ones who clung to hope of a better world.*

Outside her door, she heard the pounding of feet. Bare, small feet. And from the other side of the duraplast door, she heard Felix's voice say, "I think she's in here."

"Open it." That was Sheena.

Michaela began to quake as she heard the handle rattle. Stared from under the corner of her pillow as the latch trembled against its lock.

"Can't get in," Felix said.

Michaela closed her eyes, sucking deep breaths. Her entire body was fear-electric, her muscles trembling.

Felix? He was only eight years old. How could that eight-year-old boy they'd all fawned over become this . . . this . . . ? The words weren't there. The child whose birth they had celebrated as their own had murdered Bill Martin. That . . . *child.* Taken over, become some alien horror that had used Felix's little body to cut a man down and flay his body open.

Probably drove that ax into Anna's back. Brought her down, and then cut her throat.

That skinny bit of a boy and his . . .

"Use the ax," Sheena cried with childish glee.

Michaela trembled as the first impact shivered the door. Each whack of the hatchet's blade might have sent a spear through her heart and soul. Her body tensed, quivered as the ax smacked again and again into the duraplast.

She cried out, whimpered in desperation as the outside latch broke and clattered away across the floor.

"Dear God! Dear God!" Then she stuffed the corner of the pillow into her mouth. Paralyzed, heart bursting in her chest, she waited.

Scratching. Then something pried at her door.

"Won't open," she heard Felix complain. "Locked."

"Maybe she's not in there." Sheena sounded disappointed. Then, "Look! There's Dik! He's trying to get to the cafeteria!"

The pounding of bare feet faded as they charged down the hall. Michaela sobbed in relief.

They will be back. You know they will. And they won't stop next time.

So, what to do? In here she'd be trapped like a rat in a jar.

If only I had a weapon!

Wait. That was it. The only chance she—or any of them—had. But could she do it? Did she have the courage to open that door and make one last desperate attempt at survival?

Carefully, every muscle trembling, sobs in her throat, Michaela climbed out of bed, tiptoed to the door, and listened. The hallway was silent for once.

Shivering in fear, her broken arm cradled tight, she reached for the latch, felt it cold on her fingers, and turned it.

83

Yosh shouldn't have fought. It was his fault. That's all there was to it. Grownups had to understand. But they didn't. Yosh had tried to take the ax away, and that was unacceptable. Felix stood in the cafeteria, Sheena behind him. Each drop of blood falling from the ax blade spattered in a starburst on the sialon floor. That same bright red as the blood pooling around Yosh's sprawled body.

Sheena appeared after checking the kitchen and stopped beside Dik's bleeding body. She carefully scanned the cafeteria for any other grownups. Her eyes, like his, had been aching, changing. Now they reminded Felix of black lenses, like a camera's. Deep and bottomless. He wanted her to come hold his hand. Listen to the Song that now filled the Pod. Then they'd both get that bursting tingle of delight that made them gasp and stiffen. Instead of being Felix and Sheena, they came together, like fading into each other. He could feel her, like he was inside her, and she was inside him. Hands clasped like that, it took a couple of minutes, but he knew what she was thinking. And she said it was the same for her.

"Yosh shouldn't have tried to take the ax," he told Sheena as she stepped across Dik's bloody corpse and came trotting between the tables. She barely gave Yosh a glance and took Felix's hand. That warm, wet, and slick feeling started as soon as they locked fingers.

"Grownups don't understand. I should feel sad for Yosh."

"It's his fault. Just like it was Dik's. You heard the Voice. Yosh was going to stop us." Felix stared down at the man's body, at the gaping bloody wounds in his forearms and hands where he'd tried to ward off the ax blows. In the end, Yosh had been crying, tears running down his face as he'd held up bleeding hands and demanded, "Felix? Why are you doing this?" And, "It's me! Yosh! Don't you remember?"

Felix did. He remembered perfectly. Yosh had always been there.

Like all those times the man had held him on his lap back in Crew
Deck. And the stories Yosh told. The jokes, the clever puns. Too
bad that Yosh couldn't have been a child, too. There was room to
grow as a child. They still had time. Not like Toni and the infants
who could grow a lot, but Felix and the older girls would still be
worthwhile. Grownups just didn't have any future in the Pod.

Yosh had been like another father after Kim. All the men had
been like other fathers.

Back in that world.

Before coming here. Before the Voice and the Song had taken
over Felix's mind. And Sheena's. And all of the other children.

Down inside, some part of him was sad, even frightened, at the
sight of Yosh's slashed corpse. Felix could feel it, but that old part of
him was so remote. Sort of like knowing he had a right foot. But
he didn't constantly have to think about his right foot. He could
choose to ignore his foot any time he wanted. So, if he wanted, he
could let himself hurt, be scared. But why would he want to do
that?

"You wouldn't," Sheena told him. "Grownups don't matter anymore. They don't have a purpose. Given what's coming, killing
them is a kindness."

"Guess so."

He gave the gaping cuts in Yosh's still-bleeding body one last
look. Yosh had always been nice, had always had that laugh, that
special twinkle in the eyes. Felix would miss that. "We should get
back to the Director. Figure out a way to get that door open."

"Can't leave her loose." Sheena agreed, her large and darkening
eyes fixed on Yosh. "He told good stories."

"He did."

Felix turned, hefting the ax. When he tensed his arm, he was still
amazed at the knotting muscle that bulged there. Some distant part
of him wondered about the green splotches on his skin. Weird. The
tops of his arms were darker green than the bottoms, which had
been turning from flesh-colored to a solid white.

And he was so fast! Quick. Like the ax was a living thing. Big as

Yosh was, he'd been slow. Even when the man used a broomstick, Felix had been able to duck it, dodge, and streak his way inside to slash at Yosh's leg. Right above the kneecap. That's where the tendons were. Cut them, and a grownup fell in a pile. Couldn't get up again.

"If only they didn't plead so," Felix said as he headed for the hall. As strong as he was, he should be able to chop Michaela's door open.

He kept his grip on Sheena's hand, rubbing his fingers around on her hers, feeling the slick warmth in her palms. She understood that getting Michaela next was important. And being together like this kept that tingle pulsing through their bodies.

They made it past Mikoru's corpse where the algae now flowed out of the tube hatch from the Underwater Bay. It was Singing loudly now, humming, thrumming, and melodic. Strands of slowly moving blue-green tentacles were winding around Mikoru, slipping into rents in her clothing to run along her skin. One particularly thick one had wound its way across her chest and worked its way into Mikoru's mouth. Funny how it could push her jaw way back and how it enlarged the woman's throat as it grew down into her chest.

Felix stopped long enough to let Sheena squat and place her hand atop the thick green tentacle. For a second Sheena's slender fingers rested on the surface and then sank in. Her eyes went vacant, her slack mouth opening enough that Felix could see her tongue. Then Sheena blinked, seemed to come back to herself.

"What did it say?" Felix asked.

"Felicity is coming." Sheena told him as she pulled her hand from the algae.

A second later, through the warmth in Sheena's hand, Felix could hear the Song, knew it was true.

What a wonderful thing, to just know stuff by touching someone. It was a lot better way to be smart than just telling each other things. Being part of the Voice meant that Felix would never be alone again. Glancing at Sheena, he shared her feelings of comfort. She studied him thoughtfully, stepped close, and hugged him. That electric tingle shot through him, through her. In unison, they gasped. *You and me will be together like this forever.*

His hand pulsed warmly against hers.

Her gaze remained locked with his, as she said, "We never have to be apart again. Ever. It's just us. We're the Song."

Felicity appeared from the open hatch where the thick ropes of algae were pumping like pressurized hoses and expanding down the hallway toward the personal quarters. Water beaded on her face and trickled down her naked body. Felicity looked so different, like, totally green. The dark hair hung down, slicked back and wet; her eyes might have been large black orbs in her now much-too-narrow face. Felicity's mouth looked wider, too. Water streamed out of the gill slits above her collarbones. She stepped forward on longer legs, and Felix realized she was now a whole head taller than him.

She reached out, placed her right hand against his cheek; with her left, she took Sheena's other hand. The warmth came through her fingers, damp, reassuring. Like Sheena, he felt himself tense, his vision going dim. Then he, Sheena, and Felicity gasped and cried out in unison as their bodies merged.

Thoughts formed in Felix's head. *We don't have much time. The supports for the Pod will be gone. Maybe another day. How many of the grownups are left?*

"Michaela, Kel, Vik, Iso, Jym, and Mother." Did Felix speak or just think that?

Kel's gone. Tried to close the hatch on us. We're absorbing him now. Jym tried to take Tomaya and drive the launch through us. He was faced the other way when she hit him with a wrench. She's with Toni in the Underwater Bay. That leaves the rest. Where?

"Michaela and Iso are locked in personal quarters. We'll have to rescue Saleen after we kill Iso."

Mikoru had Saleen, so he's safe. But Iso still has Vetch and Kayle. She's our next priority. Once we've recovered the youngest, we can hunt the others.

"Come on, then, let's break Iso's door down. We can use your strength."

He turned, severing the reassuring contact of Felicity's touch on his cheek. His vision began to sharpen, his thoughts shared with

Sheena's as she held his hand and they started down the hall. To Felix's surprise, Michaela's battered door was open, the room empty.

No matter. They'd find her. The Pod was only so big.

Nor did Iso's door prove much of an obstacle. With Felicity's added strength and the ax, they pried it open in less than five minutes, advancing into the room as Iso screamed.

84

Kalico leaned against the gate that opened to the aircar field on Port Authority's west side. Capella's bright light burned down, illuminating the lines of aircars—some functional, others just abandoned hulks that had been scavenged for parts. The latter had been moved out to the perimeter, next to where Terry Mishka's field of beans, corn, okra, squash, and garlic stretched out to the verdant bush. There, silvered by mirage, the scrub aquajade and chabacho wavered and seemed to flow.

Been too long since it's rained, Kalico noted as she squinted up at the brassy sky.

Donovan's axis wasn't as inclined as Earth's. Seasons weren't as pronounced here.

In Kalico's ear bud, Talina's voice informed, *"We're coming in from the south. Be on the ground in five minutes."*

"Roger that," Two Spot replied.

Kalico shaded her eyes with a flat palm, stared south, and picked up the dot as Talina's aircar appeared over the distant bush.

A nervous tension began to wind itself through her gut. Anxious for them to land, unsettled at the changes in their relationship. She'd caught it, the change of inflection, as Talina had been talking to Two Spot on the way in. Something intimate in the way she said, "we." And lying just below the surface the words hid a familiarity, the kind shared by two people who had passed beyond the boundaries of "just friends."

But then, that's not exactly a surprise, is it, Kalico?

She filled her lungs, flexed the muscles in her arms and shoulders, letting Capella bake her black coveralls. The sweat it raised served her like the flagellation of a *penetente.*

"You've been down this road. Made your decision with your

head, so don't let your heart get in the way just because you're a jealous slit."

Nope. No matter what, she'd be the same tough and pragmatic Kalico Aguila she'd always been. Problem was, she'd been letting herself stray from that hard-hearted and cunning woman. It was well past time to bring her back.

She walked out as Talina circled, lowered her battered aircar, and the fans blew dust out from her longtime parking spot next to the fence. In the cabin, Dek was seated in the passenger seat, his tousled, sandy hair awry, eyes meeting Kalico's as the aircar spooled down.

Dek was the first out, vaulting the rail, reaching for his rifle and war bag. The former dangling from one hand, the latter slung over his shoulder, he was walking with a leonine grace in his strides that she'd never seen before.

She almost did a double take. Was this really . . . Yes. That dimple, the pink scar from where he'd blown up the Unreconciled's armed drone. The general shape of the face. But something about his eyes, still green-tinged and yellow, but the pupils where alien. Quetzal. Like Talina's and Kylee's.

"So," she mused, "It's true."

"It's true," Dek told her, the old insolent Taglioni grin bending his lips. "Sorry, old friend, but I'm Donovan's now. As much as I'd like to throw what I've become in Father's face, I'll never leave here alive."

"How's the madness?" she couldn't help but ask, a bitterness rising within.

"Under control," he told her.

Talina climbed out and plugged the aircar into its charger. Then she grabbed her own bag from the rear deck before tossing it over a shoulder, slung her rifle on the other, and headed Kalico's way. That predator's assurance filled her as she stopped short, studying Kalico with knowing eyes. "Hear we've got a problem out at the Maritime Unit. What do you need?"

"They've been out of communication. Two Spot keeps trying, but there's only silence." She turned her attention to Dek, remaining as professional as if she were addressing the Board. "If I might hire you to fly me out there—"

"Let's go. No charge."

"No charge?"

Dek gave her a look through his now-inhuman eyes. "It's what friends do, Kalico. Time's short. Tal and I need to drop off our bags, then let's get in the air. I suspect we won't get there until late afternoon as it is. If it's trouble, best to tackle it while there's still light."

"Have to charge the plane for the flight back once we're out there," Talina reminded.

Kalico told her, "Tal, I hate dragging Dek into this as it is, you don't have to—"

"Who you got who can handle trouble better than me?" Talina gave her a catlike grin. "Especially if it comes to cracking a couple of heads?"

Kalico, still uneasy with that sense that nothing would be the same between them, nodded. "Right. Let's get in the air. If it's really bad, I've got Abu Sassi on call. Makarov can have him and a couple of armored marines out there in an hour. They can fast rope down from the A-7, deal with anything we can't."

"How bad can it be?" Dek wondered. "If it's just people, like Tal says, we knock a couple of heads. If it's beasties, we've got rifles. Problem solved."

85

Heart in her throat, Michaela pounded up the stairs, burst through the topside door into the landing pad foyer, and threw herself at the weatherproof locker. Her trembling fingers botched the code the first two times, and finally got the sequence right. She slammed the door open to see only three of the rifles, the fourth already missing.

What the hell?

Didn't matter. Figure it out later.

Awkward because of her broken arm, she ripped the heavy rifle from the rack. Bracing the muzzle in the corner, and the stock on her hip, Michaela pulled the bolt back like Supervisor Aguila had shown her. She watched as the bolt shoved a long cartridge into the chamber. Should be two more in the magazine. Setting the heavy weapon to the side, Michaela grasped the box of cartridges where they sat on the shelf. Yes. The right size for the gun. She was sure. She shoved the box into one of the side pockets on her overalls and lifted the rifle, trying figure out how to raise it. Shit! Hurt like a bastard, but she slipped her broken arm from the sling, whimpered as she supported the rifle with it.

The ulna's cracked, not broken in two. The radius is still in one piece. Shooting won't snap your forearm.

But it was going to hurt like nothing she'd ever known.

On the verge of throwing up, frightened as she'd never been, she stepped over to the weather door. Looked out the window at the landing pad. Seeing no one, Michaela threw the door open.

The wind hit her as she turned and latched the door. Damn it, did she dare lock it?

"Michaela?"

At the cry, she turned, saw Casey where she rose from behind one of the supply crates. The woman looked half-panicked. The missing rifle was held awkwardly before her.

"Who else is left?" Michaela demanded, staring around with desperate eyes, expecting attack from every quarter.

"Kevina is in the seatruck. I was watching from up here as Jym tried to put out in the launch. I don't believe it! Tomaya was with him. When he turned to the wheel, she . . . my little girl used a wrench. Hit him . . . Hard. Right in the back of the head. That's my *daughter*! Jym's daughter! How could . . . ? How . . . ?"

"They're *not* our children. You get that? Our kids are *gone*! Get that through your thick head, Casey!"

"How did this happen?" Casey sobbed, her body shaking as the wind buffeted her ash-blond hair. "That clap-trapping slime . . ." She shivered. "It took the launch, Michaela. Slipped up around the sides, and just pulled the whole fucking boat down. My little girl was smiling, reaching down into that slime, and it just . . . pulled her . . . down."

"Casey. Easy. Get yourself together. We've got to think. Where are the rest?"

"Mikoru has Saleen. She's—"

"Mikoru's *dead,* and Saleen wasn't with her body."

"Michaela, I've got to go find her!" Casey began to tremble. "That's my baby. I've got to go find my . . ."

Michaela reached out, used the rifle butt to thump the woman hard on the shoulder. "Listen to me. Pay attention. Saleen wasn't with Mikoru's body. That means they have her. She's *one of them now!*"

Casey, staggered on her feet, gray eyes clearing. "Why? What do they want with her?"

"I don't know. Maybe Vik does. She still locked in the lab?"

"Last I heard."

"Come on. Let's go get her. If nothing else, the lab's the final stronghold."

"What if Saleen's down in the personal quarters, you know, left in a crib while Mikoru went—"

"Casey, the first level is *gone*! I just came from there. Barely made it. There's slime all over the floor, tendrils of it everywhere. I had to leap across thick ropes of the stuff. It was *eating* Mikoru. By now, it's covering the hall floor, slipping down toward Iso's room. We've only got the second level."

Michaela stared back at the weather door. "Seems to me the only chance we've got is to get Vik, rope our way down to the seatruck where Kevina's holed up, and fly to the beach."

Casey swallowed hard, eyes pained. "It's got my baby." She choked back a sob. "What does it want from us? Why is it doing this?"

Michaela indicated Casey's rifle. "That thing loaded?"

"I think so." Tears broke loose at the corners of her eyes.

"Let's go then. And Casey, you see any of the kids, if they start toward you, you're going to have to shoot them."

"I can't shoot one of the children."

"Then we're already dead."

86

As they flew east from PA across the rumpled forest, Talina unstrapped and walked back from the cockpit to seat herself across from Kalico in the cabin. Up front, Dek sat composed at the controls, watching the course and trim as the white aircraft jetted its way toward the Gulf.

Dropping into the seat, Talina studied Kalico, who was giving her that old ice-blue stare. Looked just like the old Kalico. The one who'd first landed on Donovan. The hard and uncompromising Corporate slit. Kalico's expression had all the give of granite; the faint white lines of scars crisscrossing her face added to the effect. The wealth of the woman's black hair was pulled back, pinned at the nape of her neck. Talina's delicate sense of smell could pick up the familiar scents of Kalico's dried sweat, the curious nervousness. The woman had perfect control of her expression.

"Let's talk." Talina kept her voice low enough Dek couldn't hear over the airplane's cabin noise. "Dek and I, that's my doing. Out at his claim, I wasn't thinking about quetzal molecules. He got more than resuscitation. On top of Flute's genetics, I dumped a whole lot more quetzal into his system. I had to keep him from hurting himself or anyone else. Things . . . happened. I let them."

"Dek's all right with this?"

"Deep down in that complicated Taglioni soul of his? I don't know. You'll have to ask him. And, yeah, I mean it. Ask him."

"That's very . . ." Kalico bit it off.

"The TriNA took him all apart, pulled a lot of bad shit out of his memory, and Dek had to put it all back. Then he had to deal with the demons in his head, both human and quetzal."

"Are we really having this talk?"

Talina pulled up a leg, rubbing her calf. "Consider me the girlfriend you and I never had as kids. Kalico, I'm too old, too filled with alien genetic material, to get tripped up in a human emotional minefield with a woman like you."

"Like me?" Kalico cocked a scarred brow. "And that means?"

Talina gave her knowing grin. "Considering that once upon a time we were committed to killing each other, when--in all that followed--did you ever become a good and valued friend? If you're having misgivings about what to do with Dek, you and he had better spend some time together and work it out."

Kalico's clever gaze didn't waver. "You really mean that, don't you?"

"Yeah. You're important to me. I don't have that many people to drink with as it is. That friend thing, you know? For another, Dek's turned into a Wild One. Even with quetzal sense, we had too many close calls out at Two Falls Gap. Who knows how long it will be before Donovan kills him? Or any of us, for that matter? And, finally, who the fuck knows what we're going to find when we get out to the Maritime Unit?"

Kalico offered her scarred hand. "Deal." She paused. "But if you tell anyone that you're the girlfriend I never had? I'll have Abu Sassi and Dina Michegan break both of your legs."

87

Rifle hanging from her good right arm, Michaela led the way down the stairs. Behind her, Casey wept, seemed to have trouble with the steps. That's who she had to rely on? Casey? After watching her oldest daughter murder Jym? Watch Tomaya pulled down into the slime? Only to learn that her infant was missing after Mikoru's murder?

Does she even know how to fire that rifle?

No time to ask now; she was at the door to the second level. Carefully, she peered through the window. What she could see of the hall was empty.

"Let's do this," she said more for herself than Casey, and flung the door open.

Michaela burst out into the hallway, swung the rifle this way and that, looking for any danger. The bare floor, the lights gleaming, doors orderly and closed . . . well, all except for the clinic.

Michaela winced. Gabarron still lay there, unattended, well past rigor by now, and probably starting to swell.

Pus and blood, we've got to get the hell out of here.

She started for the lab door, scared enough that she didn't give a damn if Casey followed or not. All that remained was getting Vik out. That, and managing to find a way to the dock that didn't involve the first level with its slime-covered floors and sprawled corpses. That's where the children seemed to be.

Didn't matter what she'd told Casey. Even if the kids were turning green, their necks swelling, and their eyes looking weird, she still wasn't sure she could shoot one.

She hurried to the lab door, used her fragile left hand to input the code, and swung the door open, hissing out, "Vik? You here? Vik! Where are you?"

"Here," the woman called, turning from where she sat at one of the microscopes. The microbiologist wore a lab coat, her hair pulled back. A grim expression left her lips tight, her forehead deeply lined. "What's the rifle for?"

"You been keeping score? The kids are murdering adults wherever they find them, and the slime's all over the first-level floor where it's eating Mikoru."

"Where's Kel?" she demanded, rising from the chair. "Where's Sheena?"

"Haven't seen Kel. Sheena's with Felix. As least she was when they were trying to chop my door open. Vik, listen to me. Pay fucking attention. We've got to evacuate. Now. Grab your notes and come. Last chance, or you can die with the rest."

"She means it." Casey held her rifle awkwardly where she stood in the doorway, tears on her cheeks. The woman kept sniffing, glancing back and forth from Vik to the hall. "I watched Tomaya murder Jym. And then the slime took her."

"Easy," Michaela said soothingly, seeing Casey start to tremble. To Vik, she added, "Get your stuff. Last call."

"My research! I can't just walk away from—"

"Finish it at PA! Now, grab what you need, and let's get the hell out of here. That's an order."

Vik leaped off her chair, grabbed up a couple of tablets, her pad, and voice recorder, a series of data cards, and finally a collection of samples that she tossed into a duraplast crate before she snapped the lid shut. As she worked, she said, "You didn't tell me where Kel is."

"I don't know. If he's not up here with you, it's not good, Vik."

"We don't know why our beautiful children are doing this," Casey whimpered from the doorway.

"It's because their brains are infected," Vik snapped. "Listen, I don't have all the answers, not even close. What I'm seeing? I don't know how this stuff thinks, let alone what it thinks it's doing, or why, but it is remaking these children. It's like nothing I've ever heard of, conceived of. That biopsy I got from the growth in the side of Toni's throat? It's gill tissue. The green tint to the skin? It allows the kids to photosynthesize."

"Why are they killing us?" Casey cried. "What's it doing to their brains?"

"I don't know!" Vik bellowed, desperation in her voice. "Making them crazy. Screwing with their neocortex, the limbic system. Maybe even rewiring their neural structure. It's sure as sin making them stronger. Adding muscle and agility. Hell, the stuff is remaking the rest of their bodies, why not their brains, too? And not only that, it's communicating with them. Mostly on a frequency we can't hear. My microphones are picking up a weird harmony that's all over the scales."

"The Song," Michaela whispered. "Felix's Voice."

Vik had her bags ready, pointing. "I need help with that one."

"Casey!" Michaela barked. "Grab a handle. I'll get the other."

It's just the ulna. The weight of the gun won't break it.

Suspending the rifle in her left hand brought tears to Michaela's eyes. Shit, that hurt. Nevertheless, she got a grip with her right on one of the crate's handles. With Casey's help, they lifted it. Followed Vik to the door, and out into the mercifully empty hallway.

Come on, God. Just let us get this to the landing pad.

As they passed opposite to the stairway down to the first level, Michaela heard the old "London Bridge" nursery rhyme from below:

> *"Now the Pod is falling down, falling down, falling down.*
> *"Now the Pod is broken down, my fair lady.*
> *"Namby Pamby is no clown, is no clown, is no clown.*
> *"All the algae's coming 'round,*
> *"Zambo! Zambo!"*

88

The rope ladder that would let them climb down to the seatruck dock had been rolled up and stuffed into a storage locker at the edge of the landing pad. It was meant for maintenance on the curving side of the Pod, to check window seals, fill cracks, that sort of thing.

Michaela set the rifle to the side and winced at the pain in her left arm as she fastened the hooks into the recesses on the landing pad. A gust of wind from the east almost toppled her off the side. She glanced at Casey, who stood wide-legged, hair wind-tossed, coveralls flapping. Windblown as she was, the rifle held across her chest made her look like a war hero on a recruitment poster.

Yeah? Not hardly.

Michaela grunted to herself, surprised she could still find the humor, and kicked the ladder loose, let it unspool down to disappear around the Pod's curved side above the dock.

Vik straightened from the crate where she'd been checking the contents. She looked worried, frail, as the breeze teased her. The third rifle was propped beside her. Something in the woman's eyes had turned wild, frantic.

Hell, they all looked that way.

"All right," Michaela told them. "Here's the plan: Casey and I climb down. We get to Kevina in the seatruck. Once inside, we spool up, lift off, and climb up to the landing pad. We set down just long enough for Kevina and me to leap out and load the crate. While we do, Vik, you climb aboard. Soon as you're on, we're off for the beach."

"You're sure about this?" Vik asked. "What if there are others? What if Kel's down there, somewhere? Maybe locked in a room? We can't just leave him behind."

Michaela stepped over, laid a hand on Vik's shoulder, and pinned the woman's frightened gaze with her own. "Listen to me. If Kel's not on the second level, he's dead. The kids have taken the first level and there's slime all over it. We're out of time. As it is, it'll be dark by the time we get to the beach. You can stay or go. Choose."

Vik nodded, wind flipping her hair. "Go."

Michaela gave the woman a reassuring slap on the shoulder, turned and strode to the rope ladder. She started to climb down, the ungainly rifle cradled in her aching left arm. Wished desperately that the thing had come with a sling. It made her progress slow, clumsy. Then she figured out a sort of rhythm. Wished the fucking ladder wasn't so unsteady. Figured it would be a miracle if she didn't flip the thing upside down and fall to her death.

But she made it, stepping down onto the dock, and turned. To her horror, thick-braided ropes of slime crisscrossed the dock in tangles of pulsing blue-green. They wound around the seatruck closest to the level one hatch, were fingering their way up the side of the portal.

"Oh, God, no." Michaela made a face, stepped warily out from the wall, rifle at the ready. "Kevina!" she bellowed. "Where are you?"

"Here!" The door to the second seatruck flung open. "I can't get back inside! The slime's got the door covered."

"Don't worry. Casey's coming down behind me. She'll fly us up to the . . ."

An anguished scream from above caused Michaela to turn. She heard the hollow rasp of metal on sialon as Casey's rifle appeared, sliding around the Pod's curve, gaining speed to fly free and smack, butt-first on the dock's decking. With a crack, the stock splintered, the barrel and action taking a half cartwheel before clattering to the hard deck between two tendrils of slime.

"Sorry," Casey cried from above. "It just slipped."

"Well, get down here! Fly us the hell out of here."

If there was any upside, it was that, unencumbered, Casey descended one hell of a lot faster. The woman made the bottom and turned, horrified as she gaped at the interlaced tangle of green engulfing the nearest seatruck's fans, and where it piled against the hatch.

"Come on!" Michaela called. "Jump the slime. Let's go."

They needed Casey. Michaela used the rifle for balance, skipping and jumping to stay as clear as she could of the thin veins of blue-green that traced out over the deck.

Behind her, she heard Casey, shoes thumping on the deck as she followed.

Michaela made the door, swung up, and almost tumbled into the seatruck's cabin. Kevina reached down, pulled her all the way in.

The look Kevina gave her was almost worshipful with relief. She pulled a long strand of blond hair out of the way as she said, "I knew someone would come. God, the waiting. I came out to see if anyone was here, figured we'd be evacuating. I was with Kel when he tried to close the Underwater Bay hatch. Someone had opened it. Let the slime out. The stuff just wound around his legs." She pinched her eyes shut. "It pulled him down into the tube. Like it was some creature, not just mindless algae."

"I don't know if hearing that makes it better or worse for Vik? At least she won't think she's leaving him behind."

Casey, whimpering again, had made it to the door. Swung up and pulled herself into the cabin. "Let's get the hell out of here." She flung herself into the driver's seat, quickly adjusted the chair to her height and reach. Then her capable fingers began flipping the switches, hit the starter, and powered up the fans.

Michaela heard it. That straining sound. Even as Casey said, "What the hell? Port side's not spinning up."

Michaela clawed her way across Kevina's lap to press her face to the transparency where it curved around the cabin. Her heart missed its beat. "Got slime in the fans."

"Powering up," Casey called. "Maybe we can chop it free."

Desperate, praying, Michaela felt like her chest was about to explode. *Come on! Come on!*

The motors whined, she could see the heat rolling out of the nacelles as the fans slowly began to turn. This was accompanied by a frantic shake as the slime reacted, tensed; the thick green vein leading into the fans convulsed. Then it let loose. A spray of water, green goo, and bits of algae spattered onto the sides of the seatruck. Michaela stared, stunned, at the star-shaped clump that slapped onto the transparency inches from her nose.

The seatruck rose, fighting for every scrap of altitude, a meter, and then two.

Michaela, still sprawled across Kevina's lap saw when the nacelle began to smoke, heard the sudden grinding. Felt the seatruck shift, losing stability.

"No!" Casey screamed. "God damn it, no!"

The gyros kicked in, the emergency override taking control and dropping them back to slam down on to the deck. The impact knocked the wind out Michaela, bounced her off Kevina's lap and onto the floor. Pain shot like lightning up her left arm. Frantically, she scrambled to her feet. Dared to stare out at the smoking nacelle.

"Must have overcooked it cutting the slime loose," Casey muttered as she stared at the temp gauges. "Think we stripped some of the gears. You heard that grinding?"

"Yeah." Michaela choked down a sob. "No way we're flying this to the beach, is there?"

Casey was staring dull-eyed at the second seatruck. It perched on the deck, no more than ten meters away. So close, and with its entwinement of slime tentacles and veins, it could have been on Donovan's moon for all the good it did them.

"What do we do now?" Kevina asked, gaze fixed on the tortured blue-green ropes of slime; they seemed to be whipping in a maniacal frenzy about where the fans had shredded them.

"God, no," Casey squeaked in a mewling voice. "It's coming!"

Michaela shifted her attention to the front of the vehicle; the ocean lay no more than four meters beyond. Every one of the rope-like tentacles were shifting, moving with that weird pulsation. They might have been pumping themselves across the salt-brined deck. Each one was now inching its way toward the truck.

Too many of them.

"Out!" Michaela screamed. "They get a hold of this, they'll drag it right over the edge and down into the depths. Just like they did Jym's launch. Move it!"

She grabbed up the rifle, threw herself at the door, and kicked it open. Dropping to the deck, Michaela gauged the distance. Took in the twisting and squirming ropes of slime between her and the ladder. Gritting her teeth, she ran. The others were either coming, or they weren't. Hell, she might not make it as it was.

At the ladder, she reached up, got a foot on a rung, and, rifle cradled, climbed.

She did throw a glance over her shoulder at the sound of the scream. Casey, the last in line, had missed a step. A wrist-thick tendril of pulsing blue-green had wrapped tight around her ankle. Her right leg was being pulled back as she tried to balance and break free with her left.

Michaela blinked away the silvering sheen of tears.

Climb! You've got to climb! It's the only way.

Kevina, every muscle trembling, her gut knotted, prayed with all her soul that Michaela would move faster, but the woman could only climb so fast with one hand; the rifle cradled in her other slowed her rate to what seemed like a molasses crawl.

Clinging to the rope ladder—the hard-curved side of the Pod more of an unforgiving cliff than a shelter—Kevina heard another scream. She glanced over her shoulder.

Casey was on her back now; the slender fingers of slime-roots were lacing their way over her body. It didn't matter how Casey screamed, how she kicked or thrashed, the inexorable pulsing ropes of slime were dragging her back toward the dock's edge.

Frozen, Kevina watched. Saw the moment when one of the green shoots flicked across Casey's face, found its way into her left nostril. The scream torn from Casey's lungs was unlike anything Kevina could have imagined. Then Casey bucked, struggled. Her body convulsed as she spewed vomit over her chest. The slime might have rejoiced, following it across the woman's breasts, up her throat and chin, to send no less than three of the green tendrils into Casey's mouth.

The next scream was muffled, half choked.

Kevina clamped her eyes shut, fought the terror shakes that sought to paralyze her. Looked up through tears to see Michaela still climbing.

"Climb. Climb."

With all of her will, Kevina made herself reach for the next rung. Somehow managed to lift her left leg, search for the next foothold. Having broken free of the paralysis, she made it. Rung by rung as the rope swayed and whipped under both of their weights.

And then, magically, the rope ladder stabilized, as if rooted at the bottom.

"Climb, woman, climb," Kevina whispered.

Her entire world shrank to that ladder, to Michaela's feet as they advanced upward, rung by rung, and the curve lessened. Kevina could see the edge of the landing pad now. Michaela was moving faster. It might have been an eternity, but Kevina was able to pull herself over the edge of the landing pad. Threw herself flat on her back, sucking air, staring up at the sky where strange tube-shaped creatures seemed to float. Illuminated from the inside by a golden light, they were unlike anything she'd ever seen. Once, she would have called them beautiful, magical even. Now, even as ethereal as the glowing cones might have been, they, too, reeked of danger and death.

Vik stepped into Kevina's field of view, asking, "Where's Casey? What happened? Where's the seatruck?"

"Slime got the seatrucks. Got Casey." Michaela's voice sounded squeaky with fear. "We're all that's left. It's just us. Up here. No way off now. No escape."

Kevina rolled to her knees, coughed. Pointed at the glowing cones that seemed to float like pulsating balloons. "What are those?"

"I don't know," Vik told her, following her finger. "Related to seaskimmers, I'd guess. They just showed up, came floating in on the wind."

"Think we ought to shoot at them?" Michaela wondered. "Every other fucking thing on this planet is trying to kill us."

"Pull up the ladder," Vik said. "It's our only way off the Pod if we lose the second level."

Kevina pivoted, grabbed hold of the ropes and pulled. "What the hell? How heavy is this?"

"Not more than about fifteen kilos, why?" Michaela asked as she panted for breath and stared worriedly at the floating cones with their wispy tentacles.

The things might have been fifteen to twenty meters high; the way they held position in the wind belied the notion they were like balloons. Now they lowered, dropping the long lengths of tentacles into the water. As they did, the slime began to react, almost churning.

Get the damned ladder up!

Kevina threw her back into it. Grunted. And felt no give in return. "It's not moving."

Michaela added her strength, sharing the duty.

"Slime's got it," Kevina realized.

A wash of defeat colored Michaela's weary eyes. "Cut it loose."

Vik cried, "But that's our only way down to the dock."

"And it's the slime's fast track up to us. Now cut the damn ladder loose. You got anything sharp?"

Vik retreated to her bag, returned with a scalpel. When Kevina took it, cut the ropes, the ladder didn't just fall, it was ripped down by the weight. A wet, splattering thump sounded from below. A lot of weight crashing down.

"What now?" Vik asked as she stared up at the glowing, floating cones. "Sort of look like squids, don't they?"

"Yeah," Michaela countered, "if squids glowed and floated. I don't like this. Come on. We're getting inside. Undercover. Kevina, the last rifle is in the locker just inside the weather door."

"But stay ready." Vik slapped a hand to her own rifle as if in assurance. "If those flying squid things are drawn to movement and drop in for a taste, shoot to kill."

Kevina struggled to her feet, her legs gone wobbly, her heart still hammering at her chest. Damn it, had she ever been this scared?

But the hovering squid things didn't follow, just changed their attitude; a couple of the silky tentacles rose from the slime, pointed toward the women as if they were observing, but who knew how, since they had no visible lens-like eyes.

At the door, Michaela glanced nervously into the foyer. Then back at the floating squids, and jerked the door open, darting inside.

Kevina was last, slamming the door behind her. As she did, Michaela opened the locker, handing her the last of the rifles and a spare magazine of cartridges.

"You know how to use that?" Michaela asked, indicating the rifle.

"Used one to cull seals off Ostrov Belaya Zemia for the polar bear feeding program." She worked the bolt, figured out how the gun loaded. "It was an automatic, not a bolt gun." She found the tang safety, flicked it back and forth. After that, it was pretty simple.

Michaela stepped up, looked her hard in the eyes. "You understand, don't you? These *things*. They're no longer our children. Felix is not your boy. It's a monster. Our kids are dead, Kevina. The slime has taken them, is directing them through some kind of sounds we can't hear. Right, Vik?"

Vik nodded where she was staring uneasily down the stairs toward the second level. "That thing that looks like my Sheena? Or the one that looks like Felix? It's taken their minds, Kevina. That's what killed Bill Martin, Anna Gabarron . . ." Her expression collapsed into a confused grief.

"Tried to kill me," Michaela added hotly. "Felix and Sheena, get it? They were chopping down my door when Dik distracted them." Michaela grabbed Kevina's shoulder, pinched. "You get a chance, Kevina, you shoot them. You with me? Your son will kill you. He won't think twice."

Kevina clamped her eyes shut, images of Felix flashing behind her lids. The feel of his fetal kicks and shifting in her womb, that miracle as she'd first placed him to her breast to suckle and all that followed. His life out of hers. All the clever antics of his childhood. That wide-eyed boy on his first boat ride out to set the buoy.

Where had it all gone wrong?

"I said: Do. You. Understand?" Michaela roared in her face.

"I . . . Yes." Kevina swallowed hard, nerved herself. "He's not my boy anymore."

Michaela nodded. "It's not even a *he*, Kev. It's a *thing*. Alien. And it's using your boy's corpse as a home."

"Couldn't have said it better," Vik agreed. She hadn't let her gaze shift from the stairs. "We can't stay here. What do you have in mind?"

Michaela rubbed her face, smearing the faint streaks of tears on her brown cheeks. "Maybe we can seal the second level? Block the door? Keep them restricted to first level?"

"If they're not already on second level," Vik reminded. "Why didn't we seal the door when we left?"

"Because we were fucking flying out of here, remember? Didn't matter back then." Michaela gestured. "Kev, you first. Be ready to shoot."

Kevina nodded, swallowed hard, lifted the rifle, and used her thumb to click the safety off. Step by step, she started down the stairs, heart hammering, blood rushing in her ears. At the bottom, she took a deep breath and stepped out onto the floor. Pivoting, she looked up and down the hall. "No one here."

Michaela and Vik eased down after her. Both cocking their heads, listening.

Michaela hurried across the hall, slammed the door to the stairs leading down to level one. Fearfully, she glanced through the window at the staircase down. "Shit! Slime's already climbing this way."

"Think that door will hold?" Kevina asked, her mouth dry as she pointed the rifle this way and that, expecting some child-shaped monster to leap on her at any instant.

"Only until someone turns the latch on the other side. How do we seal it so no one can open it?"

"Got screws in the lab," Vik said. "We can screw the door into the jamb." She hurried off.

Kevina wrinkled her nose. "What's that . . . ?" But she knew. Gabarron. Shifting her eyes to the clinic, she saw the door open. Remembered that the woman's sprawled body was blocking it. Shit on a shoe, could this get any worse?

Michaela was still staring down the staircase, eyes fixed on the advancing slime.

Kevina heard the patter of bare feet on sialon. Turned, saw Sheena coming from the end of the hall, a weird smile on her oddly green face. "Sheena?"

The little girl had a vibraknife in her right hand, her face rapturous as she hurtled down the hall calling "Got you! Got you!"

Kevina cried, "Sheena! No!"

When Michaela shot, the muzzle blast liked to have burst Kevina's ears. The pain and surprise of came as a jolt.

Sheena's face exploded into bits. Bone, muscle, tissue, and the girl's right eyeball popped loose. Sheena hit the floor face-first, momentum sliding her on the sialon. In stunned disbelief, Kevina gaped as blood and bits of brain leaked out of the girl's shattered head.

At the same moment, the door to the stairway crashed open. Michaela was thrown back, recovered, lifted her rifle, and shot. Something green, muscular, and small launched itself on top of her. A reeling part of Kevina's mind identified the attacker as an emerald caricature of Breez. But one impossibly agile, strong, and vicious as it clawed at Michaela's face and squealed in an inhuman voice. Then it ripped the rifle away, sent it clattering across the sialon. Breez batted Michaela's flailing arms aside, grabbed her by the throat, crying, "Neck: Blood vessels, windpipe, spinal cord." Her small hands dug deep into Michaela's throat.

Kevina shuddered as Breez's small hands pulled Michaela's trachea out, stretching the skin on the woman's neck. Michaela's eyes bugged, her mouth open, lungs sucking as Breez crushed her windpipe. No matter how Michaela bucked, she couldn't dislodge the clinging and squealing Breeze.

An eerie howl came from behind. Kevina whirled, seeing Felicity. Or what might have been Felicity. This time it was instinctive. Moments before the girl—her hands clawing before her—could connect, Kevina triggered the gun. At the large-caliber bullet's impact, Felicity's body spasmed, dropped nerveless. Arms, head, and legs bounced flaccidly on the unforgiving floor.

"Sheena!" The boy's scream from behind caused Kevina to whip around. Blink.

Her first thought? Her son had been in green paint, maybe dabbed some white on his under arms. He was naked as he charged from down the hall, slid to a stop, and leaned over Sheena. He took the girl's hand. Clutched it to his chest. Tears welled in his large, dark eyes.

"Baby?" she asked, heart melting. "Sweet one?"

Felix looked up, his face working. "Gonna kill you now."

Kevina vaguely noticed the hatchet in his other hand, "Felix it's me! I love you! You're my baby! Please, sweet . . . let me help you."

Vik's rifle thundered from the lab door down the hall, and

Kevina barely registered the bullet's popping impact as Breez jerked and flopped onto Michaela's motionless body.

Kevina tried to lift the rifle, memories of her son's face swimming before her eyes. This was her boy, the only being she'd ever loved with all her . . .

He leapt, the hatchet raised as an inhuman howl burst from his lips.

Kevina froze, eyes on the raised blade, at the dried blood on its sharp bit.

The words, "No, baby!" shrilled as the hatchet swung in an impossible arc.

Even as it split her skull, she didn't believe it.

90

When Felix held Sheena's hands, they were cold. Didn't matter how warm and slick and wet his palms were, nothing came in return. He heard and felt that distant and hidden part of him, knew it was shrieking, kicking, wailing out its misery and the injustice of it all.

It wasn't supposed to happen like this. He wanted to cry. Couldn't. The Voice told him not to. That it was all right. In the end, it didn't matter. Only the little children mattered. And they were down deep.

Safe.

Growing with the One.

Becoming.

Felix squatted on the floor, heedless of the blood, the bits of brain that leaked out of Sheena's broken head. He wished her one eyeball wasn't staring at him, all empty, where it lay flopped loose in the wreckage of her skull.

Down the hall, past Mother's slashed and hacked corpse, Felicity lay on her stomach, a gaping hole in her back. At the broken door to level one, Breez was bleeding. She lay slumped over Michaela's crumpled corpse, a string of intestines blown out of her side by the bullet. Michaela's throat looked weird where the windpipe had been torn out.

Even as Felix watched, a thick tendril of algae that had emerged from behind the shattered door wrapped itself around Michaela's body, was pulling it and the bleeding Breez toward the stairs. Not a second later, Michaela's head and shoulders dropped over the top stair with a thump. Breez, limp and dead, toppled loosely off of her and slipped part way down the stairs.

That left one.

Vik had locked herself in the lab. None of the other big kids were left, except maybe Tomaya. Felix wasn't sure where she was. He could have walked over, stuck his hand into the algae, listened to the Song, and maybe it would have told him. The algae knew everything.

Instead, he fought tears, picked up his bloody ax, and let go of Sheena's hand; the Voice assured him that no matter what, she wasn't coming back. He could hear the change in the Song, melodious in victory, saddened in loss. So many things communicated at once. Things Felix couldn't quite understand yet. But that he would when he and the Voice finally became one.

He didn't look down as he passed Mother's corpse. He had the memory of how his ax had felt when he split her head open. How the disbelief had filled her gray eyes, and how the blood had contrasted with her golden-blond hair. Her last words kept repeating, gone almost silent now, drifting off to some distant place in his memory. Didn't matter that down inside he hurt. He didn't have to. Could just tell it to go away, and it would. Hurting was just a curiosity, and a strange one at that. How peculiar that anyone should have to feel that way.

Not like Sheena. That hurt lay closer.

At the lab door, he reached up. Turned the latch. Locked.

Raising the ax, he took a swing. Then another. He had learned with Iso's room. This was a bigger, stronger door. Might take him a while.

"Go back!" Vik called from inside. "You break that open, I'll shoot! Just like I shot Breez."

"Got to," Felix told her. "You're the last."

"Why are you doing this?" Vik's voice sounded shrill.

> "Now the Pod is falling down, falling down, falling down.
> "Once Vik's dead we'll go around, go around.
> "My fair lady."

"Felix? Don't you get it? The Pod's compromised. The slime is eating away at the pilings. It's going to collapse, and we're all going to drown."

"Not me. I can breathe water. So can the little kids. That's where they are now. Living with the One. Underwater. The One has the Pod now. It will be safe once it's all inside and nothing can eat it. It's been waiting for a long time for a way to live all together. We'll be adrift. And protected by the Pod. Nothing can get us, understand?"

"Felix? Please. Let me help you. Maybe I can reverse this, make you well again."

"I *am* well. I don't ever have to hurt again." But he would miss the electric bliss he'd felt with Sheena and Felicity, that pricking delightful tingle that had run clear through his body. Maybe, when Tomaya came back, he could feel that again with her.

From down the hall, he could hear the Song rising and falling as the algae rejoiced over Michaela's body.

He whacked the door one more time, seeing a long sliver of duraplast peel off.

That's when the roar started. He heard it from a long way off. Barely audible to begin with, then louder. And louder. Until the entire Pod was shaking so loudly it overwhelmed the Song.

"Thank God!" Vik cried from behind the door.

"Someone coming," Felix told himself. Frowned. The last time it had been the Supervisor. This had to be her and the shuttle again. Then the shaking and sound died down to stillness. Had to be the landing pad.

More grownups to deal with. He sighed.

91

"**G** ot it!" Dek called as he banked the airplane. "About six degrees north of east and ten kilometers out."

From her seat in the cabin, Kalico stared down at the designs made by endless lines of swells. In Capella's slanting light, the surface of the sea had a platinum look, intricately textured by wind and wave. She had always loved flying over water, watching as the composition of larger patterns of swells broke into smaller and smaller patterns until the whitecaps could finally be discerned. Layer upon layer of complexity. That's what made oceans magical.

Kalico could discern the long curve of the reef, marked by the way it refracted waves, and finally she picked out the change in color, the deep royal blue edging into lighter tans, yellows, and blue-green mats of submerged vegetation.

And there, that little dot of white, that was the Pod.

"How are we doing on charge?" Kalico called to where Dek and Talina sat in the cockpit.

"Down to forty percent," Dek told her. "With the prevailing tailwind, we could just make the beach if we had to."

"Let's hope we don't have to," Talina muttered under her breath.

"Oh, ye of little faith," Dek told her, that wry Taglioni smile bending his lips.

"Yeah, we'll, I guess we'll see," Kalico told them. "It's the flipping Maritime Unit. Just a bunch of scientists, right? How much trouble can they be? And trust me, Michaela Hailwood won't buck an order. Not from me. In fact, I wonder if I shouldn't have replaced her the last time around."

"Kalico," Dek called back, "if it wasn't for her, the Maritime Unit would have died on *Ashanti*. That woman kept them together. Molded them from a disparate group of scientists into a family. Hell, they were so tightly knit that they all lived for the group. Like some sort of cultish commune. Played hell with the few of us who tried to have relationships."

"How so?" Kalico asked.

"They always went back to the family. Like, ultimately, if they were involved with anyone from the crew, it always ended up as a sort of betrayal to the others. I guess, in the end, when you think about Maritime Unit, the Unreconciled, and crew, *Ashanti* was three different worlds."

"They sure didn't take to me, and I was the Supervisor."

"So, what's the game plan when we land?" Talina asked as the airplane dropped toward the dot of white.

"We stick together," Kalico told her. "Watch each other's backs. Maybe this clannish family thing has gone over the edge. If it's us versus them, I want us on top after it all shakes out. They do have four rifles. But other than that, who knows what they could cook up."

"If it's really that bad?" Dek asked. "Say, they meet us at the landing pad and those rifles are aimed at us?"

"We scoot and toot," Kalico told him. "That tells us to leave dealing with them to the marines. This is a fact-finding trip only. If there's something else wrong, maybe they're at each other's throats but still listening to reason, I'm ordering the evacuation of the Pod. We'll come pick it up with the shuttles after they're back to the mainland."

"For all we know, it's a blown transistor in the radio," Talina added. "That, or like that idiot Weisbacher, they don't know how to fix the radio."

"Guess we'll find out." Kalico was pressing her face to the window, trying see as Dek eased them into the wind on approach.

"What are those?" he asked in awe.

Kalico craned her neck, seeing the most amazing glowing cones floating just off to the east of the Pod. Elongated and internally lit, they seemed to float just above the sea, three of them, angled into the wind and trailing what looked like gossamer tentacles at the edge of a blue-green patch of something floating around the Pod.

"Never seen the like before," Talina admitted. "Think they're a danger?"

"If they try and attack the plane," Dek told them, "we're pegging the throttle and getting the hell out of here."

"Roger that," Kalico told him. "We don't want to be stuck out here, and we sure as hell don't want to end up in the drink. I've seen what's swimming around down there."

"On approach, people," Dek told her, dropping the flaps, and letting the compact aircraft cup air as it slowed its descent.

Kalico's heart began to pound. Damn it, not only were they dropping in on a potentially hostile bunch of people, but those floating things could be crazy enough to launch themselves at the airplane. Not to mention that the landing pad looked like a tiny, tiny target in a really fucking big ocean.

"You sure you can land on that?" Kalico asked, trying to keep the tension out of her voice.

"Who do you think is flying this crate, woman? I'm Dek Taglioni."

"Yeah," Talina said dryly. "Him and all those quetzals who hate flying and water. You sure you got this?"

"Demon and the rest curled up and turned patterns of yellow and black the moment we took off," Dek told her. "They're as scared as I am."

"That's a joke, right?" Kalico asked.

All she got in return was the profile of Dek's amused smile as he eased up on the Pod, slowed, and changed his thrusters to float them gently over the landing pad. Below, Kalico could see into the clear water, got a look at the Pod before they drifted over the observation bubble. She could see the lower part of the station coated in something blue-green. Same with the seatrucks down on the dock. The launch was missing. If there was any good news, it was that the floating cones had backed off.

There didn't seem to be any sign of life, which was ominous.

"The Chinese lantern things are giving us space," Talina noted. "That's a good sign."

"Yeah. I'll take it." Dek eased them over the length of the Pod, then settled them down artfully onto the landing pad. Kalico felt barely a bump. Dek killed the thrust, letting the turbines spin down.

"Welcome to Maritime Unit," he told them. "Let's see what's happening here."

Kalico nerved herself, unbuckled, and stepped over to the door. She dropped to the landing pad; the gusting wind made her squint as she started for the access door. One hand on her pistol, she walked up, stared into the window. Nothing in the foyer. But she could see that the locker was open, rifles missing.

"Tal?" She accessed her com. Heard nothing. So, was the whole station offline?

She waited, pistol drawn. On the landing pad, the only thing out of place was a couple of packs and satchels along with a duraplast crate.

Talina and Dek came at a trot, having seen to the airplane tie-downs and having plugged the airplane into the grid to recharge. Both had their rifles. Tal kept scanning, keeping total situational awareness.

"What have we got?" Tal asked.

"Rifles are missing. The question is, who has them, and what are they planning to shoot at?"

"Kalico," Talina told her, "if they make so much as a threatening move, I'm not letting them shoot first."

"Roger that. Me either." Kalico opened the door, pistol at the ready. "This isn't right. Coming in like we did, it should have shaken the whole station. It's not like they don't know we're here."

Stepping to the top of the stairs, Kalico called, "Hello? Anyone here?"

Heart beginning to hammer, she started down.

A face peered at her from around the corner. Then it drew back. A very young face. The kind that should belong to a little boy.

92

F elix considered the problem presented by the Supervisor's return. As he did, he could hear Breez and Michaela's bodies making irregular thumps as they were pulled down each riser and tread. No help there. Surely he was smart enough to take down a single woman. She would have no clue that he was anything but a little boy.

It would be nice if Tomaya were here. It was always easier with two. Like Sheena used to do, running around behind to distract a grownup while Felix slashed above their kneecaps with the ax.

But the Supervisor wouldn't know. Sort of like with Bill Martin. He could just walk up with the ax behind his back, and when she stopped to stare at the bodies spread out on the hall floor, he'd get close. She would be distracted by the blood, the bullet-shattered corpses. That would be Felix's chance. He'd slash her above the kneecap. Down she'd come.

Carefully, Felix tiptoed down the hallway, stepped around Mother's body. Just around the corner of the stairs leading up to the landing pad, he tightened his grip on the bloody ax. He waited, listening. Heard voices, and then someone called, "Hello? Anyone here?"

As the person started down the steps, Felix peered around the corner. Not one, three!

With rifles.

Whole different problem. The ax wasn't going to work.

What to do?

The Voice didn't seem to have any idea, though the Song was ringing through the entire Pod.

"This is the Supervisor. Hello? Little boy, who are you? Where is everyone?"

Glancing around, his gaze fixed on the rifle where it had fallen from Mother's hands. He'd never shot one. Never held one. But how hard could it be? He'd seen how Michaela shot Sheena, how Mother had shot Felicity, and finally how Vik had killed Breez.

If he hadn't been so strong, he might not have been able to handle it so easily. And it was still way too long for his arms. The butt barely fit into his shoulder. His new muscles rolling under his green skin, he lifted the thing, looked down the length of it, and figured out the sights. Just put that blade on the end where he wanted the bullet to go.

They were still in the stairs but coming slowly and carefully. He would have to move really fast.

alina, a step behind Kalico, caught the odor: blood, a lot of it. Fresh. And mixed in? The scent of a putrefying body. It seemed to cloy in the staircase, thickening as they descended. The narrow confines of the sialon walls, the close ceiling, the three of them, jammed together? Nothing about this was good. Where did she go if this all turned to shit?

And there was the sound, a rising and falling humming coupled with a deep thrumming. Nothing a normal human could have discerned, not in the high and low frequency ranges her modified hearing could pick up. Even as faintly as she heard it, the almost musical tones had to be organic. Somewhat mindful of the chime. And this, she had the gut feeling, was a kind of communication. But saying what?

That fleeting glimpse of the little boy? That did nothing to ease Talina's fears. The kid had painted himself green, his thick shock of dark hair looking mussed. Filthy, even. She'd have sworn the eyes were too big for the head and oddly black. Inhuman. Dangerous.

"Something's really wrong here," she whispered.

From down below, Talina heard a different melody, familiar, the notes rising and falling. Her heart skipped, and she recognized the tune: "London Bridge." A kid's nursery rhyme. A chill played down her back.

Ahead of her, Kalico called, "This is the Supervisor. Hello? Little boy, who are you? Where is everyone?"

In answer, a child's voice sang,

> "Now the pod is fallen down, broken down.
> "Namby Pamby is a clown . . ."

Kalico, started down the steps, even faster. Talina put a hand out, grabbing Kalico's shoulder, stopping her a couple of steps short of the bottom. Leaning close she whispered, "Something's really not right. I'm smelling blood and a rotting corpse."

"Off to prison you must go, you must go, you must go.
"Now death courts the lady gray,
"My fair lady."

Talina wondered, *What kind of sick song is that?*

It happened so fast. One instant the landing was empty, the next a naked little green boy with a large rifle leaped into sight. Talina wrenched Kalico aside and down, desperate to get a clear shot.

Little as he was, the kid still held the rifle remarkably steady, the black muzzle pointed up the stairway. Right on Talina's center. She saw it as if in slow motion.

The kid's questing finger was searching for the trigger as he sang,

"Now the lady's falling down . . ."

Talina threw herself sideways in one last panicked . . .

The kid's entire body spasmed, jerked, the rifle spitting fire and ear-splitting pain. Muzzle blast patted Talina's face. But she didn't feel the impact of a bullet. How could the kid have missed?

The way Talina saw it, the kid—expression stunned—folded up under the rifle's recoil and slammed to the floor as if he'd been hammered. Or had he? Talina would have sworn there were two shots, sounding an instant apart. Looking closer, to her amazement, she could see the hole blown in the kid's right side, bits of lung, blood, and ribs blasted through the delicate green skin.

Ears ringing, Talina staggered forward. Stepped over where Kalico was crouched, trembling, her hands over her ears, to stumble out into the hallway.

Her own ears wouldn't stop ringing. She shook her head. Damn it!

The kid was on his side, mouth working; swellings on the side of his throat seemed to convulse, blood pumping from slits above each collar bone. What was that all about? His eyes were indeed over-sized, large, dark, and staring in disbelief. When he coughed, blood shot out of both sides of the bullet wound in his chest and began to bubble up past his lips.

The heavy rifle had fallen across his way-too-muscular thigh; instinctively, Talina kicked it away.

From training, she pivoted, taking in the corpses. Kevina Schwantz, bloody and limp with a split skull. Two more green chil-dren, naked. Girls this time, all with bullet holes blasted through their bodies. A blood stain smeared the floor where the door gaped open to the stairs down to the lower level. Catching movement from the corner of her eye, Talina whirled, rifle at her shoulder.

Her sights settled on a woman in the middle of the hallway. Middle-aged, white, with short hair. She approached, a rifle held at half-ready. Talina vaguely remembered her: Vik Lawrence.

"Drop it!" Talina cried, wishing her damn ears would stop squealing.

Vik Lawrence said something inaudible through Talina's tortured hearing.

Tal started forward, combat-ready. And yes, she damned well could drop Dr. Lawrence before the woman could raise and trigger the rifle.

"Put it down! Now! That's an order!" Tal barked, and the pan-icked woman, swallowing hard, seemed to finally comprehend. Carefully, she set the rifle on the sialon floor.

Lawrence spread her arms wide in surrender. Saying something.

"I can't hear," Talina shouted, pointing at her ear. "Muzzle blast."

Lawrence cupped her hands, shouted back. "We have to get out of here. Now! Before the slime kills us all!"

Glancing back, she saw Dek and Kalico, warily inspecting the bodies in the hall.

"No argument from me. This place is creep-freaked," Talina agreed.

94

Kalico's hearing was coming back, the insane ringing beginning to fade. She sat, curled in a seat in the cabin, staring at the darkness behind her window as Dek's airplane spirited them east, driven by a tailwind. The Gulf was down there, dark, menacing in a way it had never been.

They had enough charge to make it back to the beach charger. They'd have to spend the night there, recharge, and fly back to PA in the morning. But they were off the Pod with its dead and creeping algae.

Donovan was a dangerous world. Didn't matter if it was in the Number Three or out at the Maritime Unit.

Kalico glanced across at Vik Lawrence. In the dim glow of the cabin lights, the microbiologist and geneticist had a shocked look on her face, her eyes distant with nightmare and disbelief.

Vik had shot the little green boy at the last minute. The bullet blowing through his chest had spoiled his aim. Caused his shot to blast a divot out of the sialon beside Kalico's head. Saved all of their lives.

Kalico tried not to think about how close she'd come to dying. Or the kid's corpse, rolled tightly in a tarp and stored back in the cargo hold along with Dr. Lawrence's crate, notes, and specimens. The little shit might have been ready to blow them away, but he'd end up surrendering a goldmine of biological information on what Vik called "the slime."

That is, assuming the good doctor wasn't a psychological basket case.

God knew, she had a right to be. Kalico would live with the memory of the dead where they lay mangled on the floor. Two little girls, their green bodies torn by bullets. Kevina Schwantz, her forehead split with an ax. Kalico had gagged at Anna Gabarron's putrefying corpse in the smashed Pod clinic. And then there was that single glance she'd cast down the stairway to level one. She'd been fascinated and repulsed by the slime, humped up, twisting around on the stairs, and engulfing Michaela Hailwood's corpse down on the level one landing. There had been no sign of the little girl called Breez. Maybe she'd been completely devoured.

Vik had been shaking, verging on throwing up, as she told how Felix had split his mother's head, how Breez had somehow torn Michaela's trachea from her throat, how it had all spiraled out of control. She'd broken down before she could tell the whole tale, but that would come. Later, when and if the woman could pull herself together.

How the hell could this have happened? Vik Lawrence was the only survivor? A bunch of kids and algae had destroyed the Maritime Unit?

"We weren't prepared," Vik said just loudly enough to be heard over the cabin noise. Her tears had stopped. Her eyes were puffy, gaze fixed on something an eternity away.

"No one was." Kalico gave a faint shake of the head. "And did you see? When we lifted off? The moment we were clear of the landing pad, those floating cone things went drifting in. Dropped their tentacles into the algae."

Lawrence nodded. "I saw. The water was roiling. And just out from the Pod, the seaskimmers were coming in." A pause. "Seeing that, something Felix said suddenly made sense. The slime wanted the Pod for protection. A place where it could accumulate, and nothing could eat it. From now on, inside the Pod, it will be protected." She shook her head. "Can you believe it's afraid? That those floating cones eat it?"

"Glad something does."

Lawrence gave her that half-dead look. "Welcome to Donovan."

95

After the bright morning light, Dek had to blink as he stepped into the hospital hallway. Another of the light panels had burned out. Obviously one that Raya didn't have a replacement for. Either that or Sheyela Smith hadn't had time to cobble together a jury-rig fit for a different kind of light. He was still getting used to the way his eyes didn't adapt, but simply shifted to the infrared range.

"Better, yes?" That was the Rocket voice.

"We'll see," Dek told the quetzal. "Nothing comes free."

He passed the old nurse's office, then Dya's, both dark since the former occupants were dead. That was the thing about Donovan. Like his visit today. People didn't always come to Donovan to find themselves or leave. Many came to die.

He strode down the long hallway, found Raya Turnienko's office with a note on the door that stated: *IN THE LAB.*

Dek made his way down past the patients' rooms and found the lab door open. There, bent over the autopsy table, Raya, Vik Lawrence, and Shanteel Jones were crowded around Felix's body.

Dek knocked lightly at the door, and as they turned, said, "Raya? You wanted to see me?"

The tall Siberian looked up, her face distorted by a magnifying lens and mask. She wore a smock, gloves, and held wicked-looking stainless-steel dissecting tools in her gloved hands. So did the others. All were wearing biohazard suits beneath their aprons.

"I did. Thanks, Dek. Could you give me a minute?"

"Sure." Dek stepped into the room, stared down at the body on the table. Granted, he'd been the one to wrap the boy's body in a tarp and carry it up to the airplane. It still upset him. More so now that it was cut open in a classic Y incision.

"Hard to believe that's Felix," he said softly.

"It's not," Vik told him, shooting him a wounded look from her masked face. "Not any more than that was my Sheena laying on the floor beside him." The words sounded so brittle, as if Vik were on the point of shattering.

"What are we looking at here?" Dek asked.

"A whole new biology," Jones told him. "Even by Donovan's standards, or what we thought was Donovan's standards, this is a step beyond what we imagined was possible."

Dek stepped closer, stared down at the boy. "Why is his skin green? What are those things on his neck? And he looks like a weightlifter, not like the skinny little Felix I knew in *Ashanti*."

Raya turned her attention back to the body. "The closest I can come to describing it is that he's like two organisms existing side-by-side in the same body. This is a quantum leap beyond simple TriNA molecules. We're seeing prokaryotic cells forming organs alongside the human cells. Augmenting, remodeling. And it isn't random like an infection, but directed morphological change to preadapt the body to an aquatic environment. The scary thing is, not only did it modify and integrate with the boy's immune system to do this, but it had a plan. It knew exactly what it was doing, and how to do it."

"Why just the kids?"

Vik shot him another look. "Oh, I'm infected, too, Dek. We all were. Doesn't matter that my infection is dormant. I'm still in quarantine. Will be for as long as it takes to figure out if I'm contagious. Our first guess is that the slime chose the kids because they were still growing. For whatever reason, it either decided, or figured out, that the adults weren't suited for remodeling and hybridizing."

"Why green?"

Iji told him, "It would have allowed the boy to photosynthesize, not enough to support the body entirely, but it would certainly cut the amount of food he'd need to survive. Remarkably efficient, if you ask me. And looking at the skin cells, they're like a lattice of human and prokaryote cells. Every bit as flexible and resistant to tear as human integument."

"Stay back," Raya warned as Dek tried to get a better look. "The human cells are dead, as are the internal organs, but the prokaryote cells in the skin are still alive. As long as they can photosynthesize and don't desiccate, they remain viable. We think the slime is spread by contact. Especially through sweat glands in the palms."

Which, of course, was why Vik was restricted to her hazard suit and lived in a quarantined section of the hospital.

"You got it. I'm staying back. Got enough trouble with all these quetzals in me."

Into her mask, Raya mumbled, "And I thought that was bizarre? Compared to what we're seeing here? Quetzals are a cakewalk."

Dek lifted his hands, imploring. "But I still don't get it. Felix tried to kill us. He split Kevina's head with an ax. His mother, for God's sake. I *knew* that boy. Watched him grow up. Him, Sheena, Felicity, and the rest. How the hell could something turn those precious children into murderers?"

Raya shot him a sidelong look. "You're the one with quetzals in his head, and you're asking that question? How close did you come to losing yourself?"

Dek heard the chittering of quetzal laughter.

"We'll get a better idea when we get to the brain," Vik told him. "Listen, Dek, we're just at the start of this. We've got years of re-search on Felix's body. Let alone understanding what kind of life the slime is. Slime? Even the name's wrong. Disparate cells that can assemble themselves into an organism at will? That collect, trans-mit, and analyze data? That can, in a matter of days, adapt an entire immune system and alien organic chemistry to its needs? From sin-gle cells, it took over and destroyed the Pod, turned the children into its agents, and used them against us. Are you getting an idea of the sophistication? The intelligence it takes to do something like this?"

Shanteel gestured with a scalpel. "And some of the children are still missing out there."

Vik's shoulders worked, as if she was fighting off a shiver. "The little ones, they were remodeling at an advanced rate. God knows what the slime is turning them into. You ask me? The slime was willing to sacrifice the older children. Maybe, like the adults, they couldn't be modified as successfully as the younger children and

infants. The changes in Toni, Vetch, Kayle, and the rest? Well . . .
call it chilling."

"And Tomaya?"

"Still out there, Dek." Vik stared at him through her transparent
mask. "This is a guess, but my take is that after the organism first
infected Felix and the rest of the children, it saw an opportunity.
For the first time in its evolution, the introduction of the Pod into
its environment provided protection from predation by cones,
seaskimmers, and who knows what else. Better yet, it realized what
an opportunity human physiology offered. We are remarkable animals, capable of manipulating and modifying the physical world in
a way the organism can't. All it had to do was take the Pod and
adapt the human body to function in the organism's aquatic environment. Our arrival gave it the opportunity to completely change
its existence. We gave it the ability to modify its environment."

Dek rubbed the back of his neck. "Yeah, well, lot of good it will
do the slime. Kalico and Shig left this morning with the A-7s.
They're going to recover the Pod. The plan is to blow the tube and
what's left of the pilings while the shuttles support the Pod by ca-
bles. Then they're going to fly it to a rocky outcrop about an hour
east of here. Kalico wants to salvage the equipment. The microscopes and such. If she can decontaminate the Pod, she's figuring it
might be turned into a remote base on one of the other continents."

"Good luck with that," Iji muttered, studying the gill channels
that ran down the boy's neck. "How did the slime know to grow
these gills here? Why lateral to the root of the tongue and down the
side of the throat? Why didn't it choose the shoulders, or anywhere
else on the body? It's like it instinctively knew?"

Raya was fingering her scalpel, staring down at the corpse. "It
took humans a couple of million years to develop the skills and
technology to create life-forms. The slime did it within weeks.
How do you assemble that kind of brainpower from a bunch of
floating cells? This is an intelligence orders of magnitude beyond
anything we've ever encountered."

Dek rubbed his chin, considering. "We're going to have to

completely rethink how we're going to go back to Donovan's oceans. Even if we go back."

"What about the children still in the Pod?" Vik's eyes had a thousand-yard stare. "What the hell are they going to be? What does the slime intend to do with them?"

Of all the bad moods Kalico had ever descended to, this was about the worst. Never—not even in those days when she'd been alone after *Turalon*'s departure—had she felt this dispirited, defeated, and most of all, frustrated. Nothing in her life was working. The collapse of the Number Three, the mine shutdown, and idling of her smelter had her people at a standstill. The Maritime Unit was gone, a total loss. Nothing she could salvage.

And Dek belonged to Donovan now.

She walked down from the ramp on her A-7, smelling the stench of hot exhaust as she stepped onto Port Authority's heat-glazed landing field. Shuttle exhaust had seared the clay to the point that landing no longer blew dust out in great clouds to settle over the shipping containers stacked seven-high on the field margins. She jammed her hat onto her head in response to Capella's burning afternoon blaze.

As she hit dirt, Pamlico Jones was already heading her way with his skid-steer to unload the thick coils of cable that were supposed to be carrying what was left of the Pod back for salvage.

Shit on a shoe, she wanted to kill something. Stamp her feet. Scream her rage and frustration at the universe. And all she had to look forward to was Shig Mosadek, waiting patiently at the mangate. He'd been aboard the PA shuttle, had left as soon as it was apparent that there was nothing but disaster out at the Maritime Unit site.

Kalico knotted a scarred fist, wished she could strangle the universe with it.

The memory would stick with her, how the Pod looked, resting below the reef's transparent surface, maybe twenty meters down, at the edge of the drop-off to deepwater. A big, white, elongated oval splotched by patches of blue-green algae. What Vik Lawrence called "the organism." Above it, those weird glowing cones had floated, tentacles dangling, and around them, seaskimmers, their sails flashing in a riot of colors, had circled. So, too, had a flock of four-winged, polka-dot fliers.

Not a trace remained of the original location. Not even the pilings protruded from the water.

And worse, all those computers, microscopes, PCR machines, spectrometers, the diving equipment, the scanners and sonar, the com, all that wealth of technology, gone. Submerged. Ruined beyond repair.

As if we could even get to it. If the stories Vik Lawrence told were true, giant three-sided lobsters, plastic-eating slime, and murderous green children with gills who could survive underwater guarded it. Not to mention that the slime considered the Pod to be a safe haven. The predators that hovered and floated overhead notwithstanding, recovery might be forever impossible.

At the gate, Shig had that benevolent smile on his thin lips. "Might I stand you to a whiskey?"

Kalico stared down at her scarred hands, that sucking feeling of defeat draining her. "Not sure that I'm up to Inga's. Think I'll just retreat to my dome. Call it a day. Try and get a good night's sleep before I head back to the mine to see what misfortune tomorrow is going to bring." She paused. "I've got a bottle of that rye. If you'll walk with me, I'll share a shot before I send you on your way."

"I'd like that."

Sure he would. This was Shig, who rarely finished a half-glass of wine.

She nodded at Ko Lang who was standing guard at the gate and walked through into PA, her feet crunching on the gravel.

Ambling at her side, Shig said, "This is a most unpleasant setback. We had really hoped that the Maritime Unit would open new horizons on Donovan. Who could have anticipated that we would be so ill-prepared?"

"Human arrogance, Shig?" Kalico pulled her hair back, pinned it behind her neck as she walked. "Hell, for as long as I've been here, I sure didn't see it coming. Was it my fault for not pulling the plug?

I let them throw me off the Pod. Was that my arrogance? My sense of superiority and petty anger? Instead of stomping off in a huff, declaring, 'Fine. You're on your own,' I could have called Abu Sassi. Removed those people by force. They'd be alive. Those children would be alive."

"Some of them still may be," Shig told her. "Or whatever they've become. *Children* might be an inappropriate term. Our entire approach has to be rethought." A pause as he walked at her side. "It has been an expensive lesson, but those are the ones best learned."

She shot him a measuring glance as they turned on the main avenue. "You always this self-possessed in the face of disaster?" Then she barked a bitter laugh. "Of course, you are. Hell, I remember you smiling when you knew I was going execute you."

"The universe is a constant teacher," he replied. "All is illusion."

"Yeah, well, that Pod out there isn't. I looked down through that water and saw the death of dreams."

"In a manner of speaking, that's what moksha is. Surrendering dreams and aspiration in order to accept enlightenment."

"Why don't I feel enlightened?"

"You have a young soul. Not as young as Talina's or Dek's, but through the trials in this lifetime you are well on your way to a more mature dharma."

"Yeah, yeah, and all is *dukkha*. Might be that I'm starting to believe that after the month I've had."

She led the way down the block to the dome she'd bought. It wasn't much. Merely a domicile with a living room, the usual breakfast bar separating the kitchen, a bathroom, and rear bedroom. A place to lay over when she needed to.

As she led Shig in, it hit her that she'd never had a guest here before. That—in this new phase of her existence—she didn't give a flying fuck that the place was a simple dome. She took off her hat, tossed it onto the couch.

Damn. How far have I fallen?

She laughed, glanced at Shig. "Welcome to my home away from home. Funny isn't it? Once upon a time, back in Transluna, my household staff would have greeted you, fawned over you, ensured that you were impressed by the view, the luxury, the wealth and opulence of my high residence with its spectacular views of Transluna."

"I think I prefer this," he said. "Along with the woman that you are now." He seated himself on the first barstool. His high brow furrowed. "Have you spent any time with Dek since he got back?"

"A little." She walked into the kitchen, opened a cabinet to retrieve the bottle and two glasses. "You really going to drink any of this?"

Shig's smile was enigmatic. "If you would be so kind, might you pour just a tiny splash? Enough to barely wet the bottom of the glass? If that's the vintage I think it is, I heard that Inga only opened it because the last batch was so poor. That this rye is too good to waste."

She did as he asked, extending the glass, pouring a couple of fingers for herself. God knew, she'd earned it. She studied him, her suspicious side rising. "Shig? You got some ulterior motive?"

He studied the glass, his dark brown eyes thoughtful. "Always. But let us get back to Dek."

"Ah! Worried that I'm feeling like a jilted schoolgirl?"

"Are you?"

She pursed her lips. Studied the brown liquid. "Why are you bringing this up?"

Shig gave her that all-knowing smile. "I worry about you. You, Talina, Yvette, Raya. You are each, in your own way, important to me. I would have you know that this, too, shall pass. If you need anything from—"

"How about a bulletproof vest?" the angry voice asked from the bedroom hallway.

Kalico wheeled, startled to see Tadeki Ozawa—dirty and unkempt—step out. The big five-shot revolver that he held was one of Frank Freund's locally made fifty-caliber pieces. The explosive bullet it shot packed enough punch to stop a quetzal. It would burst a human body as if it were a balloon.

"Tadeki? Put that down." Kalico dropped a hand to her pistol butt. Dear God, could she draw fast enough, shoot the guy before he pulled the trigger?

"You just let her die," Tadeki said, verging on tears. His hand was trembling. "You *murdered* her! And for what? Wealth? We were having a baby, you heartless slit! She was the love of my life, and you let her die in the darkness. Wouldn't even try save her."

Kalico nerved herself, stood resolute, trying desperately to figure a way to . . .

"Might I be of service?" Shig asked softly, sliding off the bar stool and placing himself between Tadeki and Kalico.

"Stay put, you son of a bitch!" Tadeki cried. "You're just like her. One of the rulers. All of you, you just use us for what we can give you."

"I have nothing," Shig said amiably. "Anything I own, you are welcome to it."

"Shig, step back," Kalico ordered, trying to push him to the side.

"Are you out of your toilet-sucking mind?" Tadeki thundered. "I'm tired of being used by the likes of you. The Corporation? Port Authority? You and your money? Buy this, buy that? Pay for this? You hear me, you pus-sucking fuck? My wife and child are dead! I'm owed. Die with Aguila. And rot in hell."

He lifted the big fifty. The black muzzle was no more than inches from Shig's still-placid face. The muscles on Tadeki's forearm flexed under smooth skin as he took up the slack on the trigger.

Instinctively Kalico cowered away, anticipating the instantaneous explosion of Shig's head, a peculiar prickling on her skin and face as she prepared for bits of brain and blood to . . .

A loud *crack-snap-pop*. All one sound as the window broke and Tadeki's head tried to burst through his skin and scalp. The momentary image came as a flash, the man's eyes squirting out from their sockets, face puffing, ears and hair popping wide. The body, gone to rubber, thumped the floor like loose bones. The big revolver hit with a clank.

Kalico stared, paralyzed, breath stopped in her lungs, heart thumping frantically in her chest. One instant, she'd been dead, now she wavered, starved of oxygen, the beginnings of the shakes energizing her muscles.

Tadeki lay in a loose heap. Thick red blood, along with pieces of brain, were squirting out of the holes in either side of his head. The man's eyes were popped loose from the orbits, blood trickling from his nostrils, past his protruding tongue, and oozing from his ears.

The door opened. Kalico spun on her heel, barely cognizant of Shig's stunned expression, the sweat beaded on his strained face.

Allison Chomko stepped across the threshold, her golden hair piled high and pinned by a clip adorned with a sparkling diamond the size of a walnut. Her classic Nordic face wore a pensive expression. She glanced sidelong at Tadeki's bleeding body. "Sorry about your floor. It's duraplast. A couple of swipes with a mop and it'll be clean as new."

"What the hell is going on here?" Kalico demanded, the shakes taking over with a vengeance.

"Hello, Shig," Allison greeted.

Shig stepped uneasily over to the bar, lifted Kalico's glass, and sucked down a full swig of the rye. "My," he said wearily, "I didn't see that coming. Perhaps my limbic system isn't as fully under my control as I had once thought."

Allison cocked a pale eyebrow. Indicated Tadeki. "Wasn't sure about him. Didn't know if he meant the things he was saying. Talina was out of town, or I would have turned it over to her. So, I had my people keeping an eye on him. Especially after he stole Gatlin's pistol. When I heard he hotfooted it to your dome the moment he saw your shuttle landing, I thought I'd better come see."

"You knew?"

"Well, not exactly. He was said to be a deserter and swearing to kill you in all kind of ways. But then, people say all kinds of things, don't they?" Allison's brow pinched. "What if he'd decided at the last minute to go back to the mine? What if he wasn't really violent? I needed proof."

Kalico finally got a full breath. Struggled to get her shivering muscles under control and sidled over to lean against the bar next to Shig. "Ever thought about sending a message through com?"

"Wasn't my business until he pulled that pistol." Allison walked over, picked up the bottle of rye and inspected the label. "You got another glass?"

"Cabinet. The one with the brand-new bullet hole." Kalico gave a half-hearted wave.

Somehow the bullet had missed the glassware. Allison retrieved a tumbler, poured herself a finger, and sipped. "That's the good batch. That last one? Not so much." She glanced over. "Shig, you all right?"

"I suppose these things remind us how fragile the search for moksha is. It seems I've temporarily misplaced my sattva." He took another swig of Kalico's rye, placed a hand to his belly.

"Allison, what the hell are you doing here?" Kalico demanded, staring down at the bleeding corpse on her floor. Damn, that was a lot of blood. And the man's bladder had let loose, his hands were twitching, death quivers running down his legs.

Allison—preoccupied with the rye she was rolling across her tongue—swallowed, nodded approval. "Heard we lost the Maritime Unit. That you've got trouble down at Corporate Mine. That doesn't bode well. Then this toilet-sucker spouts off, figuring it's your fault his wife is dead. Shit on a shoe, we can't afford to lose you—and especially not Shig in the bargain. Next couple of years? We're going to be hanging on by a fricking thread as it is."

Kalico pried her glass from Shig's fingers, tossed off the last of the rye. Then she narrowed an eye. "But you don't even like me."

Allison gave her a deadly grin. "What's that got to do with anything?"

Shig had his eyes closed, taking deep breaths. He had the placid expression back on his face. That part of him, at least, was recovered. But looking close, Kalico could see that his hands were still shivering.

Surely it couldn't be because of his near-brush with death, let alone the body on the floor. This was Donovan, after all.

Maybe—given his reputation as a drinker—the rye just didn't sit well with him?

She didn't think of herself as Tomaya. Seemed, when she thought back, that the entire notion of a "name" defied rational sense. Life made so much more sense now, shared as it was, being part of limitless thought and understanding, the Song, and the One. She and the children were growing, rapidly. In the few moons since the Pod had become home, they were all changing, learning, acting as the "hands" for the One.

She was old enough, had better memories of *Ashanti* than the other children, and knew what it meant to have crossed the stars inside a container. Like the Pod was a container. A safe haven. A place where the hungry tentacles of predators couldn't reach.

But now, with human hands and bodies, the One could adapt; it could begin to profit from the lessons the humans had carried to it from across the stars. Humans had proved that the physical world could be manipulated, transformed, and adapted to serve the One. That threats like predators could be eliminated by violence. Already Tomaya had employed her body to make changes in the Pod, to open and close doors, to employ tools—a fascinating concept, tools—and as she did, the One learned, explored, and marveled.

There was so much to learn.

But the One was patient. First the humans had to be protected, allowed to grow and mature until they could reproduce. Only when enough of them existed could they finally be risked outside the Pod's protective walls. In the meantime, there were too many wonderful mysteries within the Pod's impregnable sialon walls. Mysteries that needed to be investigated. Like UUVs, the submarine, and the fascinating machines. That study alone would take years.

But more the point, the One, which had always needed to disperse into individual cells to survive predation, was suddenly able to reflect in peace. As predators sent tentacles to feel down the sialon walls in fruitless quest, The One no longer needed to separate and flee as a thought was coming together. Now it could concentrate billions of cells upon billions of cells without interruption. Flex its intelligence.

And in the process, it could contemplate miracles. Like the stunning new knowledge that isolated organisms like humans, each alone in its body, limited in its senses and communication, could create something as remarkable as the Pod, and more amazing, carry it across the stars.

If creatures that limited could accomplish such great things, what incredible heights could the One aspire to now that it had a redoubt that allowed it to learn, to understand, and to create? Especially now that it had harnessed humans with their remarkable bodies? Bodies that could collect, carry, and accumulate, make and use tools, create weapons, and manufacture machines? Using humans, the One could manipulate and manage its environment for the first time ever.

The future, once a mere abstract, had forever changed. The possibilities limitless.

As the One Sang in the background, the girl who used to be Tomaya swam into the observation blister, placed her hands against the transparency, and stared up at the sunlight shining through the glass. Through her and the others, the One had come to understand the extent of the world out there.

And the day would come when she would lead it back into that sunlight.

walls in fruitless quest, The One no longer needed to separate and flee as a thought was coming together. Now it could concentrate billions of cells upon billions of cells without interruption. Flex its intelligence.

And in the process, it could contemplate miracles. Like the stunning new knowledge that isolated organisms like humans, each alone in its body, limited in its senses and communication, could create something as remarkable as the Pod, and more amazing, carry it across the stars.

If creatures that limited could accomplish such great things, what incredible heights could the One aspire to now that it had a redoubt that allowed it to learn, to understand, and to create? Especially now that it had harnessed humans with their remarkable bodies? Bodies that could collect, carry, and accumulate, make and use tools, create weapons, and manufacture machines? Using humans, the One could manipulate and manage its environment for the first time ever.

The future, once a mere abstract, had forever changed. The possibilities limitless.

As the One Sang in the background, the girl who used to be Tomaya swam into the observation blister, placed her hands against the transparency, and stared up at the sunlight shining through the glass. Through her and the others, the One had come to understand the extent of the world out there.

And the day would come when she would lead it back into that sunlight.

S he didn't think of herself as Tomaya. Seemed, when she thought back, that the entire notion of a "name" defied rational sense. Life made so much more sense now, shared as it was, being part of limitless thought and understanding, the Song, and the One. She and the children were growing, rapidly. In the few moons since the Pod had become home, they were all changing, learning, acting as the "hands" for the One.

She was old enough, had better memories of *Ashanti* than the other children, and knew what it meant to have crossed the stars inside a container. Like the Pod was a container. A safe haven. A place where the hungry tentacles of predators couldn't reach.

But now, with human hands and bodies, the One could adapt; it could begin to profit from the lessons the humans had carried to it from across the stars. Humans had proved that the physical world could be manipulated, transformed, and adapted to serve the One. That threats like predators could be eliminated by violence. Already Tomaya had employed her body to make changes in the Pod, to open and close doors, to employ tools—a fascinating concept, tools—and as she did, the One learned, explored, and marveled.

There was so much to learn.

But the One was patient. First the humans had to be protected, allowed to grow and mature until they could reproduce. Only when enough of them existed could they finally be risked outside the Pod's protective walls. In the meantime, there were too many wonderful mysteries within the Pod's impregnable sialon walls. Mysteries that needed to be investigated. Like UUVs, the submarine, and the fascinating machines. That study alone would take years.

But more the point, the One, which had always needed to disperse into individual cells to survive predation, was suddenly able to reflect in peace. As predators sent tentacles to feel down the sialon